Comin' Up

Shel Weinstein

First published by Dog Ear Publishing
4011 Vincennes Rd
Indianapolis, IN 46268
www.dogearpublishing.net

ISBN: 978-1-4575-5428-5

This book is printed on acid-free paper.

This book is a work of fiction. Places, events, and situations in this book are purely
fictional and any resemblance to actual persons, living or dead, is coincidental.

Printed in the United States of America

This book was written for Joseph, Natalie and James Weinstein.

The old man looked over at his grandson and sighed.
"Things were different when I was
comin' up."

CHAPTER ONE

Chicago, 1981

Holding the glass with his thumb and forefinger, John Solberg stood next to his stool, tossed down his shot of bourbon and took a sip of his beer chaser. It was his sixth. He grimaced, catching sight of the person who mimicked him from the mirror behind the bar. That person looked haggard, old for forty-six. The whiskey burned its way down, doing nothing to calm the searing spasm of pain in his gut. *Gastritis, and the goddamn tranqs are in the car.* He held his breath and the pain nearly made him wince. Nearly. John never let anyone see him wince. The whiskey settled in, and the burning let up a little. Experience told him it would be back.

Wednesdays were slow nights at the bar, the kind of night when only regulars came in. The Bulls game had ended, and with it the 1981 season had gone into the Dumpster of history. The final loss to the Celtics was chewed on, spit out, and laid to rest. Then the bar talk went from sports to neighborhood legends, a group of exaggerated lies finessed into truths by repeated telling.

"To pull a stunt like that on Saint Patrick's Day, and him Irish!" The speaker tipped his bottle up and took a small sip of beer, nursing it so he wouldn't have to pay more rent on the barstool.

1

"Who, the cop?"

There were three of them, all a few years younger than John. "Yeah, Billy Merrin, the one they call Bugs. In he comes, tellin' Eddie Mitchell it's after hours an' he's gotta close.

Mitch looks him in the eye and says, 'There ain't no after hours on Saint Patrick's Day.' Then a couple of the boys grab Bugs by the arms and legs and toss him out inta the street. A minute later he's back, and we figure there's gonna be trouble."

One of the listeners—a small man with a nervous facial twitch and ferret eyes—broke in. "Yeah, I knew that Bugs Merrin. He was a mean bastard."

With a flash of annoyance at the interruption, the speaker resumed talking. "The boys start to go for him a second time, but Bugs holds up his arm and shows Eddie his wrist. 'The fall busted my watch, so I can't tell if it should be last call or not. So the least you can do is buy me a drink!"

The other two smiled; the story was an old one. The one who claimed to know the cop chimed in again. He spoke rapidly, glancing around like a child who was afraid of being told to shut up. "Merrin was crazy. Once, back when he was a kid, he bet Henry Fox a ten spot he could knock four teeth out of a guy's mouth with one punch. 'You're on,' says Fox, an' Bugs goes up to the first guy he sees, an' without a word, punches him square in the mouth. The poor sap drops like a stone, and Bugs leans down and peels back his lip, 'Shit,' he says. 'You win, Henry. I only knocked out three." This time there was laughter, and for some reason, the story signaled a sip break.

John had heard it told before and knew it was fiction. He turned to the group. "You got the betting part right, but the other half is wrong. The guy who thought he could knock all those teeth out was Roger Shaw, not Bugs Merrin. It was Henry Fox he made the bet with, but when Fox figured Shaw was crazy enough to do it for real, he called off the bet."

The man who'd told the story turned to glare at John, his face twitching violently. "How the fuck do you know?"

John stared at the mirror. "It was thirty years ago an' I was there."

The man rolled his eyes upward, sneered, and went back to his beer. "This was another time. A time when you wasn't around."

*****

John Solberg owned the bar. Even so, he pretended to be a customer. The lesson had come from the early days of running the tavern. Back then, friendship meant free drinks or at least unlimited credit; being everybody's pal had come close to breaking him.

He chug-a-lugged the rest of his beer chaser and set the mug down hard. Kenny, the bartender, glanced over and shot him the look that asked if he wanted another drink. He tossed a twenty on the bar and shook his head, annoyed at the flash of relief on the bartender's face. The look said that as soon as John left, Kenny could go back to giving heavy pours for bigger tips and stealing from the till.

John shrugged into his sports jacket and moved through the cigarette smoke, past the pool table, and down the small corridor that led to the parking lot. Straight-arming the back door, he pushed through in time to miss the rebound as the door hit the outside wall and bounced back partway. Grabbing it by the edge, John slammed it closed behind him. The automatic return on the door had been broken for months, but these days he never seemed to have the energy to fix things.

The night was icy cold, a stark reminder that winter wasn't ready to loosen its grip just yet. The daytime high had been over fifty, fooling John into leaving his leather topcoat in the car. Now, at two in the morning, it had dropped below freezing.

His car, a new '81 Caddy Seville, was parked to the right of the door and digging for his keys, he hurried toward it. As the car kicked over, he turned on the heater and, without waiting for it to warm up, dropped the shift into drive and pulled out into the street.

Once the road ahead straightened out, John steered with one hand so he could reach back and fish in the pocket of his topcoat for the bottle of pills that were his lifeline to pain-free serenity. He found the bottle, unscrewed the cap with his teeth and was in the process of trying to shake a pill into his mouth when a Chevy sedan pulled out in front of him. As he grabbed at the steering wheel, the bottle flew out of his hand. He stamped on the brakes and slewed sideways, barely missing the other car. The sudden stop killed his engine.

Cursing God, the Chevy driver, and the world in general, John twisted the ignition key until the engine reluctantly kicked over. The pill bottle had landed on the floor of the passenger side with most of the tablets still inside. John ignored them, instead grabbing the half-dozen that had fallen onto the passenger seat. Longing for a beer to wash them down with, he gathered spit in his mouth and swallowed the whole handful dry.

Taking 95th Street out as far as Southwest Highway, he headed for home. Somewhere along the way, the tranquilizers kicked in, and the knots in his gut began to unwind. His mind lumbered through the maze of what he saw as his insurmountable problems. Perky, the woman he should have married, had been pressuring him to dump his crazy wife Vivian, who was in and out of the nut house and, according to her shrink, too fragile for divorce. Vivian's medical bills kept flooding in, and his bartender's gambling habit was making money disappear from the till faster than usual. A lifelong grifter himself, John had expected Kenny to grant himself a five-finger raise once in awhile, but Kenny's need to pay off the bookies

4

was pushing the amount so high, it had begun to show up on the bottom line.

It was easy to look back and see where it had all gone wrong. His troubles began the day Vivian walked into his joint looking for a job. It was clear to everyone that all she wanted was a meal ticket, but her body and pretty face had turned him stupid. He'd married her within a month and been miserable ever since. The only piece of luck was that Perky, still in love with him, had stuck around.

The thoughts brought on the incessant urge to run, to just keep driving south and disappear. John tried to work out the details, but his brain was getting fuzzy, and he couldn't seem to concentrate. All he needed was a good night's sleep, and in the morning, he'd deal with it all. He'd call Henry Fox; Henry had connections. He might know someone who'd be interested in buying his bar and the two poker room operations he ran. With the money from the sale, he and Perky could just split, start over, do it right this time. Tomorrow, he promised himself. I'll take care of things tomorrow.

The tree limbs, still bare of leaves, seemed to wave and blur as he whipped by, and the white lines on the road undulated to the soft whine of the Caddy's tires. John stared straight ahead, paying no attention to the speedometer as the needle jiggled its way into the red. Seventy, eighty, eighty-five, ninety. The big Caddy hugged the highway, its quiet purr masking the sensation of speed, only the strobe-like effect of the highway reflectors giving any indication of danger. An idle thought that music would be nice crossed John's mind, but pushing the buttons on the radio seemed like too much trouble. The heater was going full blast. Leaning back into the cocoon of the leather bucket seat, he ignored the lack of traction on the icy road and lazily controlled the car with one hand.

Just past Palos Hills, the highway curved sharply to the left, but the Cadillac didn't. John didn't hear the sound of the shattering guardrail, didn't feel the jolt as the Caddy bulled its way through. His mind was in a quiet place as the car began its relentless descent into the dark ravine below. He wasn't wearing a seat belt and that was a blessing. A seat belt would have kept him alive, only to be cremated in the explosion of fire that erupted as the Caddy hit the ground. Instead, the impact sent his body twisting in several directions at once, snapping his neck and crushing his head. He felt no pain as shock, one of the few sensible design features of the human body, took over. And thus, painlessly, all of John Solberg's problems were finally over.

CHAPTER TWO

J ulia answered the phone. A harsh voice on the other end rasped
out, "Lemme talk ta Henry." Alarmed, Julia shook her husband
awake and handed him the receiver. He propped up on his pillow and
before answering, held his hand over the mouthpiece. With a mixture
of fear and concern, he asked, "Has something happened to Grandfather?"

Julia shook her head. "I don't think so. It's Patrick Delaney. He
wouldn't be calling about your grandfather."

Henry put the phone to his ear and murmured softly, "Yeah?"

The voice that spoke to Henry from the other end was uncharac-
teristically soft, and despite the phlegmy rumble, it conveyed a touch
of sadness. "That pal of yours, Solberg, the one they called Johnny Eel,
he had a car accident. He's gone, Henry."

Henry sat up straight. It might have been too soon for the pain of
loss to hit him, but he knew it was coming. "Aw, shit. When did it happen?"

The gravely tone became matter-of-fact. Henry knew Delaney
well enough to recognize that working with the details was easier for
him than giving out bad news. "He left that bar he owns in South
Shore around 2:00 a.m. Bartender says he was mildly lit, but not drunk.

Maybe he fell asleep at the wheel. Anyway, he went off the road out near Palos Hills. The car burned, but the guys at the scene told me he had to be dead on impact."

Trying to keep the quiver from his voice and failing, Henry asked, "Does his old lady know?"

Henry could hear the sounds of his business partner firing up a cigarette. Any other time, he'd bawl Delany out. The guy had a constant cough that was driving everyone in the agency crazy. "They're tryin' to track her down. No one answers at Solberg's house."

"No, not that bitch wife of his. I meant his mother. Aw, forget about it. I'll call over there. Thanks for letting me know."

Julia, who had been listening quietly, reached over and gripped Henry's hand. "John?"

He nodded and put the phone back in the cradle. "Dead, in a car accident. I gotta call the rest of the guys."

Henry shuffled into the den to get his address book and sat at his desk, staring at the phone. All of the old gang would come to John's funeral. Maybe afterward, they'd get together, even play some poker. It would be like old times. The sudden feeling of elation left and was followed by a rush of guilt. Why did a guy have to die so he could see his friends again? Twenty-five years. It had been twenty-five years since the tenement they'd lived in, the Cockroach Castle, had been torn down and the gang had drifted apart. There had been some phone calls and Christmas cards from a few of the wives, but nothing from Ben. Ben hadn't answered any of his letters, and the one time Henry had phoned and caught him at home, Ben had made it clear he wanted to be left alone.

Henry's hand shook slightly as he leafed through the pages. He made a list of the numbers he had to call, putting the most important ones first. He wrote Ben's name last, deciding that was fitting. After all, Ben had been the last one to move into the Castle.

CHAPTER THREE

Chicago
Labor Day Weekend, 1949

Henry Fox crouched on the top step of the stoop, blocking the glass front door to the building. He stared down at the other three members of the Castle gang and felt another surge of rage. They were sprawled out on the stairs below him, lazy as a pack of wolf cubs who'd just been fed. It was as if they didn't care that a kid their age, a thirteen-year-old, was moving into the fourth-floor walk-up on the Harper Avenue side. Why should they? Some new kid wouldn't be a threat to any of them.

He wiped the sweat on his forehead and ran a hand through his thick black hair. He had inherited the hair from his Mohawk father, who also gave him his reddish-tan skin, barrel chest and, a couple of times a week, bruises over most of his body.

Big Mike leaned back on his elbows, his head craned up and sideways to look at Henry. "It's hot, man. Too fuckin' hot to be lyin' out here in the sun."

Henry didn't bother to answer. He shifted slightly, and with his brooding stare, held Mike's eye until Mike turned away. What effect

9

would the new guy have on Mike? If the kid was tough and challenged Henry's leadership, would Mike stand with him?

Henry nodded to himself. He figured he could count on Mike. Sure, Mike was big, almost full-grown at thirteen. But the guy was yellow, way too scared to side with a newcomer against Henry. Andy would probably stick, too. Small like Henry, Andy had a boozer father like Henry's who bounced him around. That they had stuff in common was good and bad. Having someone in the gang who was shorter than him was a good thing. But sometimes, when the bruises were hard to hide, Andy would give Henry a knowing look that only added to Henry's shame.

Tommy was the third member of the group. A guy like Tommy would probably go along with whatever the others wanted. He was Mister Perfect, great at sports and a good fighter, but not a leader. Henry didn't much care for Tommy and would have kicked him out, but the gang was too small as it was. Besides, he wasn't sure the other two would go for it. He did the next best thing with Tommy—he ignored him.

Henry bent over and dribbled spit on a line of ants that were crawling on the stair below him. He watched them twitch and squirm, trying to swim out of the mess. With the burning sun fueling his anger, he waited for the new tenants to arrive.

*****

At half past noon, a banged up, prewar moving van came rolling down Harper Avenue. As it neared 57th Street, the driver muscled the van to the curb. A stocky, sweat-stained workman climbed down from the passenger side and smoothed out a crumpled sheet of paper. He glanced up at the building and nodded. Ignoring the boys, he lumbered up the steps and propped the heavy glass door open with a wooden wedge.

10

Moments later, a 1946 Plymouth coupe pulled in behind the van. Because the coupe's trunk was too loaded with boxes to close, the lid had been tied down with rope.

The driver of the Plymouth got out and looked around as if making sure the neighborhood was safe to park in. Squinting in the bright sunshine, he went to the trunk, untied the cord holding the lid, and grabbed one of the boxes. He slung the box onto the sidewalk and without waiting for it to land turned to get another.

A harried-looking woman slipped out of the passenger side. She frowned at the dropped box but said nothing. The woman appeared to be in her early thirties. She wore a flimsy summer dress that outlined cone-shaped breasts and a girdled but ample rear end. Straight brunette hair hung limply across her forehead, and perspiration streaked her powdered face. Henry's interest was piqued.

The front passenger seat pushed forward, and a tall, gangly kid slid out. He closed the car door and stood with his hands in his pockets. The woman dropped her cigarette on the sidewalk and ground it out with the toe of her high-heeled shoe. Henry heard her dismiss the van driver with a curt, "Four C, top floor."

The mover's beet-red face turned redder. "Don't nobody live on the first goddamn floor no more?" Henry was sure the curse word was said loud enough for the woman to hear. Swearing in front of a lady was wrong, and he was surprised when she ignored it. It was kind of sexy, a woman who let a guy swear in front of her without pitching a fit.

Henry and the boys had left a path just wide enough for one person. Now, figuring that these new people would expect them to shift to the side for the furniture, the three boys looked to Henry for direction. Almost imperceptibly, he shook his head: stay put.

Still grumbling, the mover motioned to his partner and they pulled a shabby paisley sofa off the van. Making no effort to weave

11

around the boys, they plowed forward straight up the stairs. Now the boys had no choice, it was either move or get stomped on. The three on the lower steps slid toward the railing as the approaching couch threatened to smash into them. Pretending indifference, Henry timed his shift so that the movers would think he'd be out of the way when they got to the top step. Instead, he feigned left and was still blocking the way when the lead guy got to him. Caught by surprise, the man stumbled and stopped, just for an instant. Grinning, Henry quickly slipped to one side and shrugged his innocence.

As the movers passed, Henry unrolled the sleeve of his T-shirt and yanked a smoke out of the crushed pack of Camels he'd stolen from his father. Striking a match and cupping it against a nonexistent wind, he sucked until his cigarette lit. With an elaborate exhale, he flipped away the burnt match and leaned back against the railing to watch the rest of the show.

The driver of the Plymouth slammed the trunk lid shut and got back in the car, leaving the pile of boxes on the sidewalk. The woman gave him a quick cheek kiss through the open window, then waved languidly as he drove away. Once he turned the corner, she pulled a bobby pin from her purse and pinned back the bangs that had fallen across her forehead. Lifting one of the boxes, she started for the building. She glared at the slouching boy and motioned with her head toward the pile of their belongings. The boy jerked as if coming out of a trance. He quickly picked up the largest box and shuffled after her.

The woman started up the steps with her son in tow. The kid's belt was pulled tight around his middle, causing the waistband of his baggy gray pants to crumple into accordion-like folds. Despite the heat, the dress shirt he wore was buttoned at the neck and the sleeves were rolled all the way down. His shoes were scuffed and the baggy pants were too short, exposing plaid socks that drooped around his ankles. Only his wiry brown hair was in style. It was combed into a small wave, obviously held in place by gobs of hair cream. Henry watched the kid and sighed with relief. This momma's boy was no threat.

The new kid, eyes straight ahead, started up the concrete steps carrying an open box stuffed with clothing. Glancing up as if he'd just noticed the boy's existence, Henry smirked and said, "Will ya look at mommy's little helper."

There was no reaction, and Henry wasn't sure the boy had heard. He stared at the boy and took a deep drag on his cigarette. Through the cloud of exhaled smoke, he raised his voice loud enough for the rest of the gang to hear. "Welcome ta Cockroach Castle."

The boy stopped, shifted his box to one side, and peered down at Henry. Henry figured that a kid coming into a new neighborhood would be a little scared or at least wary. This jerk was acting too dumb to be either.

"Cockroach Castle?" The boy spoke the words so softly that only Henry caught them.

"That's what we call it," Henry said. "I'll bet a smart-lookin' guy like you is gonna figure out why real soon."

The woman had stepped around Henry's puddle of spit and now stood at the glass door. She glared at Henry's cigarette. "Dammit, Ben, come on."

The boy hesitated as if he had more questions, but when his mother disappeared up into the darkened hallway, he muttered, "See you later," and hurried inside.

Henry took a final drag and knocked the lit end off with his shoe. Making sure the butt was out, he pushed it back into the rumpled pack and rolled the pack up in his sleeve. Devoid of expression, he muttered under his breath. "Yeah, I'll see ya later, all right."

CHAPTER FOUR

E ven though the momma's boy hadn't looked like much of a challenge, the kid hadn't shown fear, and that bothered Henry. He sat and fumed, focusing on the heat.

The gang watched in silence as the movers drove away and, moments later, the iceman's truck pulled into the empty space. A large, fair-haired man got out, pushed back the canvas curtain that covered the back, and jumped inside. They could all hear the sound of chipping ice as the iceman carved out a fifty-pound block. Within seconds, he emerged, the ice held on his leather-covered shoulder by a pair of iron tongs. The sun played off the melting ice and tantalized with a glistening promise of cool relief. Ignoring the boys, the iceman walked into the back alley toward the porch stairs.

"The Swede won't be back for a while," Henry said. "He's haulin' that ice ta the top floor, the new kid's house."

Mike grinned at the others. "Maybe he'll take time to stick it to the new kid's ol' lady."

Henry had the same thought, so Mike making the remark first annoyed him. "He sure as shit ain't gonna stop on the second floor an' stick it to yours," Henry snarled. "Your old lady's too fat even for the Swede."

Mike clenched his fists and his freckled face blazed red. That suited Henry just fine. The way he was feeling, kicking the shit out of Mike would be a pleasure. Before Mike could move, Tommy stepped in front of Henry. Frowning, he shook his head. "It's not right to talk about a guy's mother. You know it always ends up in a beef."

Henry sneered. He stood, pushed past Tommy, and looked up the alley to make sure the Swede was out of sight.

"Wouldn't bother me or Andy; we ain't got no old lady. Besides, it was a fuckin' joke." He pulled himself up on the back of the truck and grabbed a handful of the ice splinters that had broken away when the iceman carved out the block. Keeping the biggest piece for himself, Henry jumped back down and passed out slivers to the others. Sucking on his chunk of ice, he abruptly turned and started walking away. "It's too hot ta sit around."

The kids knew from past experience not to ask Henry where he was going. He never answered, and questions seemed to make him mad. Tommy and Mike hurried alongside, and Andy, caught by surprise, ran to keep up. Head down, Henry strode up the street fuming. *The day was ruined, and the new kid had ruined it.*

CHAPTER FIVE

H enry rounded the corner of Harper and moved up 57th Street with the others close on his heels. To their right was the row of shops that made up the ground floor of the Castle. The corner shop stood empty. "Drummond's Spot-Free Cleaners" was painted across the wrap-around front window and the floor inside was littered with faded posters and a peppering of dead flies. Next to the empty store was Angelo's, the shoemaker's shop. The door was open and the smell of leather and oil wafted out. Angelo stood behind the counter, hammering a new rubber heel onto a badly worn shoe.

Henry started to shuffle, sliding along without lifting his feet to hide the flapping of the soles of his own shoes. Alongside Angelo's was Anderson's Hardware, and next to the hardware store was the main entrance to the Castle. The name of the former hotel, Commodore Castle, could still be seen where it had been etched into the concrete header over the massive double doors that led inside. A small shed housing Herb's newspaper stand took up half the foyer. There were no late editions on Saturday, so after selling all his morning papers, Herb had closed for the afternoon. Past the building's main entrance was the tiny grocery where everyone in the neighborhood shopped. The front of the grocery store was cluttered with boxes of fruits and vegetables that spewed out onto the sidewalk, the sweet smell of produce almost sickening in the summer heat. Above each crate or box was a sign scribbled in red watercolor paint that announced the bargains of the day.

Abutting the grocery was Olsen's butcher shop. Henry stared through the butcher shop window at the display cases with their rows of steaks and lesser cuts of meat. Even though he'd never had any beef except hamburger, he just knew a steak would taste great. Behind the counter was a huge wooden cutting block with a rack of wicked-looking knives, and off to one side stood open barrels of pickles and sauerkraut.

The owners of the butcher shop and the grocery, Mr. Olsen and Stavros, the Greek were seated on the sidewalk between their respective establishments, playing chess. Perched on milk crates, they stared down at a chessboard set atop an orange crate. Flies buzzed around, attracted by Mr. Olsen's blood-stained apron. The Greek, engrossed in the game, didn't seem to notice those that marched across his bald head.

As the boys neared the grocery, Henry considered grabbing an apple. As if reading his mind, Stavros looked up and scowled at him. Andy stepped into the street and Henry knew it was to avoid getting near the Greek. When Andy was about three years old, the mean son-of-a-bitch had damned near torn off the kid's ear, and Andy was still afraid of him. Henry put an extra strut into his walk and smirked. *Let the old bastard try pulling my ear.*

As they passed the drugstore on the corner of 57th and Blackstone, Andy grabbed at Henry's arm. "Whadda ya think of the new kid?"

Henry shook his arm free and kept walking.

Andy picked at a crusted nostril and stopped for a moment to inspect the result. Satisfied, he wiped it on his pant leg and again hurried to catch

17

up. Coming back alongside Henry, he answered his own question. "The kid seems OK to me."

Without slowing his pace, Henry turned and gave him a disgusted look. "Seems OK to you, does he? Well, he don't seem OK to me, an' I'm gonna make sure he knows it."

Andy had short legs and was slightly pigeon-toed, so he had to add a skip every few paces to keep up. His body was boxy, and his wide jaw, flattened ears, and broad brow gave his head the same square shape. Mike's mother had once told Andy he had a face not even a mother could love. Henry figured she said it because Andy's mother had run out. The remake earned Mike's mother a place on Henry's hate list.

Still skipping to keep up, Andy fished in his pants pocket and dug out a piece of bubble gum. Without turning his head, Henry snapped his fingers and held out his hand. Andy dropped the gum in his palm. Before Mike could complain, Andy dug out three more pieces, gave one each to Mike and Tommy, and popped the third piece in his mouth.

Peeling away the wrapping, Mike whined, "This shit's all melted." He slipped it in his mouth, grimacing as if he thought it might taste bad. As the sweetness hit, he started to chew contentedly. "Watch this!" he said, and he blew a softball-sized, pink balloon of gum.

"Watch this!" Henry mimicked and poked a hole in the bubble. The bubble collapsed, covering Mike's face with an opaque film of pink gum.

Carefully, Mike started peeling the gum off. The heat made it sticky, but he was still able to get most of it off. He stuck the gum back in his mouth and started chewing again. "You're a fuckin' moron."

Because it was said without rancor, Henry ignored him.

Tommy took the wrapper off his gum and read aloud the joke that was printed on the inside. "Use the words defeat, defense and detail in one sentence." When no one said anything, he read the rest of it. "De feet of de cat went over de fence before de tail."

Henry sneered at Andy for giggling. Then he stared at Mike, daring him to laugh.

Andy kept grinning and hitched up his jeans. "So whadda you guys wanna do?"

Henry felt sorry for Andy. The guy just wasn't cool. A lot of it was the way he wore his clothes. If everyone rolled the cuffs of their jeans up, Andy's would drag around on the ground. If the winter style was to push the sleeves of a sweatshirt up to the forearm, Andy's would hang down to his knuckles. And the grin, the moron was always grinning, trying to make the guys like him.

Before Henry could answer, Tommy chimed in. "We could go down to the lake. Maybe go swimming off the point."

Mike shook his head. "If I go home to get a swimsuit, I'll have to stay in an' help my brother. He's cuttin' a board to put under my old man's mattress. It's for his bad back. My mom thinks if he could heal it up, he could maybe get a job."

As they crossed the street at Blackstone, Henry pointed to something on the strip between the street and sidewalk. The strip, once grass, was now cement-hard dirt. In the middle was a Baby Ruth candy bar surrounded by broken glass, cigarette butts, a few bottle tops, and assorted scraps of paper trash. The afternoon heat had melted the chocolate so flat, it looked like an empty wrapper.

He nudged Andy with his shoulder. "Hey, grab that!"

Henry knew that asking Andy to pick up the candy was silly, a joke, really.

But Andy took it seriously. "It's dirty," he said, shrinking away as if the candy could somehow come after him.

19

"No, it ain't. You can see it's still wrapped." Henry was grinning, but Andy's reaction was annoying him. He wasn't used to having Andy say no.

"Back off, Henry. It's a melted piece of shit," Tommy said.

They passed by the candy bar, but Henry wouldn't give up. "Yeah, well, maybe it would be OK if it got cooled off. The big mouth who thinks it's a melted piece of shit could take it home an' put it in his fancy refrigerator for Booger Face to eat later."

Tommy's family was the only one in the building with a refrigerator. His mother worked as a secretary for a Realtor. When one of her bosses' clients upgraded to a Frigidaire, the client sold her his old Sears Cold-Spot. Henry grudgingly gave Tommy credit for not bragging about it or laughing when one of the other guys had to go home to empty their icebox drip pans. Even so, he never passed up a chance to rib Tommy about it.

"Hey," Tommy said, "You want the candy so bad, why don't you grab it?"

"Nah," Henry shrugged, and laughed. "I'll leave it for some poor kid."

CHAPTER SIX

Without asking what anyone else wanted, Henry made the kind of pronouncement he knew the others hated. "I'm in the mood for a game of pitch."

The sun was behind him, forcing Tommy to shade his eyes when he faced in Henry's direction. "It's too hot. I still say we go down to the lake."

Ignoring him, Henry turned back toward the building. "We can play across the street against the Miller Building. It's in the shade."

Mike and Andy followed without protest, and Henry figured Tommy would go along rather than be left out.

Tommy said, "OK; my bat's on our porch. I'll go get it, but one of you guys needs to find a ball."

Andy triumphantly pulled a tennis ball out of his pocket.

Once back at the building, Henry ordered Mike to scrape the outline of a strike zone on the wall of the tenement across the street from the Castle.

The game was simple. The pitcher threw a tennis ball toward the strike zone as hard as he could. A ball inside the marked rectangle was a strike; outside, it was a ball. Three strikes were an out; four balls counted as a run. A hit ball caught on the fly was an out. If it wasn't caught, it was a run.

Because he owned the bat, Tommy was the first batter. That was the way Henry had set up the rules, and it became accepted practice, as did Henry's right to be the first pitcher. Mike stood in the middle of the street and dug the tip of his shoe in the melting tar of a patched pothole. He would pitch to Henry and bat third. Andy stood against the wall of the Castle on the other side of the street, in case Tommy tagged one.

Tommy took a few practice swings, then stared out at Henry, waggling the bat like the real ball players did. Henry kneaded the ball and grinned at Tommy. He enjoyed being the pitcher because the batter had to rely on him to call balls and strikes. The first three balls he threw were too far outside for him to pretend they were strikes.

Henry had never been to a real ball game, but he'd seen *The Pride of the Yankees* at the Kimbark Theater. Three films, a Buck Rogers short, and fifteen cartoons, but you had to have the price of admission, a dime. Slowly, he looked out at Mike and Andy, mimicking the way he'd seen the pitchers try to intimidate the batters in that film.

Mike's face was Irish red from the heat. His position was near the curb, where the sewer belched up the odor of garbage and sewer gas. "Come on, Henry, I'm dyin' out here. Just toss him a strike so's the rest of us can get to bat."

Henry smirked at Andy, then quickly turned and threw the next pitch. It was a perfect strike, and it caught Tommy by surprise. The next one, he floated in, and Tommy swung hard, foul-tipping it. Strike two. With the count full, Henry sailed in his pride-and-joy pitch, a slow-moving sinker. The ball dropped too quickly and was low, but Henry called, "Strike three! You're out," and started moving toward the wall.

Tommy acted as if Henry had slapped him. "It was a ball! You walked me, I got one run." He pounded the bat against the sidewalk a few times and went back into a crouch, ready for the next pitch.

"It was dead fucking center, man." Henry turned to the others for confirmation, but they both just shrugged.

Tommy straightened to his full height and stared at Henry. "That ball was so low, I think it bounced before it got here."

Henry stiffened. "Are you callin' me a liar?" Without a windup, he threw the tennis ball at Tommy's head. Tommy had plenty of time to avoid getting hit but waited until the last instant to duck. The ball caromed off the wall and bounced back to Henry.

"Are you crazy? You been actin' pissed off all day, an' I'm sick of it. Try playin' pitch without a bat." Tommy tucked the bat under his arm and turned to walk away.

Henry stood, tossing the ball up a few feet and catching it. Before Tommy could reach the door of the Castle, Henry called out, "Hold on, man. I'm sorry. I just got my mind on the new guy." As Tommy drifted back, Henry turned to Andy and Mike. Still tossing the ball up and down, he bared his teeth in a nasty grin. "I got an idea how we can have some fun an' let the momma's boy know who's boss around here at the same time."

CHAPTER SEVEN

S till grinning, Henry loped into the Castle's Harper Avenue entrance, climbed the stairs past his own first-floor flat and continued up to the fourth floor. He was used to the sight of cracked walls, broken banisters, and worn linoleum and no longer noticed any of it. On the other hand, the smells varied from day to day. Most days, a mildew stench would seep through the plaster and up from the wooden floors to compete with the cooking odors of cabbage, rancid fat and strange spices. Sometimes vomit, spilled booze, or urine would augment the mix. When that happened, the women of the building would eventually mop up the mess and kill the stink with Pine-Sol. This being Saturday, the smell of pine-scented bleach was heavy in the stagnant air.

On each landing, a single low-wattage bulb hung down from the ceiling and kept the hallway from complete darkness. There were no numbers on the doors, but Henry knew where everyone in the building lived.

The new kid's apartment was the first door off the stairs. Henry strode over, knocked harder than necessary, and stepped back a pace. After a few seconds, light streamed out of the apartment as the dark-haired woman opened the door on the night chain. When she saw who it was, she pushed the door closed again, and for an instant, Henry thought she was going to ignore him. Then he heard the chain rattle and the door jerked fully open.

She stood glowering, one hand on the doorknob and the other on her hip. The armpits of her dress were dark with sweat stains, and a few strands of hair that had escaped the bobby pin were plastered to her forehead. "What do *you* want?" She spit out the words, her voice edged with exhaustion.

Even with his reputation as a bad influence on the other kids, Henry's smile was sometimes enough to soften the hearts of women in the building. He started to smile now, but appraised the new woman's look and quickly changed his mind. Instead he mumbled, "Uh, can your kid come out?"

Shifting to one side, the woman shrugged and let Henry in. "Ask him yourself. He's in the back."

Like most of the apartments in the building, the four rooms were in a row, railroad fashion. Henry wove his way around the half-emptied boxes and headed through the kitchen to the back room. The new kid was sprawled on a mattress that hadn't been set in its bed frame. A Cubs game blared from the radio, drowning out Henry's footsteps. He stood in the doorway and took a moment to observe his victim. This, he decided, was going to be fun. When the boy looked over and saw Henry watching him, he jerked upright into a sitting position and switched off the radio.

Henry fought to keep his voice level. "Ya listen ta ball games?"

The boy shook his head. "Nothing else on."

They stared at each other until Henry looked away. "Ya wanna come out? Your mother says it's OK."

The boy stood up and moved past Henry. "Mom, can I go out?"

"Oh, go ahead, Ben. God knows, you're no help to me lying around listening to the radio."

Henry forced a casual tone, but couldn't quite hide his anger. "I already told ya she said it was OK. Did ya think I was lyin'?"

Ben shrugged. "Nah; it's just she gets funny sometimes."

Henry followed Ben to the front door. When they passed the boy's mother, Henry pasted on a smile and said good-bye with a slight wave of his hand. She ignored him.

She called after her son. "I saw that kid smoking. You know what I think about that. Smoke and you'll wind up a shrimp like him."

Henry pushed in front of Ben and started down the stairs, two steps at a time. Ben paced him and it turned into a race. Ben was faster, but Henry had the advantage of having gone down hundreds of times. He used the banister to pull himself along and leaped the last few steps of each landing. They were neck and neck at the top of the final flight when Henry flung himself forward and jumped the final eight stairs. Ben shrugged and slowed to a walk. Henry opened the front door with a smirk and a slight bow, letting Ben precede him out.

They crossed the street to where the other three waited. Henry whispered, "I told the guys you might be Ok. So try not to act like too big an asshole."

CHAPTER EIGHT

B en gave Henry a nervous nod and dropped a pace behind. As they approached, he felt the eyes of the other three boys staring at him. The big one with the red face full of freckles turned away first and let fly with a gob of spit. "Them's some stupid-lookin' pants."

Ben went rigid, but his new friend Henry put an arm around his shoulder.

Henry told the big one, Mike, to shut up. "Ya want Ben ta think we don't like him?"

Mike let fly with another gob of spit, but he kept quiet. Henry squeezed Ben closer. "Look, Ben, we're goin' over ta the victory gardens in the park ta get some tomatoes. You wanna come with?"

Ignoring the tingle of warning that crawled across his scalp, Ben shrugged and mumbled, "Are there still victory gardens there?"

"Yeah, after the war, no one ever bothered ta dig up the stuff that was planted. They just left things to rot. So whadda ya say? Ya wanna come?"

When Ben nodded, Henry made a fist and gave him an approving punch on the shoulder. It was a hard shot, and Ben had to bite down to keep from reacting. Forcing a smile, he followed the group toward the park.

They crossed Stony Island Avenue and pushed through the lilac bushes that bordered the park. Tomatoes were the hardiest of the vegetables that still grew there. Snaking their vines between high weeds and the dead stalks of other plants, they extended far beyond the plots originally laid out for them. Stopping at the first row, Henry waved his arm in a broad sweep that included the entire garden. "Pick as many as you can. We'll divvy 'em up later."

Ben moved away from the group and began collecting tomatoes. He tried to find good ones, thinking that the tomatoes were to be eaten, but noticed that the others seemed to concentrate on picking the most rotten ones they could find. Within an hour, the boys had each filled a bag. Heading back to the Castle, Ben pushed past the others and walked alongside Henry the entire way. They hid their bags in the alley behind the building and agreed to meet after dinner.

Ben tried to damp down his excitement at being included in whatever the group was planning. After all, Henry was the only one who had actually talked to him. Maybe the others thought he was an asshole, like Henry said they might. He decided he hadn't done or said anything wrong. Even so, he knew from having bounced around different neighborhoods that you never knew when some kid would be offended. He promised himself he would keep his mouth shut when they got together again. That way, he couldn't say anything stupid. With a quick wave to Henry, he headed home.

*****

The sun settled into the evening haze, and a slight onshore breeze helped drop the temperature a few degrees. The neighborhood quieted, and the street lamps blinked on.

Once dinner ended, Ben wandered out to the stoop. The group was already there, lagging pennies. They stood shoulder- to-shoulder, aiming for the sidewalk line two squares away. After each toss, the closest penny to the line took all the money. Ben fingered the few coins he had in his pocket and watched the game with envy. No one had asked him to join in, and something warned him that lagging for pennies was a sacred ritual, too special for outsiders.

After almost an hour of lagging, Ben was fighting boredom. He was about to tell Henry he had to get home when Henry threw a final penny directly on the line. With that, the boy Ben had come to recognize as the leader collected his winnings and nodded for Ben to follow him. They retrieved the bags of tomatoes and moved across the street.

Puzzled, Ben watched as Henry reached into his bag and pulled out a huge tomato. Taking aim at the chalk rectangle they'd used earlier for the game of pitch, the boy went into a full big league windup. As he released the gooey mess, he came to a forward crouched position and yelped as it splattered on the wall directly in the center of the strike zone. Then he put a tomato in Ben's hand. Ben hesitated, worried about being caught.

Seeming to sense his concern, Henry motioned toward the target and said in a low, menacing tone, "Go ahead an' throw." Then, leaning in close, he whispered, "Unless you're a fuckin' chicken."

Ben wound up and threw, but his tomato dropped a few feet short of the wall. Embarrassed, he looked over at Henry, who had already turned away and was throwing another tomato of his own. In a frenzy, the others joined in, and tomatoes flew everywhere. Some accidentally landed on parked cars and first-floor windows, but no one came out to stop the game, so they all kept throwing.

When fewer than half the tomatoes remained, a contest appeared to develop between Mike and Henry. "That's three inside the square," Henry said, stepping back and waiting for Mike to throw. "We're even."

Mike grinned at Ben, then lampooned checking the wind direction by wetting his thumb and holding it up in the air. Acting satisfied, he closed one eye, sighted down his arm and lobbed a tomato so rotten he had to keep his grip loose for fear of squashing it. It hit the wall just outside of the line.

"Ya missed; we're still even," Henry said. "My turn."

The others remained silent.

"Hey, I think it's touchin' the line," Mike said. "I'll go look."

Henry frowned at Mike. "Nah; I don't trust you." He gestured to Ben. "Let the new kid look."

Ben was too happy to be cautious. Grinning, he tossed the tomato he'd been holding and started to run across the street. Behind him, the other four silently waited for him to reach the wall.

The first shot aimed at Ben was a miss. Black with rot, it slapped against the bricks, exploding in all directions and splattering him with seeds and liquid. The second one connected. Just as he was turning back toward the group, it caught him full in the neck and gave off a stench that almost gagged him. The next tomato hit a foot lower, its juices splashing red like blood against the white of his shirt. He stood frozen, like a thief caught in a watchman's flashlight, as pieces of the soggy mess ran down inside his collar. More followed. A few missed, but others, better aimed, hit him in the face and chest.

Ben bowed his head and didn't move. A choking sensation gripped at his throat, warning him he was about to cry. He had been so sure Henry liked him, so sure he'd found a friend. Swallowing deeply, he forced his head back up and stuck his chin out in defiance. He couldn't fight all four of them, but he wasn't going to give them the satisfaction of seeing him run.

He heard the big one scream, "Run, you stupid fuckin' sheeny, run!" And, as Ben watched, the boy wound up and threw the largest tomato yet. It struck him in the chest with a solid thump, and its force made him stagger backward a few steps. This was the first one that had

30

caused physical pain, and in that instant, he thought maybe he should run.

Then, Henry stopped in mid-windup and let his arm slowly drop to his side. Tommy, the one who had seemed nice, also stopped, and they both stared at Ben with puzzled expressions. Runny-nosed Andy hadn't been throwing at all. He was standing behind the other three, hands in his pockets, staring down at the sidewalk.

Only Freckle-Face was still throwing. Either he hadn't noticed or didn't care that the others had quit. Ben saw him pull another tomato from his bag and proudly display it to Henry. He grinned at Ben and shifted the tomato from his right hand to his left, shaking the right hand free of the dripping juice. Ben jammed his eyes shut to keep from wincing and forced himself to stand still. The tomato never hit. Instead, Ben heard Tommy holler, "Gus!" and when his eyes flew open, he saw Mike drop the tomato and all four boys took off running.

Ben stood wiping the mess from his eyes, trying to understand why they had run away. Part of him wanted to sit down on the curb and cry. Another part was urging him to move, to leave before they changed their minds and came back. Scraping some of the pulp off his shirt, he started to turn when steely fingers gripped the back of his neck. He tried to struggle loose, but before he could get away, an open hand slammed into the side of his face.

CHAPTER NINE

"**S**on-uf-a-bitch." Along with the curse came another ear-ringing roundhouse slap. "You vill clean up dis crap, or I kick shit out of you."

Terror gripped Ben. He wanted to scream, but his throat was so tight he could barely squeak. He again struggled to break away, but the janitor just tightened his grip and gave the boy a final stinging slap.

At a solid six foot three, Gus looked like a giant. His iron gray hair was cropped close to the skull, and his face was etched in an unforgiving frown. His gray work clothes were smudged with coal dust, and his blackened hands were hard with calluses.

Gus shouted again, "You vill clean up dis mess," and before Gus had the words fully out, Ben was nodding as fast as he could.

Gus let go.

"Who vas dose udder boys?" He spun Ben around and grabbed him under the chin.

Ben tried to nod again, but Gus held his chin too tight. His voice had come back but his teeth were chattering so hard, he couldn't stop stuttering. "I'll cl—cl—ean it up; I pro—pro—mise."

A window on the second floor of the Miller Building slid open, and an elderly woman leaned out. Her voice was shrill with outrage. "I watched the whole thing. There was five of 'em, but he's the ring-leader."

Gus looked up and waved dismissively. "You vatch, but you don't say nothing?"

The window slammed down and Gus looked back at Ben.

Pushing him in the chest, he forced the boy up against the wall. For a moment, the sulfuric smell of coal overcame the stench of rotten tomatoes.

Ben fought desperately to keep from crying. "I'm sorry. I swear I'll clean it up."

"Gottdamn right you clean up. You and doze udder boys. Who vas dey?"

Ben shook his head and shrugged stupidly. "I don't know. I'm new here."

Gus's rage seemed to flare up again, and Ben knew he wasn't buying the obvious lie. "I know who you are! I run da building what you live in. I know your momma, and I tell her vot you do. You tell me who vas dose udder boys." He pointed at Ben's tomato-splattered shirt. "Vhy dey throw stuff at you?"

Ben stared down at his shoes and shrugged.

Grabbing the boy by the upper arms, Gus shook him so hard, his head snapped back and forth. He let go and shook a finger in Ben's face. "You be out here tomorrow; vash valls, vash cars, vash vindows. You be here, or I tell momma and den I kick your ass."

*****

Ben met the janitor the next morning, and, without a word, accepted a scrub brush, bucket, and broom. With Gus watching, he went to work. The job turned out to be easier than he thought. The few tenants whose windows were spattered probably didn't know Ben had been caught, because they had cleaned up their windows themselves. On Sundays, cars

33

were needed to get families to church for early Mass, so all but one had been driven away. Ben sloshed the wall and the sidewalk with buckets of water and scrubbed them clean with the broom. Once, he glanced across the street and saw a curtain on the first floor of the Castle pull away, then flutter back. He figured that the whole gang was up there watching and laughing at him. Face burning with shame, he ignored them and went about washing the lone car as best he could. By noon, the job was finished.

As Ben headed home, Henry and the rest of the gang strolled out of the Castle. They stood in front of the side entrance, and Ben realized he'd have to walk past them to get in. He watched as Henry got a penny out of his pocket and started lagging. The one named Tommy joined him.

Ben knew he could avoid them by going around the block to use the main entrance on 57th Street, but he didn't even consider it. He balled up his fists and walked across the street toward the side door. He couldn't fight them all, but he promised himself that he'd keep fighting until he was either knocked out or killed. Henry seemed to be concentrating on his throw, and he let loose just as Ben stepped up on the curb. The coin landed on the line. Without looking at Ben, Henry stooped to pick up his winnings. Ben strode by with his head up, staring straight ahead. When he was almost to the door, Henry called, "Hey, you, new kid…uh, Ben."

When Ben looked back, all four boys were smiling at him. Henry shrugged and said, "You wanna lag?"

CHAPTER TEN

B en propped the living room window open with a two-foot piece of broom handle. He stared down, oblivious to the warm morning breeze blowing into the flat. Across the street, a couple of girls flounced out of the Miller Building's side entrance. They wore full skirts and white blouses and clutched their schoolbooks so tightly against their chests that Ben couldn't see if they had breasts. He watched as they tilted their heads together and giggled. Another girl joined them, and the three turned the corner and headed west toward the local grammar school.

It was Thursday. School had opened the day after Labor Day, two days earlier.

Ben's mother was in the bathroom, putting on her makeup. The bathroom door was open, and he turned to look at her as she rolled on her lipstick and rubbed her lips together to even out the bright red smear. Without turning away from the mirror, she called out. "Benjamin, you are going to school today if I have to take you by the arm and drag you there."

Ben moved away from the window and flopped onto the couch. The steel in her voice and her use of his full first name left him no hope. He decided to try anyway. "I've got this really bad stomachache." Grimacing, he grabbed his middle, moaned, and doubled over.

He could tell she was watching him out of the corner of her eye, and the sneer on her face showed him his performance wasn't convincing her. She forced a smile to check her teeth for lipstick, and with a final flounce of her hair, walked over to Ben. Gripping his chin firmly, she tilted his head up. "You'll meet people, make new friends."

He started to object and she stiffened. "The discussion's over. You're going to school."

Ben swallowed hard and went back to his room to get dressed. Talk of meeting people and making friends was crap. He didn't give a damn about making friends—he just wanted to keep from getting the shit kicked out of him. They'd lived in four different places over the last seven years. Each move had meant a new school, and each new school had meant proving himself all over again.

He pulled on his pants and cinched his belt as tight as possible. Fear of having them fall down was stronger than his shame at the way they looked all bunched up. Most of Ben's clothes were hand-me-downs from one of his many "uncles," and his mother assured him he'd grow into them. He was already taller than the uncle who had given him the pants, so that didn't seem likely. He pulled on a polo shirt and left it hanging out to cover the baggy waistline of the pants.

By the time he finished dressing, his mother was gone. She hadn't bothered to saygood-bye, but there was a glass of milk, a bowl of Wheaties, a sack lunch, and a dime on the table. He gulped down the milk, poured the Wheaties back into the box, and grabbed the dime and his lunch. Stopping at the bathroom, he put his things down and peered in the mirror to see if pulling on the polo shirt had mussed his hair. It was so heavily greased with hair cream that it was unmussable, but he did a final re-comb anyway.

As he left the safety of the flat, his stomach fluttered and brought up the sour taste of undigested milk. He swallowed hard and walked quickly along the corridor to Andy's door. He hoped to catch Andy and Henry before they started the five-block walk to school. Henry said that they could all go together, but Ben's having missed Tuesday and Wednesday put that in doubt.

Henry was leaning against the wall next to Andy's door. Ben hid his relief. He didn't want to walk to school alone, but he couldn't admit that to Henry. Henry would think he was chicken.

"Hi," Ben said, and Henry nodded.

"Hi, yourself. Where ya been?"

Ben sidled up and put his back against the wall, imitating Henry's stance. "Sick."

Henry smirked, "Me too, but my old man booted my ass out anyway."

With nothing left to say, Ben stared at the linoleum-covered floor. Finally, Henry pushed forward and banged on the door. "Come on, asshole. We're gonna be late. Mike an' Tommy already gave up on ya an' went ahead." Moments later, several locks clicked, and the door flew open. A disheveled Andy charged out, still tucking his shirt in. His hair fanned out wildly in all directions, and one of his shoes was unlaced.

For some reason, seeing Andy's hair made Ben think about his. He pulled out his comb and swept it across, first one side, then the other.

Andy skipped along on one foot, trying to tie his shoe. He looked up and mumbled, "Sorry," to Henry. Then he caught sight of Ben. "Where you been?"

Before Ben could answer, Henry grabbed Andy's arm. "Let's just go."

Herb stood at the newsstand. He grinned at the kids and waved as they charged by.

The sunny day did nothing to lighten Ben's spirits as the three headed down 57th Street toward Ray Elementary. Some of the shabbiness of Hyde Park was hidden by the rows of oaks and elms lining the streets, but high above the trees, he could see the aging tenements that comprised most of the neighborhood.

Ben felt comfortable with Henry, despite his bossiness. "Can I ask you somethin'?"

Henry shrugged. "Yeah?"

"When I moved in, you called the building the Cockroach Castle, an' you said I'd figure out why it was called that. Well, I figured out the cockroach part, but I don't get the castle part."

Henry frowned. "You got lots of roaches?"

Ben gave a mock shudder. "Yeah, the little fuckers are everywhere."

Andy chimed in, "And bedbugs—and water beetles—and silverfish."

Henry reached over and tousled Andy's hair. "You an' your scummy brother are the only ones with bedbugs. Ya probably got cooties and crabs, too."

Andy flushed, but it seemed to Ben he liked the teasing.

They walked for a moment in silence. "OK," Ben said. "So we all got bugs, but what about the castle part? How'd that dump get a name like the Castle?"

Henry shrugged again. "The dump started out a high-class hotel, with a lobby and doormen an' everything. It was named after some guy named Commodore, an' I guess he thought it was his castle or somethin'."

Ben laughed. "Commodore's not a name. It's a rank, like captain or admiral. You know, like Commodore Perry."

Henry stopped and his face turned red. The anger in his voice was unmistakable. "You sound real smart, Benny. Just don't get too smart."

Ben just shrugged, but Andy seemed concerned that Henry would stay angry. He tugged at Henry's arm. "He didn't mean nothin' by it, Henry. Don't go gettin' all mad."

Ben nodded. "Yeah, I didn't mean nothin'. I was just…let's forget it, OK?" He held his hand out, palm up, and Henry lightly slapped it. They started walking again, faster now, suddenly remembering how late it was.

As they neared the school, Henry said, "Look out for the guys with maroon jackets. They belong to a gang called the Dukes. Most of 'em are pussies, but if ya get into it with one, ya gotta fight 'em all."

"An' keep away from the playground," Andy advised. "If you stay cool an' don't smart off, most of the guys'll leave you alone."

Henry waved to a girl who was walking so fast she was almost running. "That's Anita. She ain't got such big tits, but one of the guys said she let him touch 'em at the movies."

Ben stayed silent. Not even the thought of touching tits could ease his mounting panic.

At Kenwood Avenue, a patrol boy was supervising the street crossing. He wore a white belt that circled his waist and slashed diagonally across his chest. Standing with his arms outstretched, he held back the kids until the street was clear. As the three of them reached the curb, they watched a car start into the intersection. The patrol boy put up his arms, and when the car came to a stop, he waved them across. Ben couldn't believe it—the car had stopped for a kid. Once they made it to the other side, the driver of the car went on across, smiling at the patrol boy as he passed. Ben decided he'd become a patrol boy as soon as they'd let him.

"Whadda moron," Henry sneered. "Gets up an hour early, puts on that stupid belt, an' every day he stands out there. Rain, snow, colder than a whore's heart—it don't matter, he's gotta stand there.

39

An' what's the sucker get for it? Shit!! That's what he gets. My old man says ya always gotta ask, 'What's in it for me?'"

The threesome turned the corner at Kimbark Avenue, walked past the girl's entrance to the school, and headed for the boy's entrance on the other side of the building.

*****

Ray Elementary looked more like a penitentiary than a school to Ben. A three-story brick and granite building, it loomed above him like something out of a horror movie. On each side were gravel-covered play areas surrounded by a spiked iron fence. The playground to the south was for the girls, while the one on the north was filled with boys.

The first bell rang just as Ben, Henry and Andy reached the boy's entrance. When the doors flew open, Ben was caught by surprise. He stood undecided for a moment, and in that instant, Henry and Andy were swept away with the crowd.

Ben tried to catch up to them, but the hall became even more congested as the swarm of girls coming in from the other side mingled with the boys. At first, the noise was deafening, each kid yelling louder than the other trying to be heard over the din. Then the crowd began to thin as everyone—except Ben—moved into classrooms or headed up the stairs to other floors. One by one, the rooms filled and doors closed. Within moments, the tornado of a thousand pushing, shouting children passed through and left only a silent, empty hallway. Ben stood stranded in the middle of the main corridor, completely alone.

CHAPTER ELEVEN

A woman with blue-gray hair pulled tightly back in a bun seemed to appear from out of nowhere. She wore a dark blue dress buttoned all the way up and smelled faintly of mothballs. Snapping open the watch locket around her neck, she tapped her finger on the dial and said, "It's late! You'd better get to your class."

Ben was flustered. He knew the number of the room he was supposed to be in because they had told his mother when she registered him. But no one had bothered to tell him how to get there. "Uh…I…uh"

The watch clicked closed. "New here?"

Ben nodded.

"Know your homeroom number?"

"Uh huh."

"Well, spit it out. What is it?"

"Uh, 204."

With a smirk, she pointed to the stairway. "As you might expect, 204 is on the second floor. It's next to the library."

When Ben's face still registered confusion, the woman sighed. "I'm Miss Lynn, the librarian. I'm going to the library now. If you'd like you can follow me."

Ben felt a rush of gratitude and stammered, "Thanks."

The half-glass door marked 204 had been propped open with a metal garbage can. The room was in chaos. Some of the girls were huddled together chattering loudly, while others were combing their hair or applying makeup. The boys pushed, shouted, ran around the desks, and threw paper balls at each other. There was no teacher in the room.

Ben slipped through the doorway and stood to one side, waiting for the teacher to come in and assign him a seat. He agonized over the teacher's absence. She might be sick and not show up. He saw himself without a seat, forced to stand against the wall for the whole homeroom period. Choking back the tightness in his throat, he shoved his hands in his pockets and slouched forward, quietly looking down at the floor.

The chaos eased when a tall, middle-aged woman in a long gray dress rushed into the room. Her head jutted forward and her shoulders were rounded as if her height was an embarrassment to her. Once at her desk, she began shuffling papers.

Cold sweat dribbled down Ben's face and he felt in need of a bathroom.

Everyone took a seat and the noise level dropped but suddenly there were loud whispers.

A boy looked over at Ben, turned to the boy behind and asked, "Who's that?" There were other murmurs and echoes of the same question.

Someone said, "Look at them pants," and the class burst into laughter.

When the laughter died out, one of the girls said, "He's kinda cute!" and several others hid their giggles with their hands.

The buzzing continued until the teacher, still frazzled, looked up from her papers and surveyed the classroom. The room quieted and a few of the students glanced over at Ben.

The teacher distractedly waved in his direction and reached into her top drawer for the class roster. She pointed to an empty seat. "Name?"

Ben moved to his assigned desk and mumbled, "Ben Kahn."

"Speak up. I'm sure you can speak louder than that."

The whole class seemed to titter and the murmuring started up again. When the teacher snapped at Ben a second time the class fell quiet. At the same instant, Ben shouted to be heard over the noise. "Ben Kahn!"

The class exploded with laughter. The teacher rapped sharply on her desk and the class settled down. She frowned at Ben. "Everybody please say hello to Ben Kahn."

In ragged unison the class giggled out a garbled, "Hello, Ben Kahn."

*****

The top of Ben's desk was so carved up he knew he wouldn't be able to write on it without something firm under the paper. The country's favorite bad word had been repeatedly scratched in and then altered to hide its existence. The most common disguise was the"F" changed to a "B" and the "U" to an "O" forming the word "bock." No one had changed the next word, so "Bock you" was repeated in several spots. The word "love" was also gouged in a few times, and hearts with initials appeared all around the edges. An empty hole in the corner had been designed for an inkwell, and there was a space for books under the desktop.

The homeroom period lasted just long enough for the teacher to take attendance and pass on information about an upcoming assembly. Then the bell rang and the students rushed out to their first class.

Ben's next two classes were more of the same. Girls giggled, boys sneered, and his urge to pee got stronger. Finally, during the recess

43

between the second and third period, Ben found the first-floor boy's bathroom and locked himself in a stall. The room had just been washed down, and the smell of bleach partially blocked the stink of urine. Thinking about Andy's warning to keep away from the playground, Ben decided the bathroom would be a good place to hide. He peed into the commode standing up. Then, worried that someone might peek under the stall door and wonder why he was just standing there, he dropped his pants and sat down on the toilet seat. The stall was covered with scratched initials and badly drawn pictures of breasts, legs with dark triangles, and penises. Someone had written, "Here I sit brokenhearted, came to shit and only farted." Ben thought that was pretty funny and tried to think up one of his own. He pulled out his pencil and wrote, "Different foods go in your mouth, but it's all the same when it comes out south." Deciding it sounded stupid, he used his eraser to smear it away.

*****

After fourth period, the bell rang for lunch. Ben ate his sandwich dry rather than risk standing in line to buy milk. One of the worst fights he'd gotten into at his old school had been when a boy tried to extort money from him in the milk line.

The day's weather was mild, so most of the kids ate their lunch out on the playground. Ben went to the basement lunchroom instead. The room was long and narrow, with empty benches and limited lighting. It felt cave-like and safe. Wrapping his arms around his knees, he tucked himself into a corner. He would have stayed there until the bell to end lunch sounded, but a hall monitor showed up and told him to finish and leave. He thought about hiding in a bathroom again, but he didn't know where the basement bathroom was and was afraid to ask. That left the playground.

CHAPTER TWELVE

A s Ben walked out onto the boy's playground, he spotted a group of kids who were spinning tops on the concrete apron in front of the school doors. Standing away from the main crowd, a boy younger than Ben was winding the string around his top. He was small and skinny, with droopy eyes, and he seemed harmless.

The kid held one end of the string, and with a flip of his wrist, he set the top dancing over the concrete. When it finally started to wobble, he picked it up and started winding the string around the top again. Ben had never had a top, but the process of making it spin looked simple. Staring down at his feet, he risked asking, "Can I try?"

The boy stopped winding and looked up at Ben. He stared for several seconds, then slowly shook his head no and moved away. After he'd put some distance between himself and Ben, he finished winding the string. With the same practiced whip of his wrist, he released his top again. This time, the top whirled further away, seeming to pick up speed as it spun.

Suddenly, another top slashed through the air. This one had its point sharpened into a spike. It hit the already spinning top and split it in two. The group watching gave a roar of approval, and the kid with the broken top started to cry. No one paid any attention to him. Instead, the sharpened top became the object of interest.

"Lemme see!" They circled around, pushing and shoving, trying to get a look at the spiker.

"Back off." The owner was big, almost as tall as Ben, and heavier. With a flourish, he waved his top and grinned with pride. "That's the fifth one this baby's split. This top's a killer."

Ben craned his neck to get a look at the killer top and was forced by the crowd to brush up against its owner.

The proud grin faded. The large boy looked over at Ben, sizing him up. "You got a top?"

Ben took a step backward and shook his head, "Uh-uh."

"Then get the fuck outta here."

As Ben turned away, there was laughter and a clucking noise that was supposed to sound like a chicken. Ben wasn't afraid to fight. Four different schools in seven years had toughened him up. Given an opponent who was close to his size and age, he was able to hold his own. But he hated fighting. It never seemed to end. As soon as he fought one kid, another one would want to see how tough he was. He'd decided two schools ago that it was better to keep quiet and try not to be noticed.

Hoping to find Henry or one of the other Castle kids, Ben wandered aimlessly out onto the gravel surface of the schoolyard. Circles for marble games had been scratched in the gravel, and kids ringed around to watch. Players took turns using one marble to knock another marble outside the circle. Once a marble was out of the circle, it became the property of the kid who had knocked it out. Like pool, a player kept shooting until he missed. The game went on until all of the marbles had been cleared from the circle. To start a new game, each kid had to drop five marbles into the circle.

Ben thought about it. He considered himself good with marbles and debated bringing some the next day. The fierce intensity on the faces of the players made him decide against it.

He spotted an empty set of monkey bars and figured they were used to do chin-ups. Chin-ups were something Ben could do and do well. He had strong arms and had once done fifteen in a row. Climbing up one side, he swung onto the first rung of the horizontal bar. A larger boy climbed up the other side, mirroring Ben's movements. Lazily, the larger boy swung toward Ben. Someone started shouting, "Monkey fight! Monkey fight!" and kids stopped what they were doing to gather around the bars.

Confused, Ben dropped to the ground and started to move away, but the larger boy dropped down next to Ben and blocked his path. His face had a mean, mottled look, and his crooked teeth were yellow. He stiff-armed Ben in the chest, knocking him back a step.

"How 'bout a monkey fight?"

Ben didn't know what a monkey fight was, but the crowd surrounding him was so thick, it was impossible to back away. "OK, I'll do it, but how's it played?"

"It ain't played, 'cause it ain't no game. It's a fight," someone offered.

Ben still looked confused. Finally, a boy with dark curly hair smiled and pushed forward.

"There ain't no rules. You go up on the bars an' swing out till you reach the middle. The idea is to get past the other guy, an' the only way to do that is to make him let go. You can kick, punch, wrap him with your legs, anything goes. First one that falls is the loser."

There were nods of agreement, and the large boy started rubbing his hands in the dirt. Terrified of being embarrassed, Ben did the same, then they went to opposite sides of the apparatus and began to climb.

Before he had time to think, Ben's opponent was swinging hand-over-hand toward him.

The shock of the first kick made him forget his fear. It came flashing at him from the left side and would have ended the contest had he been facing the larger boy squarely. As it was, his swinging motion had him turned sideways, and his hip absorbed most of the blow. Even so, he almost fell. Stunned by the pain of the kick, his first impulse was to shout that he wasn't ready. Then he remembered the curly-headed kid saying there were no rules.

Ben kicked out blindly. It was a feeble attempt and fell short. The awkward move came close to pulling him off the bar. There was laughter from the crowd as he struggled to readjust his grip. The bigger boy seemed determined to end the contest quickly. Instead of trying to kick Ben again, he suddenly swung with his legs apart and wrapped them tightly around Ben's waist. With a snort of triumph, he completed his scissor hold by crossing his ankles and squeezing. Wrenching from side to side, his mottled face reddening with the effort, the boy tried to weaken Ben's grip. Ben gritted his teeth, and despite the wracking pain in his shoulders, he grimly held on. Finally, the boy seemed to tire. His legs loosened slightly and Ben used the slack to swing backward and wiggle free.

Learning fast, Ben copied the move his opponent had made. He wrapped his legs around the other boy's waist and crossed his ankles.

The crowd started to cheer, and Ben decided they were rooting for him. Back and forth the two swung as the noise of the spectators became a background roar. Time slowed, and all the fear and pain of the day eased away as Ben reveled in the crowd's approval.

Then his body betrayed him. The cheers couldn't overcome the numbing exertion of the fight. Slick with sweat, his fingers slowly began to slip until he was holding on by the knuckle joint only. The cords in his neck bulged with the effort, and he struggled for a firmer grip. He tried taking the weight off his hands by tightening his leg hold, but the pain was too much and he slipped even further. Sensing victory, the bigger boy let go with one hand. Swinging wildly, he punched Ben in the face. Ben's nose erupted with blood and his hands slipped off the bar, but his legs were still locked at the ankles and refused to release. He went over backward, head hanging down toward the ground. The larger boy tried to hold on, but the combined weight was too much. His fingers tore open and he dropped to the concrete on top of Ben.

Technically, this should have been called a draw. But the sickening thud of Ben's skull hitting the ground eliminated any concerns about who had won the contest.

Through a haze of pain Ben heard someone shout, "Ya killed the fucker. He's dead for sure!"

Another voice, this one filled with authority came in response. "Nah, he's just knocked out."

There was more shouting and then a hushed voice said, "Look at the blood. He's gonna bleed to death."

Then the voices became jumbled and Ben no longer could separate the speakers.

"His fuckin' head sounded like it was hit with a baseball bat."

"Back off, give him air!"

As if in response, instead of backing off, the crowd pushed in closer. The larger boy quickly rose to his feet, wiped his runny nose, and backed away.

Ben was too stunned to understand what had happened. He lifted his head slightly and looked up at the circle of moving mouths surrounding him. A volcano of agony erupted, but he couldn't cry. It just wasn't allowed. Instead, he sat up and groaned, feeling the back of his head. When he pulled his hand away, it was covered with a thick film of blood.

"I gotta go home," he mumbled, staggering to his feet.

Someone said, "You'd better sit down."

"Nah, I gotta go home."

He tried to take a step, but a hand took his arm and the curly-headed boy started walking him toward the school. He followed, still dazed, insisting that he had to go home. Paying no attention, the boy led the way to the nurse's office.

By now, the blood had flowed down his forehead and into his eyes, obscuring his vision in a red haze. To the untrained eye, his injury might have looked serious, but the sight of blood didn't seem to impress the school nurse. She pushed Ben's head under a faucet and briskly washed most of the dirt out of the cut. The pain was excruciating, but she squelched his protests.

"Quit squirming, it's gotta be cleaned. If it gets infected, they'll have to cut your head off." She laughed and added, "Might be an improvement at that."

Aware of others in the room, Ben bit down hard and tried to hold still.

The nurse took one quick look before the blood started up again. She muttered something to herself and gave Ben a towel to hold against the wound. "You're gonna need stitches."

Ben had only a vague recollection of the trip to the hospital. He remembered the driver of the car snarling a warning, "Hold the goddamned towel on that cut. You get blood on my seat, I'll make you clean it up."

Despite the pain, Ben pushed the towel tight against the wound.

Once in the hospital, a white-coated intern came into the screened area, frowned at Ben, and started to probe the wound. Ben let out a yell and jerked away.

"Hold still. Grit your teeth and pretend you're a wounded soldier."

After rubbing his runny nose with a blood-encrusted cuff, Ben managed to keep from moving. Twelve stitches later, he was driven back to school.

The nurse paid Ben little attention, but she wouldn't let him go back to class. Instead, she made him lie down on a sheetless, gray-striped cot in the sick room. Still stunned, he quietly waited for the final bell. Noticing his silence, the nurse laughed. "They oughta bang a few more of you kids on the head. It shuts you up."

Finally, three o'clock came, and with a surprisingly gentle stroke on the cheek, the nurse asked him if he felt well enough to make it home on his own. When he said "Yes," she stared into his eyes for a moment, then nodded and let him go.

Ben wandered back to his homeroom, got his books, and slowly shuffled out of the deserted building. Feeling the bandage that covered his wound, he thrilled at the thought of the scar it would leave. A cut on the forehead would have been better, but this was pretty good.

Outside, the curly-haired kid was bouncing a tennis ball against the wall. As Ben approached, he fell in step. "Lemme see the cut."

Ben bowed his head, exaggerating the difficulty.

"Wow, how many stitches?"

"Twelve."

"Twelve?"

"Yeah."

"Did it hurt?"

"Nah."

They walked in silence for a few minutes.

When they reached the corner, the boy stopped. He motioned up toward Woodlawn, the opposite direction from where Ben was headed. As he turned to leave, he stuck out a grimy hand.

"My name's John, John Solberg. You wanna be friends?"

CHAPTER THIRTEEN

"S'posed to snow tonight." Henry was sprawled sideways on Ben's bed, his hands intertwined behind his head. He was staring at the far wall, his eyes tracking a cockroach as it crept behind a torn spot near one of the seams in the wallpaper. Ben was on the floor reading a book, his back against the radiator. The room was tiny, barely large enough for a twin-sized bed. An orange crate served as a nightstand and the drawers of the dresser could only be opened when the bedroom door was closed.

Ben scratched his back against the cold cast iron. Gus took Saturdays off, so the heat wouldn't come on until the evening. He looked at Henry and cocked his head. "So?"

Henry sat up. "So…there's a bunch of richies livin' over by the university. We can pick up some bread shoveling their walks. One time last winter, me an' Mikey made a buck an' a half apiece. You and me could do even better 'cause you ain't lazy like him. Whadda ya say, you in?"

Ben looked down at his book. "Yeah, I guess so."

Henry got up and grabbed his coat. Pausing at the door, he pressed against the loose wallpaper where he'd last seen the roach and dragged his hand along the surface for a foot or so. There was no sound, but when he peeled the paper back, Ben saw he'd managed to kill at least a dozen of the repulsive bugs. Henry grinned. "They like the paste; it's made from flour." He smoothed the paper back into place. "I gotta go. Saturday nights, it's safer ta sleep at my grandfather's house. Meet ya in front tomorrow."

After Henry left, Ben tore the loose piece of wallpaper down and used a rag to clean up the dead roaches.

*****

The snow started just after dark. The temperature stayed in the twenties all night and the big fluffy flakes piled up, camouflaging the filth of the city with a fresh coat of pristine white. By 6:00a.m., Henry was pounding on Ben's door. "Come on, come on," he muttered under his breath. The door finally inched open and revealed Ben standing in his underwear, shivering in the cold that blew in from the hallway.

"Whadda you want?"

Henry pushed inside. "Where's your old lady?"

Ben shrugged. He looked around as if he thought she might be hiding somewhere. "I guess she didn't come home last night." He didn't sound worried, so Henry dropped it.

"I told ya it was gonna snow. Come on, get dressed. We gotta go to the basement an' get Gus's shovels."

While Henry paced, Ben used the bathroom. Then, still half asleep, he shuffled back to his room and took his jeans and shirt off the radiator. The heat had started up an hour earlier and the clothes were pleasantly warm. He pulled them on and shoved into his heavy shoes. Grabbing his coat and gloves, he followed Henry down the stairs.

Henry led the way past the sulfuric stink of the basement coal pile to the boiler room. A single lightbulb barely gave off enough light to make out the furnace. Behind the grated feeding door, the fire roared and glowed like hell itself. Ben hesitated, but Henry pushed him inside. "I got a deal with Gus. He lets me use the coal shovels to shovel snow, but first I gotta shovel the walk in front of the Castle for free."

Several coal shovels were stacked against one wall and Henry grabbed two of them. Handing the largest one to Ben, he led the way out of the building.

"We gotta hurry. A bunch of the richies go to early Mass. If we don't get to 'em before they leave the house, we're outta luck."

To most kids, snow meant fun, snowball fights, sledding, and building snowmen. To Henry, it meant money.

The snow was wet, the kind kids called "good packin'." While the moisture made it heavy, it was easily shoveled. Within half an hour, they had completely cleared the Castle sidewalks. Gus came out as they were finishing and didn't say a word. Henry knew that a lack of complaint from Gus was overwhelming approval.

Runny-nosed and red-cheeked, they hurried west to the nicer homes near the university. When they reached the corner of 58th and Woodlawn, Henry spotted John, the curly-headed kid Ben had met at school, standing in the middle of the street.

Ben had been bringing him around the building for the past few months, and the jerk was acting as if he was one of the gang. It was OK with Henry if one of the guys made a friend at school. And once in a while, those friends could even come around the building and hang out. But John was with Ben all the time, and Henry didn't like it. Besides, he couldn't figure the guy out. He seemed gutsy enough, but he never got angry and always talked his way out of stuff. Like when Mike started pushing him around. Instead of decking the asshole, John made a joke of it and walked away. He even acted like he didn't mind Andy. The guy was weird. Henry decided it was time to let Ben know who said what guys were welcome and what guys weren't. He'd tell Ben that he didn't want John coming around so much. If that turned out to be a problem for Benny boy, that would be just too bad.

CHAPTER FOURTEEN

J ohn Solberg was running a game, a scam. It was the one thing
that made him truly happy. He made a note on the pad he was
holding and moved to the middle of the street. As he looked up, he saw
two figures with shovels on their shoulders coming up Woodlawn. He
recognized them immediately and muttered, "Oh, shit."

He raised his hand in a halt gesture, and the "oh shit." feeling
began to subside. A game was a game, even when Ben and Henry were
involved. The trick would be to work the scam, still keep Ben as a
friend, and not have Henry beat the crap out of him. John felt the
tingle of elation he sometimes got when one of his games turned dangerous.

Henry and Ben stopped, their hot breath puffing clouds into the
cold air. They stood with their shovels over their shoulders and stared
at John. Before they could ask what he was doing, John threw his arm
around Henry's shoulder. He used a chiding but friendly tone. "You
guys are late, but it's OK. I went and knocked on the door of the
second an' third house for you, and they're gonna pay you a buck for
cleaning their walks." He nodded toward a couple of red brick homes
with walks that went straight from the sidewalk to the front porch. It
was an easy thirty-minute job.

"Whadda ya mean?" Henry asked. "That ain't the way we did it last year."

John smiled and pointed at two boys who were scurrying down the street with shovels on their shoulders. "The other kids were gonna beat you guys to all the easy walks, so I signed up some of the houses for you. I already got the bread from that one an' the one next to it. I'll give you the buck when you finish."

John made a head motion toward the other team. "Better hurry before they finish and try to get the houses I already signed up."

As they moved away, Henry still wasn't satisfied. "Don't make sense. How'd he know we was comin'?"

Ben shrugged and they went to work without another word.

The first house went fast. Side-by-side, they pushed against the snow like a pair of snowplows. When the pile got too heavy to move, they stopped and shoved the snow sideways onto the lawn. The whole thing took less than ten minutes. At the second house, a severe-looking colored maid in an overcoat stood outside and supervised the job. After they finished, she handed Henry a broom and made him sweep the walk clean of every last trace of snow.

When the two houses were finished, they walked over to get their money from John. He paid out the four quarters and asked if they wanted to do another set of houses at the far end of the street.

"Did you get the same deal from them?" Henry asked, "Half-a-buck each?"

John nodded and tried to avoid looking at Henry straight on. The other team of kids was due back, and he wanted to get rid of his friends before the second team showed up. Henry seemed to catch on that John was trying to rush them. "A half-a-buck a house is pretty good bread. How come so much?"

John couldn't help preening a little. "It's all in how you ask. I start out offering to do it for lots more. The suckers figure I'm just a dumb kid an' I let 'em Jew me down to what I wanted in the first place—no offense, Benny."

He stopped talking, surprised at the flash of anger he saw in Ben's eyes. "Whoa, it's just an expression. I didn't mean nothin' by it."

Ben frowned and John hoped he'd let it go.

At that moment, John saw Henry's glance shift up the street, and he realized he'd talked too long. The two kids who were there when Ben and Henry first showed up came over with their hands out. John gave Henry an uncomfortable shrug, paid the kids each a quarter, and directed them toward another house.

Ben was baffled. "What's goin' on?"

John shuffled from foot to foot and looked down. He could tell that Henry had caught on. He smiled a shark's smile at John and seemed content to wait for Ben to figure it out on his own. When Ben finally did, John flinched at the explosion.

"You son-of-a-bitch!" Ben screamed.

John backed away. "Hey, if it wasn't for me, the other guys woulda got all the jobs and you two would've been standing around with shovels on your shoulders."

To John's relief, the tough guy was still grinning. He'd gotten to know Henry well enough to figure that a smile meant he wasn't going to knock your teeth out.

Ben's face, already red from the cold, went purple. "You let me think you were doing us a favor comin' out early an' all, but what you were really doing was making chumps outta Henry an' me. Havin' us do all the work while you sat on your ass."

John backed up another step to get out of the range of Ben's fists. He put his hand in his pocket and jingled a bunch of quarters. "I gave you an' Henry the easiest jobs, an' I paid you half a buck each. I only give the other guys a quarter. I made less on you than on the other guys."

The sun had begun to peek out, and despite the sub-freezing temperature, Ben started sweating under his wool cap. He pulled it off and wisps of steam rose from his head. "I thought we were friends."

John winced at the hurt tone in Ben's voice. He shrugged his shoulders, knowing it would be hopeless for him to explain. "We are friends, but this is different. This is money."

Henry pulled Ben away, and with a backward wink at John, he stomped up the street toward the next job.

Hours later, Ben was still fuming, swearing that he and John were no longer friends. Henry quietly calculated John's take. Twenty houses at between twenty-five and fifty cents per house worked out to anywhere from five to ten dollars, and all of it without pushing one shovelful of snow. As they put the shovels back in the boiler room, he pulled out the twelve quarters they'd gotten for the day's work and said, "This is the best I've ever done shovelin'. Mostly, me and Mike would do the walk an' let the guy who owned the house give us what he thought was right, kinda like a tip. None of the cheap bastards ever gave us half-a-buck each. I'm glad ya brought that Johnny around. We need a grifter in the gang with that kind of smarts." He grinned and nodded at Ben. "Only ya gotta make it clear ta him—next time, he cuts us in."

CHAPTER FIFTEEN

On the morning of the coldest day of the year, the boiler at Ray Elementary broke down. The temperature in the classrooms dropped below freezing, and the principal sent the children home.

As the Castle kids huddled outside the school, John announced that he wanted to take advantage of the enforced holiday. "I seen these pictures of the lake shore in Sunday's paper. A bunch of freakish ice sculptures was formed by the waves an' there's ice caves an' everything. We outta go see it before it thaws."

Mike shoved his gloved hands deep into his pockets and grumbled. "It's too fuckin' cold to go down to the beach. It's below zero."

The wind whipped at John's face, shooting needles of pain at his exposed skin. The lobes of his ears, peeking out from under his earmuffs, ached with cold. He pulled the muffs down, then shoved his gloved hands back under his armpits. "It's almost March. A couple more weeks an' most of the ice'll be gone. We gotta go now or we'll miss out."

A worried frown crossed Tommy's face. "Last time the boiler broke, they made us wear our coats in class. My teacher said this cold snap is so bad, it's gonna break a record, gonna go to fifteen below. That's why they let us out early."

Backs hunched against the wind, the boys stood in a semicircle. Their breath billowed out in gusts of white, only to fade and disappear in the frigid air. Henry made the final decision. "We can go ta my house and play cards. My ol' man got a job, so he ain't home."

With a shrug of resignation, John turned toward the lake. "We're all gonna freeze if we keep standin' here arguing. I'm goin', but if you guys don't wanna go, it's cool. I'll come by Henry's place when I get back."

When his buddy Ben didn't immediately leave with the others, John waited quietly for him to make his decision. It was almost too cold to breathe. An inhale brought a sharp stab of icy air as the fine hairs in his nostrils froze. His whole face hurt and his feet had long since lost any feeling except for a tingling numbness. *Maybe Mike and Tommy are right—it is too cold.*

He watched Ben shift from foot to foot, obviously torn between going with the group or staying with his friend. Finally, with a groan, Ben grabbed John's arm. "I think you're nuts, but let's go and get it over with."

The two of them were dressed alike in navy surplus pea-coats, blue jeans stuffed into unbuckled galoshes, and earmuffs instead of hats. John had a scarf wrapped around his neck and tucked inside his coat. It was considered sissy to wear a scarf, but he hadn't been able to get out of the house without it.

As they crossed Stoney Island Avenue and plowed into Jackson Park, their world lost color. Except for the trees with their skeletal fingers of leafless limbs, white was everywhere. Not the welcoming white of cotton sheets but the cold blue-white of a marble tomb. Dodging cars with complete confidence in their indestructibility, they crossed the Outer Drive and walked along the storm fence bordering the beach.

Lake Michigan never completely froze over, but a blanket of snow-encrusted ice extended out for hundreds of yards. The actual shoreline was hidden, so there was no way of knowing if there was sand or water beneath the crust. After a few tentative steps, John decided that the ice was strong enough to hold them, even if they were over water.

He started out onto the ice shelf, talking as he went. "When we was little kids, we used to go skating on the lagoon. The ice was thick and OK for skating, except the cops didn't like for us to go out there. So this one day, we're all on the ice, and along comes that prick Delaney in Car 109. 'Get the fuck off the ice!' he yells. And most of the guys, me included, take off, but there's this guy I know named Roger, Roger Shaw. He's really tough, an' he figures if Delaney decides to come after him, he can get away seein' as how Delaney would be on foot an he's on skates. Also, Delaney's got all this crap on his belt so he don't run so good. Anyway, Roger yells back. 'Fuck you, Delaney' and goes on skatin'. He's keepin' an eye out in case Delaney parks and gets outta the car, but what he don't figure on is Delaney gettin' so pissed off he pulls his car right onto the ice. The Ford Delaney's drivin' must weigh a ton, but he don't care. He drives straight across the lagoon an' pins Roger up against the bank before Rog can get his skates off. Delaney grabs Shaw and gives him a couple of slaps for bein' a wiseass. I'm standin' on the bank, starin' at Delaney's car sittin' out on the ice, an' I say real polite-like, 'Officer Delaney, how come we can't skate here?' He looks over at me, smilin' with that mean face of his, an' he says, 'It's too dangerous. The ice might break an' we might lose a couple of you punks.'"

John broke up remembering the scene. Ben scuttled sideways through the slushy snow. "It woulda been great if the whole fuckin' car had gone through."

"Yeah, with Delaney hangin' onta the fender, tryin' to hold it up."
John imitated Delaney struggling with the car.

"How's he gonna break it to the captain?" Ben puffed out his chest. "Uh, Chief," he said in a deep, gruff voice. "My squad car sank in the lagoon. Should we pull it out now or wait till the ice melts in spring? I'd wait—

In mid-sentence, Ben disappeared from sight.

Unlike clear ice, the crusty snow ice they were walking on didn't crack and shatter. It softened from underneath and gave way in isolated patches. The surface where Ben had been walking collapsed and Ben, windmilling his arms, spun around and fell through the ice butt first. The impact caused the hole to widen and he dropped beneath the water without a splash.

John saw the pratfall and waited a beat, expecting his friend to bob back up. A moment passed and he dropped to his knees, leaned over the hole, and started screaming Ben's name. The water was crystal clear beneath him, and John could see Ben on his back, thrashing wildly. He reached in and grabbed the collar of Ben's coat. Leaning back, he braced his feet on the edge of the hole and pulled with all his might. Ben's sputtering face came bobbing up through the icy water. Upright, with John's help, he finally got a foothold on the bottom and was able to stand. The water was only neck deep.

Earmuffs knocked askew over one eye and hair plastered to his head, Ben would have looked comical if his face hadn't turned deathly white. He needed both hands to get out of the hole, so he reached up to hand his earmuffs to John. John tried to grab the front of Ben's pea-coat, but the sodden wool had started to freeze and John lost his grip. Just as Ben began sliding back into the water, John wrapped his arms around his friend's chest and managed to haul him halfway out. Ben rested for a moment to catch his breath. Getting a second wind, he lifted his knee over the side of the hole and scrambled the rest of the way onto firm snow.

The boys stared at each other. John took in Ben's pale, ghostly skin and his stiffening, wet hair. "Shit, I thought you was a goner, dead for sure."

Ben got to his feet and stood dripping, staring down at the hole that had almost swallowed him. He seemed stunned but otherwise unhurt. His first attempts to speak came out slurred, but finally, John was able to make some sense out of what he was saying. "Uh, at first, it was like…like electric, then I got really numb…an' I couldn't straighten up."

The water had filled Ben's galoshes, and his feet were encased in half-frozen socks. Within seconds, his jeans froze solid, and wearing the ice-encrusted earmuffs became worse than going without. He began to shake and his teeth were chattering so hard, John thought he might break a few.

He took off his scarf and wrapped it around Ben's head. "We gotta get somewhere warm.C'mon"

After crossing the Outer Drive, John's first thought was to try to save time by cutting across the snow-covered fields. After a few steps, it became obvious that the crust over the foot-deep snow was too thin to hold them. Giving up, he motioned to Ben that they had to go back the way they'd come, on the asphalt path. It began to snow. Hard tiny crystals, whipped sideways by the increasing wind, seemed to come at them from all sides. Ben moved behind John, and with their heads turtled in, they continued in single file.

Just before they reached the Inner Drive, Ben slumped down in the middle of the pathway. He stretched out and started mumbling so low that John had to get down on his knees to hear what he was muttering. "Lemme lay here awhile. I'm really tired."

John panicked. "Get up, ya fuckin' moron! If ya stop now, you'll freeze to death."

Ben rolled over on his side. "Nah, I'm really warm. Toasty warm. I'm just sleepy."

John yanked at Ben's arm, yelling in his ear and shaking him as hard as he could. "You'll die here. Get the fuck up!"

Ben grumbled some more about wanting to be left alone but finally pushed his way off the ground and onto his feet. He staggered so badly that John had to tuck under his friend's arm to hold him upright.

Their progress was slow, with Ben stumbling and almost falling at each step. John's muscles were screaming; and while the cold didn't seem to be bothering Ben, John felt like his own body was turning to ice. He stepped in front of Ben and pulled him with both arms. He was yelling again, but it was barely audible over the shriek of the wind. "Come on, asshole, move!"

With John tucked under Ben's arm again and both boys staggering as if they were blind drunk, they finally made it to Stony Island Avenue. John half pulled and half carried Ben toward the restaurant on the corner. He pushed inside and led Ben, tripping and stumbling, to a back booth. The warmth of the Greek-owned restaurant meant safety. The smell of greasy food, wet wool, and cigar smoke comforted John, convincing him that everything was going to be all right.

He let Ben sink down onto the booth's cracked plastic cushions and walked up to the counter. Pete, the counterman, was Stavros the grocer's teenage nephew. He swiped at the counter in front of John, spreading the crumbs of a former customers' toast. "What'll ya have?"

John shivered, still chilled. "Two hot chocolates," he mumbled, and he waited while Pete filled the order. Pete set the steaming cups on the counter and dropped a marshmallow into each one. "Cold as a witch's tit out there, huh?"

John nodded, grabbed the hot chocolates, and rushed back to Ben. He tried to get Ben to drink, but he was shaking so badly, most of it spilled on the floor. John's ears, fingers, and toes began to ache with a hurt as sharp as the wind itself. He figured Ben's pain must be even worse. He moved next to his friend, holding him tight to control the convulsions.

As the ice on his clothes thawed, melted water began to drip on the floor. Pete stared first at the growing puddle under Ben and then at Ben himself. With a disgusted snort, he yelled over to John, "Get that kid outta here, he's sick an' pissing all over the floor."

Before John could explain, the owner, Tony, came over. Without a word, he put a hand on Ben's forehead. "Son-of-a-bitch, thees kid, he's a-freezin'!" The boss whipped off his apron and screamed at Pete, "Get a blanket!" Tony was a big man, strong in the way men who have labored hard all their lives are. Without waiting for Pete, he pulled the nearly unconscious boy out of the booth and slung him over his shoulder. Pete met him halfway to the door and wrapped the blanket around Ben as best he could. Then Tony was outside, running the half a block to Illinois Central Hospital. John stumbled to the door and started after them, but Pete stopped him with an upraised arm. "You're all wet, too. Better stay here, warm up. The boss is gonna take care of your friend."

John nodded and went back to the booth. He finished the first two hot chocolates and had two more before he left.

The wind was at his back and the warmth of the restaurant stayed with him all the way to the Castle. He went upstairs to Ben's apartment, knocked, waited, then knocked again. He felt sure that Ben's mother was home, but he knew from past experience she was a sound sleeper. While he waited, he scratched his initials and the date in the wood of the door jamb. He admired his handiwork for a moment, then knocked again. Finally, he gave up and sank down with his back braced against the wall. He sat for a moment not knowing what to do. Then he dropped his head between his legs and began to cry. He was still there crying when a disheveled and bleary-eyed Mrs. Kahn opened the door.

CHAPTER SIXTEEN

John sniffed the early spring air. The fragrance he first recognized was the heavy perfume given off by the blooming lilac bushes that bordered Jackson Park. John sniffed again and smiled as he detected the equally exciting smell of money.

The scheme John devised needed at least two other guys. Mike was too chicken, Andy too dumb, and Tommy too honest. He settled on Henry and Ben. Henry because he had guts, and Ben because ever since he'd saved Ben's life, they had become even closer friends.

"It's easy, we get the flowers free an' we sell 'em for fifty cents a bunch."

Henry didn't hesitate. "I'm in. How 'bout you, Benny?"

John could tell that Ben was scared. When John told him that they would have to steal the things they needed, he started getting jumpy. "I don't wanna wind up in juvie."

John squinted and slowly stroked his chin as if he had a beard. He nodded and said solemnly, "Dot's vhy chu shoot not get caught."

Henry laughed, then let his smile fade. He turned to Ben, and his voice went flat. "Ya ain't chicken, are ya, Benny?"

*****

To start, they needed some empty milk crates, and the place to get them was Stavros's grocery store. Stavros usually had a dozen or so set out in the alley, waiting for pick up by the dairy man. The Greek wouldn't give the crates up willingly, but John figured if there were a diversion, it would be easy to walk off with a few.

Once a week, the refuse collection truck drove into the alley to empty the trash cans piled high with the rotting produce Stavros hadn't been able to sell. On most pick-up days, Garbage Maggie and Crippled Gene would sort through the cans long before the truck arrived, but today, they had either been late or the garbage truck had come early.

Gene lost his legs in the First World War, and he rode around on a roller-skate platform. That put his head far below the lip of the cans. Normally, Maggie would hand things down to him, but today, his job was to distract the garbage man while she grabbed as much stuff as possible.

The driver tipped a can on its edge, rolled it to the truck, and lifted it over the side to dump it. Gene cursed and tried to place his wheeled contraption between the garbage man and the remaining cans. The garbage man ignored him. All the while, Maggie was hauling heads of lettuce, soft tomatoes, and withered potatoes out as fast as she could.

Seeing that the cursing wasn't doing any good, Gene tried pleading. "Just give Maggie a few minutes. If you don't, we're gonna starve."

From Ben's porch above the alley, John watched like a vulture waiting for his prey to die. He couldn't tell if Gene had managed to squeeze out any tears, but he knew the old drunk could do it at will. He nudged Ben and got a nod in return. This could be the commotion that would give them cover while they snatched the empty milk bottle crates. John stayed on the porch while Henry and Ben moved nonchalantly down the stairs. Heads together in conversation, they crossed in front of Stavros's back door to the side where the crates were stacked.

"Yer throwin' away good shit," Gene whined as the third can was upended into the back of the truck. He rolled himself along with his hands and, in desperation, tried to block the garbage man from the next can.

The garbage man put his gloved hands on his hips. He was swathed in ragged grease-stained pants and shirt, the fronts of which were protected by a full-length leather apron. On his head was a knit watch cap, and around his neck he wore a sweat-stained, knotted rag. He reeked worse than the garbage.

"Get the fuck outta my way, Rummy." He reached down to shove Gene aside, but with surprising speed, Gene wheeled back out of his reach.

"Please, help an ol' vet out here, just a couple more minutes ta get somethin' ta eat."

"You're too old ta be a vet. You're nothin' but a fuckin' wino. Now get outta my way." The garbage man reached over and grabbed Gene by the shoulder. He shoved him sideways and moved past. Before grabbing the next can, he wiped his gloved hands on his apron as if touching Gene was worse than touching the garbage.

"You bastard, I was in the Great War. Got my legs blown off while you was still jizzum in your old man's dick." Reaching into one of the remaining cans, Gene threw a handful of rotten produce at the garbage man.

Knowing Stavros couldn't keep from butting in, the boys stood alongside the crates and waited. Their problem wasn't getting the containers—it was getting past Stavros and out of the alley without being seen.

The screen door exploded outward and Stavros burst out, cursing. He had his back to Henry, and as he waved his arms and screamed,

Henry made his move. Calmly, he slipped his hands into the grip of two empty crates and walked away from the Greek's door to the porch stairs. Ben grabbed two more and followed. Stavros was shaking his fist and shouting at Gene. The garbage man had stopped dumping the garbage and was shaking his fist at Stavros. Gene was shaking his fist at Stavros and the garbage man. All three were screaming at the top of their lungs.

The boys quietly carried the crates back up to Ben's porch and joined John. They leaned over the porch railing and watched as Maggie, ignoring the tumult, kept stuffing half-rotted food into her sack. John smiled down at her in sincere admiration of a fellow thief. Turning to the others, he rubbed his hands together. "Now comes the hard part."

CHAPTER SEVENTEEN

John decided that cutting and preparing the lilacs for sale required wire, a wire cutter,and a small branch trimmer. He pleaded with Ben. "You gotta be the one to do it. Anderson's is the only hardware store near enough to walk to. The thing is, both ol' man Anderson and his kid Donnie know me an' Henry."

"Shit, he knows me too, "Ben said.

"Yeah, but he thinks you're a good kid. Besides, he's hot for your mom. If he does catch you, he'll probably just smack you around a little and let you go."

John could have bitten his tongue after he said it. A beating wasn't something Ben would look forward to, but the logic of his argument was solid. It had to be Ben.

"OK, Benny, here's how we play it. Henry an' me'll go in an' distract Donnie an' his ol' man. You come in after an' pick up the stuff we need. Slip everything into your armpit. Keep your jacket on, an' they won't see nothin'." John demonstrated by stuffing a tennis ball under his arm. Then he had Ben try it a few times. When he was satisfied that Ben could carry it off, the three of them walked over to Anderson's.

The door to the hardware store was wedged open. On either side were dirty display windows showcasing dusty power tools, some small hand tools, and a pyramid of paint cans. Inside the store, three narrow aisles were formed by two free-standing merchandise counters that held the hand tools and large power items. Along the walls, shelves were laden with trays of nails, screws, nuts, bolts, and assorted small items. The floors were wooden and worn clean of any wax or varnish. Little sprinkles of sweeping compound that the broom had missed gave the place an oily pine odor.

Mr. Anderson, dressed in a button-straining white shirt and food-stained tie, stood by the cash register. His son Donnie was the floor man.

Henry strolled into the store and veered left up one of the side aisles. He picked up a pair of locking pliers, turning them over and examining them as if he'd never seen anything like them before.

Donnie was on him like a shot.

"Whadda you lookin' for? Maybe I can help."

"Nothin', just lookin'. My dad's birthday's comin' up, an' I might wanna get him a hammer or somethin'. I'll call ya if I need help." Henry wasn't surprised when Donnie didn't move. He kept walking deeper into the store, touching things as he passed. Gripped by suspicion, Donnie followed.

While Mr. Anderson watched his son, John slipped in and went down the other aisle. Now the Andersons had a problem, they weren't sure which kid to watch. Donnie looked over at his dad and nodded in John's direction. Anderson Senior slowly nodded back.

Ben strolled in. He picked up a spool of copper wire and headed for the small tools display. At first, it looked as if Ben wasn't going to get a chance to snatch the tools. Mr. Anderson watched John, but he stayed rooted to the front, and Ben was in plain view. Then, just when Ben was about to give up, a man in paint-spattered overalls and a painter's cap walked in.

Anderson turned to the new customer and smiled. Sensing an opportunity, Henry asked Donnie where the nails were, knowing that they were against the back wall.

John moved in front of Ben to shield him.

The painter asked to see a color card, and Mr. Anderson left his post to get one. With both Andersons out of the way, John gave Ben a nod. Wire cutter, wire, and plant trimmer all went under Ben's jacket; the wire into one armpit and the tools into the other. John and Ben turned and headed for the door.

Henry saw them about to leave and turned away from Donnie. Muttering about needing to go home and get his money, he ran to the door ahead of Ben and John. With a wave at Donnie, he disappeared. John hesitated, glancing back to see Donnie's reaction, and Ben, also looking back, walked into him. The spool of wire was jarred loose and fell out directly in front of Mr. Anderson, who was returning with the paint chart.

For a stunned moment, the store owner, his customer, and Ben all stood and stared at the spool of wire. It rolled leisurely down the aisle, and they watched, transfixed, as it slowed to a stop. Anderson snapped out of it first. He grabbed Ben by the arm and pulled the boy toward him. The pull caused Ben's other armpit to open and the two tools dropped out. John quietly faded backward into the store. He watched from behind an end unit, unable to help his friend.

"You fuckin' thief!" Mr. Anderson slapped Ben in the mouth, and Donnie came running up to help his father.

"Call the cops," the customer said. "These little shits need to be taught a lesson."

Ben said nothing. John may not have turned him into a good thief, but he had taught him to keep his mouth shut. He tried squeezing out a tear to get some sympathy but had to rub his eye to make it look as if he'd been crying. He let himself be pulled by the arm over to the cash register desk. Head hanging down, he watched Anderson pick up the telephone.

"Hold on, Dad." Donnie pulled his father aside and whispered in his ear. His father listened with mounting disgust and slammed down the phone. He turned to Ben and started slapping him again, but Ben wrapped his arms in front of his face and took most of the slaps on his forearms.

None of them noticed John as he slipped past the group. With a final look of pity for Ben, he got out the door and hit the sidewalk at a run.

John's move caught Mr. Anderson's attention, but it was too late. He turned back to Ben. "I'm gonna give you a break. You get your ass outta here and don't come back. Next time, I'll call the cops for sure."

The instant the man released his arm, Ben whirled and ran out of the store, just barely avoiding the kick Anderson aimed at his backside. He stumbled out onto the street, breathing as if he'd run a mile, and headed for the corner where John and Henry were waiting.

"I can't figure out why he let me go." Ben's face and arms were red from the slaps, and he was still shaking.

John examined Ben's face, looking for blood. "Cause you dropped the shit inside the store. It ain't stealin' unless you leave the store. You could've told the cops you meant to pay."

Henry fumed. "Johnny's right, but look out, Donnie'll try ta catch ya outside the store an' kick the shit outta ya."

"I really fucked up. Now how we gonna get the stuff we need?"

With a grin, John pulled the two of them into the alley and produced the three items. Ben's mouth dropped open, and even Henry was stunned. "Wipe the shit-eatin' grin off your face and tell us how the fuck ya did that?"

John grinned even wider. "Easy. I picked 'em up while they were busy slappin' the crap outta Ben."

CHAPTER EIGHTEEN

Being in the lead felt odd to John. He kept glancing back at Henry and Ben lugging the crates as they moved up Stony Island Avenue toward 59th Street. When they got there, Henry wanted to start cutting the stalks of purple flowers from the street side, but John convinced him that by working from the park side, there would be less chance of being seen by other kids who might want to horn in on their racket. Dragging the crates, they pushed through the bushes to the grassy area beyond.

Using the hedge clipper, John started cutting off large bunches of lilacs. A number of bees, annoyed at being disturbed, buzzed angrily around his head, and Ben and Henry backed quickly away from the bush. John waited until the bees settled on other blooms. Using his hand like a comb, he brushed the hair back off his forehead and went back to cutting.

John was careful around Henry, never quite knowing what would set him off. Suggesting that Henry was afraid of something could be tricky, so he directed his words at Ben. "Don't be scared. Them bees won't hurt you 'less you make 'em really mad."

To his surprise, Henry shook his head and backed away even further. "I ain't gonna go near no bees. I hate the little fuckers."

John nodded without looking at Henry. "You guys can bundle the flowers up. I'll do all the cutting."

He went back to clipping the flowers and the other two took over sorting the flowers into bouquets, then wiring their stems together. Moving along quickly, John stripped half-a-dozen bushes of their blooms. Within thirty minutes, all four crates were filled, each with twelve huge bunches of lilacs.

John set aside two of the crates and slid the other two toward Ben and Henry.

"You guys try to sell the flowers in those two crates. I'll get rid of these."

Ben glanced over at Henry, then back at John. "How come you got twice as much as us?"

John grinned at him. "It ain't a trick, Benny. No offense, but neither one of you been hustlin' as long as me. Don't worry, everything gets split three ways." He shifted one crate up onto his shoulder and grabbed the other one by the slot in the side.

"Meet ya back here when you get everything sold. Don't forget, no less than four bits a bunch, an' try to get more. Start out with a buck, an' let 'em Jew you down." Not until he saw Ben's ears flatten did John remember the last time he'd made the remark. "I meant to say Scotch 'em down. Scotch 'em down is OK, ain't it, Benny?"

Still grinning, John sauntered off. He knew there was no sense in trying to peddle the flowers at the Castle. Castle residents wouldn't spend a dime on flowers, let alone fifty cents. He decided on one of the newer apartment buildings facing the park. He hid the crates under a stairwell, taking only two bunches with him. The first floor had eight apartments, four on each side of the carpeted hallway. John jounced along, knocking on each door until one opened.

He greeted the woman who answered with the largest smile he could manage. "Would you care to buy some flowers? My mother's got a garden full of these lilacs, and she said for me to go out and give the neighborhood a chance to buy 'em."

When he'd sold the two bunches, he went back for more. Near the end of the hall, two people answered at the same time. John gave them the same spiel and added, "If you both wanna buy, I'll give you a special price, six bits instead of a buck." They both bought. By the time he finished with the building, he'd sold a full dozen.

His next stop was the real estate office on the corner of 61st and Stoney. He shouldered the crate and slid into the busy office. In a loud sing-song voice, he called out, "Flowers, get your lady friend some flowers. Only a buck a bunch."

A man in shirtsleeves and a vest came rushing out of a glass-enclosed office. He wore rimless glasses and his mouth was set in a purposeful frown. Two other men got up from their desks near the front and were also moving toward John. John felt the beginnings of panic. He held up his hand and had started to scuttle backward when the first man snarled at the office in general. "I'm first. I get first pick."

When Henry and Ben got back an hour later, John was already sitting on the bench waiting for them. His crates were empty and next to him, piled neatly on top of a dollar bill, were four stacks of coins—nickels, dimes, quarters,and half dollars.

"I got over seventeen dollars an' fifty cents. I got six bits for most of 'em, an' one lady gave me a buck and asked for change. I pretended I didn't have any, so she let me keep the buck."

Henry and Ben stared at the money. Ben added ten dollars and fifty cents to the pile and admitted they'd been unable to sell the last three bunches.

John wasn't disappointed. The money didn't mean as much to him as having outsold Ben and Henry. His grin carried a hint of condescension. "I'll sell those last three and then we'll beat it."

Ben sank down next to John. "Can't we just go? This shit's too much like work."

John faked a stricken look. "Benny, you should know better. A buck's a buck." Grabbing the three bunches before Henry could stop him, he headed for one of the buildings directly across the street from the park.

Stepping into the foyer, he rang the first bell he saw and waited for the tenant to buzz the inside door open. When there was no answer, he rang another bell. This time, the door buzzed, and John slipped inside.

"Who is it?" A man's voice floated down from the floor directly above him.

"Wanna buy some flowers?"

Men didn't usually buy, but this one said, "Come on up."

A soft-looking, middle-aged man in a bathrobe was standing in the doorway to his apartment. His eyes lit up when he saw the flowers.

John figured him for a fruitcake who probably liked boys, but he said, "I bet your lady would really like these."

The man kept staring at John. Finally, he reached into the pocket of his robe and pulled out his wallet. "How much?"

Thinking that fairies liked it when you talked softly, John smiled and lowered his voice. "Only a buck six bits."

The man looked away and wet his lips. "I'll give you a dollar for two bunches."

John turned as if he were about to leave. The man said, "A dollar and a quarter."

With a resigned shrug, John looked down at the flowers and shook his head ruefully. "Seein' as it's my last three bunches, I'll give you two for a buck an' a half."

"Done."

Almost chortling with glee at the thought of rubbing it in to Ben and Henry, John went to the next apartment. He knocked and stepped back, having noticed that standing too close seemed to worry people.

"Who is it?" The voice was female, elderly, and timid.

John answered loudly, assuming that anyone who was old was deaf. "Wanna buy some flowers?"

The door flew open and a wild-looking hag stood in the doorway, shaking her finger in his face and glaring at him.

This was trouble. John's first thought was to get the hell out of there, but he couldn't figure out what he'd done wrong.

"You filthy little beast." She spat the words at him. She looked frail, but her rage stunned him, and he moved even further away.

"I saw you through my window. You thought you were hidden, but from up here, I could see everything. You destroyed those bushes. I called the police, but you got away before they came. Now I'm going to call them again."

"The police, what for?" John's sincere tone seemed to confuse the old lady.

"What for? What for?" Her face flushed and she gasped for breath. "You ruined those beautiful flowers. I loved to look at those flowers. They were planted for people to look at, and you cut them down."

John still couldn't understand it. Did this crazy old lady think she had the right to keep him from making a buck just because she liked to look at a few flowers? "Hey, they're public property. I didn't do nothin' wrong."

"We'll see what the police say about that, you vandal." She shuffled back into her apartment, and John decided it was time to go. He ran back down the stairs and across the street to where Henry and Ben were waiting. "Some crazy old bitch wants to call the police on us 'cause we cut down the flowers. Let's split."

*****

Later, sitting on the stoop in front of the Castle, John still couldn't get over the old lady's attitude. "We're supposed to go broke just so some loony can look out of her window at a few fuckin' flowers. What a bitch!"

"Maybe she's got a point," Ben said. "I wonder if we could get in a jam for cuttin' the flowers."

John frowned and turned to Henry. "Whadda you gonna do with your dough?"

Without hesitation, Henry said, "Eat! Me and Benny are gonna buy us a feast. You can come with if ya want. Right, Benny?"

Ben grinned.

John sprang his trap. "So Benny, as far as you're concerned, it's OK for this old lady who likes flowers to keep poor kids from eating. Maybe it'd be better if we just stuck some guy up for money."

Ben shook his head. "All I'm saying is I can see her side of it. She don't know we're hungry, an' she don't have nothin' to do with our bein' poor. My not havin' an old man ain't her fault. Henry's dad bein' a drunk ain't her fault, and your father getting killed in the war ain't her fault either. She just knows she's gotta wait another full year before she can see the flowers again. And that's if we didn't cut them up so bad they won't grow anymore."

"Yeah, well, I think it's bullshit." John spoke without looking at Ben, as if he were trying to convince himself. "There's always someone that's gotta screw up somethin' good."

They divvied up the money. Ben and Henry went in the Castle, leaving John with the last bunch of flowers.

*****

The thought of the old lady still nagged at John as he headed up 57th Street toward home. He wondered about what she'd said, about the flowers being for everyone. He looked down at his lilacs and decided he'd give them to his mother. That would shut up the old lady. If he met her on the street, he could say, "I cut those flowers down for my poor mother, who's sick in bed. Now what's better than givin' them to a poor sick lady who can't get outta bed so she can enjoy them flowers?" His mother wasn't sick, but what if she was? Then cutting flowers would be a good deed. That's what he'd do, he'd give them to his mother.

Near the entrance of his building, he noticed a young couple strolling along the other side of the street, holding hands.

He thought for a moment, then shrugged and turned away from the door. He crossed over to them, smiling. "Wanna buy some flowers? Only a buck-fifty a bunch."

CHAPTER NINETEEN

"Let me do the talkin'," Henry warned as he and Ben approached Olson's butcher shop. They stood to one side of the entrance and Henry, palm up, waggled his fingers until Ben gave him all of the money they'd collected selling lilacs.

Ben's face scrunched up into a frown of distrust. "What're you so worried about? I bought stuff from Mr. Olsen before, and he never gave me any trouble."

Henry pocketed the money and patted his friend's shoulder. "Yeah, but you was buyin' for your mother. When a kid goes in ta buy for himself, Olsen cheats 'em."

"The prices are right in front," Ben said, using the tone of condescension Henry hated. "How can Olsen cheat?"

"Ya never heard of puttin' a thumb on the scales?" Henry sneered. "Ya act like a dumb hillbilly."

Henry led the way inside and stood looking down at the gleaming white refrigerator case that held the meat. He liked the sawdust and dill smell of the butcher shop, particularly when Mr. Olsen had just opened a new barrel of pickles or sauerkraut. He pushed up closer to the case and nudged Ben, nodding toward the chicken necks and backs that were separated from the more expensive pieces of chicken by a row of fresh parsley.

The boys were the only customers in the shop. Olsen, a fullback gone to fat, stood behind the refrigerated showcase and stared down at them. Bald and hatless, he wore a white shirt and dark trousers, protected by a full-length apron that was covered with smears of animal blood.

Henry reached into his pocket and pulled out a crumpled piece of paper. Smoothing it, he pretended it was a note from his mother. "My mom says you should gimme ten pounds of chicken necks and backs for soup."

Mr. Olsen said nothing. He turned away and trudged toward the back. The heavy freezer door swung open with a hiss, and a thin cloud of frigid air swirled out. Henry caught a quick flash of hanging sides of beef before the door swung shut.

"See that?" Henry said. "He's gonna get the fresh stuff 'cause he thinks it's for my mom."

Ben laughed. "Olsen ain't got ten pounds out here, and you ain't got no mom."

Before Henry could get mad, the freezer door swung back open and Mr. Olsen came shuffling out. He was carrying a sheet of pink butcher paper piled high with a mound of chicken necks and backs. Using both hands, he threw the package on the scale. After the needle settled, the dial read eleven pounds. Mr. Olsen started to remove some of the chicken.

"Nah, that's OK," Henry said grandly. "You can make it eleven." Mr. Olsen didn't even look up. Instead, in one rolling motion, he wrapped the chicken with the sure hands of an expert. Going to the cash register, he punched the keys and handed the package over.

"Dollar ten."

Ben tapped Henry from behind and whispered, "Don't forget the pickles an' the sauerkraut."

Henry shot him a glare, then turned back to the butcher. He pretended to read from his note. "Oh, I forgot. Six pickles an' two pounds of sauerkraut."

The butcher said nothing. Using the tongs that hung on the side of the barrel, he fished out a half-dozen pickles. From a second barrel, he scooped out enough sauerkraut to fill a white cardboard tray. He weighed the sauerkraut, wrapped both items in butcher paper, tapped the price into the cash register, and handed Henry the additional packages.

Mr. Olsen was one of the few people in the neighborhood Henry couldn't figure out. He never smiled and he never frowned. He just shuffled around with the same frozen look on his face. To Henry, the guy seemed OK, in a creepy kind of way.

"Pickles nickel apiece, sauerkraut fifty cents. Whole thing, dollar ninety."

Henry paid and they left.

When they got to John's house, Henry yelled up to his window. "Come an' get it 'fore I throw it ta the hogs." It was a line he'd picked up from a Ma and Pa Kettle movie. He thought it was funny, but when Ben groaned and grimaced as if he were in pain, he decided not to use it again. With John in tow, the three of them strolled to the Castle.

Henry's dad was sleeping off a drunk and too dangerous to be around, so they went to Ben's place. His mother hadn't been home for a few days, and while Ben admitted to Henry that there was no telling when she'd get back, he swore it didn't matter. "She didn't leave me any money for food, so she can't complain about me feeding myself."

Henry did the cooking. Lighting a stick match with his fingernail, he fired up one of the burners on the stove. In a huge iron frying pan, he melted some butter, then browned about half of the chicken. Setting the browned chicken to one side, he browned the other half, loaded the whole mess into the skillet, added water, and covered the pan. Within an hour, he served up a soggy, half-fried, half-boiled, unseasoned mess of chicken necks and backs.

Ben started eating so fast, Henry was afraid he was going to choke on his food. "Slow down, man. For once, we got enough ta eat, an' there ain't anyone around ta take it away from us."

After a few minutes of silent eating, John patted his stomach and burped. "Where'd you learn to cook, Henry?"

"Don't remember, just always been doin' it." Henry wiped his greasy fingers on his shirt and grinned. "This is the first time I ever pushed back with stuff still on the table."

Henry got up, and after an "OK" nod from Ben, pulled a couple of Cokes out of the icebox. He poured about a third from each bottle into a glass and handed the glass to John. The bottles went to him and Ben. "What'll we do with the extra money?"

"Let's hang onta it," Henry said. "An' we'll spend it when we're all together." He looked at John for confirmation, and when John said nothing, he added, "The flowers was your idea, Johnny, so it's for you ta say."

John smiled. "OK, by me. Who's gonna hold the dough?"

Henry gave a noncommittal shrug. "I got it now, but I'll hand it over ta Benny. It's safe with him 'cause he's too dumb ta steal."

John laughed and looked over at Ben.

Ben picked up a neck bone and started sucking on it.

Henry tilted his chair back and put his foot on the edge of the table for balance. "What about it, Benny? Is it OK with you?"

He expected a quick "yes" and scowled at Ben when he didn't get one.

Ben paused, then, almost in a whisper, he said, "Maybe we should use some of it to pay Mr. Anderson for the stuff we stole."

Henry stared at Ben, too stunned to say anything. Finally, he shook his head slowly from side to side. "Man, you are the biggest pussy of all time. How're we gonna do that without tellin' him we took the stuff? If we did, ol' man Anderson would call the police for sure. It ain't like we stole from someone who was broke. Anderson's got bucks up the ass. Besides, guys like him jack up the price of their stuff ta cover shopliftin'."

Ben shrugged and grabbed another neck bone. "Don't get all pissed off. It was just an idea."

Henry leaned back even further in his chair and chugged his Coke. He tried to catch Ben's eye, but each time he looked over, Ben put his head down and ate more chicken. "If the flowers are still fresh enough next weekend, I say we go back and get some more of 'em."

He reached over and gripped Ben's shoulder. "The only thing is, we're outta wire. It's too tricky ta go back ta Anderson's. There's a hardware store on 55th an' Dorchester. Let's go there instead. They don't know us, so they won't be lookin' for us ta steal. That OK with you, Benny boy?"

Henry locked eyes with Ben. If the kid was going to go Boy Scout on him, he needed to know. John looked away and busied himself eating a pickle. Ben finally nodded. "It's OK by me, but it seems stupid to take the risk now that we've got enough money in our pockets to buy what we need."

Henry was torn between punching Ben for calling him stupid and admitting that Ben was right. Before he could make up his mind, John helped make the decision for him. He reached over and ruffled Ben's hair. "Stealin' more wire was my idea, Benny. But you're right, buyin' it makes a lot more sense." Forking a scoop of sauerkraut onto his plate, Henry grinned at Ben. So much for worrying about the kid going sissy on him. He nodded and went back to eating.

CHAPTER TWENTY

I t was the day after the Ray School graduation, and summer boredom had already set in. At fifteen, Andy was a year older than the other five Castle boys, but because he had been held back a year, they all graduated together. Now he sprawled on the bottom step next to Mike. On the steps above them were Henry, Ben, Tommy, and John.

Andy stood, dug in the pocket of his jeans, and fished out a penny. With a backhand flip, he lagged the penny two squares up, dropping it an inch from the line. He was hoping Mike would lag with him because he could sometimes beat Mike, but Mike ignored him and turned to Ben.

"Only pussies like Ben go to Hyde Park High. You gotta be tough to go to Carmel.

John got up, and Andy's shoulders sagged. Here was the one guy he could never beat. John lagged and his penny hit the line square. Andy picked up both pennies and handed them over.

Ben sneered, "Yeah! I heard those nuns at Carmel are really tough. They whack you with a ruler every time you get somethin' wrong. Dumb as you are, Mikey, you won't have any knuckles left."

Mike responded with his usual "Fuck you!"

Ben glanced over at Andy and winked. "That brilliant retort shows why Mikey's goin' to Carmel. They won't let him in a free school 'cause he's too stupid. He's goin' to a school where if you pay, they gotta let you in."

Andy cringed, saying nothing. He'd never told Ben that Father Donahue had tried to get him a scholarship to Mount Carmel. The catholic school had rejected him because of his low test scores.

He fondled the blue and white ribbons pinned to his jeans. They proved that he was among the students who had graduated. He knew the rest of them thought the ribbons were stupid, but he wore them because he was proud of finally getting out of Ray.

School wasn't easy for Andy. Each year, he promised himself he'd really try to get good grades, but the school wouldn't let him stay after to do homework, and studying at home was next to impossible. Between his father's drunken rages and his brother's sneering abuse, "Asshole Andy's turnin' inta a bookworm," they had made it clear that his job was to wait on them, not waste time on schoolwork.

Being rejected by Carmel was embarrassing, but deep down, Andy was glad. He hadn't wanted to go there in the first place. He wanted to go to Chicago Vocational with Henry.

"I'm goin' to CVS 'cause I wanna learn auto mechanics. Me an' Henry'll fix your cars if any of you guys ever get rich enough to buy one."

Everyone laughed, and Henry tousled Andy's hair. "Maybe they'll steal 'em."

Ben got up and hip-bumped Andy out of the way. He lagged and landed a foot away from the line. "It's none of Mikey's business, but I'm goin' to Hyde Park because Vocational doesn't give you enough required subjects to get into college. College is my ticket out of this rat-fucked neighborhood."

John nodded his head as if that went for him, too. Andy was surprised, since John had told him he was going to Hyde Park because his mother insisted. He caught John's eye and shrugged to let him know that he wasn't going to blab to the guys. John tossed his penny and grimaced when it hit next to Ben's.

Andy threw his penny, and this time, he tossed a liner. He started to pick up his winnings, but John put his hand on his arm. Andy caught him winking at Ben and knew John was figuring on hustling him. John said, "How 'bout we go double or nothin'?"

Andy sighed, acting as if he was already resigned to the loss of his pennies.

Tommy stood and stretched. "I'm goin' to Hyde Park for the swim team. They've got the best diving coach in the city. If I can place in the city finals, I can get an athletic scholarship to Illinois."

John's second coin landed even farther back.

"So whadda you guys wanna do?" Andy threw and again hit the line.

John shook his head. "You're hot, Andy. How 'bout we leave the pennies there and go for nickels?"

Andy shook his head. "Can't. I ain't got a nickel." With that, he picked up all the pennies and grinned to let John know he'd just hustled the hustler.

Andy sat down next to Henry. "So, whadda you wanna do?"

Tommy pulled out a nickel and started to flip it. "How 'bout we go swimmin' at the poles?"

Mike dug in his pocket and pulled out some coins. "The ladder broke last week, and it ain't been fixed yet. It ain't no fun just swimmin' around."

Andy nodded. He was used to Mike always finding an excuse to keep away from the poles.

The poles were all that was left of an old boat pier. Three poles, fifteen-feet-high, stood clumped together twenty yards out from the edge of the Lake Michigan rock breakwater. The kids used them as diving platforms. Andy had gone there with Tommy a week earlier. He'd followed Tommy up the mossy ladder of the first pole and moved to the slippery top of the one that faced out into the lake. Some kids dove, some jumped, but they all went off because there was a line of kids behind them pushing to get to the diving pole. Andy had watched with a combination of pride and envy as Tommy executed a perfect swan dive. Then he'd swallowed his fear and followed Tommy with a straight dive, stabbing the water squarely and slipping under the surface with hardly a splash. Even Tommy had said he was impressed.

Andy smiled to himself. He knew Mike was a good swimmer and that he probably had the skill to dive the poles—what Mike lacked was the nerve.

Ben stretched his legs out, locking his hands behind his head. "I don't care what we do."

John, Mike, and Tommy kept lagging.

"Some of the older guys are supposed to play softball at the schoolyard," Andy said. "If they're short a few guys, they might let us play. Even if they don't, it'll be fun to watch."

Henry got up and lagged his only nickel. It landed on its edge and rolled into the street. Without a word, he turned and started walking away.

"Where you goin'?" Andy called.

Henry turned and shrugged as if it were a stupid question. "Ta the ball game, like ya said. It's better than hangin' around watchin' John grab our dough."

Andy called out, "Wait for me," and scrambled to catch up while the others fell in behind.

*****

90

The ball game was just getting underway. Most of the players were wearing street gang jackets, so it almost looked as if they were in uniform. What was confusing was that members of the same gang were on both sides. Andy figured it was what kept the game from turning into one huge fight.

All six of them got to play. Because they were younger, they were split up, three on each side. To Andy's amazement, one of the older guys had seen him throwing strikes in the schoolyard and talked the others into letting him start as pitcher.

The minute they handed Andy the twelve-inch ball, he knew it was going to be his day. He strode out to the mound, checked to make sure his teammates were all in place, then whipped an underhand pitch straight down the middle. There was no umpire, so his perfect strike went uncalled and unappreciated. But on his next pitch, the batter swung and dribbled a grounder to short for an easy out. The next two batters fell to his fastball and his wicked curve, one on a pop-up and the other on a line drive to Mike at second base.

During Andy's team's turn at bat, Tommy slapped a double and Mike singled him home. One of the other kids hit a home run, and the second inning started with them up by two runs.

The first batter in the second inning was big, bad Roger Shaw. Roger was easily the toughest kid in the neighborhood. Fully grown at fifteen, he had the reputation of being so mean, even his family was afraid of him. The whole neighborhood talked about how Roger had broken a kid's arm because he wouldn't let loose of his lunch money. That incident had bought him a year in Saint Charles, but Andy knew that there were a whole lot of other times when kids had been too scared to squeal.

Roger crowded the plate, waving the bat and grinning. "Just get it over the plate, Pip-squeak. I'll take it from there."

Andy brushed him back with his first pitch.

The catcher called time and raced out to the mound. "Hey, dumbshit. Can't you see who you're pitchin' to? Do that again, an' Shaw'll fuck you up good."

Andy kneaded the ball with both hands. "He's crowdin' the plate. What am I supposed to do?"

The catcher, a high school sophomore, shook his head and hustled back behind the plate.

Mike moved in from second. "If it was me, I'd just walk him."

Andy thought about the poles, about how Mike was afraid to dive, and how he had been scared too, but he'd done it anyway. He remembered how it felt when Tommy had said what a good dive he'd made, and how for just that moment, he'd felt good, like one of the guys. This was his day, and Roger Shaw wasn't going to ruin it for him.

He snapped the ball high and inside, again trying to brush Roger back. This time, the ball got too far inside and hit Roger on the arm. Roger dropped the bat and rushed the mound like a maddened bull. His face was red with rage and both hands were pumping to give him more speed. Andy froze, watching mesmerized as Roger charged. He had a fleeting regret, recognizing that his good day was over. Then, almost as an afterthought, he stuck his left arm straight out, and Roger, running head down, plowed into Andy's fist. It caught him on the forehead just above his nose and stopped him dead in his tracks.

Ignoring the pain in his hand, Andy stood staring as Roger, dazed and glassy-eyed, shook his head from side to side. When Roger's eyes seemed to clear, Andy fought off his paralysis and took off running. Roger roared with rage and started after him. Both teams and all the spectators followed, including the Castle gang.

Roger Shaw was the fastest runner in the neighborhood. He caught up with his quarry before Andy's pigeon-toed feet got him past right field. At over six feet, Roger was a foot taller than Andy and outweighed him by at least forty pounds.

In full stride, he reached out and slammed his hand down on Andy's shoulder. Terrified, instead of slowing down, Andy swung around and threw a roundhouse right that caught Roger in the throat. Roger stumbled and almost fell. He stopped and tried to breathe, but the punch had hit him in the windpipe.

Andy spun away and kept on running. He glanced back over his shoulder and saw Roger bent over, sucking air in hoarse gasps. He almost wept when Roger straightened up and started coming after him again.

Roger caught up again two blocks farther away on Dorchester. He got so close, Andy could hear his labored breathing, and while Roger didn't seem to be running as fast, he was still faster than Andy. This time, Roger launched himself in the air, trying to bring Andy down with a knee-high tackle. Andy high-stepped out of his grasp, and Roger hit the pavement chin first. Once again, Roger pulled himself up and continued the chase.

Andy felt that his life was in danger, and the danger pushed him on. He was aware of Henry and Tommy being in the crowd that was following, but he knew neither one would interfere. This was between him and Roger Shaw, and Andy figured he didn't have a chance of coming out of it alive.

He passed Harper Avenue and kept going east toward the lake. At Lake Park, Roger managed to grab the back of Andy's shirt, and when Andy spun around swinging, he stepped back and blocked the punch.

"Not this time, ya fuckin' little shit."

Andy tried to back away, but by now, the crowd had caught up with them, and they were surrounded. He put his hands up in a traditional fighter's stance.

Roger smirked. "You got a lotta guts, kid. I admire that. Whadda ya say we call it quits." He put out his open hand.

Stunned and relieved, Andy didn't hesitate. He smiled sheepishly and grabbed Roger's hand. Roger gripped tightly and jerked Andy forward, throwing an arm around his neck. Making a fist, he started throwing uppercuts at the side of Andy's head and full in his face. There was the sickening sound of fist on flesh, loud, popping smacks that turned wet as blood began to spew from Andy's nose. Roger finally released him, and Andy slid down to his knees. Roger grinned at the crowd and stepped back. Then he landed a kick between Andy's legs. Screaming, Andy grabbed his crotch and curled into a ball.

Roger laughed out loud and hauled back his leg, starting another kick. This one, had it landed, would have broken ribs. Instead, Andy, retching on the ground, saw Roger suddenly stumble backward. Through the haze of pain, he realized that Tommy had grabbed Roger's jacket and yanked him off balance. Tears of love and gratitude welled up in Andy's eyes as Henry moved around and stood in front of him. Ben, fists clenched, moved to stand next to Tommy. Andy watched as the three-to-one odds convinced Roger Shaw it wasn't worth the risk.

"So that's the way it is, huh? Well, you assholes can't hang together all the time. I'll catch up with ya one at a time."

Henry helped Andy to his feet. Then he turned toward Roger Shaw. His face looked as if it had been carved from stone. To Andy, Henry's black expressionless eyes made him seem all the more deadly. Henry put his arm around Andy's shoulder. "It's gonna be the other way around, Rog. We owe you a bloody nose and a cut-up face. Lucky for you Tommy stopped ya, or we'd have ta add a couple of busted ribs. You couldn't beat the kid fair, so ya had ta cheat, and we're gonna get even—no matter how long it takes."

Once they got Andy back to the Castle, Tommy ran upstairs and wrapped a couple of ice cubes in a dish towel for Andy's busted nose. The cuts were minor but his face was puffed up, and it looked as though both eyes would blacken. Andy soaked up their admiration as they clucked at him and called him stupid for tossing at Roger. At that moment, he loved them more than he'd ever loved anyone or anything in his life. One by one, they took their regular places on the steps. Andy leaned back and through swollen lips rasped out, "So whadda you guys wanna do?"

CHAPTER TWENTY-ONE

H enry ambled up to the group and plopped down on the stoop next to Mike. John noticed that he sported a bruise on one cheek, a mouse under his left eye, and a split lip. He acknowledged Henry with a nod, then looked away. Henry hadn't come from inside the building, so John figured the cops had forced him to sleep at his grandparents' house. That was usually the case when his father got hauled away to the drunk tank.

John was bored and nervous. Tomorrow was the end of summer vacation. Instead of going to Ray School where he was among the oldest, he'd be going to high school where he'd be among the youngest and most picked on.

He started to stand up and lag a coin, but thought better of it and sank back down. There was no sense in trying to get the others to play—he had long since taken all their change. He spoke without looking at anyone in particular. "I hate Labor Day. It ain't a real holiday 'cause it comes during vacation. Columbus Day, Armistice Day, Thanksgiving, Christmas, New Year's, Washington's Birthday, Lincoln's Birthday, Memorial Day—those are real holidays. Today oughta be a day of mourning 'cause we gotta go back to school tomorrow."

For once, Ben didn't come up with some wiseass remark, and John took it to mean that Ben was as nervous as he was.

He stood and moved in front of Henry. "There's a Swedish Day picnic goin' on over by the lagoon. My mom said there's gonna be a ton of people, so no one'll notice a few extra. They give out Swedish food like at a smorgasbord, all you can eat."

Henry stared up at him in disgust. "No talkin' about food. My old man drank up his paycheck again. Unless I go back to Grandfather's place an' listen ta a bunch of Mohawk crap, I ain't gonna eat for a few days."

"So come to the picnic. You can load up on Swedish meatballs."

"I just told you, the old man drank up all the money in the house. I'm flat broke."

"You got it all wrong. It's a picnic. You don't have to pay nothin'. Every Labor Day, all these Swedes get together and toss a big shindig. There's gonna be food, games, an' dancin', but mostly food. Swedes aren't big on havin' fun."

Ben got off the stoop and started pulling Henry to his feet. "Free food, Fox. What're we waitin' for?"

*****

It was cool for September, mid-eighties. A breeze blew in off the lake, whispering promises of a perfect day at The Rocks. Mike remained sprawled out on the top step. "A bunch of the girls from Sacred Heart are gonna be at the beach. I'll probably get to score with one of 'em. I'd pass up food for pussy any day."

John caught Ben's eye, and they both started to laugh. To keep Mike from seeing the smirk on his face, John turned his head toward the others. "What about the rest of us, Mikey? You think the rest of us can get pussy from these Sacred Heart girls?"

"There's this one broad, Mary Ryan, an' she puts out. I already nailed her, but I ain't sure you guys can. For sure not Booger Nose."

Andy shot up, hands curled into fists. His hairline pulled back and his face went white with cold rage. John was surprised. Insulting Andy was so accepted, Mike's remark had gone by without him even noticing. Andy's deadly quiet words shocked him even further. "Call me that again, and a lot more than boogers is gonna come outta your nose."

Leave it to Mike to screw things up, John thought. *Now him and Andy are gonna fight, an' we'll never get to the picnic.* He got very interested in his fingernails and watched as Tommy and Henry got fascinated by their shoes. Mike sat up and hugged his knees. He caught John's eye, hoping for some kind of help, but John turned away.

Mike's voice quivered. "Ever since Shaw kicked your ass, you been actin' fucked up. "Anyway, I didn't mean nothin' by it."

The tension seemed to ease out of Andy like air from a tire with a slow leak. John slowly sank back down next to Andy and threw his arm around Andy's shoulder. "I wouldn't say Shaw kicked anyone's ass. The only way he won that fight was by sucker-punching my pal here."

Henry Fox had finally started to grow. He was still five inches shorter than Mike, but when he moved up a step, he and Mike were at eye level. "When it comes ta Mary Ryan, you're fulla shit. The only pussy you ever got was Rosy Palm and her five daughters. I know for a fact Mary ain't never put out to you. Last time I screwed her, she told me she thought you was a punk."

He faced the group. "I'm bettin' I'm the only one here what even got tit, let alone pussy."

Ben and Tommy shrugged, and Henry took their silence as confirmation. John grinned and shook his head. "You lose. I got tit from Edna Moran. But unlike Big Dick Mike, I ain't got her to go all the way...yet."

Henry smiled as if accepting John into the fraternity of guys who scored. "I nailed Edna at the beach last month. Keep tryin'. If ya get a finger in her, she'll roll over for ya. Once ya get a finger in a broad's pussy, they get so hot, they can't say no."

Tommy blushed and shook his head. "You know what, Fox, it isn't right to be bragging about stuff like that. Anyway, who wants some tramp who's been with every guy on the block? I'm gonna wait till I get married." With that, he got to his feet and started off in the direction of the lake. He called back over his shoulder, "It's too nice a day to waste time crashin' a picnic."

Mike ran after him. "Hey, Tommy, wait up."

John stood staring at Henry, waiting for an answer. It wasn't long in coming. "I guess that leaves the four of us. Swedish meatballs, here we come."

*****

John didn't spend much time thinking about his mother. Gretta Solberg was just there, a person who bought him clothes and provided his lunches. Mostly, his conversations with her were short, polite, and marked by obvious indifference. She rarely smiled, and he hadn't heard her laugh for as long as he could remember. John figured she was like that because of his dad getting killed in the war. He was nine when she got the telegram, and from that time on, she acted like she knew nothing good would ever happen to her again. She worked as a private nurse. When she had a client, things at the Solberg house were peaceful. This Labor Day, she was out of work.

The picnic table was spread with more food than John had seen in a long while. Deviled eggs, Gretta's famous Swedish meatballs, fried chicken, and a fruit salad with lingonberries were all set out on the checked oilcloth cover that was normally draped over their kitchen table. His mother stood with her arms crossed over her chest, her face was wrinkled in a deep frown. John waved Henry and the others to a stop. He eyed his mother. "You said I could bring some friends."

His mother's frown deepened. "I said *a* friend, not every bum in the neighborhood."

John moved around her, thinking this mood would pass. He grabbed a deviled egg, popped it in his mouth, and turned to his mother. She stared pointedly at Henry, then back at her son. John locked eyes with her for a moment, and for the first time saw past the flat, pale blue irises to the fear lurking behind. "The kind of people you have for friends. This won't do, John. This just won't do. What is that boy, some kind of Arab?"

John felt his throat grab and he swallowed back the tears. He stared at his mother and, shaking his head, began to slowly back away. "He's my friend." He grabbed Henry's arm and turned to walk away. Face flaming with shame, he looked back at his mother. "Next time, I'll bring you pictures of everyone before you invite them. That way, my friends won't have to put up with a bunch of crap."

Ben and Andy were also moving away. Ben had a funny look on his face, and John flashed on all the times he'd joked about Ben's being Jewish. He wondered if Ben and Henry thought he was like his mother. Suddenly, Ben started laughing. "She thinks Henry's an Arab. He's the 'Sheik of Araby.'"

Andy shouted, "No, he's a Norwegian." Then he started chanting at the top of his lungs. "Ten thousand Swedes went through the weeds, chased by one Norwegian."

One of the men standing near Mrs. Solberg heard the chant. His face drained of what little color it had. "What does he say?" Fists clenched, he started after the boys.

Andy glanced back and nudged John. "One of the guys is comin' after us, maybe we should run."

John slowed and refused to look back. "Fuck him, fuck my mother, and fuck all the Swedes in Sweden."

Andy glanced back again. "It's OK, the guy gave up."

The four of them walked back to the Castle side-by-side. They dropped down on the stoop and Andy nudged John. "Don't feel bad, Johnny. My old man talks that shit all the time, an' he goes out drinkin' with Henry's dad."

Henry nodded. "No one's blamin' you, Johnny boy. Some people are just ignorant."

John wasn't sure he should let Henry call his mother ignorant without saying something. He thought for a moment, then decided he didn't really care what anyone called her. He wiped his eyes and frowned. "You know what's really fucked? School starts tomorrow."

CHAPTER TWENTY-TWO

Tommy loved the smell of chlorine. Like swimming itself, the smell of chlorine on his body made him feel cleansed and free of sin. In church, the priest talked about being washed in the blood of the lamb, which sounded disgusting to Tommy. He grinned, thinking he'd take washing in chlorinated water over blood every time.

Today, he had been sensational, hitting every practice dive perfectly. Even coach Olsen had been forced to give him an approving nod. It was rare praise, and it put Tommy in a really good mood.

Waving back at a couple of teammates, he shrugged on his letterman's jacket and used his shoulder to bang open the swinging door that led from the pool area to the hall.

As the door flew open, it slammed into something that brought it to an abrupt stop and sent it swinging back sharply. The backswing caught Tommy as he was turning forward. Off balance and stumbling, he dropped his athletic bag and almost went down.

He was barely able to choke back a curse when he saw who the door had slammed into. Anita Gibson was in Tommy's English class. She was easily the best-looking girl in the class, maybe in the entire school. Ringlets of blonde hair cascaded down her forehead, stopping just above the bluest eyes Tommy had ever seen. Her nose was pert, her lips bowed, and at fourteen, she had breasts that challenged the cashmere sweater she'd probably shoplifted from Marshall Field's.

"Jeez, are you hurt?" Face flushed with embarrassment, Tommy leaned down and grabbed his bag.

"No, I'm OK, I think." Anita moved her hand away from her forehead and pushed her face uncomfortably close to Tommy. "Is my head cut?"

"Nah, just a little red." He flushed again, this time because the closeness of her body was sending a fiery heat through him. "I'm really sorry. I shouldn't a slammed out like that."

He shuffled awkwardly to one side, then started to pull away.

Anita grabbed his arm. "Uh, I think it's starting to swell. Could you get me some ice?"

Tommy looked around as if ice cubes should be within reach. Not seeing any, he turned back to her in desperation.

She smiled. It was a beaming smile that created deep dimples, and flashed almost perfect white teeth. The tiny flaw was a smudge of lipstick on one front tooth. Pouting playfully, she stood looking up at him. "Oh, I guess it'll be all right."

The thing Tommy hated about girls was that they wouldn't just come out and tell a guy what they wanted. It seemed girls expected guys to figure it out by themselves. He mumbled, "Uh, we could go to Walgreen's an' get a Coke with ice. You could drink the Coke and use the ice for your head."

Anita seemed to waver, then allowed him to take her arm as the two of them left school and headed for the drugstore.

Tommy ordered a couple of cherry Cokes and carried them to a back booth. He dug a piece of ice out of his glass, wrapped it in a napkin, and pressed it against Anita's head.

She held it there for a few moments, then bent her head and sipped at her straw. "It's a lot better now."

They sat in silence. Tommy sipped his Coke and avoided Anita's eyes.

Anita must have decided Tommy would never start the conversation on his own. "I remember you from Ray School. You were always with a bunch of hoodlums. Are they going here, too?"

It felt disloyal to ignore the hoodlum remark, but Tommy didn't want to start an argument. "You're probably talkin' about Henry Fox. He an' my other buddy Andy are goin' to Vocational. Ben and Johnny are goin' here, but they hang around the back of the school with the…uh…you know…the ones who aren't welcome in front with us."

"What about the big one? I think his name is Mike?"

Tommy felt a flash of jealousy. She'd noticed Mike enough to single him out, even remembered his name. "The poor sap, he went to Mount Carmel. A nun who thanks God for givin' her kids to torture is probably smacking his knuckles with a ruler right this minute."

Anita giggled and took Tommy's hand. "You're really funny."

For the next hour, they talked about school, their mutual friends,and Tommy's diving. "I'm hoping to win City. If I can do that, I can get a scholarship to Illinois."

Anita told him she wanted to become a film star. "If I can get to Hollywood, I know I can get a screen test. They say Lana Turner was discovered in a drugstore." She looked around at the pharmacy counter. "Can you imagine? A drugstore!"

The Cokes were finished and the ice had long since melted when Anita said she had to go.

They left the soda fountain and stepped out onto the sidewalk. Reluctantly, Tommy said good-bye. He took her hand and then, not knowing what to do with it, he ended up shaking it. She smiled and started to walk away.

When she'd gone a few steps, she turned back as if she'd had an afterthought. "Are you going to the sock hop?"

Tommy faced her with a shrug. "I don't know how to dance."

She hesitated. "I could teach you."

Tommy shuffled slowly toward her, stopping within a few feet. "You could? I really want to learn."

Anita scribbled her address on a piece of paper. "My mom's divorced. On Tuesdays, she's got a second job as a waitress, an' she's gone until ten. We'd have the apartment to ourselves. Come after dinner, around six." She smiled and started leaving, walking backward. "I hope I can trust you."

Tommy turned and headed toward the Castle in a daze. He clutched the note tightly in his fist and prayed that his heartbeat would slow down before six o'clock.

*****

Anita met him at the door. Leaning against the jamb, she swayed and bit her bottom lip, blocking him from coming in. For a moment, Tommy thought she'd changed her mind. Then, as if making a big decision, she stepped back, and he slid past her.

"Hi."

"Hi."

She was dressed in jeans and the same cashmere sweater. There were some records next to the phonograph, and she put on a slow fox trot. Showing him how to hold her, Anita paced off a basic step, and they started trying to dance. At first, Tommy held her at arm's length, but as they shuffled along, she pulled him closer and closer.

"The girl's got to feel your body to know how you want her to move."

105

Tommy buried his face in her neck, inhaling the womanly smell of her. He was on fire. Sweat began to run under his clothing and his face went beet red. He wanted to take off his sweater, but he was afraid that the armpits of his shirt were wet. He'd never had a feeling like this. Flushed and lightheaded, his breath coming in short gasps, he clung to Anita, convinced that if he let go, he'd fall flat on his face.

As they swayed to the music, Tommy's body rubbed against hers and her breasts pressed into his chest. Suddenly, he became aware of his penis. It began to stiffen, and he couldn't control it. He pulled back to avoid the rubbing, but it was too late. There was an unmistakable bulge in his slacks. He expected some kind of reaction from Anita, but she seemed not to notice.

"Let's sit down for a while, OK? You look really hot. Should I get you a Coke?"

Turning away from her to shield the front of his pants, Tommy slid onto the couch. "Yeah."

When she returned with the bottle of Coke, she slid down next to him. They kissed, lips tightly closed. Tommy's idea of a passionate kiss was to press as hard as he could. Anita seemed to think differently. After several minutes with their mouths closed, Tommy felt Anita's lips part and her tongue push lightly against his. Tommy's erection became painfully hard. Anita tasted of spearmint and smelled like some sweet perfume mixed with a hint of perspiration. Every time a movement rubbed his clothing against his crotch, he almost passed out. After what seemed like hours, Tommy casually dropped his hand from her shoulder and tried to stroke her breast. She firmly pushed him away, and they went back to kissing.

Anita was flushed, too. Her clothing was rumpled and her swollen lips were surrounded with a pinkish stain. Tommy again reached for her breast, and again, she shoved his hand away.

106

"Why can't I touch you there?"

Anita didn't answer. She got up, straightened her clothing, and walked into the bathroom. When she returned, she sat next to him and refused to kiss.

"I think it's time for you to go."

Cursing himself for trying too soon, he reluctantly got up and started toward the door.

Anita didn't walk him out, but as he pulled the door open, she said, "If you still want to learn how to dance, you can come over again next Tuesday."

*****

A routine was established. A few minutes of dance lessons followed by a lot of heavy necking. After a while, Tommy was allowed to touch her breast, but only from the outside of her clothing. He began wearing a jock strap to hide his erections, but it didn't help much. If anything, the telltale bulge looked larger.

After the necking sessions, Anita always wanted to calm down and talk. She talked about the future—about marriage, goals, and children. Somehow the idea of a career as a film star would mesh with motherhood. The talking as much as the petting convinced Tommy that he was in love.

One night, Tommy said, "I wanna see you without any clothes on."

"Oh, you do, do you?"she teased. "Why? You know I'm not gonna do it with you till we're married."

"I dunno. I think you're beautiful an' I'd just like to see what you look like underneath." Tommy paused, not daring to hope. He was sure that if he could get her naked, she'd let him go all the way. Clothing was his enemy.

Anita rose and walked to the phonograph. She was quiet for a long time. Then she said, "If someone were to climb onto my porch at night and look in my bedroom window, they'd get a real eyeful."

"Whadda you mean?"

"Sometimes I undress and dance around in front of the mirror. If someone was out on the porch, they'd see me, because I never pull the shade all the way down."

Tommy had trouble talking. He looked through the doorway of Anita's bedroom and saw that her bedroom window did indeed look out onto the porch.

"I...uh...what time do you go to bed?"

"Nine-thirty every night. Exactly at nine-thirty."

At nine the next night, Tommy tiptoed up the wooden stairs that led from the back alley to the Gibson's porch. Anita lived on the top floor of a four-story building, and the chance of someone seeing him increased with each floor he passed. When he reached the top, he was confused as to which side Anita's apartment was on. The idea of being caught peeking into a stranger's window almost stopped him. He was standing in the dark, trying to guess which one was Anita's, when a light went on in the apartment to his left and the shade slowly moved up a few inches.

Tommy dropped down on all fours and crept toward the window, making sure he was beneath the bottom edge. Rising slightly, he cautiously peered over the sill.

Anita was sitting on her bed, idly picking at the top button of her fuzzy pink sweater. She seemed almost hypnotized, staring off toward a side of the room Tommy couldn't see. Suddenly, she undid the top three buttons of the sweater and peeled it slowly upward and off. She laid it carefully on the chair next to her bed, then lowered the side zipper of her skirt, inch by agonizing inch. The skirt had a waistline button, and to undo it, she pulled it around so that the button was in the front. She unbuttoned it, gave a slight wiggle, and the skirt floated to the floor. She stepped out of it and was then dressed only in her bra and white panties.

Tommy's heart was thundering, and he forced back a groan of excitement. Anita walked slowly to the side of the room and stood posing in front of a mirror. His vision was limited by the small opening beneath the shade, but his view of Anita from the rear was complete.

Her movements became even more sensual. She seemed to undulate as her hands moved to the back of her bra and undid the eye hooks. As she shrugged slightly forward, the bra came off, but with her back toward Tommy and the mirror's reflection blocked by her body, he was unable to see her breasts.

Anita held her arms up and began to sway from side to side. It wasn't actually dancing, but it was close. Tommy choked back a moan and stroked his crotch.

Now she hooked her thumbs into the waistband of her panties and slowly pulled them down past her thighs. From there, another slight wiggle made them drop the rest of the way to her ankles. Anita stepped out of the panties with the same graceful motion she'd used when she stepped out of her skirt. She stood upright with her hands at her sides and stared into the mirror. The tan that ended at her bra line began again just below the perfect curve of her buttocks. She was completely nude but remained with her back toward Tommy.

Minutes passed. Tommy's mouth went completely dry and his breathing was hoarse and so loud, he was sure Anita could hear him. His penis felt like a steel rod, and he worried that if he didn't open his pants, it might be damaged. Silently, he begged Anita to turn around. As if she heard him, she suddenly pivoted toward the window and stood fully revealed for an instant.

Her breasts tilted upward as she threw back her shoulders. Hands behind her neck, she thrust her hip to one side and stood for a moment, posing. Then, as if coming to her senses, her face took on a look of horror. Frantically, she leaned over to the bedside lamp. Fumbling with the switch, she finally managed to turn it off. The room went black, and Tommy staggered back. He waited, confused by the sudden darkness. Then he turned and ran down the stairs.

The dance lessons continued, and the porch event was never mentioned. Tommy returned to the window a couple of times, but the shade was always all the way down, so he gave up.

After a few more weeks, Anita let him slip his hand under her bra and feel her naked breast. Then one night, Anita met him at the door dressed in a skirt for the first time.

"Hi, Tommy greeted her.

"Hi."

"You look really nice."

Anita stepped away from him and pirouetted sharply. The skirt, a red pleated plaid, whirled out, exposing a flash of thigh and a blur of white panty. It happened so fast, Tommy didn't have time to look away.

They sat on the couch and tongue-kissed, his hand slipping underneath her sweater and undoing her bra. She pretended not to notice, helping instead by exhaling to make the release of the hooks easier. He stroked her nipples and wanted to kiss them, but when he tried to take off her sweater, she wouldn't let him. Still kissing, he slowly slid his fingers under her skirt and moved up her thigh until he touched the front of her wet panties. As he pulled the edge aside and ran his hand over her fuzz, he found the source of the wetness. He edged past her panties and pushed his finger inside. At that moment, Anita seemed to awaken. Her legs slammed together, and she shoved him roughly away. Before he could react, she was off the couch and into the bathroom with the door slammed shut.

Tommy groaned and sank back onto the couch.

When Anita came out a few minutes later, tears were running down her cheeks. She shrank back when he tried to hold her. "You'd better leave."

"I gotta use the bathroom."

Anita wiped her eyes with a Kleenex and looked away.

Once in the bathroom, Tommy smelled her faint odor. It met him with such a rush of warm familiarity that he had to sit on the toilet seat to regain control. He undid his pants and stroked himself until he came. Afterward, he felt the hot sense of shame that hit him every time he masturbated. He flushed the toilet, washed his hands, and went home.

*****

In bed, staring up at the ceiling, Tommy recalled how he and Anita had parted. She was still crying, and as she clung to him in the doorway, she'd said, "I got too scared. Next time. We'll do it next time."

CHAPTER TWENTY-THREE

Henry Fox thrived at Chicago Vocational. The school pecking order was detrmined by how well you handled your fists, not how well you studied. He joined CYO, took up boxing, and discovered that just being one of the kids who hung out at the Dorchester Gym kept the tests of manhood down to a minimum. Vocational also had the advantage of attracting mostly poor kids, so he and Andy fit right in.

It was Friday afternoon and Henry was heading home from school later than usual. He'd hung around chatting with one of the girls in his study class and missed the bus. The driver had pulled away just as he ran up, and Henry was convinced the guy saw him. The bus door swishing closed in his face put him in an ugly mood.

He was crossing Stoney Island Avenue when Tommy came strolling up. Hyde Park was within walking distance of the Castle, and the thought of Tommy not having to deal with buses blackened Henry's mood even more.

He had mixed feelings about Tommy. The whole neighborhood was talking about his diving. Word was he had a lock on some kind of City diving championship. Henry still considered Tommy a member of the gang, but the guy never seemed to have the time to hang out. It was beginning to feel as if Tommy thought he was too good for them.

"Tommy, my man. Whadda ya doin' home this early? Ya don't usually get here till after dark."

Tommy shifted his books to his left hand and exchanged palm slaps with Henry. "Coach cancelled practice and gave us the weekend off. He says we're as ready for the City meet as we'll ever be."

Henry lightly punched his shoulder. "You're a cinch ta win. We're all pullin' for ya."

Tommy shrugged. "You don't even know what my event is, but thanks anyway."

There was a strained pause, and Henry couldn't tell if Tommy was uncomfortable being seen with him or just nervous about the coming meet. Andy's dad had heard that Tommy's mother wanted to move to another building to get her son away from the riff-raff in the Castle. Henry was pretty sure he knew who the woman meant by riff-raff.

"There's gonna be a Pom-Pom game down at the Midway," Henry said. "Ya wanna go? The other guys are there already."

Tommy shifted from foot to foot, and for a moment, Henry thought he was going to cop out. Then Tommy nodded. "Coach would kill me if I got hurt the day before the meet. But I guess it would be OK if I go an' just watch."

Henry said, "Cool," and waited at the corner while Tommy went to his flat to let his folks know where he was going. When Tommy came back outside, they started off in the direction of the Midway.

A new game was about to begin when Henry and Tommy showed up. Tommy hunkered down at the top of the bowl-shaped grassy field and stretched back on his elbows to watch the action. Henry retied his sneakers and pulled his pants belt as tight as it would go. He pumped his shoulders up and down a few times to loosen up and grinned over at Tommy. "Watch me go kick some ass."

Henry loved Pom-Pom because it took guts to play. It wasn't the roughness he enjoyed, it was the chance to show that he was fearless. The action was just starting. A player Henry didn't know stood in the middle of the field while all the other players lined up on one side, waiting for the kid to give the signal to try to run past him. On the first trip across, the center player tackled one of the older boys. The rules were that the tackled guy stayed in the middle and became a tackler. On the next run, the two became four, then the four became eight, and so on. Henry bulled his way across time after time without anyone bringing him down. He stood, ready to cross again, when Ben and Andy shifted over.

The smell of freshly mowed grass mixed with perspiration as Henry put his hands on the front of his thighs and bent over, catching his breath. "Where's Mike?"

Andy waved toward the center of the field. "He got tackled on his first run. Now he's gunnin' for us."

The center guy gave the signal, and a brave but stupid kid was the first to go. He got creamed. Henry hung back, waiting for just the right moment. Waiting too long could mean being isolated and an easy target. The ideal was to be in the middle of the pack and slip by unnoticed.

Henry gave a nod, and the three of them started across together. At midfield, Mike came gunning for Henry. Henry let him commit, then hip-checked him at the last second and was out of the zone before Mike could recover. But Andy was too slow, and Mike nailed him. On the next run, Mike and Andy ignored Henry and went for Ben. Henry was so focused on avoiding them that he let a kid sneak up from behind and take him down.

More and more boys showed up to play, and it began to look as if the game would go on forever. Then Roger Shaw swaggered onto the field.

Henry huddled with the others. "You see who I see?"

He watched Andy's eyes go mean. "I still got a score to settle with Mister Shaw."

For most of the kids, Roger was too tough to mess with, but a few of the older boys weren't afraid. Henry wasn't afraid either. With the help of Andy and a couple of guys he knew from Vocational, he managed to pen Roger in long enough to grab him around the waist and bring him down to his knees. Roger immediately got back up and kept running. Andy grabbed at his legs, but he was too light to hold Roger back. Dragging Andy halfway across the field, he trotted over the end line and raised his arms in triumph.

Andy turned to the crowd and said, "His knee touched the ground. Look at the grass stains."

Shaw shoved him away. "Fuck you."

Someone yelled, "Come on, Shaw, you been tackled. You belong out in the middle."

"Who tackled me?" Roger said, pushing close to Andy. "This little piece of shit?"

If Roger had expected Andy to cower, he was disappointed. Andy just sneered and turned away. "You always cheat, Rog. That's the only way you can win."

Roger started for Andy, but Ben stepped in front of him. "Come on, let's keep the game goin'."

Roger looked first at Ben and then at Henry, who had come over to back his guys up. Shaking his head, Roger turned away. The rest of the kids walked to the center of the field.

Henry spoke quietly, "No one tackles Roger. Leave him for last."

As the word spread down the line, a few of the boys smiled grimly, and the game took a more vicious turn. The tacklers started taking kids down hard, hitting high and low at the same time. Noses

115

bled and elbows were scraped, and as each new kid came into the center, they were told to lay off Roger Shaw. Finally, only Roger was left. He stood defiantly facing almost fifty kids spread across the field in three lines. Henry moved to the back of the crowd and waited for Roger to break through. Everyone got quiet as Roger started to run. Then the entire field erupted in shouts of encouragement. "Get 'im! Cut 'im off! Don't let 'im get by!"

Roger moved first to his left, then dodged quickly to his right. He spun past the first line of kids and stopped dead, faking the second line into diving for him. He slipped between the two biggest kids, avoiding their tackles, and passed the second line. When he was sure everyone was committed, he spun left again, digging in so sharply that his body was almost parallel with the ground. Two of the tacklers were fooled completely. They grabbed at him and were rewarded with air. Then he straightened and ran all out for the other end of the field.

Only three boys from the third line were left—Henry, Andy, and Ben. This was just the way Henry wanted it. His upper lip curled in a sneer while he directed Ben left and Andy right. Roger backed up, then jerked to the left and went to the right. Ben wasn't fooled. He and Andy forced their prey back toward the middle. Again, Roger reversed his field. He ran back a few yards, stopped for a split second, then sprinted for the safe line full-out.

Henry launched his tackle with Roger heading straight for him. He hit Shaw below the knees, taking the bigger boy's legs out from under him. It was timed perfectly, and Roger crashed down. Andy and Ben both piled on to keep Roger from getting up and cheating again.

In a wave, the rest of the kids stormed in. Someone on the ground screamed, "Nigger pile, nigger pile," and in a frenzied rush, the ones nearest took up the cry. One after another, they piled on, crushing Roger and all of the kids who had piled on before them.

"Get off, get off," someone screamed, but no one moved.

"They can't breathe," someone else shouted, but the piling on continued.

Tommy ran down from the sidelines and started pulling bodies away from the tangled heap.

"Get the fuck off!" he yelled.

The first kids he pulled off started helping him, and the pile slowly unfolded. The boys who had been near the bottom rolled away, unable to stand as they gasped for air. Roger was the last one to get up. His face had deep red welts, and his nose was gushing blood. His white shirt was in shreds, and grass stains and dirt were ground into his pants at the knees. When he started to move, he suddenly grimaced in pain and held his side.

"Some fucker kicked me. I think I got a busted rib." He wiped at his nose and stared down at his blood-smeared hand. "Somebody punched me, too. I find the guy, I'm gonna kill him." Roger glowered at everyone within striking distance, but he wasn't sure who'd done it. Still in a rage, he turned away and limped up the embankment, signaling the end of the game.

The Castle group started for home. Henry brushed off his pants and smiled at Andy. "We got even with the fucker, didn't we?"

Andy nodded. He swung his leg in a whip kick, then lashed out with a hard right hook. "After you screamed 'nigger pile', too many guys jumped on. They pinned me down an' I couldn't hit him no more. The only thing that could make it better would be if we could tell him."

Henry leaned over and ruffled Andy's hair. "Best not to press your luck."

When Henry looked up, Tommy was glaring at him. "You caused that pile on purpose? What the hell's the matter with you? Someone could've been killed."

Henry recoiled as if Tommy had slapped him. "The pile was meant for Shaw, he was the only one who got hurt." He turned to Andy. "Tell him how we planned it so we could get even with Shaw."

Tommy stopped walking and stared at Andy. "You're almost sixteen, but you still follow Henry around like some kind of sniveling baby. It's time you stopped taking crap from everybody and started thinking for yourself."

Henry's face tightened and he started to move toward Tommy. Andy shoved in front of him, splaying his pigeon-toed feet outward and putting his hands up to stop Henry. Henry leaned past him and faced Tommy. "Andy don't take crap anymore, Tommy. But that ain't somethin' you'd know about, 'cause you ain't been around. We ain't good enough for ya anymore; we been dumped for your new friends." He looked around at the others and saw Ben nodding. "Just 'cause you're smart an' ya can dive and a few broads think you're cute, ya think it gives ya the right ta tell the rest of us how ta act. It's like you're some kinda prince or somethin'." Henry's voice had softened, but when Tommy tried to speak, he waved him quiet. "Here's the way we see it." He waved his arm at the others in an inclusive gesture. "We don't take any shit from anyone, an' we never back down. When someone like Shaw fucks with us, we stick together an' get even any way we can. If ya can't do that, then ya don't belong hangin' out with us."

No one said anything. Then Henry shrugged and started walking toward the Castle while Ben, Andy, and Mike fell in beside him.

Tommy followed, calling out to Henry's back. His voice cracked and he sounded as if he was ready to cry. "You think I got it made? Well, you're wrong. There's pressure comin' from all sides. My coach, the kids at school, my mom, even you, Henry, even you're sayin' as how I'm sure to win City. What if I don't? What if I screw up? You don't know what it's like to be worried all the time. I didn't mean all

118

that stuff I said to Andy, and I'm sorry I haven't had time to hang out lately. I don't blame you if you wanna kick me out of the gang. But I'm sorry. I want you all to know I'm sorry."

Before Henry could decide what to do, Andy turned and ran back to Tommy. Grinning his goofy grin, he grabbed Tommy in a bear hug. Henry walked over. "Yeah, I guess we're sorry, too. You was right about the pile up—someone could'a got hurt."

He put his arm around Tommy's neck and lightly rubbed his knuckles across his head. Then the five of them walked side-by-side back to the Castle.

CHAPTER TWENTY-FOUR

The spring day was blustery and overcast. Mike and Tommy were strolling along the staggered line of granite blocks that bordered the lake, deep in conversation. "The Rocks," as the kids called them, were stacked like giant steps, a pyramid effect that acted as a breakwater and kept Lake Michigan from swamping the Outer Drive.

The area held a fascination for Mike. In the summer, he'd swim off the 55th Street Promontory despite the signs that warned against it. And when it was too cold to swim, he would stand for hours and watch the waves crash in against the lower tier. He was still afraid to dive off the poles, but the severe winter weather had torn away the makeshift ladder and he was hopeful no one would ever take the trouble to repair it.

This was a great day for wave-watching. Breakers of icy water five and six feet high roared in, and every set had at least one wave that was so high, the two of them were forced to scramble up to the second tier to avoid getting soaked.

Mike liked talking to Tommy. He was the only one of the gang who would listen to him and not crack wise. "I hate my old man. He's on my ass all the time. My brother says I can go downstate to live with him when I get outta high school, an' I'm gonna go. Shit, I'd do anything to get away from here."

Tommy nodded and said nothing. Mike knew his friend's home life was pretty good, but one of the great things about Tommy was that he never bragged about having it better than anyone else.

Abruptly, Mike changed the subject to what he really wanted to talk about. "You ever get any pussy?"

Without breaking stride, Tommy shook his head. "Nah, not all the way. I got my hand there an' my finger partway inside once, but the girl made me stop."

Mike felt a stab of jealousy. A finger inside was a lot further than he'd ever gotten. He couldn't keep the skepticism out of his voice. "That's weird. Henry says if you get your hand on it, they get so hot they can't quit."

"Well, that wasn't the way it was with this one. How about you? You ever get any?"

If it had been anyone but Tommy, he would have lied. He dodged a puddle and confessed. "Nah. I got tit off of Mary Ryan once, but that's as far as I ever got."

Mike inhaled the mossy smell of the lake spray and thought about how good he felt. Tommy Davis, the All-City spring board diving champion, was his friend, and they were walking together, talking about girls. "I wonder if any of the guys besides Henry has gone all the way?"

A wave crashed a hundred feet ahead of them, leaving pockets of wet on the smooth stone breakwater. Mike was looking down, gingerly inching along the wet rocks, when Tommy slipped and started to fall. He made a grab for one of Tommy's flailing arms, but missed. At that instant, the lake sent in a killer wave. Much bigger than those before, it slammed up head high and knocked both of the boys off their feet.

Mike's fingers caught on a broken edge of one of the rocks, and he clung there desperately, trying to keep the sucking backwash of the wave from dragging him in. He turned his head to one side just in time to see Tommy lose his grip on the slick stone, slide by him, and disappear into the water.

Once the wave passed, Mike scrambled to his feet and moved to the edge of the breakwater. On some days, the water was crystal clear, but not this day. This day, the storm-tossed waters gave Mike no clue of what was happening beneath them. Frantically, he searched for some sign of Tommy, not accepting what his senses were telling him. The thought formed in his head that his friend was just playing a trick on him. He was underwater, holding his breath, and would come up in a minute, laughing.

Before the thought could take root, Tommy's body bobbed to the surface, face up. Like a piece of flotsam, it swayed in rhythm with the waves. Mike started to take off his loafers, having heard that you should remove your shoes before trying to rescue someone. He slid off his right shoe and put his stockinged foot down onto the wet rock. Already soaked from the wave, he barely felt the stab of icy cold that shot up his leg. He raised his left leg to remove the other shoe and then, perched like a crane, he caught a glimpse of the water churning below and his entire body went rigid with fear.

Mike slowly sat down on the rock surface and wrapped his arms around his knees, pulling them to his chest. Too paralyzed to move, his lips began to quiver and the terror gripped him so hard, he moaned. Staring at the floating body, he was convinced that he could see Tommy's heart beating. In that moment, he was certain that his failure to dive in killed his friend.

Finally, he stood and scrambled off the rocks. Hysteria hit as he ran through the tunnel that led under the highway bordering the lake.

He started screaming, "Help! Somebody help!" and as he emerged from the tunnel, a Park District policeman stopped him.

*****

They found Tommy right away. The waves that had dragged him in now pushed his body against the rocks, within easy reach.

The policeman called the Coast Guard, who arrived on the scene in a motor launch and directed the retrieval from the water. Mike watched from the edge of the rocks as they looped a huge rubber lasso around the body and hauled it in.

As they pulled Tommy up onto the ledge, Mike turned away. He wandered around the park for a long time, shivering in his wet clothes and too dazed to grasp what had happened. He had a feeling he should do something, but couldn't decide exactly what—maybe go and tell Tommy's mother. He nodded vigorously. That was it—go and tell Tommy's mother. He turned and headed back to the Castle.

When no one at Tommy's flat responded to his pounding, his confusion came back. What now? He was set to pound again when Ben's mother came down the stairs. She moved over to where Mike stood and pushed a strand of hair off his forehead. "There's been an accident, Mikey. The police came and took Tommy's mom away."

Tears filled Mike's eyes. He nodded and headed for Henry's apartment. When Henry opened the door, Mike swiped at his eyes and whispered, "Tommy, he's dead. He drowned."

CHAPTER TWENTY-FIVE

M ike did everything he could to get out of going to
Tommy's funeral. In the end, his father gave him no
choice. "The whole buildings goin'. I even saw that drunken Indian an'
his kid headed over to Cacher's Mortuary." With a disgusted slap to
the back of Mike's head, the decision was made.

By the time the McManns arrived, most of the people had gone
into the chapel and been seated. Mike wanted to slip in unnoticed, but
a few heads turned as he walked down the aisle, and the whispering
started. More and more heads turned until his mother finally found a
pew to her liking and the three of them sat down.

The casket was open, and Mike's mother forced him to walk past
the coffin. The thing that used to be Tommy had its eyes closed, but it
didn't look like Tommy was sleeping. Most of the face had a waxy
look, and only the cheeks and lips had color. They were pinkish, like a
black and white photograph that someone tinted.

Bile started to rise in Mike's throat, but he swallowed hard and
looked away. Back in the pew, he watched with envy as Henry, Ben,
and Andy filed by and stared down at Tommy's body without hesitation. All of the women, Mike's mother included, were gripping tissues
and dabbing at their eyes. In the front row, Tommy's mother and

Anita Gibson wept openly. Mike stared at Anita. She was beautiful, and Mike flushed with disgust at himself when he wondered if she was the one who had let Tommy finger her.

The chapel fell quiet as the minister rose to speak. Even the muffled sobbing of the women faded. The minister had a soft, calming voice. He told of God's love and the mystery of death and urged Tommy's mother and friends to treasure what little time they'd had with him. Then Tommy's coach got up and seemed to have trouble keeping the anger out of his voice. He spoke about Tommy's dedication to his sport, his incredible athletic talent, and he questioned why this perfect child had been taken.

The weeping became noticeable again, and with a cold glare at the minister, Tommy's coach left the altar. The McManns didn't go to the cemetery. It was too far to walk, and Henry Fox's grandfather was the only one who had a car. His mother was about to ask for a ride, but to Mike's relief, his father refused to let her. "You'd beg a ride from a bunch of Indians? The stink in the car would kill us." They walked home.

After the burial, the adults were invited to a gathering at the Davis apartment. Mike sprawled with the rest of the gang across the street on the steps of the Miller Building. He felt a total disconnect between the funeral of Tommy and his friend Tommy. Even viewing the body didn't end the feeling that this hadn't really happened. Mike's hands shook as he raised a cigarette to his lips and took a deep drag. "Tommy's the first dead person I've ever seen."

Henry reached over and took the cigarette out of Mike's hand. He took a deep drag and then returned it. "I saw a drunk once that I thought was passed out, but he was really croaked. I didn't know the guy, so who cared."

Without taking a drag, Mike dropped the half-smoked cigarette on the ground and looked over at Henry. "What's that supposed to mean?"

Henry got to his feet and stared across the street at the Castle. "Just that this is different 'cause Tommy was a friend an' he was cool."

"I don't see what some drunk's got to do with Tommy's bein' dead."

Mike felt Ben take his arm. "Let it go, Mikey. Henry's just talkin' to keep from thinkin'."

Henry nodded at Mike as if in a trance. "Yeah, Benny's right. Benny's always right."

"I wonder what it's like to be dead," Andy said. "I wonder if there's a heaven like the priests say."

Mike turned his head away. He wiped angrily at his eyes and turned back to Andy. "If there is, Tommy's there for sure."

Henry sat back down and offered Mike a cigarette. "What I can't figure is how a great swimmer like Tommy could drown. I seen him swim out to the pumping station an' back. I don't know how many miles out it is, but it's far."

Mike felt the sick feeling starting up again. He looked over at Ben and John, who were bobbing their heads in agreement. "Well, he fuckin' drowned, didn't he? Maybe he wasn't as great at swimming as you guys think. I mean, just because he could dive, that didn't make him a great swimmer."

Andy shook his head. "No, you're wrong, Mikey. He was a great swimmer, all right. I never told you guys, but one time, I got cramps about a mile out, an' Tommy pulled me all the way in. He never told no one about it—not you guys, not no one. He hauled me over a mile, and he never said nothin' 'cause that's the way he was." Tears began to dribble down his face, and he started to sob.

Mike looked away.

"Well, he still drowned, great swimmer or not."

He stood and lagged a nickel. It rolled off the curb and into the gutter. "That girl Anita, she told Tommy's mom she couldn't figure out why God took Tommy instead of me." He retrieved the nickel and lagged it again. This time, it hit close to the line. He thought about Anita and spoke under his breath, not really aware that anyone could hear. "Sometimes I wonder the same thing."

Ben got up and lagged, falling short of Mike's nickel. "Anita's a fuckin' bitch. Don't pay no attention to her, Mikey."

Mike stood and stared at the two nickels. "The cops said they was gonna get really tough about guys walkin' down on The Rocks."

Henry picked up the money and stuffed the coins in Mike's pocket. "Yeah, I seen 'em paintin' "No Swimmin'" signs all over the place where Tommy got killed." He smirked at Mike. "That'll keep all the kids away, for sure."

Mike turned away from them, head down, and walked back across the street.

For the next couple of days, Mike hung around the house after school. He listened to the radio and stared at the ceiling, trying to make sense out of the accident. He replayed what had happened over and over, seeing his hand miss Tommy's arm and watching Tommy's body slide over the edge of the breakwater. At night, he dreamed that Tommy was angry at him for not jumping in and saving him. A sad voice came through the fog of sleep. "I saved Andy. Dragged him a mile, and I never said a word about it."

When Mike did come out to the stoop, he was pale and subdued. He said nothing to the guys unless he was asked a direct question. Even then, his answers were one-word mumbles. When he tried to explain that he just didn't feel like talking, the others seemed to take it personally, and Ben started pressing so hard, Mike couldn't take it. He quit going out to the stoop at all.

At school, he moved through the halls with his head down. Every free period was spent on his knees in the chapel. The boys' dean, Father Healy, tried to get him to open up, but Mike just shrugged and kept silent. Like the memory of pain, the truth of his paralyzing fear also passed. It became harder and harder for him to understand why he hadn't saved his friend. The image of Tommy's beating heart kept coming back to him, and as the days passed, that vision became more and more real. It finally became so fixed in his mind, he could think of nothing else.

*****

The start of summer vacation was a week away. Mike had gotten home early and was stretched out on his bed with the radio on. He ignored the banging on his door until he remembered that his mother wasn't home. When the knocking didn't stop, he slowly trudged to the door and opened it halfway.

Henry Fox smiled in at him. "Where's your ol' lady?"

Ben and Andy were standing back a few feet, one on each side of Henry.

Where was his mother? He tried to remember and felt relieved when he was able to come up with an answer. "Church."

"On Wednesday?"

"She's prayin' for me."

He realized Henry was staring, and it bothered him. He started to close the door, but Henry put his hand up to stop him.

"So, whadda ya doin'?"

Mike shrugged. "Listenin' to the radio."

"What's on?"

Mike shrugged again. "Jack Armstrong."

Andy looked as if he were about to jam his finger up his nose. Instead, he shoved his hand into his pocket. "Can't be. Jack Armstrong ain't on till four. Captain Midnight is on now."

Mike shrugged.

Henry said, "We're up at Ben's an' we need a fourth for poker. Ya wanna play?"

Mike couldn't quite understand what Henry said. "Huh?"

"Poker, ya wanna play poker?"

Mike shook his head and closed the door.

He heard Ben through the closed door. "He's goin' nuts. He didn't even know what program he was listening to. An' did you see how skinny he's gotten? The guy's definitely goin' nuts."

Mike trudged back to his bed.

*****

Sleeping all day wasn't permitted in the McMann household, so when Mike's mother forced him to go out, he usually went to the Post Restaurant for a Coke.

He was sitting at the counter when Detective Delaney walked in. Delaney smiled and clapped a hand on the boy's shoulder. "How they hangin', Mikey?"

Mike slowly turned his head. The last time he'd seen the policeman was before Delaney's promotion to detective. It took a moment for recognition to kick in. As a patrolman, Delaney in Car 109 had been a source of fear to the kids in the neighborhood, but like the stern priests at Saint Thomas, there had always been something reassuring about his presence.

Tears started at the corners of Mike's eyes. It was as if something broke inside of him. In an instant, the answer to everything presented itself. *A cop*, he thought. *I'll tell a cop an' they'll put me away, where I belong*. He whirled around on his stool and blurted out his personal truth. "I killed him."

Delaney seemed to freeze. His smile faded and he slid onto the stool next to Mike. "Whadda you mean, you killed him?"

Mike felt the tears running freely down his face as the story came pouring out. "Tommy was alive in the water, an' I was too scared to dive in to save him."

Delaney's shoulders slumped and his head went to one side. "He was dead, Mike. You couldn't a done nothin'.'"

Mike started to blubber. Having gone this far, he didn't want to stop. The guilt that had been poisoning him came to the surface in a purging flood. "No, he was alive. I seen his heart beatin'. I fuckin' let him drown because I was scared." He pounded his fist against his head, softly at first and then harder and harder. "I was so fuckin' scared, I let him drown."

The policeman reached over and took hold of Mike's wrist, forcing his arm down on the counter. His voice sounded hollow to Mike, as if Delaney were speaking through a megaphone. "Look, you goofy jerk. First off, your buddy didn't drown. His head was crushed by the rocks. He was dead a few seconds after he hit the water, and there was nothin' anyone could've done to save him. Secondly, if you had jumped in, we would've had a double funeral, 'cause you'd be as dead as Tommy."

Delaney's face was blurred through the wash of Mike's tears. He shook his head, wanting to believe. "I seen his heart beat. Maybe his head got smashed later."

The far-away, hollow voice flattened, and Delaney came into sharp focus. "Listen to me, McMann, you can't see someone's heart beat. There was no water in Tommy's lungs. He didn't drown. He was killed by hittin' his head on the rocks."

When Delaney stood, Mike felt his hand on his shoulder. The detective leaned in close to Mike's ear and spoke quietly. "It was not your fault." Then he turned and walked out of the restaurant.

Mike stared at himself in the mirror behind the counter and slowly finished his coffee. Suddenly, he was very hungry.

CHAPTER TWENTY-SIX

During the summer of 1950, Ben pitched a tent at the Indiana Dunes State Park and spent the better part of three weeks alone. He climbed the sand dunes, swam in the tepid waters of Lake Michigan, and slept out under the stars almost every night. The campsite was free, and by doing odd jobs for the other campers—mostly families who only came in on the weekends—he was able to pick up enough money to pay for food. John came down for a few days, and Ben thought he would be glad for the company. Instead, John's presence turned out to be a disruption. After two days, Ben couldn't wait for him to leave so he could get back to his comfortable routine and be alone again.

When he got home near the end of vacation, there were letters from both Henry and Andy waiting. They'd gone to a Salvation Army resident camp for kids—a benefit of having alcoholic fathers. They weren't chatty letters, just short notes that said "Hi" and "You should be here" and "See you soon." Mike had spent his summer downstate on his uncle's farm, but he hadn't bothered to write.

The day after school started, Ben went out to the stoop. The rest of the group was there, lagging nickels in the hot September sun, acting as if they had never been separated.

Reaching for Henry's cigarette, Mike said, "Give me a drag."

Henry pulled it back out of Mike's reach and took a deep drag before handing it over. "Don't nigger-lip it."

Mike shrugged and took a drag.

Ben frowned at Henry, tossed the winning coin, and picked up the nickels. He'd been away from the group for so long, he'd forgotten how crude they could be. Instead of going back to the line and lagging again, he straightened up and abruptly walked away. He was halfway to the corner when Mike looked up and yelled, "Hey, where's Benny going?"

Ben decided not to look back. He called over his shoulder, "You guys talk like a bunch of assholes."

He heard footsteps behind him and turned to see Henry and the others coming after him.

John was the first one to catch up. "What's with you?"

Ben stopped at the corner and waited for the rest of them. "Nigger, nigger, nigger. That's all you guys say. Nigger-lip, nigger pile, nigger rich, nigger, nigger, nigger. I'm getting sick of it. People with brains don't talk like that. Besides, I know lots of *negroes* in school, and they're cool."

Mike smiled. "Yeah, like who?"

Caught off guard, Ben stammered out the first name he could think of. "There's a guy on the football team named Robinson. He's cool."

John laughed. "You mean Pork Chops Robinson?"

Ben shrugged. "I guess, but I never heard anyone call him that."

John leaned against a car parked at the curb. "He's in my history class. The first week, he showed a rubber to this jig, I mean this Negro broad, an' she pretended she didn't know what it was. He tells her, 'It's a skillet.' An' she says, 'A skillet?' An' he says, 'Yeah, it's where I fries my pork chops.' Now all the guys call him Pork Chops. He's one of my good customers. Buys test papers and sells me all kinds of shit I can fence. Ben's right, Pork Chops is cool." Everyone laughed—except Ben.

Henry pinched the coal from his cigarette and put the butt behind his ear. "OK Benny, from now on, no more nigger talk. From now on, we call 'em coons."

John leaned over, his eyes watering with laughter. "No!" he blurted. "They're buffaloes."

Andy chimed in with "tar babies," and he and John laughed harder.

Ben stood silent, and slowly, the laughter died out. "They're people just like us. You all just show your ignorance by talking like you do."

"Who's teachin' you this shit?" Mike asked. "Your commie mommy?"

"You mean my mother?" Ben said, slowly turning toward Mike.

"Yeah, like I said, your kike old lady."

Ben knew that the summer had changed him. Roughing it, living hand to mouth, relying on no one, he'd decided he could do anything he wanted. The first day back in the city, he had gone to the army-navy store and stolen a pair of Levi's and some white T-shirts. If he could have figured out how, he would have stolen shoes, too. Instead, he pilfered five dollars from the wallet of his mother's latest boyfriend and bought a pair of the square-toed loafers that all the kids were wearing. Before the summer, he'd been willing to take a lot of guff to avoid confrontation. Now he felt differently. Seconds after Mike called his mother a kike, the difference in him was clear to everyone in the group.

The solid right hook caught Mike on the temple. His head snapped sideways, and before he could get the rest of his body out of the way, Ben swung again. This time, the punch was an uppercut to the stomach. It angled up toward the solar plexus and seemed to bend Mike almost in half. He went down with a whoosh and curled into a ball. Rasping hoarsely, he fought to suck in air. Ben danced back and was set to swing again when Henry pushed in front of him. Without saying anything, he helped Mike to a sitting position on the curb and made him put his head between his knees. Ben took Henry's interference as disapproval but he didn't feel ashamed. If anything, he was pleased with himself.

Mike's gasping for air slowed, but he remained bent over. He moaned, "That Jew fucker sucker punched me."

Henry retrieved the cigarette butt from behind his ear, lit it, and took a deep drag. He passed the stub over to Mike. "Maybe ya better refer ta his mother as just plain mother."

"Yeah, drop the kike talk," John said.

There wasn't enough of the cigarette left to get a strong pull, so Mike held it between his thumb and forefinger and sort of sucked at it. "All because Henry said nigger."

Ben saw John take a quick look at Henry. "My mother always says coloreds. Is that OK, Benny?"

His anger felt so good, Ben didn't want to let go of it. "Would you call Illinois Jaquette a colored?"

"Jaquette's different," Henry said. "He's a musician."

Then John distracted everyone. "I saw him play last week."

Henry said, "Bullshit! Where'd you see Jaquette?"

Mike stood up and they all started moving back toward the stoop. John pulled in front of the group, walking backward to face them.

"At the Beehive. I was—"

"Henry's right, you're fulla shit," Ben interrupted, rubbing at the abrasions on his knuckles. "They'd never let you in, even with a phony ID. You don't look anywhere near twenty-one."

"I didn't say I went in. I was on the loading dock in back. When it's warm, they leave the back door open, an' you can see the stage an' hear the music through the screen door. Next week, we can all go."

When they reached the Castle, Mike went inside without a word. A minute later, John and Andy called it a day and Henry turned to follow Andy, but Ben took his arm and held him back.

"I gotta talk to you, Henry." He began gnawing at his thumbnail.

Henry waited without saying anything.

Ben motioned to the stoop and they sat back down. Even though there was no one around, Ben leaned in close. "My, uh, aunt married a…uh…a Negro."

Henry nodded. "Is that why ya hit Mikey?"

Ben shrugged. "Nah, I hit him 'cause of what he called my mother. She's not much, but I'm the only one who's got a right to say it."

He offered Henry a cigarette. They lit up and Ben puffed quietly for a few moments. "I'm scared of the way the other guys might act if they find out about my aunt. Andy's not so bad, but Mike and John both act like they hate anyone who isn't white."

"So what if they find out? You didn't marry no jig; it was your aunt."

Ben sat forward and took a drag. He'd been practicing letting smoke drift out of his mouth and sniffing it back in through his nose before it escaped. The kids called it French inhaling, and it was a skill in which he took great pride. "Mike's mother would spread it all over the neighborhood, an' it would be one more thing they got against my mother. They already call her a whore."

Henry stood. "I don't hate colored guys. It *is* nuts, though. Why would your aunt do somethin' like that? I mean, she's white, right?"

A twinge of disappointment went through Ben when Henry didn't seem to notice how well he handled inhaling. He nodded. "Of course she's white. She's my mother's sister. The thing is, I like the guy. He's really cool to me, an' he's a war hero. He was at the Battle of the Bulge, and when they were losin', they gave the cooks an' everyone guns to go fight. He got a bronze star 'cause he helped a bunch of wounded guys. When I'm around him, I kind of forget he's, you know, colored."

"Yeah, some colored guys might be cool, but that don't mean white girls should marry 'em. It's against nature an' all. I mean, if they're married, she's gotta screw 'im an' everything."

Suddenly, Ben was sorry he'd told Henry. "Just forget it, OK?" He turned to go.

Henry took his arm. "Well, I ain't gonna tell any of the guys about your aunt or about you liking the jig she married. If you're smart, you won't, either."

Ben yanked his arm away. He nodded slowly and went inside.

CHAPTER TWENTY-SEVEN

J ohn Solberg loved jazz, especially jazz that featured the tenor
sax. In one of her rare good moods, his mother had told him that
before the war, his father had played the saxophone in a jazz combo.
After that, the sax was his favorite instrument.

One hot night in early July, as John was strolling down the 55th
Street alley between Harper Avenue and Lake Park, the wailing sound
of Sonny Rollins's saxophone came blaring out and hit him like a fist.

At first, he thought someone was playing a radio loudly, but when
he crept in close to the loading dock of The Beehive Show Lounge, he
realized he was hearing a live musician. After that, John spent every
free summer night listening to the sounds that came pouring out The
Hive's back door.

The boy felt that the music was his alone, and the spot behind
The nightclub his secret. He never considered sharing it with the gang,
thinking that having them there would ruin it for him. Then the argument with Ben over what to call colored guys changed that.

*****

On the second Friday in September, John reluctantly led the
group to the loading dock. At first, the guys wouldn't shut up, and
within minutes, the manager came out and warned them not to make

trouble. With his head bowed, John responded with a polite, "Yes, sir. We're just here for the music." The manager seemed satisfied and, with a final threat to kick them out if they made noise, let them stay.

For the rest of the summer, John and the Castle group crowded onto the loading dock of The Beehive Lounge every Friday and Saturday night, listening to jazz.

They heard Lester "Prez" Young, and arguments over who was the greatest saxophone player raged for days afterward. When Stan Kenton was booked, John had to drag Ben away from the screen door because he couldn't get enough of June Christy. He told John that the song "Something Cool" made him think of his mother.

*****

October came and the group was all set to call it quits when John read on the marquee that the saxophone player he considered the greatest in the world was going to play the Hive. Charlie "Yardbird" Parker was coming to Chicago.

John dressed up for the event. Despite having to stay in the alley because of their age, he decided it was important to show the greatest saxophone player in the world the respect he was due by not wearing jeans. Instead, he wore pegged slacks, narrow at the bottom and full at the knee, with a four-inch drop waist and a cuff that broke perfectly over his square-toed, spit-shined black shoes. His shirt was a yellow dress shirt open at the neck, with the sleeves rolled up two or three turns.

None of the others had dress clothes, so John had to put up with their razzing. He didn't care. The thought of hearing Parker play had him so excited that nothing could dampen his mood. John arrived first and found a couple of wooden boxes for him and Henry to sit on. Andy and Ben came a few minutes later and made do with garbage can lids. Mike sat alone on the edge of the dock.

When the music started, John pulled his crate up to the screen door and squinted into the smoky depths of the club to watch the musicians perform. The crowd seemed to be more respectful than they had been on other nights. Occasionally, someone would grunt encouragement or clap loudly after a solo, but mostly they sat quietly, not even sipping their drinks, while Parker was playing.

It was a hot Indian summer night, but as the jazz pumped out into the alley, John forgot any discomfort and focused on the split-reed wailing of his hero, "The Bird."

The set ended, and Parker leaned into the microphone to announce a break. Mike jumped down off the dock and turned to leave. When John didn't move, he stopped. "Whadda you waitin' for? It's over."

John stood and straightened the crease in his pants. "They're just takin' a break. Be back in fifteen minutes."

As Mike started to argue, John heard voices coming from inside the club. The screen door opened and three men, all talking at once, filed out onto the dock. The lead man was Charlie Parker. His round, cherubic face was slick with perspiration, and the front of his suit jacket was rumpled from collar to waist. Still talking, he leaned against the wall and paid no attention to the boys. Parker nodded at the last man out. "Got a smoke?"

The man out reached into his shirt pocket and produced a pack of cigarettes. He passed it to Parker, who took one and passed the pack on to the other man. Parker lit a match and held it out for the other two. After they lit up, he blew out the match. Laughing, he lit another one for himself.

"Three on a match, I don't need no bad shit like that."

John stared at the three men leaning against the building, smoking. Finally, Parker seemed to become aware of the group.

"Why you kids hangin'around here?"

The boys turned to John, designating him their spokesman. He shifted slightly and, swallowing his fear, looked up at Parker.

"We're too young to get in. So, uh, we sit out here an' listen to your music."

Parker took a deep drag on his cigarette. He stared down at the burning tip for a moment, seemingly lost in thought. Then he dropped his smoke on the ground, put it out with his shoe, and smiled. "You know what? That's cool, that's really cool."

He glanced at his watch, and the other two men put out their cigarettes. Then all three turned and went back into the club.

Ben said, "That was Charlie Parker."

"Charlie Parker," John shook his head from side to side. His heart was pounding so hard he could hear the beating in his ears. He kept staring at the screen door, wondering if Parker had ever heard of his dad. Then he decided that he probably had, because all great musicians knew each other. "Charlie Parker talked to me, told me I was cool."

"Nah," Mike said. "He meant us all, he meant we was all cool."

"Yeah," Henry said. "Mikey's right, he meant we was all cool."

John nodded agreement at Henry, then smiled. Deep down, he knew better.

CHAPTER TWENTY-EIGHT

The week before Halloween, Indian summer gave way to iron gray skies and icy winds. The change was so sudden, it caught the group by surprise, leaving them shivering in their summer jackets. They huddled in the doorway of the Castle, trying to come up with a plan for Halloween. John was convinced that they were too old to wear costumes and go door to door trick-or-treating.

Like Ben, Henry, and Mike, John was fifteen, and Andy was a year older. He talked to Henry, knowing that whatever Henry decided would fly with the rest of them. "We'll get laughed at. Remember last year, a bunch of the richies wouldn't give us shit."

Mike shoved his hands in his armpits. "If they do that, we can really do some damage. I got a couple of cherry bombs left over from the Fourth."

John ignored Mike and spoke directly to Henry. "It's time we quit actin' like babies an' use our brains to make some bread. Let's tell the shops that we'll spend the evening watching their places so other kids won't do any damage."

The look of approval that beamed out from Henry made John feel great. He offered to be the gang's spokesman, explaining that he was the only one who had the finesse to convince the local merchants to sign up with the group.

His bragging about the scheme made what happened all the harder for John to take. Mr. Olsen, the butcher, simply turned his back and walked away, while Angelo the shoemaker sneered and told him to get lost.

The Greek grocer's attitude was more pronounced. He stomped out from behind the counter, shaking his fist. "Son-of-a-bitch, I kick you ass. Stavros don't pay no protection to mobsters, you think he gonna pay punk kids?" With that, he quickly aimed a kick at John's retreating backside that just missed.

Henry stood in the doorway and didn't move. Maybe it was the look John saw in Henry's black eyes that convinced Stavros to avoid trying a second kick. Still, Stavros didn't change his mind about paying.

The only one who might have agreed to pay was Herb at the newsstand. The problem was, all the kids in the neighborhood liked Herb, so no one would have bothered him.

It was the first scheme of John's that flopped, and it hit him hard.

*****

The next day, John and Andy were sitting on the Miller Building's steps waiting for the others. Andy said, "We all figured it was a great idea, an' it could still work. We'll tape Mike's cherry bombs to the Greek's windows, and when the rest of 'em see the damage, they'll pay up."

John was one of the few people who usually stuck up for Andy. There was something about the guy that made him feel protective. Today was different. He couldn't get past the black mood caused by the failure of his plan. The mistake was so hard on his ego that he lashed out at the nearest target. "How come you always gotta be a fuckin' moron? Are you too stupid to figure out that any damage to the Greek would get blamed on us? It's just the opposite of what you said.

143

Henry and me gotta stand guard most of the night to make sure nothin' happens. An' they ain't gonna pay us one red cent."

John immediately felt guilty, but Andy didn't seem too upset by the outburst. He stood and shoved his hands in his pockets. "I'll do it, Johnny, I'll watch for ya. That way, Henry won't be mad."

The innate goodness of Andy made John feel worse. "Just get the fuck away from me. Go home."

He was staring down at the sidewalk, so he was unaware of the change in Andy until he spoke. "How come everyone thinks it's OK to pick on me? I'm gettin' fuckin' sick of it."

John didn't answer. He wasn't sure whether Andy meant it to be a statement or a serious question.

Andy moved down to the bottom step so they would be at eye level. He snapped out his arm and pushed against John's shoulder. "So, whadda you think? Why is that?"

"Why is what?"

"What I said. Why does everyone figure it's OK to give me a load of shit?"

John felt trapped, embarrassed by the truth of what Andy was saying. "Some of the guys pick on Mike more than you."

"That's bullshit, an' besides, I don't mean just the guys around here. I mean everywhere. At school, I'm in a fight every other day. If it wasn't for Henry, it'd be every day. What is it I do that makes all you guys wanna push me around?"

The tone caught John's attention. At first, he smiled, then the smile slowly faded. He looked directly into Andy's eyes. "It's the way you walk."

"The way I walk!" Andy screeched incredulously. "That's it? People don't like the way I walk? What the fuck is wrong with the way I walk?"

John leaned back on his elbows and warmed to the subject. "Everythin's in the way a guy walks. You take Tommy—may he rest in peace—he used to move fast. His shoulders were back and he kinda bounced. Full of energy. Any fool could tell Tommy was really somethin'."

Andy sat down again and fought back a tear. The mention of Tommy's name always seemed to start him crying.

"Now, Henry, he walks slower. His hands are always out and curled into fists, an' he sort of sways like he's really bad or somethin'. His head pushes forward like he's darin' you to take a swing.

Mike, he tries to move like Henry, but he knows he ain't as tough so it comes out in a kind of a hesitatin' stroll. The thing is, Mike's big. So even though he ain't got a great walk, guys who don't know him give him space.

Me, I try to step lightly. You know, so's people won't notice me. I like bein' in the background. Half the time, when I pull some shit, no one remembers what I look like."

"What about Ben?" Andy asked, rubbing at his eyes.

John cocked his head to one side. "Benny's walk is really weird. He don't walk like a kid at all. He don't slink, and he keeps his shoulders back. Now that I think of it, Ben mostly walks like a grown-up. And, he always has his head down like he's thinkin' about really important stuff."

Andy mulled it over, calmer and a bit intrigued. "So how do I walk?"

"I don't wanna hurt your feelin's, Andy, but you kind of shuffle like a whipped dog. We all know you don't take shit anymore, but your walk says, 'Hey, I'm already beat so you might as well go ahead an' take your shot.'"

Andy looked stunned. He was quiet for a long time, then finally said, "Show me how I oughta walk."

John nodded and jumped to his feet, pulling Andy up alongside him. "OK, throw your shoulders back." They both stood straight, and when John was satisfied, he started walking. "Keep 'em back, keep 'em back. Now swagger a little. Not too much. Just enough to say, 'I ain't lookin' for trouble, but I'm a bad motherfucker so don't mess with me.'"

Andy tried to swagger.

"No, no, swagger don't mean shimmy. You're walkin' like a girl." He stopped Andy. "Watch me." John moved up the sidewalk and back again with a purposeful stride. His arms were slightly forward and he seemed to be lifting his legs a little higher than normal.

Andy had to admit it, John did look really mean. He tried to copy John's walk.

"Better," John said. "Takes a little practice, but you'll get it."

Henry, Mike, and Ben rounded the corner and came up behind them.

"Get what?" Henry asked.

John started to answer, but Andy cut him off. "Nothin', nothin' at all. John was just showin' me some stuff."

The five of them sat down on the steps. John avoided Henry's eyes, thinking that his edginess was because of the Halloween screw-up.

Henry said, "I can't stick around. My old man wants ta get in early. Grandfather's comin' over."

Mike nodded. "It's cool, I can't stay out anyway."

Andy looked over at John. "If we're not doin' nothin', I'm gonna split. Sissy's cookin' dinner an' I ain't had a cooked meal in a week." He got up and started walking across the street. After a few steps, he threw his shoulders back, slowed his pace, and tried to swagger.

"What the fuck's he doing?" Henry asked.

John grinned. "He's practicin'."

"Practicin' what? How ta walk with a broom up his ass?"

Ben lit a cigarette and they watched in silence as Andy reached the door of the Castle and slid inside.

John cleared his throat. Almost under his breath, he said, "Scotty MacDonald's quittin' Edelstein's drugstore."

Ben shifted on the stoop to look at him. "So what?"

John tightened up. He sat forward. "So I might try ta get his job."

Henry laughed. It was a humorless bark. "You givin' up on bein' a thief an' gonna be a soda jerk instead?"

Mike nudged Henry. "You're half right, the jerk part."

John shrugged. "Henry's got a right to be pissed at me 'cause I screwed up with the Halloween idea. But you got a right to shut your face." He pulled his knees up to his chest, put his arms around them, and started rocking back and forth. No one spoke, and John stared at Mike until Mike looked away.

Mike said, "I gotta go."

"Me too," Henry sighed and looked over at John. "An' I ain't pissed."

He stood up, slapped John on the back with a "Catch ya later," and followed Mike into the Castle.

Once he and Ben were alone, John moved closer. Still holding his knees to his chest, he shifted his weight from one buttock to the other nervously.

"Spill it," Ben said. "Just spit it out."

"I don't want you to get mad at me," John said, letting go of his legs.

"I can't tell if I'm gonna be mad or not, 'cause I don't know what you're gonna say."

John spoke in a rush. "I already got the job. I tol' Edelstein I was a Heb. I mean, I didn't tell him that; he just figured I was, an' I didn't tell him different. I kind of mumbled my last name an' the 'Sol' part of 'Solberg' got lost. He heard 'Berg' an' figured I was a Jew."

Ben raised his hand to stop the flow of words. "What the fuck are you talkin' about?"

"The job at Edelstein's. Scotty's old job. I got it 'cause old man Edelstein thinks I'm a Jew. Are you pissed off?"

Ben laughed. "Why would I be pissed off? It's cool with me. Just don't let Edelstein see you up close when you're takin' a leak."

John looked relieved. "I'm glad you ain't mad. Tell me what you Jewish guys do so I won't screw up."

This time, Ben didn't laugh. "I'm probably only half Jewish, an' my old lady doesn't believe in that stuff, so I don't know much about it. If the subject comes up, just put on a sad face an' tell him your folks aren't observant. Say that they don't keep Kosher and that they wouldn't let you go to Hebrew school. That way, he'll feel sorry for you, and your ignorance won't show."

John looked thoughtful. "Write that shit down for me, OK?"

CHAPTER TWENTY-NINE

T he pharmacy was on the corner of 57th Street and Blackstone. Directly above the entrance a faded yellow and blue sign read "Edelstein's Drugs"

John had been Edelstein's soda jerk for a week. White apron tied around his waist and striped army-style paper hat on his head, he surveyed his domain. The stainless steel double sinks, the stork-necked sodawater dispensers, and the marble counter were all spotless. The freezer lids were clamped tight over the four flavors of ice cream, and John had wiped up any telltale spills that would have revealed which one held the chocolate, strawberry, vanilla, or mint. At one end of the counter, the gleaming red enamel Coke machine competed for attention with the lime-colored Green River machine. Syrup holders lined John's side of the counter, and three malted milk shake blenders stood ready to whir into action. Behind him, built against the mirrored wall, shelves held flat sundae dishes, inverted cone-shaped soda glasses, and soft drink glasses bearing the name Coca-Cola in flowing script. There were enough glasses for all of Hyde Park, and one of John's tasks was to rotate them so the glasses in back wouldn't get dusty.

A young couple walked in, the boy wearing jeans with turned-up cuffs and a white dress shirt and the girl in a tight-fitting sweater and flared skirt. John smiled at them. He had become superstitious about the first customer of the day. If they tipped, it would be a good night, and if not, it wouldn't. They decided on chocolate sundaes with mint ice cream. John scooped out the green stuff, squirted thick chocolate syrup over the top, added cherries, and filled in the spaces with whipped cream. Two glasses of water and a couple of packaged cookies went with the sundaes. The boy, a few years older than John, paid with a dollar bill. After John rang up the sale and gave him his sixty cents change, the boy casually dropped a dime back on the counter. John smiled again, broader this time. He picked up the dime and flipped it high in the air. Then, spinning around, he caught it behind his back. The girl laughed her appreciation, and the two went over to a table.

John didn't steal the forty cents they paid for the sundaes. He only stole when he was given the exact amount. His system was to leave the cash drawer open a slight crack and drop even money in without ringing it up. He kept a running total in his head. And at the end of each shift, when he cashed out his register, he would pocket the two or three dollars he'd filched that night.

He watched the couple as they lapped up the sundaes. The girl was cute, with a Liz Taylor-style pixie haircut and deep dimples when she grinned. He stared for a moment at the cone-shaped breasts pushing out of the pink wool sweater and wondered if the two of them were doing it.

Edelstein came out from behind the pharmacist's window. John chuckled to himself, watching Edelstein walk. It was a kind of splayfooted sway, with each foot going sideways while the pharmacist headed forward. He was a tall man, wider in the middle than the shoulders. Over his shirt and tie, he wore a white doctor's jacket, and his suspenders showed darkly through the thin material. Little tufts of hair stuck out on either side of his head, emphasizing his lack of hair on top.

Heavy-framed glasses flattened his bushy eyebrows and gave him a scholarly look.

John pretended he didn't see Edelstein heading over. He backed up against the cash register drawer, using his body to close it, and busied himself shining the chrome on the soda dispenser.

Edelstein said nothing. Instead, he pulled down a Coke glass, dropped in two doses of Bromo-Seltzer from the counter dispenser, and filled his glass with fizz water. He drank without waiting for the crystals to disintegrate. A belch and sigh later, he put down the empty glass and turned to John.

"When I expanded the shop and wanted to put in the soda fountain, my father, may he rest in peace, said it would never pay. I decided to go ahead anyway. He was a good man, but risks weren't something he liked to take. Now, I see the kids come in here every day, the cash register rings, and it makes me feel good to know I was right and the old man was wrong."

Until Edelstein spoke, John had been afraid that the old man had noticed him closing the cash drawer. Now he relaxed. He picked up the Bromo-coated glass and started washing it.

Edelstein patted him on the back. "You should only know how good it is to have a Jewish boy working here." He smiled at John and nodded. "Since you started, the soda fountain is making fifteen to twenty dollars more a week. I think that goyisher gonif Scotty was stealing me blind."

John forced himself to smile, and Edelstein waddled out of the soda fountain area and back to the pharmacy counter.

*****

After school the next day, John sat on the bottom step of the stoop in front of the Castle talking to Ben. They leaned back on their elbows, side by side, not looking at each other. "Yesterday, old man

151

Edelstein tells me he's happy he's got a Jewish kid workin' the fountain 'cause now it's pullin' in twenty more bucks a week." He shook his head in disgust.

Ben said, "So?"

John straightened up and glared at him. "So it pisses me off. Scotty must have been skimmin' way more than me. If the dumbshit had told me, I could've done the same. But he never said nothin', an' now it's too late. If I try to up the take now, Edelstein'll get wise."

Ben nudged John with his elbow. "I feel really sorry for you, Johnny. Finding out that someone else stole more than you must be damn near killin' you."

Laughing at himself, John leaned back again. "Well, I've got a rep to uphold. I've gotta figure out a way to steal at least as much as Scotty."

John's last period at school ended at two-thirty in the afternoon, so he was able to get to the store by three. Edelstein always seemed apprehensive about the arrangement. Each day, he stood there, hands clasped behind his back, looking out the plate glass window as his new soda jerk dodged the traffic crossing 57th Street. When the boy came through the door, Edelstein would flash a smile of relief and hand over the apron as if passing the baton.

There was usually a short burst of activity as the grammar school kids walked by on their way home. John would sell a few Cokes, a soda or two, and then came the dead period.

It started around four o'clock and lasted about an hour. Some-times, customers would come in during the lull because the place would be deserted. They would slink to the rear of the store and talk to Edelstein in low tones, usually asking for items that embarrassed them—men buying Kotex for their wives, women with hemorrhoids. They woud speak in furtive whispers. "Since the baby, it's so bad I can hardly sit down." Or, "He's got such gas. Isn't there something you can give him? Believe you me, I'm ready to move out." John would lean in close to the pharmacy window and listen to the secret complaints. It broke the monotony.

This afternoon, it was a teenager John didn't know, a greasy-looking kid with a duck's ass haircut and black motorcycle jacket. The guy was trying for nonchalant, but John could see he was really nervous. His first guess was "cigarettes" as he watched the kid shuffle over to where Edelstein was filling prescriptions.

The teenager's voice started out deep, then squeaked and sounded ridiculous. "Gimme a pack of Trojans."

Edelstein looked up and shrugged. John knew him well enough to recognize when the druggist was trying to ease a customer's embarrassment. "Believe me, I wish I could, but I can't. The law ties my hands. You got to be twenty-one."

The kid's shoulders slumped and he left. Edelstein sighed and came out from behind the glass. He stepped behind the soda fountain counter, made himself a Bromo, and stared out the front door while he drank it. John waited. The Bromo finished, Edelstein leaned over the sink and started rinsing the glass himself.

"Does it make sense to you? All you need to schtup is a stiff prick, but if you want to keep from getting the clap or making a baby, you got to be twenty-one." Edelstein shook his head. Without waiting for an answer, he set the glass on the drainer and went back to work.

John smiled at the simplicity of the idea that came to him. He pulled off his apron and waved at Edelstein. "Back in a second," he hollered, and ran outside. The kid was all the way to Harper Avenue before John, breathing hard, caught up with him. "I can get you rubbers. Half a buck, pack of three."

The boy looked skeptical. Dealing with someone his own age, he lost his nervousness. "You're fulla shit. How you gonna get 'em?"

John ignored the question. "Meet me in the alley in back of the store, by the garbage cans. Ten-thirty. If you're late, I'm gone."

John wiped all the stainless steel fixtures completely dry as he prepared to close up. Edelstein and his son Barry were finishing off some last-minute prescriptions. Once the sinks were dried, it was John's job to sweep the shop. He got a can of sweeping compound out of the closet and spread it over the entire floor. Sweeping fast to keep the oil in the compound from staining the wood, he pushed his broom behind the cigarette and candy counter and quickly grabbed at the packages of rubbers Edelstein kept out of sight. He threw a handful into the trash can and covered them with the pile of sweepings. When he finished the floor, he dumped all the garbage outside in the alley trash bin.

The boss picked this night to offer John a ride home. Staying cool, he thought fast. "Hey, thanks, but I gotta go over to a buddy's house to do some homework." When Edelstein finally pulled away, he went around back.

The trash from the tailor shop on the other side of the alley had been dumped into the container after John's cleanup, so the rubbers were buried under small pieces of cloth and the remains of the tailor's lunch. John pulled out his hidden loot, using his shirtsleeve to wipe a glob of mustard off one of the packages. Stuffing the condoms into his jacket pocket, he waited for Mr. Duck's Ass to show up.

The kid was right on time. They moved back into the darkest part of the alley, and John showed him the rubbers.

"Hey, those are Sheiks! I wanted Trojans." He said it loud, and John shushed him with a hiss.

"As if you can tell the difference. You want 'em or not? Don't waste my time."

154

The kid hunched his shoulders and turned cagey. Through squinted eyes, he took a moment to size John up. John straightened to his full height and clenched his fists. The moment passed. Using the body language of the streets, the kid turned sideways and broke eye contact. "I'll give ya a buck for four packs."

John snorted and turned to leave.

The kid grabbed his arm. "OK, OK. How much do ya want?"

"Fifty cents a pack. Just what you were gonna pay inside." John paused for emphasis. "Where they wouldn't sell them to you."

The money changed hands, and the kid turned to walk away. John called after him, "Tell your friends I can get any kind they want."

The kid looked back and sneered, "Next time, get Trojans."

*****

As time went by, John started adding other things to the trash. Magazines, candy bars, fancy soaps, and perfume. He sold to anyone with money, and for everything except rubbers, he charged half price. When Henry or Mike needed a family birthday present, they would go to the drugstore and pick out the stuff they wanted John to steal. By Christmas, between the cash register and the trash items, he was clearing twenty-five bucks a week.

"Hey, boychik," Edelstein sang out. "I bought a bike. Now you got no excuse for taking so long on deliveries."

The bike was used, a rusty, beat-up Schwinn with a huge basket in front. Standing out in the cold in front of the store, Edelstein displayed it to John as if it were brand new.

John had been the one to suggest using a bike. Now he wasn't so sure it had been a good idea. "Sorry, boss, but it's a piece of junk."

Edelstein looked hurt. "OK, so it don't look so hot. But at least when you leave it outside, no one's gonna steal it."

John shrugged and the old man went to the back to finish preparing a prescription. "Give the bike a try. Take this to Mrs. Ryan." He handed John a bottle of cough medicine with the receipt wrapped around the bottle and held on by a thin rubber band. John took off his apron.

Edelstein counted out three ones, two quarters, and a penny. "Here's change for a five. That's all you'll need. No one ever handed that one more than five dollars in her life. Don't give her the prescription until she gives you the money. Otherwise, you're out of luck. Those Irishers drink up every spare nickel. Then, when they need medicine, they expect me to give it for free."

John nodded with impatience. He liked making deliveries and riding the bike might work out better than walking, but it was almost nine o'clock, and he wanted to get off work on time for once.

The streets were covered with huge mounds of blackened snow and ice, and the only way to ride a bicycle was to stay in the ruts created by automobile tires. That method worked up to a point, but problems developed when a car came. Headlights flashed behind him, and John had to pull the bike over to the side and wait for the vehicle to pass. It was only three blocks to the Ryan apartment, but there were so many cars, John figured the trip would have been faster on foot.

The building was a tenement like the Castle, only worse. It was four stories high, and each level had its own unpleasant smell. The Ryans lived on the third floor, where the overriding stink was boiled cabbage. John hoped that Mary Ryan would answer the door. She had great tits and didn't seem to care if her blouse opened up and showed a little skin. The odds were against it, there were six Ryan children and any number of guests bunking in. Old man Ryan had skipped out years ago, but that hadn't stopped the babies from coming.

The door opened a crack, and a hand reached out for the medicine. John pulled back. "No, I gotta get the money. Buck forty-nine. I gotta get it, or I can't leave the stuff."

The cabbage smell was coming from the Ryans' place and it almost gagged him when Mrs. Ryan threw the door open wide. Mary's mother looked terrible. Her eyes were dark holes sunk deep in her head, and her hair, partly pinned, was mostly loose and hanging down onto her face. She wore no makeup, and as she stood in the doorway, she made a halfhearted attempt to push her hair back up under her barrette. Her stained housedress looked as if it were on a wire hanger rather than a person. From the room behind her came a hoarse coughing sound followed by an exhausted whining.

"It's the baby. She ain't stopped coughing since yesterday. She can't sleep and she's gettin' worse an' worse. Tell the Jew I'll come in an' pay tomorrow."

John tried to hold out. He knew he should just walk away, but the hacking cough and the pitiful crying broke him. He handed over the cough syrup. "Tell Mary that John said 'Hi.'" The door slammed.

On the way back to the pharmacy, it started to snow. Rather than ride the bike in the ruts again, John stayed on the sidewalk and pushed it back to the drugstore. As he trudged through the wind-whipped snowflakes, he tried to think of an excuse to give Mr. Edelstein. He knew Mrs. Ryan wouldn't be in to pay, and he had no way to explain why he'd given her the medicine.

He decided to pay for it himself. That seemed better than facing Edelstein. The problem was, he always left his wallet next to the cash register when he went on deliveries because he was afraid of getting robbed. Now he had to get to his wallet without Edelstein seeing him. John stood outside in the driving snow and watched Edelstein through the storefront window. When the old man went from behind the prescription counter to the back, he slipped inside the door and moved quickly over to the soda fountain. Snatching a five-dollar bill from his wallet, he carried it and the receipt to the back just as Edelstein, holding a huge bottle filled with some kind of liquid, came out.

Coat and hat dripping with melted snow, John handed over the five, and Edelstein rang up the sale in the prescription cash register without saying a word.

John was sure he'd pulled it off. Not bothering to take off his wet coat, he started washing down the equipment so he could go home. A moment later, Edelstein came over and joined him. He made himself the usual Bromo and downed it in one long gulp. "From now on, if I think a customer don't pay, I'll send Barry."

John moved over to the sink and started drying glasses. He couldn't look Edelstein in the eye.

Edelstein made a placating gesture. "What? You think this is a bad thing? You think it's bad you got a heart? No, boychik, sometimes, it's good to be a softy. The only thing is, I can't have my fountain kid paying for the customer's medicine. Barry, he ain't got as big a heart as you. So from now on, if I think a customer don't pay, Barry goes."

Edelstein pinched John's cheek, turned, and walked to the back.

John wiped the glasses, and the next night, he nicked the cash register for an additional two bucks to make up for his loss.

With the demands John's job put on his time, he and Ben rarely saw each other outside of school. To keep in touch, they started meeting in the lunchroom at Hyde Park.

John had bragged to Ben about most of his high school schemes— fencing stolen goods, buying and selling completed homework, and providing crib sheets for most exams. But John could tell by Ben's beaming face that this drugstore scam was the best thing he'd done so far. "So you made money on the deal, and Edelstein thinks you're some kind of saint."

"I'm a saint and a softy with a good heart. Plus, I got the added bonus of having Miss Mary Ryan deeply grateful to yours truly. I may never quit this job."

CHAPTER THIRTY

The order was for ice cream, a lot of ice cream. Edelstein had taken it over the phone, and now he helped John package up the cartons for delivery. "The building is across from the park," Edelstein said, and John nodded. He knew the place. He'd once tried to sell some lilacs there, and some old biddy had almost called the cops. It was a ritzy building. In fact, they had recently installed a doorman to keep out the riffraff.

The blizzard-force wind sent sharp crystals of snow pecking against John's face. They slashed at him as he pulled the bike over the frozen mounds of ice on the street. There weren't many cars out, so he rode for two blocks before he was forced to pull over to the side. Back in the ruts, he pushed past Lake Park Avenue. The snow had thickened and was making it hard to see, and the wind whipped in so strong, it forced him to a standstill a few times. Finally, he reached Stony Island. He turned south toward 59th. The last two blocks were brutal, but somehow, he found himself in front of the building. He dropped the bike in a snowbank, half hoping someone would steal the damned thing. Cradling the package against his chest, he hunched sideways and fought his way through the blizzard to the building's main entrance.

The lobby was tiny. A maroon carpet with wet footprints led from the entrance straight to the elevators. To the right were a table and chair for the doorman, and on the left were rows of brass-plated mailboxes covering the wall. The doorman was standing by the mailboxes, staring out at the snow. Nodding, John started past him toward the bank of elevators. The doorman snarled out of the side of his mouth, "Where do you think you're goin'?"

Making a show of looking at the order slip, John said, "Number 303," and kept moving toward the elevator.

The doorman thumbed toward the desk. "Leave it. I'll get it up there."

John knew the game. If the doorman delivered the package, the tip would be his. He pulled off his earmuffs and took a firmer grip on the package. "Sorry, I gotta collect for the delivery. It's ice cream, an' it's already melting."

Neither statement was true. It was a charge order, and the weather outside had, if anything, made the ice cream harder.

John was wearing his frayed war surplus navy peacoat with two of the four buttons missing. His nose was red and running from the cold, and his wet hair leaked hair cream down his neck. In the warmth of the lobby, his clothes and shoes started dripping melted snow on the already soaked carpet.

"All right, but make it snappy."

The elevator was the new self-service type. John stepped in and pushed the button for the third floor with a mild flourish. He said, "Third floor, ladies' underwear," and grinned at the frowning doorman just before the elevator door closed.

The hallway was tastefully austere, with thick paisley carpeting on the floor and dark wood paneling halfway up the wall. There was an oil painting across from the elevator depicting men in red jackets on horses chasing dogs through a woodland scene. The lighting was subdued, and John had to get close to the doors to make out the gold numbers. He found 303 and knocked lightly on the varnished mahogany door. Through it, he could hear laughter, talking, and music, and his gentle rapping was drowned out by the noise inside. He knocked again, louder this time, and when there still was no answer, he pounded on the door. Then all sound except the music stopped and the door slowly opened.

Standing with her hands on her hips was Maxine Sommers, a girl in John's homeroom at Hyde Park High. Behind her, the room was full of kids John knew. There were no adults. Suddenly, he became aware of his appearance. He ran his hand through his hair and brushed ineffectually at his peacoat. Maxine took the package without looking up and turned to go back to her party.

Everyone seemed frozen in place. As if remembering something, Maxine stopped and turned back. He smiled, but she didn't seem to notice.

"Please wait," she said and turned away from the door. John waited and dripped.

After an excruciatingly long minute, Maxine returned, and with a grand gesture, she held out a small coin. "This is for you," she said, handing him a nickel. John's face flamed and he started to stammer, but the door closed abruptly and the sound of laughter followed him long after he could no longer hear it.

In the elevator, he looked down at the nickel in his palm and wished he'd let the stupid doorman make the delivery. Had the guy known how cheap the Sommers people were? Was that why he let John make the delivery? Flipping the nickel up and snatching it out of the air, he pushed the button for the ground floor.

Before the elevator door opened, John reached into his wallet and pulled out a dollar bill. He kept it in plain view as he walked past the doorman. Rubbing the bill between his thumb and forefinger, he opened the door with a flourish and pushed out into the storm.

A few days later, John met Ben in the school lunchroom. He nibbled at what the Hyde Park kitchen staff called a hamburger. "Maxine Sommers is a bitch. She gives me a fuckin' nickel. I shoulda tossed it back at her an' told her ta buy herself a heart. The cheap bitch."

Ben knew better than to laugh. "But a goodlooking bitch. I'd sure like to get in her pants."

John wadded up the remains of his burger in a napkin and basketballed it into the garbage. "That bitch is so cold, she'd freeze your dick off."

CHAPTER THIRTY-ONE

John looked up when Dumb Eddie walked in. His stomach did a little twist, but he resigned himself to what was coming and tried to smile. Dumb Eddie reached up and wiped a blob of drool from the corner of his mouth. "Wanna unday."

That meant an ice cream sundae. John had learned to understand most of what Eddie said the hard way, with lots of repeating, pointing, and frustration on both their parts.

"Like before?" John asked, and the answering nod set him in motion.

The first time he'd served Dumb Eddie, Edelstein had told him to make as large a sundae as the glass would hold, and if Eddie forgot to pay, that was OK, too. Edelstein's comment was, "Boychik, you think you got trouble? Thanks God you ain't like that one."

The retarded man was hard to wait on. His sheepskin coat was filthy and he smelled of urine. While he ate, he drooled and spit into the glass, and his nose ran constantly.

He had an unbreakable routine when he came into the store. First, he would order his sundae, then, while it was being made, he'd go to the public phone and push his finger into the coin return slot. Edelstein told John that a few years back, Eddie had found a nickel in the slot, and he still remembered.

Two of the younger kids had seen Eddie coming. Using tweezers and a cigarette lighter, they had heated several pennies red hot and thrown them in the coin return. John started scooping ice cream into the dish, trying to ignore what was going on. It was no skin off his nose if the retard got burned—served him right for being so disgusting.

John watched as the two kids stood to one side, choking back laughter. And then something in him snapped. When Eddie headed for the back, John came out from behind the counter and waved his arms to head him off.

"The coins are hot!" Shaking his head, John reached out and tried to stop Eddie. He pointed at the two gigglers. "Those kids, they made them real hot. You'll get burned."

He couldn't get Eddie to understand. The retarded man pushed past John and reached into the slot. His hand flew back and he looked stunned. Then he tried again, and again he got burned. When he started to try a third time, John grabbed his arm and pulled him away.

Edelstein had seen most of what had happened from behind the prescription window. Now he came roaring and shouted at the kids, "Get the hell outta here, you hooligans, and don't come back."

The two ran out, still laughing.

John took Dumb Eddie's hand. It was filthy and heavily calloused. His nails were thick and black underneath. There didn't seem to be any real damage, just a couple of small red spots where the fingers had come into contact with the pennies. He led Eddie to the counter, gave him a piece of ice for the burn and finished making him his sundae.

Dumb Eddie spit and drooled and wiped his nose with his sleeve. It was obvious he'd forgotten what had happened seconds after he'd been burned.

Later, when John was drying the sink, Edelstein came behind the counter and shot fizzy water into a glass. For once, he drank it without the Bromo-Seltzer.

"How long you been working here, boychik?"

John held up his hand and counted the months. "Started in September—five months."

Edelstein nodded. "Good thing it wasn't six. You'd run out of fingers."

John grinned. He liked the old man's sense of humor. "By next month, I'll figure out how to use the other hand."

"Five months." Edelstein nodded again, this time as if he were impressed. "Five months is a long time." He paused and turned, setting his empty glass in the sink. As he walked away, he said over his shoulder, "For such a long time as that, a person deserves a raise."

John didn't say anything. He just kept wiping the sink.

CHAPTER THIRTY-TWO

It was Saturday morning. Normally, Edelstein was at the drug-store long before John showed up, but not today. Today, it was five below zero, one of the coldest days of the year, and Edelstein was late. John stood outside huddled against the March wind and pulled out a cigarette. *In like a lion, out like a lamb. Well, the lion part is sure true this year.*

He tried to light a match by cupping his hands around the flame, but the wind caught it and blew it out. It was the last match in the book, but John had another book. It was a large double-size, picked up during one of his fencing endeavors with a couple of rich kids at the South Shore Country Club. This time, he turned his whole body away from the wind and curled into a comma while he again tried to light a match. The match flared, the wind gusted, and the book caught fire. A blowtorch of flame poured out of the side of the matchbook, turning John's palm into blistered meat.

The pain hit John so hard, he almost threw up. He gripped the wrist of the burned hand with his other hand and looked down at the phosphorous ash residue coating his palm. Just then, Edelstein walked up. He didn't notice that John was hurt and started to apologize for being late.

"OK, so I'm a little late. You been late—"

John was still holding his burned hand by the wrist, and he raised it to almost eye level to show Edelstein.

"Oy! Boychik, what did you do?"

"Matchbook," John muttered, and he let himself be led into the pharmacy.

With the gentleness of a woman, Edelstein applied salve to the burn. He bandaged it loosely and gave John the tube of salve for later.

"You can't work the fountain with a hand like that. Get in the car, I'm gonna drive you home."

John knew he wasn't all that badly hurt, but he liked the way Edelstein was taking care of him, so he nodded and let himself be escorted out. Edelstein pulled the car out of the parking space in back and motioned John into the front seat. When they reached John's house, he ran around to the passenger side and opened the door.

"You'll go inside and you'll lie down. It's a shock and you'll need to be quiet for a while."

The last thing John wanted to do was get in bed. He decided that as soon as the old man was gone, he'd go out and see what the guys were doing. In the living room, he could hear the druggist conferring quietly with his mother. She sounded annoyed, and John could tell that her concern didn't run as deep as Mr. Edelstein's. He looked at the bandage Mr. Edelstein had wrapped around his hand and relived the feeling of the salve being rubbed on. Cradling his injury, he sank back on the bed. A choked feeling started in his throat, and tears began running down his face. He forced his lips closed so that when he cried, it was without making a sound.

*****

John was sitting with Ben and Henry on the third-floor landing, just outside of Henry's flat. It was still too cold to sit on the stoop in front of the building. The original plan had been to play cards, but Henry's father was drunk again, and when he got drunk, it was best to keep away from him.

"But why do ya gotta quit?" Henry asked, "Just because Edelstein's nice to you?"

John had his back against the wall. He looked around as if he were afraid of being overheard and tried to explain. "He acts like I'm his kid or somethin'. I just can't steal from him anymore."

Ben shook his head. "So why quit? Why not just stop stealing?"

John smirked and lampooned a look of shocked horror. "Stealing's what I do. Why the fuck would I keep a job where I didn't steal?"

CHAPTER THIRTY-THREE

The week before his fight at the Memorial Day CYO boxing finals, Henry started keeping away from the stoop. Lately, Benny seemed to be able to read minds, and Henry didn't want Mr. Know-It-All to figure out how worried he was. He wasn't afraid; nights of waiting in bed for the old man to come home and beat the shit out of him had taught him how to swallow back fear. Besides, being afraid was shameful, disgusting, and not possible for a badass like Henry Fox. What he was, was resigned—resigned to getting his first loss. His only hope was to keep from getting beaten so badly that the loss would eliminate him from a spot on the Golden Gloves team.

So instead of hanging out with his friends, he spent all his spare time at the Dorchester Avenue Gym. He pounded the heavy bag, made the speed bag dance, and sparred with anyone he could coax into the ring with him.

Henry was scheduled to fight a three-round prelim against Sherman "Blacky" Thatch and he knew he couldn't win. After all, the guy was eighteen years old, and Henry had a month to go before he turned sixteen. Besides, Thatch had a record of six wins and no losses, and all of the guys Thatch had fought were older and bigger than Henry. Not that Henry considered himself a slouch. He had a five-and-zero record himself, and a couple of the guys he'd out-boxed had been marked as real comers. Still, the word was that Thatch was crazy and had a punch that said "lights out" in blood-red letters.

Thatch hadn't gone to Ray School because he was out of the district, but Henry had run into him at Chicago Vocational. The neighborhood had him as the second-baddest kid in a crew of bad boys from 47th Street. The leader of the gang, Roger Shaw, was supposedly the only one who had ever beaten Thatch in a fight.

One of the things that made Thatch so feared was his lack of front teeth. The teeth had been knocked out during a Pom-Pom game. A dentist recommended having a plate made, but the cost was too high, so his parents passed on the offer. Henry figured that being toothless would embarrass most guys, but not Thatch. Thatch was the opposite. He seemed to enjoy rolling back his eyes and curling his upper lip to expose the gaping hole. The result was a frightening caricature of an insane person.

After the boxing card was announced, Henry seemed to run into Thatch every time he walked down the hall at school. The maniac would spot Henry, do the upper-lip-raise thing, and cackle like a madman. Henry tried to ignore it, but the ugly grimace and sneering cackle that went with it had him badly shaken.

*****

The match was held at the American Legion Hall. Every seat was filled because the democratic alderman of the 5th Ward had contributed the money for beer and hotdogs, besides the main event had a couple of promising heavyweights.

The smoke was so thick, Henry could barely see the ring. He shrugged his shoulders as he'd seen other fighters do, and he and Thatch strode down the aisle with Father Donahue between them. They were almost unnoticed by the crowd. Benny, Andy, Mike, and

John were in the last row, and they let out a cheer as Henry went past, but the chatter of the crowd almost drowned them out. Henry grinned their way and raised his gloved hands above his head in triumph.

In his other five fights, Henry's approach had been methodical. He worked flat-footed and had just kept circling away to his left. There were two things that set him apart—his arms were long for his size, and he could switch to southpaw at will. The extra arm length let him lope jabs over his opponent's guard while falling back. Usually, by the time his adversary reacted, Henry had danced out of range. It was a good scoring move. He'd get credit for a hit, and the other fighter would look silly trying to counter as Henry backpedaled away.

Henry's drawback was his speed. He didn't have any. He was a short, skinny kid with big bones and was too slow to be an effective counter-puncher. But Henry could take punishment. His father had been showing him how to deal with pain almost all his life.

In his coaching, Father Donahue maintained that in a defensive stance, the boxer was fully protected. The problem was, in order to throw a punch the fighter had to open up. To make up for his lack of speed, Henry learned to sucker his opponent into swinging. He'd take the punch, roll with it as best he could, and go for the opening. In two of his past matches, he'd connected with countering rights solid enough to end the fight.

Henry had seen all of Thatch's fights, three of which had resulted in bout-ending knockdowns. In all of them, Thatch had fought like a tank. Head down, he'd plowed forward, absorbing punishment until he got close enough inside to deliver one devastating punch. Henry's plan for this fight was to keep from getting killed by staying out of Thatch's range.

When Thatch got in the ring and dropped the towel that Father Donahue had draped over his shoulders, Henry saw that his body was

172

almost blue-white and his broad chest was covered in tightly curled black hair. The manliness of chest hair was one thing Henry knew he would never have. His already reddish skin flushed even redder as he imagined how the contrast between he and Thatch looked to the audience.

They moved to the center of the ring and stood facing each other as the referee rattled off a bunch of instructions they'd both heard before. Thatch had his mouthpiece in, and the white rubber covered his lack of teeth. He kept raising his upper lip, but the scary snarl was gone, and in its place was the swollen grimace of a goofy clown. The harder he tried to sneer, the funnier he looked.

That was enough to ease away Henry's nervousness, but not enough to make him change his fight strategy. That change came as they touched gloves and started back to their corners. Thatch did a little shuffle step and faked a punch at Henry. When Henry flinched, Thatch laughed. "Poor little Injun. They should have let you grow some cock hair before they put you in the ring with a man."

Henry calmly swallowed his rage and decided he was going to win the fight or get killed trying.

When the bell for the first round rang, Thatch rushed out as if eager to get the bout over with. Henry danced away and flicked out a left. Thatch ran into it and swung wildly. Henry ducked under and they fell into a clinch. The referee separated them, and Thatch pushed away with both hands. Henry backpedaled, keeping his left jabbing at Thatch's face. As Thatch bulled his way in, Henry looped his right over Thatch's guard and scored hits that did no damage but gained him points. Each time Henry connected, he felt a little more confident. He started mixing in combinations: left jab, left jab, left hook, right cross. He landed punches with ease, and near the end of the second round, the crowd began to notice. Thatch was unhurt but completely out of control.

173

In Henry's corner, the black man who helped with the fighters patted Henry's shoulder. "You gots this fight. Just keep away from him. He gonna try ta get in close an' end it wit' one punch."

Henry nodded.

The instant the bell rang for the third round, the bigger man charged. Henry danced away, keeping his left flicking in Thatch's face. When Thatch stopped charging, Henry moved in, scoring with a few solid shots before dancing away again. The bull charged again, and Henry slipped back, taking punches that had no steam because they landed on a retreating target.

About a minute into the round, Henry knew he'd won the fight. Thatch's face was bright red from punches and frustration. He was flailing away at Henry, unhurt but frustrated, hoping to land a fight-ending miracle. Henry was watching Thatch's eyes, so he knew exactly when the guy snapped. A kind of wildness flashed on Thatch's face, and suddenly, he grabbed Henry in a headlock and tried to wrestle him to the ground. Henry was slick with sweat and easily slid out of the hold. He instinctively shifted into a southpaw stance and danced back as Thatch swung a wild left hook. In the southpaw stance, Henry's right hand was forward, and he easily deflected Thatch's punch. He dropped his shoulder and put everything he had into a solid left cross.

Father Donahue had called it Henry's double-cross; no one expected a right-handed fighter to switch stances in the middle of a bout and lead with the right instead of the left. The punch caught Thatch flush on the chin and put him down with a dislocated jaw. The referee raised Henry's hand in victory and the crowd went nuts.

Laughing, Henry's corner man whispered, "I's glad y'all listened ta me an' kept away from him."

Benny was the first one in the ring, and the others were right behind him. Mary Ryan tongue-kissed him on the way back to the locker room, and in one blaze of glory, Henry's neighborhood reputation was made.

*****

For a few days after the fight, Henry expected Thatch to come after him to settle up. He stopped carrying books in the school hallway so his hands would always be free, and on the street, he never let anyone get behind him. After hearing that Father Donahue had tossed Thatch out of CYO for poor sportsmanship and that Thatch's family had moved to the West Side. He was able to relax

Henry's next bout was a tryout bout for the Golden Gloves team. A small Asian kid peppered him with so many punches, he was confused as to which hand the kid was hitting him with. The black man who had been in his corner at the Thatch fight took pity on him. "Maybe by next year, y'all grow enough ta fight white boys who be slow like you."

CHAPTER THIRTY-FOUR

On the Saturday before Memorial Day, Ben and Henry went to the small strip of lakefront known as 57th Street Beach. From the waterline to the sidewalk, side-by-side pale winter bodies stretched out on rectangles, each laying claim to their small patch of sand. It was so crowded that the boys chose to lie on the rocks along the southern edge of the Outer Drive breakwater.

Belly down and elbows bent, they both kept their heads high enough to watch girls wearing this summer's new one-piece bathing suits. The unspoken hope was for a glimpse of breasts as some young lovely bent over to smooth out her blanket.

Ben wore a bathing suit, but Henry, unwilling to further darken his Indian skin, was fully clothed. He even wore a baseball hat with a bill that shaded his face from the sun.

Henry said, "If I can get my freshwater merchant marine papers, I can score a job on the ore boats. It's supposed ta be beaucoup bucks."

A couple strolled by looking for a place to set down their blanket, and Ben tried to will them away. "I thought you were going to box CYO again this summer. After the Thatch fight, I thought you'd be a shoo-in for the team."

The couple hesitated, the man staring at Henry. With a shake of his head, they moved on. "Nah, some skinny Jap kid kicked my ass, and

Father Donahue says I need time ta grow inta my body. There's no sense in spendin' the summer chasin' a bunch of little guys faster than me. He figures I'm due for a big growth spurt."

Grinning at him, Ben said, "'Bout time."

Henry thought about smacking him, but it seemed like too much trouble. "Anyway, if I go on the boats, I won't have ta watch my old man drink himself ta death. Doctor says a few more good blackouts and it's curtains."

"Is it cirrhosis?"

Henry thought for a moment. The word sounded familiar, but he wasn't sure. "Nah, it's his liver."

If it had been anyone else, Ben would have explained, but he knew how much Henry resented being corrected. He settled for a shrug. "Oh."

"There ain't gonna be any of the gang around the neighborhood this summer. Andy got on as a dishwasher at that Salvation Army camp we went to last summer. Mike's goin' down on his uncle's farm again, and Johnny's got a job as a busboy at one of the Benton Harbor resorts. He claims there's a lot of rich young pussy that gets bored hangin' out with their folks, and scorin' with 'em is a cinch. I think he's got the right idea. At least he ain't gonna spend another summer sittin' around sayin' 'So whadda ya wanna do?'"

Henry rolled over on his back and lit a cigarette. "How 'bout you, what you gonna do?"

Ben watched a girl shuck out of her jeans. She unbuttoned her blouse, folded it carefully, and laid it down on her blanket. The cups of her bathing suit held tightly to her chest. "I dunno, I was thinkin' of hittin' the road. Hitch out to California."

Henry spun his head to face his friend. "You're fulla shit."

177

"No, actually, I'm kinda light in that area. Had a huge shit before we came, a real bowl-winder. Nothing like a good shit ta put a smile on your face."

Henry grinned. "I take it back. You're not fulla shit, you're nuts. And don't start a speech about nuts."

They went quiet for a few minutes, Ben in his own world and Henry drinking in the shrieks of children playing in the chilly water and the rhythmic sound of the breakers crashing against the shore. "Your mother ain't gonna go for you hitchin' out West, is she?"

Feeling the skin on his back begin to heat up, Ben was about to turn over and get some sun on his chest. Then another girl started to strip down to her bathing suit, and he decided to stay put. "I could slip a pillow under the blanket on my bed an' she'd never know I was gone."

Henry sat up and lightly punched Ben's arm. "Why don't ya try out for the boats, like me?" A light breeze kept the beach temperature down, and the soft smell of the lake waters wafted over them with each breaking wave.

Ben dropped his head to his folded arms and felt as close to content as he would allow himself to be. "You gotta be sixteen. Besides, those boats are dangerous. I heard the cooks like to play with the little cabin boys."

Henry had forgotten that Ben was a few months younger. By the time his friend turned sixteen, summer vacation would be almost over. "I ain't worried. I got me a pig sticker." He reached into his pocket, pulled out a switchblade stiletto, and pressed the button. With an ugly click, four inches of steel shot out. "Besides, hitchhikin's a lot more dangerous than workin' the ore boats. Your mother would be as nuts as you if she let ya go."

"My mother's the reason I'm thinkin' about it." Ben moved onto his side and raised his hand for Henry to shake. "Meet Ben Kahn, my mother's new kid brother. She nailed a rich guy an' lied about her age. She went from thirty-four to twenty-six. I went from fifteen to seventeen and from bein' her son to bein' her kid brother. To top off her load of horseshit, she gave the fool a story 'bout how she refused to put me in an orphan home after our parents were killed in a car accident. The jerk thinks she's some kind of saint."

Henry stared out at the lake. "Does it bother ya? I mean her bein' like that."

Ben rocked upright and wrapped his arms around his knees. "I dunno, sometimes. But then I think about you not even knowin' who your mother was, an' Andy's mother takin' off without even sayin' good-bye, an' I figure I don't have it so bad."

*****

The weather turned miserable in June, raining almost every day. Ben faked a cold as an excuse to keep away from the stoop and stay in his room. He didn't want the gang to know that he was studying for finals.

Andy also had a secret, a secret so shameful that if the guys found out, they would never stop razzing him about it. The head cook at the camp had promised to teach Andy how to work the grill, providing he did a good job with the dishes. He was determined to excel, and in order to excel, he decided he had to practice. A couple of times each day, he would fill the sink in his apartment with clean dishes and wash them, timing himself to measure his improvement. By mid-June, Andy could finish off the entire sink load in five minutes without so much as chipping a single plate.

John didn't spend much time around the Castle either. He was busy shopping for expensive beachwear so he could pretend to the Benton Harbor girls that he was rich. He explained to Ben that by limiting his purchases to bathing suits and matching shirts, he could afford to go for the name brands. "Runnin' a game in this neighborhood's a waste of time. Nobody has nothin' to rip off."

A week before school was out, Henry's hopes of a cabin boy job were dashed by the news of a mining iron ore strike. No mining, no ore, no ore, no ore boats.

*****

Ben forged his mother's name in his report book and turned it in on the last day of school. He'd pulled all Superiors and had maintained his 4.0 grade average. His biggest fear was that if he kept his grades up during his coming senior year, he might wind up class valedictorian. Hiding that from John would be impossible, and John would gleefully squeal to the rest of the guys. He wondered if anyone had ever turned the honor down.

The next morning, Ben banged on Henry's door. When no one answered, he tried Mike, then Andy. Mike's mother informed him that Mike had already left for the farm, and Andy's brother was pretty sure Andy had gone to camp. Ben knew John was home packing, so he didn't bother walking over there. Instead, scuffling his feet at the torn places in the linoleum, he slowly trudged down the stairs and headed outside.

Henry was on the stoop. Without looking up at Ben he said, "If ya wasn't just bein' fulla shit, I'm with ya."

Ben dropped down beside him. Sometimes, when he wasn't sure what others were talking about, he faked it. Noncommittal responses eventually gave him enough information to figure out what was being discussed. "Well, I'm not fulla shit."

"Then ya wanna go?"

"Sure."

"So, when?"

"Well, when do you wanna go?"

Henry threw his arm around Ben's shoulder. "Right now. There's no sense in hangin' around. How much money you got?"

"I'm not sure. How much do you think I'll need?"

Henry coughed up a wad of saliva and let it fly. "Ya don't got any idea what I'm talkin' about, do ya?"

Ben eyed the spot of spit some six feet from the bottom of the stoop and let loose a gob of his own. It fell short of Henry's by an inch or so. "Nope. Not the foggiest."

"Hitchin' ta California. I'm ready. The old man's in the hospital with the DTs, an' Grandfather says it's OK for me ta go." Henry straightened, and in a sonorous tone, imitated the old Indian. "'You have no choice, Henry. This is a knowledge quest to learn who you are.'"

"Now you're the one shittin' me."

Reaching into his pocket, Henry pulled out five ten-dollar bills. "Does this look like I'm shittin' ya? Grandfather peeled these bills off his roll without battin' an eye."

Jamming the bills back into his jeans, Henry stood and raised his arms in a parody of his Mohawk grandfather. "Then he says, 'A journey without an end will continue forever. It is better to have a destination.' An' he gives me the address of this Indian guy he knows who lives in a town in California called Lodeville. Supposed ta be not too far from San Francisco. He says this guy, George Red Cloud, could get us jobs pickin' fruit."

Ben started getting excited. "I'm stone broke, but I'll bet my moth...excuse me, my *sister* would come up with some bread to get rid of me. I'll try to get fifty, but if I can't, do you still wanna go?"

"We only need enough ta get out there. Then we can pick fruit an' earn enough ta get back. You get as much as ya can, an' we'll pool it."

"Damn! We're goin' to California. I can't believe it. What else did your grandfather say?"

"He said…" Henry put his hand over his heart and stared off into the distance. "'Don't tell your grandmother.'"

CHAPTER THIRTY-FIVE

Convinced that hitching rides was easier on a holiday weekend, Henry talked Ben into hitting the road on the Friday before the Fourth of July. Ben carried a canvas satchel with a strap that let him sling it over his shoulder. Inside were two pairs of jeans, three T-shirts, two pairs of Jockey shorts, two pairs of socks, a light jacket, and toiletries consisting of a toothbrush, toothpaste, a razor, and a tube of Wildroot hair cream. His comb and the twenty-five dollars he'd managed to scrape up stayed in his pocket. Except for the razor—Henry didn't shave—Henry's small duffel bag held identical items.

Herb, the operator of the newsstand next to the Castle, had been stationed near Los Angeles during the war. Not knowing the boys were headed for Northern California, he told them the best route to take was south on Highway 66. With that sketchy information, they hit the road.

The closest South-bound street out of the city was Stony Island Avenue. They headed for it, and with a grin of encouragement at Ben, Henry threw out his thumb. Because Henry had hitched rides before, Ben accepted that he knew the most about hitching. He stayed behind Henry and tried to look as inoffensive as possible.

The day was typical Chicago ugly—ninety-plus degrees with humidity to match. They trudged along at the curb, with Henry turning to face each passing car, waving his thumb and grinning hopefully. If a car was parked blocking the oncoming driver's view, Henry would run around it and stand in the street.

At first, the indifference of the drivers didn't bother him, but as car after car rolled by without so much as a glance in his direction, Henry's smile began to fade.

He wiped a sleeve across his face. "We gotta split up. No one's gonna stop for two of us, 'specially when one of us is Indian-lookin'. I'm gonna go ahead of ya. Try ta look pitiful and harmless. When ya get a ride, talk the driver inta pullin' over for me. If ya can't, make him stop an' let ya out."

Ben was too miserable to argue. His T-shirt was soaked through and his feet ached and burned at the same time. He sat on the curb and pulled off his shoes, checking the backs of his heels for blisters. The skin was red but had not yet bubbled. He pulled his socks up and put his shoes back on, making sure that the laces were tight to minimize the rubbing. Limping slightly, he moved to the street side of the parked cars and put out his thumb.

A Chevy panel truck with two men in the front slowed as it approached, and it looked as if the driver intended to pull over. Ben stopped walking and waved, forcing a broad smile. The man in the passenger seat said something to the driver, and the truck swerved sharply, forcing Ben to leap up on the hood of a parked car to avoid getting hit. Laughing and nudging his buddy, the driver hit the gas and pulled back into traffic.

Henry heard the squeal of tires and looked back. The truck swerved again, this time aimed at him. Forewarned by the noise, Henry was able to squeeze between two parked cars. He screamed at the laughing occupants. "Ya chickenshit motherfuckers! I dare ya ta stop." The passenger flipped Henry his middle finger and the truck kept going.

Henry ran back to Ben and gave him a hand as he slid off the car hood. "The dirty fuckers! they coulda killed ya. Are ya OK?" Ben nodded, his face drained of color. After that, they stayed together.

*****

It was past noon and they had walked almost three miles, from 57th to 79th, before they got their first ride.

It was a dark green 1949 Mercury convertible. The top was down, and the driver had an arm slung over the back of the passenger seat. He rolled a toothpick from one side of his mouth to the other and grimaced. "How far ya goin'?"

Ben started to say California, but Henry spoke up first. "Far as you'll take us."

The toothpick rolled and the driver's eyes squinted slightly. "Hop in."

They piled in, Henry up front and Ben sprawled across the back seat. The driver headed south on Stony. They caught a red light at 81st and the driver spoke out of the side of his mouth while they waited for the green. "How much gas money you guys got?"

"None," wasn't the right answer. The driver pulled over to the curb, reached past Henry to open the car door, and thumbed the two of them out.

They walked another six blocks. Ben began to lag behind, and finally, Henry turned around. "What're ya doin'?"

"I gotta get something ta drink. The way I'm sweatin' I'm gonna die of thirst. Let's stop at a store and grab a couple of Cokes."

Henry shook his head and turned away. "We can't be wastin' money on Cokes. You're thirsty? Drink water."

"You see any drinking fountains around here? Jesus, Fox, we can't go all the way to California without eating and drinking."

They stopped at a drugstore and shared a chocolate soda. It cost fifteen cents, and like the sodas John fixed at Edelstein's, it came with a package of two cookies and a glass of water. Ben had the fountain boy refill the water glass four times.

Back on the street, with sweat pouring off his face, Ben moved over to the curb and leaned against a parked car. "This ain't workin'."

The surface of the car was hot to the touch, and traffic whizzed by, belching exhaust fumes into the stagnant air. Henry dropped his bag and pushed up onto the car's fender. "You're the one with all the bright ideas. What else we gonna do?"

They caught the CTA bus home. Henry knew where his father kept a spare key, so they decided to spend the night at his apartment. The place was musty and stank of stale alcohol and vomit, but the water was still running, and it was a place to crash.

They bought a couple of cans of chili at the Greek's, but the gas bill hadn't been paid, so the stove was dead. That meant spooning out the chili cold. Ben forced his down, figuring that it would have to last them awhile. He spent most of the night groaning with a stomach-ache, but the cold dinner didn't bother Henry at all.

In the morning, Ben stayed on the toilet for a half-hour, and when he came out, he told Henry that he felt lots better. "You got the most money, Fox, so you get to decide, but I say we check out taking a bus to California. Not as cool as hitchhiking, but at least we'll get there."

They walked to the Greyhound bus station on 63rd, wishing they'd had the sense to stop there when they'd passed yesterday. Inside the station, they learned that the fare to Sacramento was thirty-eight bucks apiece. Henry put on what he supposed was an innocent face. "Hey, I'm only twelve, do I gotta pay full fare?"

The bald-headed clerk stepped back from the grated ticket window and grabbed at his crotch. "I'd sell you a half-price ticket on balls alone, but the driver would take one look an' toss you out on your ass."

Even if they had been able to come up with the seventy-six-dollar total, it would have left them with zero for food. They headed back to the Castle, gloom dogging every step. Ben was frantic. Having to beg his mother to let him back in the apartment was almost inconceivable. "Maybe we could go as far as St. Louis, an' hitchhike from there."

Henry shook his head. "For a guy who's supposed ta be a brain, you can be really stupid. If we can't get a ride in St. Louis, there won't be any CTA bus ta bring us back home. I feel as shitty as you. The first thing my old man is gonna do when he gets outta the hospital is tie one on."

The blazing noonday sun put an exclamation point on their decision to give up trying to thumb a ride. Round-shouldered with dejection, they passed the Post Restaurant, turned down 57th Street and headed for home.

John was sitting on the stoop as Henry and Ben crossed the street. He jumped up, waved excitedly, then ran over to meet them. His grinning face was flushed with triumph, and he started yelling while he was still twenty feet away. "Man, am I glad I caught up with you guys before you left. I got you a ride downstate, all the way to Champaign."

CHAPTER THIRTY-SIX

B en caught Henry's eye and gave a quick shake of his head. He was afraid Henry was going to spill about their failed attempt at hitchhiking. The humiliation of failing to catch a ride was more than he could take right now. Henry slowly nodded back.

"This guy, Ricardo, he's a med student at Illinois who's got a buddy there in Champaign, and it's right on your way to California. He don't even want gas money, but the thing is, you gotta do the drivin'. The guy's kinda squirrelly. He can't leave till after supper, and he's scared to drive at night."

Henry shrugged. "I can drive. Grandfather taught me so I could haul the old man home when he was drunk. Dark don't bother me."

The offer of the ride was a mixed bag. On the one hand, it got them going. On the other hand, they could wind up stranded a hundred and fifty miles from home. The boys moved across the street to the Miller Building so Ben could keep an eye on the Castle door. He wasn't sure where his mother was and didn't feel like having to explain why he wasn't halfway to California.

"How'd you find this guy?"

John had a shopping bag from Marshall Field's with him. While he talked, he dug into the bag and pulled out a shirt and bathing suit.

"My mom. She knows the guy from the hospital. The thing is, she's so relieved I got a summer job, she'll do just about anything for me. When I told her what you guys were doin', she mentioned Ricardo. That's the guy's name, Ricardo."

The fashionable beach set John held up for approval consisted of a flowered shirt and a solid-colored matching bathing suit. Henry reached over and felt the material. "What'd that sissy outfit run ya?"

Grinning, John rammed the clothes back in the bag. "Thirty bucks for both, an' they were on sale. I also got a pair of sandals, sunglasses, an' a fancy beach towel. This *sissy* stuff is what the richies wear to sit around the resort pool." He raised his finger as if tapping an ash off the tip of a cigar and did a poor W.C. Fields impression. "Ah, yes, my little chickadees, let the plucking begin."

Ben threw his arm around John's neck and held him in a loose headlock. "Plucking or fucking?"

"Let me go, fool." John stepped away and took an elaborate bow. "As much of both as possible."

John waited on the stoop while Ben and Henry went up to the Fox apartment to get their things. Ben was all for going. The thought of seeing the campus of the University of Illinois was reason enough for him to risk it. "If we get stuck in Champaign, we can always catch a Greyhound home. We ain't got enough to get to California on the bus, but it's gotta be a lot cheaper just getting from downstate to here. Besides, if we turn Johnny down, we'll have to tell him we bombed out on hitchin'."

The three of them walked to the address John's mother had reluctantly given them, saying. "I can't imagine what your parents are thinking, letting you run all over without any supervision."

John rang the bell, and they waited until the med student came trotting down the stairs, grinning and waving. A skinny, brown elf of a man with a mouth full of bone-white teeth, Ricardo jabbered at them in sing-song English. "You put de luggage in de trunk, an' den we go."

Henry whispered to John, "What is he, some kind of Jap?"

John shook his head. "He's a Filipino, like the guys in *Back to Bataan*."

Ricardo's car—a '48 Ford sedan—wasn't actually Ricardo's. It belonged to the buddy he was going to meet up with in Champaign.

They said good-bye to John and piled in. Henry started it up, shifted into first, and let the clutch out too fast. The engine sputtered and died. A second try got them into a lurching forward motion, and they headed out of the city.

A worried frown had replaced Ricardo's smile. He was gripping the armrest tightly and shoving his foot down on an imaginary brake. Henry was too focused on driving to notice, so it fell to Ben to calm the little guy down. "The car's new to my friend. It's gonna be OK once he gets used to the clutch."

The frown deepened. "Dees not my car. If he don' learn soon, de clutch be burn up."

They had to stop in Kankakee for gas. Coming off the highway, Henry managed to downshift without too much trouble, and Ricardo began to look slightly less frightened.

They loaded up on potato chips and candy bars at a small market and got back on the road. Henry raced through the gears and almost killed the engine trying to get into third too soon. Instead of down-shifting again, he punched the gas. After an agonizing wait, the speedometer slowly crept past fifty and the feel of control returned.

Relaxed now that he was in high gear, Henry used his left hand to steer and draped his right arm over the back of the seat.

"Uh, Ricardo, do ya think your friend would mind if we slept in the car tonight? It's gonna be too late ta try an' hitch a ride from Champaign, an' we ain't got enough money ta be rentin' hotel rooms."

190

"My friend got apartment near de campus. You could sleep dere."

Henry reached over and clapped Ricardo on the shoulder. "That's cool, man, really cool."

Ricardo grinned for the first time since they'd left Chicago. "My friend ees name Martin. Ees from Manila, an' he fly back dere for de summer from San Franceesco. Dis da car he buy here, an' he want to send it on a boat to his home. You drive pretty good. Maybe he take you weet him to California. Dat way, you take turns driving, no got to stop for sleep. Get dere faster."

Too excited to even speak the boys said nothing.

*****

They rolled into Champaign after midnight. Martin's two-room apartment consisted of a kitchenette, living room, and one tiny bedroom. It was sparsely furnished, but clean. Martin was already asleep in the bedroom, so Ricardo grabbed the couch and offered the floor to Ben and Henry. More tired than hungry, the boys collapsed onto a throw rug and fell fast asleep.

*****

Ben awoke to a gentle push on his side. A light-skinned Filipino stood above him, nudging him with his foot. "Who are you?"

Henry's eyes popped open and he sat up. "Friends of Ricardo's. Are you Martin?"

The man stepped back, his head cocked to one side and his face scrunched with suspicion. He was an inch or so shorter than Ben's six feet and about twenty pounds heavier. "Where is Ricardo?"

Just then the door to the bathroom opened and Ricardo walked out. Beaming a Cheshire Cat smile, he introduced the boys. "I was afraid to drive in de dark, so dese guys do de driving. Maybe dey help you drive to San Franceesco?"

Martin said nothing and Ben took that as a good sign. He nudged Henry and whispered, "He didn't say 'no.'"

Henry nudged him back, hard. "He didn't say 'yes' either."

The four of them went to breakfast at a run-down diner not far from the apartment. It was a typical greasy spoon, with the heavy odor of burned grease to prove it. They shoved in around a table with so many cigarette burns around the edge it looked as if the pattern was by design. Henry pulled the ashtray toward him and took a pack of cigarettes out of his shirt pocket.

Martin sat next to Ricardo, facing Henry. "If you are going to smoke, we cannot drive together. I am not a smoker and the odor bothers me."

Ben went rigid. It was the kind of confrontation that could set Henry off.

Henry stared at Martin for a moment. Then, with a flourish, he flipped the pack to Ben. "It's your car, an' I wanted ta quit anyway."

Ben tried not to whoop with joy. They had a ride all the way to California!

The blonde waitress seemed to know Martin, smiling at him seductively when he waved her over. She wore a food-stained chef's apron over her street clothes, capri pants and a scoop-neck blouse. As she leaned over to hand out menus, she treated Ben and Henry to a brief glimpse of cleavage. She straightened, then ran her finger slowly across the back of Martin's neck. "I thought you were heading home."

He reached up and took her hand. "I am, as soon as I get the money order my father swears he sent me a month ago. There is no sense in leaving Illinois if I cannot afford to buy a plane ticket when I get to San Francisco."

Ben shot Henry a nervous glance. He returned it with a nod and a cynical scowl.

They ordered and ate in silence. Ben and Henry both settled for bowls of oatmeal. When they finished, Ricardo and Martin ordered coffee. Martin wrapped his hands around the coffee mug and looked straight at Ben. "I have been told by my friend Ricardo that you boys are going to California. Is there some particular spot?"

There was an edge to Henry's voice when he answered. "Yeah, we're headed for a town called Lodeville. My grandfather has a friend there who can get us work."

Still singling out Ben as the one to talk to, Martin sipped his coffee and shrugged. "I can drive you as far as Sacramento, but Lodeville would add a hundred and fifty miles to my trip. I would not normally mind, but the boat I am shipping my car on leaves in one week. I called my father last night, and he said the money had been sent. I explained to him that, because of the July Fourth holiday, there is no mail delivery until Tuesday. He said if it does not come then, he will send money to me by Western Union. That will give me less than four days to drive across the country and arrange shipment. If you wish to…" Martin hesitated, as if looking for the right words. Then he smiled and nodded. "To 'hang around' and wait with me, I will allow you to stay at my apartment until we leave."

The sigh of relief Ben let out seemed to be all the answer Martin needed. He picked up the check and offered his hand to seal the bargain. Ben started to slap at it the way they did at home, then caught himself and gripped Martin's hand, adult-style.

"You go to school here, right?"

"Yes, Illinois has an excellent engineering program. In September, I will enter my fourth year."

"I'm gonna go here too. Could you maybe show us around? I mean, if you've got nothin' to do but wait."

*****

193

With Martin as their guide, they strolled from the student union onto the main quad. Their benefactor identified the buildings as they passed. Ben was fascinated, but Henry made it clear to both of them that he was bored. At the far end of the campus, Martin led them around the back of the domed auditorium to show them the statue of Alma Mater. It seemed to Ben as if her outstretched arms were beckoning to him personally. He motioned to Henry. "Lorado Taft did that. He's the same guy who did the fountain near Washington Park."

Henry looked away and sneered, "Who gives a shit?"

Martin didn't change expression. "That is correct, Ben. Lorado Taft was a great artist. And, Henry, you should care. Art is what separates us from the animals."

Henry said, "Woof, woof," and turned away.

The next morning, the boys awoke late. Martin was still in the bedroom with the greasy spoon waitress, and Ricardo, who was going to sublet from Martin, had gone out to look for a roommate.

Ben rubbed his face and grinned at Henry. "So, whadda ya wanna do?"

They went to the same restaurant as the morning before. As they walked in, a beefy bald guy in a filthy apron yelled out that there was no table service. "Waitress didn't show up." He moved to the counter with a pad in his hand. "Goddamn college kids."

They ordered oatmeal again because it was cheap and filling. Ben smothered his with sugar and butter. "How come you're acting like such an asshole? This Martin guy is giving us the break of a lifetime, an' you treat him like crap."

Henry sat hunched over with his arm around his breakfast as if he thought someone would try to take it away. "I dunno, the freak rubs me the wrong way. His stupid way of talkin', an' not lettin' me smoke in the car. He keeps messin' with me, I'm gonna take a poke at him."

Ben knew it was more than talk. He'd seen Henry like this before. "Well, if you wanna screw up this deal, go ahead and get it over with. If we hang around here spending our bread on meals, we won't have enough money to take the bus back home."

"That's bullshit, Benny, an' you know it. You just like this guy 'cause he acts hoity-toity. There's gotta be other guys goin' West. We ain't even tried yet."

"Other guys who pick up the tab at a restaurant? Who don't say nothin' about gas money an' let us crash at their pad free? Go ahead, find me someone like that."

They finished eating in silence.

When they got back to the apartment, Martin was dressed and alone. "I am going to a farm not too far from here. The young man whose father owns this farm is a former classmate, and he is indebted to me for the amount of fifty dollars. I would like to collect this money before I start my trip home. I visited this farm once with a few other students, and his father loaned us shotguns to go rabbit hunting in the woods that border his property. Perhaps he would do so again. Would you two like to go?"

Martin asked Henry to drive. "I will not lie to you. This is a test to see if I will be able to sleep while you are at the wheel."

It was the kind of challenge Henry thrived on. He ran the Ford through its gears as if it were equipped with an automatic shift. If Martin resented the smug smile that crossed Henry's face, he hid it well. "Now if you stay within the speed limits, Henry, I will sleep like a child all the way to California. Turn here, and when you come to Route 45, take it south toward Savoy."

The farm was just north of Tolono. As they pulled off the road and headed toward the property, the first thing that came into view was a barn that looked as if a sneeze would finish it off. Next to the barn was a henhouse that didn't look much better. In contrast, the white farmhouse at the end of the drive, with its green trim and Adirondack porch chairs, could have graced the cover of *Farmer's Monthly*. They pulled up to the house, and Martin reached over to toot the horn. The screen door opened and a sullen young man stepped out on the porch. He scratched at the crew cut on his volleyball-sized head and stood eyeing them as if they were invaders from another planet. He was large—not fat, just big all over. An Illinois U T-shirt was stretched tight across his massive chest, with the words "Wrestling Team" silkscreened across the front. Martin got out of the car and motioned for Ben and Henry to follow him.

"Hello, Ron."

Ron didn't move. He squinted into the sun and buried his hands in the back pockets of his jeans. "Whadda *you* want?"

Martin stopped at the foot of the porch steps. "I am forced to stay in Champaign for a few more days. I thought I would come by and pick up the money you owe me. And perhaps we could do some rabbit hunting again."

Cocking his head to one side, Ron seemed to be thinking it over. "Who're the punks?"

Henry reddened and started to move forward, but Martin held both arms out to block the boys. "They are friends of mine, Ron, and they are not punks. You seem in a bad mood. Just give me my money, and we will go back to town."

An older man appeared in the doorway behind Ron. Despite the wrinkles and grizzled beard, the resemblance between the older man and Ron was obvious. "Hell, Ronnie, what you doin' keepin' company out in the hot sun? If your mother was here, she'd have your hide for not bein' social." He stood to one side of the door and waved the visitors in.

Before Martin could move, Ron turned to his father. "They come for me to take them on a rabbit hunt. Is it OK if I loan them our shotguns?"

The old man shoved his hands inside the bib of his overalls and grinned. "Damn, son, you don't gotta ask. Anytime you can get someone to shoot them furry rats, you go right ahead."

Ron motioned for them to stay on the porch while he went inside and got the guns. Claiming that his father's twelve gauge was too much for city kids to handle, he grudgingly parted with two shotguns, a sixteen-gauge for Martin, and a four-ten that he told Ben and Henry to share.

They moved away from the house and into a heavily wooded area. After a brief set of cautions from Martin—stay lined up, keep your hand off the trigger, and always know the whereabouts of your fellow hunters before firing—the three of them set off.

Ben had first crack at the four-ten, and as far as Henry was concerned, he could keep it. Guns were not high on Henry's list of favorite objects. He liked to settle things with his fists, and guns took away his advantage.

The temperature was in the nineties, but a light breeze kept it pleasant among the trees. The thick underbrush made keeping quiet almost impossible, and after an hour of seeing nothing, Henry was ready to call it a day. They had been walking alongside a shallow river for a mile or so when the water darkened and slowed, widening into a pool. Ben looked longingly into the cool depths. "I say we quit this hunting crap and grab a quick swim."

Henry and Martin agreed, and soon the three of them were buck naked and splashing around like little kids.

That's where Ron found them. He was carrying his twelve-gauge shotgun under one arm and shaking his massive head. "I told my daddy it was a waste of time having you fools try to hunt."

There was something about being naked in front of a man who was dressed that bothered Ben. He stayed in the water as long as he could, then waded out, hunching over and casually covering his privates. It didn't seem to bother Henry or Martin.

They both got out quickly and began drying themselves with their shirts. Ron tilted his head to one side and openly watched the three of them get dressed. When they were clothed, he snorted with disgust and handed them the guns they'd left leaning against a tree.

He tried to give the smaller gauge to Henry, but Henry thumbed him over to Ben. Ron sneered, "What's the matter, little sissy, afraid of guns?"

Henry's eyes squinted down to slits. "I ain't afraid of nothin'. An' if you call me sissy again, we're gonna see what you're afraid of."

It was like a mouse threatening a rhino. Ron laughed and started toward Henry, who stood his ground. Martin pushed between them. "Henry, please calm down. Take the gun, and let us go hunting."

They started through the woods again, this time, with Ron slightly in the lead. Henry carried the shotgun under his arm and pointed it toward the ground the way he'd seen Martin do. They came to a shallow depression with a narrow creek running through it and thick foliage along the opposite bank. Martin and Henry were shoulder-to-shoulder when a rabbit bounded out of the brush. Henry was so startled by the sudden movement, he shouted, "There! There!" Pointing his shotgun in the general direction of the rabbit, he yanked at the trigger. The gun bucked with a tremendous explosion that sent Henry reeling backward. He felt something slap hard against his face, and when he grabbed at his cheek, he dropped the shotgun. Martin fired an instant later—unlike Henry, he aimed. By then, the rabbit had made it as far as the creek. It flipped a few feet in the air, rolled, then collapsed to the ground. Martin and Ben scrambled down the bank to the twitching creature and Martin snapped its neck.

Grinning with triumph, Martin grabbed the rabbit by its ears and held it up for the others to see. Ben stared at the pitiful thing. He stroked its soft fur and silently vowed that he would never hunt again.

They turned to see Ron pointing at Henry and laughing. "Couldn't handle a baby shotgun, a four-ten." Ben saw the blood running down Henry's face at the same time as Ron did. Lumbering over to pick up the gun, Ron stared at the barrel for a moment, then waved the gun in Henry's face. "Ya Goddamn moron. Ya blew up my shotgun. You musta gotten dirt up the barrel. Now the fuckin' gun is ruined."

Henry examined the business end of the shotgun's barrel. It was flared out like a flower in bloom, and it was obvious that one of the pieces had broken off in the blast and flown back, cutting his cheek.

Henry wiped at the injury and stared at the blood on his hand. "I told ya I didn't like guns."

Ben ran over and checked out the cut. "It's not too deep—probably won't need stitches." He turned to Martin. "Four big hunters got one bunny rabbit, blew up a shotgun, and got one of our safari injured. Can we quit now?"

Ron collected the guns and cradled all three under one arm. In the other hand, he held the dead rabbit by its back legs. As he started back toward the farmhouse, he called over his shoulder. "Someone's gonna pay for that gun. That gun cost twenty bucks. One of you owes me twenty bucks."

When they got back to the farmhouse, Martin asked Ben and Henry to wait in the car while he went inside to talk to Ron. Within a few minutes, he came back out. His jaw was clenched so tight, knots of muscle bulged on both sides of his face. "I offered to deduct the price of the gun from the fifty dollars he owes me, but he claims he does not have any money at all. He promised to send it to me in the Philippines, but he did not ask for my address. When I said that was not good enough, he physically forced me out of his house."

He motioned to Henry to start the car. "Let us go. I have had enough of that...that..."

"Deadbeat." Ben chimed in.

"Yes, that is it, that deadbeat."

Henry made eye contact with Ben. "Jeez, Martin, I can't hit the road without takin' a leak. I'll be back in a minute."

Ben pushed the driver's seat forward and got out. "Me too; my eyeballs are turnin' yellow."

From the roar of a tractor, Henry knew that Ron's father was out in the fields. They pushed up the porch stairs and through the screen door without knocking. Ron was sprawled on the living room sofa with the radio blaring Johnny Ray. *"If your sweetheart writes a letter of good-bye..."*

Ben really had to go. He motioned to Henry to wait for him, then moved down the hall to use the bathroom. Henry had planned on stealing something he could peddle to get Martin his money, but the sight of Ron on the sofa got him so mad, the plan went out the window.

"It's no secret you'll feel better if you cry." The radio was near the living room doorway, almost within arm's reach.

Henry stepped over and snapped it off. "Martin was nice enough to loan you the dough. An' it was cool of him to take off twenty for the gun. You oughta pay him back the thirty bucks."

Ron charged off the sofa faster then Henry would have thought possible. Hands outstretched in a wrestling pose, he faced Henry. Ron had the kind of skin that burned and never tanned. Anger turned his face so red, Henry thought the guy's nose might start bleeding. "Ya fucking spic punk. Get your dirty wetback ass outta my house."

With both massive hands, he slammed out at Henry's chest. Henry staggered back and Ron advanced, aiming a second shove at him. This time, Henry dropped under the thrust and threw a sharp left jab. It caught Ron on the side of his jaw but didn't seem to faze him. He roared and rushed forward, arms outstretched as if he were trying for a waist-high tackle. Henry sidestepped and chopped down with a hard right. It stopped Ron for a moment, and Henry spun into the hallway. Like a crazed bull, Ron ran at Henry again. Dancing out of range, Henry scored with lefts and rights almost at will. He moved into the kitchen, dodging around the table and chairs to stall Ron's charges. In his blind rage, Ron tripped and almost fell. Henry moved in, using both hands to slam down on Ron's head. If the blow had any effect, Ron didn't show it. He shook it off and charged again. In a boxing match, Henry would have easily won on points, but this wasn't a boxing match. Like a pit bull cornering a rat, Ron kept backing Henry up until he managed to force Henry into a corner.

Huge arms outstretched, he faked left and moved right, finally grabbing Henry around the middle in a bone-crushing bear hug. Henry pounded away with both fists, trying to break Ron's grip, but Ron just laughed and squeezed tighter. It felt to Henry as if his ribs were being shoved into his lungs. He couldn't breathe and the pain kept getting worse as he started to black out. If he could have said something, he would have begged Ron to let him go, but he couldn't make a sound. Instead, he pushed past the pain and went limp, thinking that if he played dead, Ron would get scared and release him.

Just then, Ben walked out of the bathroom and sized up the situation. Moving fast, he came up behind Ron and buried his fist in the wrestler's kidney the way Henry had taught him. As Ron rocked back in pain, Ben threw his arm around the wrestler's thick neck in a choke-hold and screamed, "Let him go!"

Ron threw Henry aside and clawed at Ben's arm. Unable to break the hold, he tried to slam his head backward to smash Ben's nose. Ben had been in too many fights to get caught that way. He moved his head sideways and hung on. Bucking and roaring with rage, Ron pulled Ben off his feet and tried to shake the boy loose. Ben kept his hold, shifting slightly to get his arm directly across Ron's windpipe.

Henry finally managed to get his breathing under control. With his voice raspy and barely above a whisper, he got right up in Ron's face. "For your information, asshole, I'm a Mohawk." He took a step back and threw a bolo uppercut that landed just below Ron's rib cage.

There was a hoarse inhale of air as Ron curled over. Ben let go, and Henry threw another uppercut, this time at Ron's jaw. The shot caught Ron in his throat, and he crumbled to the floor. Henry took out his switchblade and held it upright. The snick of the blade was muffled by Ron's groans. He pressed the point against Ron's cheek just below his eye and snarled, "That final bone crusher is gonna cost you the price of the shotgun. Now you're gonna cough up the whole fifty bucks or be blind in one eye." The knife tip dug in, and a small stream of blood started down Ron's cheek. Ron froze.

Hiding his disgust at the intimacy of searching through another man's pockets, Ben found Ron's money clip. "I dunno, looks like about twenty bucks in all."

Moving the knife so it pressed against Ron's throat, Henry grabbed him by the ear. "Thirty more bucks or you're a dead man." Recoiling, Ron managed to bleat out, "My wallet's on the dresser in the bedroom."

*****

202

As they raced back to the car, Henry snarled, "I shoulda scalped the guy ta prove I was a real Indian."

Ben laughed and shook his head. "Nah, the guy's head's so hard, it would've dulled your blade."

Martin looked puzzled as Henry hurriedly slid behind the wheel. Still laughing, Ben shouted from the back seat, "Go, go!" just as Ron, his left cheek running with blood, came charging out of the house.

Henry popped the clutch and the Ford spun rooster tails of dirt all the way to the road.

Ben dropped a wad of bills in Martin's lap. "Ron found some money after all. He wanted you to have it."

CHAPTER THIRTY-SEVEN

Martin's check came before the banks closed on Tuesday. A little after two in the afternoon, he stood next to the Ford, saying his good-byes to Sally the waitress and Ricardo.

Sally had fixed him a bag of sandwiches and filled his Thermos with coffee. "Will you write?"

Martin tapped her lightly on the nose. "Angel, the mail service is so poor in the Philippines, I will be back for the fall semester before a letter can reach you." They kissed long and deep, with Martin gripping her buttocks and pulling her body tightly against his.

Henry was in the driver's seat of the car and Ben was in the back. Henry whispered, "If he don't quit rubbin' on her, I'm gonna have ta go inside and jack off."

They were laughing when Martin slid into the front passenger seat. "I have missed a joke?"

As Sally sobbed and little Ricardo excitedly waved them off, Henry popped the clutch, peeled rubber, and they were on their way.

*****

They drove between seventy and eighty miles an hour, stopping first for gas and later to grab a few dozen ears of corn from a field near the road. The boys had never eaten raw corn, but Martin assured them it was edible, so they tried it. After three ears, Henry announced, "Needs butter." Spewing a trail of corn cobs along the highway, they pushed on, crossing the Illinois border into Iowa a few hours into the trip.

The miles and miles through the flat fields were so dull, it was a relief when the sun went down.

Martin had done some things that started to change Henry's opinion of him. He had stuck up for them in front of Ron, offered to pay for the shotgun, and had even split the fifty bucks with the boys. "You two have earned this money. I never would have tried bargaining with that giant."

The one thing that still annoyed Henry was the snooty way Martin talked.

Martin tapped his brights on and off and passed a slow-moving station wagon. Ben was snoring in the back, but Henry wasn't taking advantage of the driver rotation to sleep. He sat in the passenger seat and stared out of the window while Hank Williams whined about someone having a cold, cold heart. Henry hated what he termed "hillbilly music," but it was Martin's radio. "Hey, Martin, I never did get your last name."

It seemed to take a while for Henry's voice to register. He was about to ask again when Martin reached over and turned down the radio. "My name is Ramos, Martin Ramos."

"Sounds Mexican."

Martin nodded. "It is Spanish. It sounds Mexican to you Americans because the Spanish invaded the Philippines in the sixteenth century and gave the natives Spanish surnames, just as they did in Mexico."

"So how come you speak English all hoity-toity an' don't got a accent like the Mexicans?"

Martin shifted in his seat and glanced over at Henry. "*Hoity-toity* English? Is that what I speak?"

"No offense."

"None taken. After the Spanish-American War, my country was taken over by America. Most of the Tagalog families have English as a second language. When I came to this country, I wanted to be an actor, so I took speech lessons. Those lessons helped me to overcome the kind of accent Ricardo has."

"Again, no offense, but even without a accent, ya talk funny." Henry affected a nasal tone. "Ya say things like 'are not' and 'you are,' instead of 'ain't' and 'you're.'"

Martin turned the radio back up. "Perhaps on this trip, you will help me to sound more acceptable."

*****

By the time they reached Nebraska, it was a little before midnight. Martin was still driving, and he smoothly downshifted as the highway led them into Lincoln. Henry rolled down his window and hung his head out for a breath of night air. "This is the cleanest town I've ever seen. The streets ain't all fulla garbage like back home. I'll bet this would be a good place to live."

Martin pulled onto a side street and parked. "The oncoming headlights are beginning to bother my eyes. I wish to stop for a few hours of rest." He slid his seat back, and within a minute, seemed to be asleep.

For a few moments, it was quiet in the car. Then Ben began fidgeting. Underneath his jeans, his crotch and legs were on fire with the worst itching he'd ever felt. When he started scratching, Henry sat up. "What's the matter?"

"Dunno, I'm itching like crazy. Maybe I walked into some poison ivy."

Henry spoke softly so he wouldn't wake Martin. "Same here, it's all the way up to my balls."

Martin groaned, "I will treat you both to some calamine lotion in the morning. Now try to get some sleep."

Henry unbuckled his belt and opened his pants. He grimaced with relief as he scratched at his groin. Then he turned toward Martin and said, "*I'll*..."

The word hung in the still air. Finally Martin let out an exasperated hiss. "You will what?"

"Ya said '*I will.*' What I was tryin' ta tell ya was if ya wanna talk like one of us, ya gotta say '*I'll.*'"

Martin sighed and closed his eyes again. "Thank you, Henry."

*****

An hour later, hard rapping on the driver's side window woke the three of them. A policeman shone his flashlight inside and stepped back with his hand on the butt of his gun. "Driver, step out of the car."

Henry started out of the passenger side, but the cop growled, "Just the driver. You other two stay in the car."

Martin got out, showed his identification, exchanged a few words, and got back in the car. "He explained to me that the streets of Lincoln were not to be confused with a flophouse and suggested that unless we wished to spend the night in jail, we should move along."

The highway was better now. It was an hour past midnight, and oncoming headlights were few and far between. "If we drive straight through to the Salt Lake area, I will..." He paused and grinned at Henry. "*I'll*...pay for a room, and we can all shower and get some sleep." He elaborately sniffed at the air. "I am sure we could all use both. After that, we should be able to drive the rest of the way without stopping."

Because Ben didn't drive, he had become the official map reader. "That's close to a thousand miles. We won't get there till tomorrow night."

207

"If we become too tired to drive, we can again pull over and nap. This time, we will use the open highway so that the local law enforcement personnel cannot complain."

Henry gave an exasperated huff and said, *Can't.*"

*****

After a quick breakfast in Cheyenne, they headed south to pick up Highway 40. The car started acting funny as soon as the elevation began to rise. Finally, halfway up an incline, it sputtered to a stop. Martin popped the hood and poured water on the carburetor. A few minutes later, the car kicked over, and they started to climb again. It stalled three more times, and each time, the treatment was the same—water on the carburetor—wait a few minutes, and go.

According to Martin, it was part of the car's normal operation. "Vapor locks. I simply use the water to cool the carburetor and all is well. It is nothing to be concerned about."

Once they descended out of the mountains into the Colorado Desert, the temperature moved up toward the century mark. By noon, Martin was too sleepy to drive, and Henry wasn't in much better shape. They pulled to the side of the road, but even with all the windows wide open, the heat in the car was unbearable. After a half-hour of simmering in sweat, Martin gave up and suggested they push on to Craig, Colorado.

As they drove into town, Henry spotted a diner with the ubiquitous "Eat" sign over the entrance and pulled into the unpaved lot. "I hope they mean eat an' drink, 'cause if I don't get a Coke, I'm gonna die."

The counter was directly opposite the entry and there were several booths along the wall. A large oscillating fan was next to the door. With a loud hum, it swept back and forth, cooling the booths but not quite reaching the counter. Except for the waitress, the place was empty.

The three of them piled into a booth and ordered Cokes for Ben and Henry and coffee for Martin.

Ignoring the flies that buzzed around, thirsty for sweat, Henry cradled his head in his arms and instantly fell asleep.

Ben waved limply at the flies and glanced over at the waitress. "We better not drive any farther. Both of you guys are beat, an' I can't drive good enough. Even if I could, I'm just as tired."

Martin wiped at his face with a handkerchief. His eyes had drooped into slits, and he seemed to be having trouble keeping his head up. "Several cups of coffee will keep me awake until this evening."

Ben started to object, but the waitress interrupted with their drinks.

She was a plump, fresh-faced girl with straw-colored hair and bright blue, knowing eyes. Smiling at Martin, she said, "I bet a whole lot of folks tol' you that you look a lot like Tuhran Bey."

Martin smiled back and nodded. "When I first came to this country, I did not know who he was. Then I was told I resembled him, and I went to see the film *Song of India*. I found him to be very handsome, so I am flattered to learn you think I resemble him."

The girl stared into Martin's eyes, blushed, then busied herself with her order pad. "Just the drinks?"

Martin held out his right hand. "I am Martin. My friends and I have driven without stopping from Illinois, and we are very tired. Could we perhaps nap here for an hour or so?" The girl seemed hypnotized. She fumbled her pad into the pocket on her apron and took his hand as if intending to shake. Martin smiled and raised her hand to his lips. Then, as he released her, he lightly stroked her palm.

The waitress pulled her hand away as if she'd been burned and glanced around as if to confirm that the place was empty. "Sure. Won't anyone be around till four or so."

*****

The slam of the screen door brought Ben instantly awake. Henry was still next to him, snoring away, but Martin had disappeared. With a feeling of panic, he checked outside to make sure the Ford was still in front.

A beanpole cowboy stood just inside the doorway and pulled off his straw Stetson. He looked around in confusion. A few remaining gray hairs were plastered flat on his head by sweat, and his craggy face was scrunched into an angry red frown.

He bellowed out, "Lucy, where the hell are ya?" There was no answer. He turned, glaring at Ben and Henry. His voice was tinged with suspicion. "Y'all seen the girl who works here?"

Ben said, "Maybe she's in the John." Then he reached over and shook Henry awake.

Eyes squinting into deep crow's feet, the man moved toward the door behind the counter. "She ain't supposed ta be in the shitter with customers out here. For all I know, you two might clean out the till while she's takin' a damn crap."

Henry stretched his arms in the air and yawned. "What business is it of yours?"

The man turned back to face Henry. The tendons in his neck had popped out, and when he clenched his fists, his whipcord muscles seemed to swell his forearms to double their normal size. "It's my place, my daughter, and the one whose business it ain't is you."

Ben grabbed Henry's arm and pulled him toward the diner entrance. "We're not lookin' for any trouble, mister." At that moment, the swinging door to the kitchen flew open and Martin rushed out, buttoning his shirt. He charged past the startled diner owner and headed straight for the front, pushing Henry and Ben ahead of him.

As they slammed through the screen door and broke into a run, Martin lateraled the keys to Henry and shouted, "Drive!"

Henry got behind the wheel as Martin and Ben piled in. From the diner came a high-pitched squeal followed by what sounded like an open-handed slap. An enraged shout of "Ya little slut!" was the last thing the three of them heard as they spewed gravel all the way back to the highway.

Henry was laughing and banging his hands against the steering wheel. "I'm guessin' ya didn't get a whole lotta sleep."

Martin was looking back in the direction of the diner. "Ah, my young friend, there are some things that are far more important than sleep."

Henry drove the rest of the way, and by eight that night, they pulled into Provo, Utah. Martin spotted a small courtyard motel with a neon **No Vacancy** sign. The **Vacancy** part was blinking, and the **No** wasn't lit.

Martin told Henry and Ben to scrunch down so they couldn't be seen. "I am paying to rent the room. I see no reason to pay for extra persons."

When he returned with the room key, they parked the car and Henry and Ben slipped inside the tiny room. Ben grabbed his nose in a gesture of disgust, and Henry nodded his agreement. The place reeked of stale urine, some kind of room deodorizer, and mildew. Shoved into one corner was a twin-sized bed covered with a stained, beige bedspread. Next to the door was a faded green armchair.

Henry pulled the bedspread off the bed and tossed it on the floor to cover the filthy rug. Using his bag as a pillow, he curled up in a ball and fell asleep. Martin loosened his belt, collapsed on the bed, and within minutes, was snoring softly. Ben stripped down to his Jockey shorts and stretched out in the chair. His legs and inner thighs itched so badly, he couldn't stop scratching. Each dig of his fingernails broke loose scabs from the places where he'd scratched himself raw and bloody. Convinced that the itching would keep him up all night, Ben closed his eyes. His last thought was regret at not asking Martin to make good on his promise to buy him a bottle of calamine lotion.

Moaning from the room next door woke him. At first, it sounded like a person in pain. Then the groans subsided momentarily and were swallowed by heavy breathing and giggling. Slowly, the giggling faded away and it grew quiet. Ben had just started to close his eyes again when the moaning burst out loud and clear.

Ben recognized the voice as female. She groaned, panted, said, "Yes, yes," and then there was a loud "Oooh," followed by quiet. Heart pounding, Ben held his breath and prayed there would be more.

The moaning began again, and this time, it was a man. "Yeah, mmmmh, yeah!" An annoyed female voice hissed, "Let go of my ears." A few moments of silence, then more moaning, then a final, "Oh yeah!"

Ben stroked himself, excited beyond control and hoping that the noise of the next-door neighbors wouldn't wake Henry or Martin. A new set of sounds began coming through the paper-thin walls—first a rhythmic thumping, then both the man and the woman groaning and shouting "Oh, oh!"

The volume rose until Ben heard a fist hammering on a wall and a distant voice shout, "Shut the fuck up!" The moaning subsided, but the thumping kept on. Finally, it stopped and there were a few moments of whispering, then the motel again grew quiet. Ben slipped off his shorts and put his pants back on without underwear. He slid the soiled shorts under the chair and went back to sleep.

They were up at five. While first Martin and then Henry took showers, Ben stood at the window, hoping to get a glimpse of the woman he'd heard during the night. He saw her in his mind as Gail Russell—all innocent looking, like in *The Angel and the Badman*. And sort of like Merle Oberon, all smoky and hot-eyed in *Temptation*. His breath caught when he heard voices and the door of the neighboring unit opened. A balding, middle-aged man with an Abe Lincoln beard and a bulging paunch waddled out, followed by a Two-Ton-Tillie with her hair in a bun. The woman was wearing a faded housedress that hiked up in back, coming within inches of failing to cover an ass that bounced like the elephant's bottom in *Dumbo*, another of Ben's favorite films.

When it was Ben's turn in the shower, he scrubbed himself clean, rinsed, then scrubbed himself clean again. He probably would have washed a third time if Martin hadn't shouted for him to hurry up. "I am in a great hurry. I want to be on the road by six."

Ben heard Henry call out, "Say *I'm* Martin, not *I am*."

*****

After stopping for gas, they picked up Highway 50. Outside of Hinckley, Utah, they were blocked by a flock of sheep being herded across the highway. The drovers seemed indifferent to cars and made no attempt to move the flock faster. The stench of wool and the blinding dust forced them to roll up the windows.

The temperature inside the car crept up until Henry couldn't stand it. "Run the goddamn things down, they'll move."

Martin began to inch forward slowly. The sheep also inched forward slowly. Henry leaned over and punched the horn, cursing the drovers, the sheep, and Utah, in that order. The men and the sheep ignored him. Now they were surrounded by the smelly beasts, and Martin got nervous.

Henry slid his foot over on the gas and the car jumped. Martin fought to shove Henry's foot off the accelerator. "What are you doing? Are you crazy? You will kill those sheep." Henry ignored him and kept pushing on the gas. Just as it seemed the car would hit an animal, the sheep managed to get out of the way.

213

Encouraged by the success, Martin held the horn down and sped up. Now sheep began to scatter in all directions. The drovers started yelling and were forced to spread out to keep the fringe animals from wandering too far. Martin gave the car more gas, and they moved past the edge of the flock just as one of the drovers turned back, shaking his fist at the car. With a final burst of speed, they roared down the highway.

Martin rolled the windows down and opened the wind wings as far as they would go.

Ben stared back at the dust cloud. "This is one really weird state."

*****

They crossed over into Nevada and stopped at Ely to eat. Ben and Henry got chili and loaded their pockets with extra crackers. Martin settled for a burger. By late afternoon, they were nearing Reno.

Henry was driving while Martin napped in the passenger seat. Ben scratched at his legs and studied the map. "We're comin' into Fallon. Another fifty miles an' we'll be in Reno. Maybe we should stop on the outskirts for a while. My mother had this boyfriend who was a big-time gambler. He said the slots outside of town are rigged in the sucker's favor. It's to pull guys in to Reno."

Martin sat up and asked for the map. "We are not going toward Reno. I am going to follow Highway 50 to Sacramento. The road branches in a few miles."

Henry shook his head and grinned. "Marty, you keep sayin' things the wrong way. Not we are, *we're*. Not I am, *I'm*."

Folding the map, Martin nodded but didn't smile. "In any case, Sacramento is our destination."

They stopped for gas outside of Carson City. As Ben walked to the bathroom, he paused to put a nickel in one of the slot machines that lined the wall. Three lemons popped up, paying twenty nickels.

He started laughing, "Shit! Mom's boyfriend was right. If we'd gone toward Reno, we coulda been rich."

The terrain began to change as they headed back up into mountains. Tall trees lined the road, and as they turned south, Lake Tahoe came into view. The beauty of the lake and the surrounding pines stunned Ben into silence. He decided the blue of the lake was the most intense color he'd ever seen. A forest of trees grew right up to the water's edge, and the breeze rippled the surface of the lake into a million sparkling diamonds.

Ben turned to Henry. "This is the place for me. One way or another, I'm gonna live here someday."

Henry gave him a quizzical look. "What for? There ain't nothin' ta do here."

"There's fishin', swimmin', an' hikin'. Besides, just lookin' at the lake makes me feel good all over."

The quizzical look turned into a sneer. "Ya got fishin' an' swimmin' back in Chi-town, an' if ya wanna go hikin', ya can stroll on down ta 55th Street. The city's excitin' 'cause there's always some kinda shit happenin'. Me, I ain't never gonna live no place else."

Outside of Placerville, Martin grew quiet. His usual serious expression became a worried frown. He gripped his chin, deep in thought, and finally shook his head. "I must leave you at Sacramento. As things are, I still may not reach San Francisco before the boat departs. If I were to make the one-hundred-and-fifty-mile round trip to Lodeville, I would have no chance to get my automobile on board."

Henry started to interrupt, but Martin held up his hand. "I have come to think of you two as my brothers, and it saddens me to leave you like this. I will drop you on Highway 99. That road is heavily traveled and provides the best opportunity for hitchhiking. Please be very careful. Do not go with those who do not seem trustworthy. Truck drivers offer the best chance of a ride. They often welcome company."

Martin pulled over before crossing the Sacramento River and let them off at a diner. He insisted on giving Henry five dollars to pay for their meal. They exchanged addresses and shook hands. Then Martin swiped at his eye with his sleeve. "I will send you a letter as soon as I arrive in the Philippines."

Henry smiled, gripped Martin's shoulder, and said, "*I'll.*"

"*I'll?*"

"Us friends say *I'll*"

CHAPTER THIRTY-EIGHT

As the Ford faded into the distance, Ben was hit with the realization that they were stranded in a strange town seventy-five miles from the only person in California who might be a friend.

He snatched the five-dollar bill from Henry. "Better not spend this. We could need it to buy us bus tickets to Lodeville."

Henry shrugged, hoisted his duffle bag up on his shoulder, and stood looking at Ben as if waiting for instructions.

Ben said, "We better hurry an' get a ride. It'sgettin' late, an' the chances of someone stoppin' are gonna go down with the sun."

They waded through the brush alongside the highway with their thumbs out, surprising grasshoppers and picking up assorted seedlings on their clothing. Cars, trucks, and even a few buses whizzed by, but no matter how hard Henry waved his arms, no one slowed or even gave them a second glance. Soon, the sky faded from gold to purple, and the headlights of the passing cars blinked on.

Ben gave one final frantic wave at a graybeard in a station wagon, and when the old man steadfastly kept his eyes forward, Ben gave up. "We should've found a spot where they had to stop. These guys are movin' so fast, they'd have a dozen cars up their ass if they tried to pull over."

Henry nodded and lowered his arm in defeat, trudging along behind Ben until they found a gas station. One attendant was pumping gas into a Pontiac sedan, and another one was busy checking the air pressure in the tires. The occupant of the car had the window down and seemed hypnotized by the spinning meter. When it hit two dollars, the attendant clicked the pump off and screwed the gas cap back on. "Check your oil?"

With a bored shrug, the driver gave permission. While one attendant wiped his windows, the one who'd pumped the gas popped the car's hood and pulled out the dip-stick. He wiped it with a rag and reinserted it. When he pulled the stick out a second time, he showed it to the driver. "'Bout a quart low."

Two dollars changed hands, and the car engine rumbled to life. "Catch it next time."

Hands on hips, the older of the two attendants watched the car head toward Sacramento.

Sum-bitch never did intend to buy no oil." He waved lazily at his co-worker. "Cheap bastard, Hope his goddamned engine burns up."

Now the station was empty. The attendant looked over at the boys, then abruptly turned and went into the station office. They scurried after him.

Ben called out, "Excuse me, excuse me. Can you tell us how to get to the nearest bus depot?"

The man went behind his desk and sat down. He stared at Ben for a moment, then swung his feet onto his desk and rocked back in his chair. He wore a filthy, grease-stained gray uniform with a Texaco star over one pocket. "It's in town, quite a ways back." The man motioned toward their bags. "Too far to be walkin' carryin' all your stuff. Tell ya what I'll do. I got my wrecker out there, an' right now, things is pretty quiet. Gimme a dollar for gas, an' I'll drive you."

Ben slipped the man a handful of coins before Henry could stop him. "Are ya crazy? Gas money, my ass. A buck's enough for four gallons."

Too tired to argue, Ben cut him off. "It's my slot machine money. I get to say what we do with it." The man added up the twenty nickels, nodded as if that settled it, and shuffled out to his tow truck. They piled in the front seat and headed back the way they'd come.

"Where you boys from?"

Henry was enraged at Ben. They'd been sharing their money since the trip began, so Henry figured that Ben had no right to separate out the dollar just because he won it. "My dumb buddy blew a buck of *our* money ta get a ride, not ta answer a bunch of questions. That OK with you?"

The man turned and glanced over at Henry. "Sonny boy, I'm gonna give you some hitchhikin' advice. Polite don't hurt, but smart-aleck can get you booted out on the highway an' back to walkin'."

Ben quickly mumbled, "Chicago, we're from Chicago."

They rode the rest of the way in silence.

The bus station was a dusty room with a row of benches facing the ticket counter. Flypaper spiraled down from the ceiling, and cigarette butts overflowed the bench arm ashtrays, littering the floor. There was a working bathroom that reeked of bleach. Ben checked the chalkboard schedule; a bus going south to Fresno was leaving at 7:00 a.m.

"Anyone asks, we're goin' to Fresno in the morning. That way, we got a reason to crash here for the night. We can try hitchin' again tomorrow."

"What if somebody asks ta see our ticket?"

Using his bag for a pillow, Ben stretched out on a wooden bench and stared at the initials, dates, and protestations of love carved into

219

almost every available inch of the backrest. "Just mumble and pretend you're too sleepy to dig it out." He turned to one side and closed his eyes.

Minutes later, neither boy would have needed to pretend.

*****

The noise of people bustling around the station woke them. It was morning, and the huge clock above the ticket counter announced that it was after eight. They breakfasted on the crackers from yesterday's chili and used the bathroom. Both boys stripped to their shorts and dug the foxtails out of their clothing. The bathroom was empty, so they grabbed the opportunity for a cold water paper towel bath to clean up and ease the fire in their itching legs. Then they headed back out to the highway.

Almost immediately, a stake bed truck loaded with empty crates pulled to the side of the road ahead of them. The driver, a stocky Mexican farmer wearing a sweat-stained straw hat and neck bandana, stared straight ahead and waited for them while the truck rattled at idle.

Grinning their thanks, the boys piled in the front and sat with their bags on their laps. The bench seat was cracked and the gear shift made it difficult for Henry to stretch out his legs, but it was a ride.

The driver pulled back onto the highway and said, "Hola, muchachos¿Para donde van?"

Henry said, "Huh?" and over the loud rumble of the engine, Ben whispered, "'Hola' means 'hi' in Spanish."

Ben knew that his two years of high school Spanish weren't going to fool the man. He shouted, "We, uh, no comprendo espanol."

The driver seemed surprised. Curiosity in his voice, he waggled a thumb at Henry without taking his eyes off the road. "¿No Mexicano?"

"Nope, I'm an Indian."

The driver switched to heavily accented English. "You Indio, but you no speak Spanish?"

220

Henry shook his head, then realized that the driver was figuring him for one of the Spanish-speaking Southwest tribes. "No Spanish Indian. I'm Eastern Indian."

A look of wonder crossed the Mexican's face. "Oh, Eastern Indio, no Spanish?"

"No, no Spanish."

The driver grinned at Henry and nodded. "Hokay."

Ben choked back a laugh, and leaned in close to Henry's ear. "He thinks you're from India. That's where the term 'Indian' came from in the first place."

An hour later, they rattled their way into a small town called Marysville. The driver pulled over and shrugged, indicating that this was as far as he was going. They thanked him and got out forty miles closer to their goal.

"Our first real hitchhikin' ride, and the guy only stopped because he thought I was Mexican. I figured when he found out I wasn't one, he'd toss us out, but he was cool."

Ben shrugged. "Most people are cool if you give 'em a chance." Ignoring the annoyance on Henry's face, he said, "I'm starvin'. Let's get a bowl of chili or somethin'."

It was almost noon, and the sun was blazing down with an intensity Henry wasn't used to. "It's almost as hot as home."

Wiping his face with the shoulder of his T-shirt, Ben said, "Yeah, but it's a dry heat. Back home, there's times when the humidity is higher than the temperature."

Henry pushed his arms through the straps on his duffel bag and hoisted the bag up on his back. "Would it kill ya ta let somethin' I say slide by without tryin' ta show me how fuckin' smart ya are?"

Ben was already red from the heat, so his flush of embarrassment didn't show. He hiked up his own bag on his shoulders and said nothing.

The first diner they came to was so tiny, it had a counter with six stools but no tables or booths. A young man was outside leaning over the fender of a truck with its hood up.

Ben tapped the guy on the back and gestured toward the eatery with his chin. "Place looks pretty small. Is the food any good?"

The guy pulled his head out and started wiping his hands on a greasy rag. He nodded solemnly. "Best in town."

They pushed in through the screen door and sat down. A teenage waitress in a stained uniform slouched against the kitchen doorway and yawned, ignoring them while they debated what to eat.

It was a discussion they'd been having the entire trip. Henry wanted oatmeal, but Ben was arguing for chili. "You get crackers with chili, an' it's cheaper."

Henry shrugged. "Oatmeal's more fillin', an' ya can get crackers with it, too. I'll bet if ya had ta sleep next to yourself after ya ate chili, you'd switch ta oatmeal too."

Ben set his menu down. He called over to the waitress. "I'll have chili an' my stupid buddy'll have oatmeal. Could we please have crackers with that?"

The waitress shrugged. "Coffee?"

Ben tried smiling at her, but she didn't seem to notice. "No thanks. Just the chili and oatmeal."

A heavy-set older woman in a print housedress and apron came bustling out of the kitchen, grinning. "I hear Midwest, and by God, it sounds good. Where you boys from?"

Ben braced himself for Henry's snarl, but it seemed as if he'd learned his lesson. Henry politely repliled, "Chicago, ma'am."

"I knew it. I could hear it all the way out in the kitchen. I'm from St. Louis myself, but I've been to Chicago lots of times. You boys plannin' on stayin' out here, or are you just passin' through?"

Henry scratched at his leg and managed to keep his hands off his privates. "We're hitchin' our way up ta Lodeville ta visit a friend."

With a frown at the teenage waitress, the woman went back into the kitchen. After a minute or so, she came out with two steaming bowls filled to the brim. She set the chili in front of Henry and the oatmeal in front of Ben. When she reached down under the counter for the crackers, Ben switched the plates. "Lunch is on me, boys. Probably the last good thing that'll happen to you out here. Most California people are mean as snakes. It ain't like home. Sometimes I think about sellin' this place an' headin' back to St. Louis."

Ben scooped up a mouthful of chili with a cracker. Still chewing, he looked up at her. "Thanks for the chow."

To show Ben he'd been listening, Henry asked, "How come ya don't go back?"

The woman sighed. "My kids'd kill me. They were both born here an' they figure it's home. My oldest boy is almost married. Maybe when I get this one hitched"— she thumbed over at the waitress—"I'll pull up stakes."

Henry spooned cinnamon over his oatmeal and topped it with a couple of pats of butter. "I know what ya mean about people around here. We had ta pay a guy a buck just ta drive us a few miles, an' the only real ride we got was from this farmer who thought I was a Mex."

The woman cocked her head thoughtfully to one side, then spun around the counter and waddled out the front door. As Ben scooped up the last few bits of chili, she came back in. "That's my boy out there workin' on his truck. He's on his way up to Lodeville to see his lady friend, an' he'll be glad to let you boys go with. Only thing is, he's got the front seat piled high with junk, so you'll have to ride in back. That bother you?"

Ben couldn't believe their luck. "No, ma'am, we don't mind at all. Fact is, we enjoy the open air."

The woman went out front to let her son know that the boys had taken him up on his offer.

Henry couldn't keep the sneer off his face. "'Enjoy the open air?' Asshole, it's close to a hundred *dry heat* degrees out there."

"Walkin' or ridin', the heat's the same. An' ridin' gets us out of the sun sooner."

Smiling at the young man, they tossed their bags in the back of his truck. While Ben waited for Henry to get, in he started scratching again. The woman gave him a sympathetic smile. "Skeeters got ya?"

Ben shook his head. "Don't know what it is, but it's not mosquitoes. We showed a drugstore guy in Provo, an' he said it wasn't poison ivy, either. Claimed he's never seen anything like it. I've got sores all up my leg, an' Henry's got 'em too."

She came around to the back of the truck. "Pull up your pant legs an' lemme see."

Ben no sooner got his pant leg up to his knee than the woman started shaking her head and *tsk-tsking*. She motioned for him to let the pant leg back down.

"Bad news, sonny boy. You've got chiggers. It's no wonder that druggist didn't know what he was lookin' at. Those little devils don't come out West. You must've done some walkin' in the woods before you came out here. Some folks say they burrow into your skin, an' the only way to get rid of 'em is to put airplane glue over the pore. You can try that, but the truth is, nothin' really helps. Try not to scratch and they'll die off by themselves in a week or two."

*****

Sitting on the flat bed of the moving truck was almost impossible. Every shift of the gears bounced them forward and back, and every curve in the road slammed them against the sides. Finally, they gave up and stood. Ben faced forward with the wind in his face. "So we got chiggers. Ron's revenge."

Henry scratched at his crotch. "It ain't revenge if he don't know about it, an' he ain't never gonna know."

Less than an hour later, the truck pulled onto Lodeville's Main Street and stopped. The St. Louis woman's son got out and came around back. "Any particular place I can drop you guys?"

Ben looked over at Henry, who shrugged. "I guess this'll do."

They got out, thanked him, and waved good-bye. As the truck rolled on down the road, Ben sat down on the curb. "Tell me what I'm thinkin' isn't true. Tell me you do know where this pal of your grandfather's lives."

Henry sat next to him. "Man, I wish I could. I really wish I could."

CHAPTER THIRTY-NINE

I t was hot and dry, with a soul-parching wind that swirled the dust and gave no relief from the heat. Ben was incredulous. "We've gotta hit the first pay phone we come to so you can call your grandfather and get the number. Maybe we can do it collect."

Henry's look of dejection was so pronounced, he needn't have said anything to Ben. "He's gone on vacation up ta Michigan. They was packin' when I left."

With a snort of disgust, Ben picked up his bag and started walking toward the center of the town.

Henry snarled, "Wait up!" and ran after him.

The straps cut into Ben's shoulders and the weight of his few belongings seemed to increase with each step. Being stymied within a few miles of their goal did more to exhaust him than the relentless heat.

They stopped at the first gas station they came to and went inside. The attendant was a friendly kid with a watermelon smile that slowly faded with their question. He scratched at the back of his head and seemed disappointed at not being able to help.

"Red Cloud? Nope, I never heard of no Red Cloud."

He let them look in the county phone book, and when there was no such listing, he used his wall phone to call someone named Emma.

"Emma, it's Dwayne Hooper, down at the gas station. Got two boys here lookin' for a friend named Red Cloud. You know anyone around here named that?" There was a long pause. "Well, I figured if anyone would know, it'd be you. Sorry to bother you." He turned to Ben. "Emma runs the post office. If she don't know someone, they don't exist."

He dug into the soda pop cooler that stood to one side of his chair and offered them each a Coke. "On the house. You both look about to die of thirst."

Ben and Henry gulped down their Cokes, thanked the gas station attendant, and having no idea what to do next, they continued walking toward the center of town.

If anything, the Coke made Ben hotter. He trudged on without speaking, each painful step seeming to emphasize the hopelessness of their situation. He figured Henry was expecting him to come up with some kind of plan, and the pressure of that made him even angrier. Going from door to door asking about George Red Cloud seemed to be their only option, and Ben was sure that would turn out to be a waste of time.

Henry nudged Ben, pointed with his chin toward a small park across the street, and headed for a tree-shaded bench. Plopping down as if never intended to get up again, he shrugged out of his duffel bag and stretched out on the bench. When Ben sat on the other end, Henry propped up on his elbows. "That guy at the station was cool. Not mean like the St. Louis lady said all California people was."

Ben just kept staring off into space. Henry swung his feet around and sat up. "OK, so I screwed up not gettin' George's address from Grandfather. You gave away a buck an' damn near got us roasted ta death in the back of that truck. Let's call it even an' figure out what we're gonna do." He sank back down and wrapped one arm across his eyes. "OK?"

Ben crossed his legs at the ankles. He sighed heavily and rubbed at his forehead. "Maybe this George guy is new in town and that Emma lady hasn't met him yet. Let's ask in the stores along this street. If we still can't find him, we'll hitch back to Sacramento. That place is big enough for us to maybe get some work so's we can earn enough to head back home."

A green and white sheriff's car pulled up to the curb, and a man in a hat like Smokey the Bear's got out. Backlit by the afternoon sun, he strolled over to the bench and stared at Henry. "You boys lost?"

Henry sat up.

Ben shaded his eyes and tried looking straight at the policeman. "We're here to visit a friend, but we don't know where exactly he lives."

The cop tucked his thumbs inside his belt and kept staring at Henry. The weight of his gun pulled the belt lower on one side, and the holster had a strip of rawhide that was tied around his leg. "Funny kind of friend, don't give you his address."

Henry cocked his head to one side. "I had his address, but I lost it. That some kind of crime in this town?"

The cop's eyes widened and he drew his head back. "Took you for a Mex fruit picker, son. My mistake. Still, Mex or no Mex, we don't allow vagrants in town. Particularly ones with smart mouths like yours."

Ben started to pull out his wallet to show the cop they had some money, then thought better of it. "Our friend's name is George Red Cloud. He's an Indian like my buddy here. Maybe you know him?"

The deputy made a sound that was halfway between a laugh and a sneer. "Indian George Red Cloud, huh?" Then his voice hardened, and he jerked his thumb toward the squad car. "Get in back."

Ben picked up his bag, but Henry didn't move. "What for? We ain't done nothin'."

The car was a four-door '49 Ford, almost identical to the one Martin owned. "Gonna check out your story. If you're tellin' the truth, you got a free ride. If not, you get a boot in the ass, a stiff fine, and a rail to ride out of town on. I know every livin' soul in Lodeville, and none of them's named George Red Cloud. There is an Indian named George though."

He stood to one side, his hand near his gun, and the boys got in the back of the sedan.

Unlike the police cars in Chicago, there was no metal screen divider between the front and back seats. While the cop walked around to the driver's side, Henry whispered to Ben. "This is the dumbest setup I've ever seen. I could slit this hick's throat and grab the car."

The cop settled in and turned to face them. "I reckon you're wonderin' why I didn't bother to check for weapons. It's 'cause before one of you little chickenshits could get somethin' out of your pocket, I'd have my pistol drawn and shoved halfway down your throat. Stay on my good side by sittin' back and not givin' me no trouble."

They rolled down Main Street past six or seven blocks of shops, including a movie theater, a couple of diners, a courthouse, and the post office. When they were almost to the end, the cop turned and took a side road that led out of town. After a mile or so, they pulled onto a gravel path and came to a dust-cloud stop behind a rusty tow truck parked in front of a farmhouse that had seen better days. There was a chicken coop to one side and a small vegetable garden on the other. In back, a fenced-in field of weeds stretched far into the distance. A white horse with black patches stood at the fence placidly eyeing them, while a collie-mix dog crawled out from under the house and started barking hysterically.

The screen door of the house flew open as they got out of the car, and a middle-aged man clomped out onto the porch. Bare from the waist up, he wore faded jeans with the knees shredded out and western-style boots, high-heeled and pointy. His ponytail whipped around as he quickly checked right and left. Then he focused in on the three people in front of him. "Vince, you're scaring the shit out of the chickens. What the hell do you want?"

Vince grinned. "George, I'm just clearin' up a misunderstanding with these vagrants. They claim to be lookin' for an Injun named George Red Cloud. Now, about fifteen years ago, I went to high school with a George Willette, who suddenly decided he wanted to become a big, bad Injun and started calling himself Red Cloud. I never heard of that name becomin' official. So I figure these boys for liars, but I wanna make sure. You don't know these punks, do you?"

Ben swallowed, worrying about the fine for vagrancy and Henry's temper. Henry, fists clenched, glared at the cop. The man called George Willette put his hands on the porch rail and leaned forward, staring at Henry. His only sign of tension was the strain of his weight on his forearm muscles. He nodded and a smile creased his face. "Damn straight I know 'em. Reason why you're confused is when I'm around my people, I use my real name, Red Cloud. Come on in, boys."

The deputy lost his grin. "Hold on, there, George. Maybe you'd better tell me their names so it's for sure you know 'em and can guarantee they ain't some troublemakers." George nodded and gave Henry a quick wink. "Tell the nice policeman your names, boys. He's here to protect you." Before Vince could interrupt, Henry blurted out, "Henry Fox, an' this here's Ben Kahn."

Vince took his hat off and used his handkerchief to wipe up the perspiration around the band.

"That was pretty slick, George. One of these days, you're gonna regret takin' in every stray this side of Fresno. I'll guarantee you the mean-lookin' little one's got a shiv. If I was you, I wouldn't turn my back on him. Still, if you say they're friends and'll vouch for 'em, I'll back off. But I'm givin' you fair warning, George. Any trouble out of these two, an' I'll be coming after you."

The farmhouse was as shabby inside as out. A worn plaid sofa with a coffee table in front and a couple of mismatched chairs filled the small front room. The floor was patterned linoleum with cracks where the wooden planking underneath had buckled. George led them back to the kitchen. "Beer?"

Both boys eagerly nodded yes.

Henry took the church key from George and popped open his beer. "We're from Chicago. My grandfather—"

George interrupted, "Sonny boy, you don't have to tell me who you are. Knew you right off. Your granddad wrote an' tol' me you might drop in. Your granddad, he's a great man. A credit to our people."

Ben sipped at his beer, trying to hold back a belch. "What's with the cop? He acted like he wanted to run us outta town."

"Nothin' to worry about. There's been trouble between the Mexican pickers and the Filipinos. Flips work fast but they're expensive. Braceros are cheap but slow. Both are being exploited by the growers. Been goin' on for years, gonna go on for lots more. Vince is like an old dog; if he can't eat something or fuck it, he pisses on it. I know him pretty good. Played football with him back in high school. He ain't a bad guy, just worries too much."

George got up and went to the refrigerator. "You boys hungry?"

Three peanut butter and jelly sandwiches apiece later, George broke out their second beers.

"So, what are your plans?"

Ben and Henry exchanged glances, and Ben shrugged. "Don't really have any plans. We just wanted to see the country. Money's getting low, though. We need to find some kind of work."

231

George rubbed his chin. "Only way to earn money around here is pickin'. It's hot, back-breakin' work that don't pay spit. You interested?"

Both boys nodded.

"Should start picking the peach crop in a few days. I got a friend what's the foreman out at one of the bigger places. Name's Danny Miranda, one of them Flips I tol' you about. He's a good guy, an' there's a bunkhouse next to his place where he might put you up. I'll run you out there tomorrow."

Ben slept on the sofa while Henry bunked on a cot in George's spare room. In the morning, George was up before the sun. The slam of the screen door woke Ben and he went into Henry's room. "Wake up."

"I'm awake, been awake since that chicken started sounding off."

"Rooster."

"What?"

"Rooster, that was a rooster crowing. They—"

"Benny, just for once, shut the fuck up. What difference does it make whether I call it a chicken or a rooster? The goddamn bird woke me up."

Ben sat on the floor next to Henry's cot. "You think we should offer to pay George somethin'? I mean, we're eatin' the guy's food an' sleepin' here."

Henry sat up and pulled on his loafers. "How much we got left?"

Ben pulled out his wallet and took a quick count. "Twenty-two bucks."

Henry shook his head. "We better hang on ta what we got."

The screen door banged and George called out, "You guys want some breakfast?"

George fixed them scrambled eggs with toast and thick, chicory-laced coffee. Ben wolfed the food down, then sat back to sip the coffee.

"George, we don't have a bunch of money, but we ain't mooches, either. We'd like to pay you somethin' for helpin' us out like this."

Mopping up the last of his eggs with a piece of toast, George glanced over at Henry. "I should've known you'd offer. You're your grandfather's boy, all right. No need to pay me. I'd be insulted if you was to insist, so say no more about it."

Ben was annoyed. After all, it was he who had made the offer. "Well, OK, if you say so. But I still think we should pay something."

Again, George turned to Henry. "I met your grandfather at a pow-wow in New Mexico. Back then, a powwow was a way for me to meet Indian women, get drunk, and raise hell. Your grandfather straightened me out. We talked for days. He made me proud I was born a Cheyenne. Turned me into an activist, an' helped me hook up with others who felt the same way. The Native Americans of this country are gonna start makin' some noise. Just you wait an' see if we don't."

Henry was bored. He'd heard it all before from his grandfather. "How 'bout us doin' some chores? Maybe we could help ya out that way."

Ben's coffee had gone cold, so he went to the pot and poured another cup.

George held out his cup and Ben filled it, too. "There is one thing you boys could do. But we can talk about it later, after we get back from seein' whether Danny needs pickers."

George jammed on a black leather cowboy hat with a hatband made from a rattlesnake skin, and they climbed into his tow truck. They chugged along the highway for a few miles, then left the paved road for a dirt one, laying a trail of billowing red dust for miles. The peach ranch was like an oasis of green in a world of rust reds and browns. "Tormino's place. He's one of the biggest ranchers in the area. Treats his pickers better than most, which ain't sayin' much."

Danny Miranda was a compact, bald man who kept his jaw clenched so tight it looked as if a smile would crack his face. He wore jeans and a denim shirt with short sleeves that had been ripped open to fit his bulging biceps. He listened to George, grunted, thumbed toward the back of his house, and walked away.

George led them around to the bunkhouse, a large one-room shack with plasterboard walls and a corrugated metal roof. There was no solid front door, just a screen door with the bottom panel torn out. A few feet to the left was an outhouse and next to it, a water pump. In front of the shack, set on bricks over a fire pit filled with ashes, was a black metal pot large enough to hold several people. There was a huge woodpile of lumber and logs to the right of the pot.

Ben nudged Henry. "We've stumbled onto a bunch of cannibals. Feet, don't fail me now."

Henry scowled, but George laughed. "You'll learn to love that big ol' pot." He pulled open the screen door and they stepped inside. Along the walls were canvas cots, a few of which looked usable. A dry musty odor hung in the air along with the faint whiff of some long-dead animal. The floor was littered with dust, dead flies, and rat droppings. Spiderwebs were the only coverings on the windows.

George looked around with a worried frown. "This gonna be all right with you boys?"

Henry waved away a fly and grimaced. "Just like home. Right, Benny?"

Ben went over and stretched out on one of the cots. "Even better...no uncles."

CHAPTER FORTY

A s they walked back toward George's truck, Danny came out of his house. "Picking starts Monday. Bring 'em out early so they can clean out the bunkhouse before they move in."

Inside the truck, George lit a cigarette and offered the half empty pack of Camels to Henry before starting the engine.

"No thanks, George. I don't smoke no more, but Benny does."

The pack was passed over and a grateful Ben pulled out a cigarette and lit up. Their money had been too tight to include luxuries, especially since Henry had decided to quit when Martin convinced him it was stunting his growth. Ben fondled the pack and was tempted to sneak another cigarette for later, but decided against it. As if reading his mind, George said, "Keep the pack. I got a carton at home."

They drove in silence until they left the dirt road and pulled onto the two-lane highway. "If you boys was serious about wantin' to do somethin' to help around the house, I got a job for you."

Ben nudged Henry, who jumped and said, "Yeah, sure, whatever ya want."

"Well, here's the thing. My bitch collie got knocked up by a coyote some time back. She went inta the crawl space under the house and dropped four pups, nursed 'em for a couple of months, then got fed up with the mother thing and walked away. Three of the pups come out, no problem, an' I give 'em away. The fourth won't move. He's gonna die under there, and the stink'll be in the house for a month."

George flipped his butt out the window and turned to Henry. "I'm too big to fit in that crawl space, but you just might make it. I was hoping you'd go under there and drag the poor thing out."

*****

Ben knelt at the opening to the crawl space and listened to Henry complain. "You're the one who figured we owed George a favor, but I'm the one who's gotta do the work. There's spiders and all kinds of shit in here." The dog was in a shallow depression just a few yards from the opening. Ben held the flashlight as Henry crawled forward. "OK, little puppy, time ta see the real world."

The light reflected in the creature's eyes and the animal made a noise that sounded more like a squeak than a growl. Henry reached out his hand. "Here, puppy. Ow! Goddamn it, the little son-of-a-bitch bit me." He reached for the pup again, but this time it slithered under a series of pipes. Henry backed out, holding his hand. A ring of bloody pinpricks circled the area between his thumb and forefinger. "I can't get the little fucker outta there. He squirrels back just outta my reach. George is gonna have ta shoot him and drag out the carcass."

While Henry went into the bathroom to get a Band-Aid for his hand, Ben got a six-pack of hot dogs out of the refrigerator. He knew Henry would freak out over owing George a replacement package, but he wasn't going to let them kill the dog without trying to save it. He yelled in to Henry, "Stay in the house. I'm going to try to coax the thing out."

Ben moved to the opening and started talking in a soft, sing-song voice. "Here, puppy. Come on out and eat some food." He set the flashlight down on its side so that it would provide light but not shine directly in the animal's eyes. The puppy stood and gave a squeaky puppy growl. He watched Ben warily, but he didn't move away. After half an hour, he settled back down.

Ben broke off a piece of hot dog and gently lobbed it toward the pup. The dog jumped to its feet and disappeared into the maze of pipes. Ben stayed where he was. The day was another scorcher, but the farmhouse provided shelter from the direct sun.

After about twenty minutes, Ben rolled over on his back and his eyes started to flutter closed. He was almost asleep when a slight rustle alerted him. Slowly turning his head, he watched as the pup crept on its belly toward the food. This was his first good look at the animal. It had gray and white markings on its chest and a head like a collie, but it had the shorter hair and ears of a coyote.

Suddenly it pounced, grabbed the piece of hot dog, and scurried back out of the flashlight's fading glow. Ben rolled over on his stomach and tossed in another larger piece. This time, he let it land a few feet closer to the opening. Less time passed before the dog came back, but the pouncing and retreating stayed the same. Ben put out another piece and began singing. He started with Brahms's lullaby. *"Lullaby and goodnight, may the angels surround you."* Deciding it was as good as anything else, he just kept repeating it.

By sundown, Ben had the dog eating the meat where he threw it without rushing back under the pipes. The flashlight batteries had long since died and there was no moon, so Ben gave up for the night, went inside, and crashed on the sofa.

He awoke before either George or Henry. Pulling the remaining hot dogs out of the refrigerator, he headed back to the crawl space. It was as if the puppy had been waiting for him. Instead of moving back to the lair, the dog was on his belly only inches from the opening. Ben

237

knelt down and started singing again. He broke off a piece of the meat and dropped it just outside the crawl space. The puppy scooted forward and snatched it up. Then Ben put a piece in the palm of his hand and held it out as an offering. The dog sniffed at the hand and cautiously grabbed the food. Ben wanted to shout with triumph, but he forced himself to stay still and keep singing.

After the puppy finished the hot dog, he licked the moisture off Ben's hand, and Ben stroked his head as he gave him the rest of the meat.

George fixed them French toast with jelly for breakfast. "That is one fine-lookin' pup. Gonna be big, too. I won't have any problem findin' someone to take him. Spooky as he was, I can't figure how you got that creature to come out." He put his hand on Ben's shoulder. "I think your totem must be the coyote. He saw your soul."

The puppy was tied up near the crawl hole with a rope that was long enough for him to get back under the house. Ben had fed him a full meal of kibble and put out a bowl of water. He wanted to keep the puppy so bad, his stomach ached with it, but he knew it was impossible. Even if he could have somehow gotten the animal home, his mother would have sent it to the pound the minute she saw it. She had no use for animals of any kind, especially dogs. Well, at least George would find him a good home. He went quiet and sipped his coffee.

Suddenly, an eerie yipping howl sounded from outside. George's forehead furrowed and his mouth turned down. "Uh, oh. Sounds like that pup got more coyote than collie."

Ben felt a prickle of fear. "Is that bad?"

George avoided his eyes. "Hard to say. Some things is wild an' there's nothin' anyone can do about it. I wouldn't go namin' that dog just yet."

Ben looked out the back door screen at the pup he'd named Smoke; he didn't tell George it was already too late.

CHAPTER FORTY-ONE

It was still dark on Monday morning when George drove them out to the peach ranch. The radio was on—Les Paul was trying to find out how high the moon was with an electric guitar. Henry asked if they could change the station.

"You don't like jazz music?"

"The guy playin' use ta be a real jazz guy. Then he sold out an' went for the big bucks."

George changed to a news station. "Can't blame a guy for that."

The news was all about the war in Korea, and with a frown, George snapped it off. "That 'police action' keeps goin' much longer, you kids'll get your asses drafted."

They pulled onto the ranch road and stopped at Danny's house. George signaled the boys to stay in the truck while he went to Danny's door. "Danny can be kinda funny sometimes. It's best not to surprise him."

Danny came out and nodded George and the boys toward the bunkhouse. They dropped off their belongings, unfolded a couple of the less beat-up cots, and made a halfhearted attempt at sweeping up the place. George seemed reluctant to leave them, but when he saw Danny and a group of Filipinos heading for the grove, he quickly urged the boys to follow the crowd. Dawn was just breaking as their only friend in California waved good-bye and drove off.

Earlier, George had lent them each a long-sleeved shirt and bandana, urging them to keep the sleeves down and the shirt buttoned to the neck. "Keeping that peach fuzz off your body's gonna trump putting up with a little extra heat."

Before the dust from George's truck had settled, Henry rolled up his sleeves and unbuttoned the neck of his shirt. As he walked along, he tied the bandana around his head, pirate-style, and gave Ben a satisfied grin. "Now I'm lookin' cool."

Danny wore bib overalls and an undershirt that exposed his freakishly overdeveloped shoulders and arms. His pant legs were tucked into high rubber boots. Carrying an irrigation shovel on his shoulder, he took long, purposeful strides that made it hard to keep up. No one spoke as the group trotted along the dirt road. A few of the pickers, shirts buttoned to the neck and sleeves rolled down, took quick glances over at Henry and grinned. To Ben, their interest seemed more curiosity than hostility, but Henry didn't like it. He let his facial expression go flat and stared straight back. Those who caught his eye quickly looked away.

"That guy Danny ain't got his arms covered."

Ben did a quick double-step to catch up. "He's the boss. Bosses don't do any picking."

When they reached the edge of the grove, Danny motioned for them to pick up ladders that were unlike any ladder either boy had seen before. The ladders had three legs. There was the kind of ladder you would put up against a wall, with a center pole that extended out for additional support.

The foreman assigned each of them a group of four trees.

Stacks of lug boxes, well-worn cotton gloves, and empty sacks with a shoulder strap were set at the entrance to each row. Henry pulled on a pair of gloves, grabbed a sack, and threw the strap over his shoulder. Then he leaned his ladder against one of the trees and scampered up to the top.

The morning was just starting to warm up, and it was noticeably cooler in among the leaves. The limbs of the tree sagged under the weight of peaches that were twice the size of any Henry had ever seen in Chicago. They were rose-colored where the sun hit them, more golden where the leaves provided shelter.

In a grudging tone, Danny had warned them not to pick any fruit smaller than four inches across. But that was no problem; the peaches on Henry's tree were the size of baseballs. Henry started grabbing peaches and stuffing them into his sack. Within minutes, the weight of the sack cut deep into his shoulder. He climbed down and emptied it into one of the lug boxes, half filling it, then he climbed back up the ladder.

This time, it was not so cool within the shade of the leaves. He wiped at the perspiration on his face and kept on picking, up and down and up again, nonstop. An hour later, Henry took a break. He chugged water from the bucket put out for the pickers and propped his back against a tree. The pickers weren't paid by the hour. They earned twelve-and-a-half cents per box. Henry had picked two full boxes. After almost two hours of back-breaking work, he'd earned a quarter.

During the next two hours, Henry tried to hit a rhythm. He went up and down the tree fewer times, waiting until he could barely manage the weight of the sack before heading for the boxes. The bottoms of the trees were easier because he didn't have to use the ladder.

The sun was blazing by the time he decided to break for lunch. His face, neck, and arms tingled with what felt like a sunburn, and every muscle was numb with fatigue. His total count was ten boxes, a dollar and a quarter for half a day's work.

He moved over to a shady spot beneath some unpicked trees and stretched out.

Ben came over and sank down next to him. "I'm either dyin' or dead. No, I must be dyin', 'cause I wouldn't hurt this much if I was dead. How many boxes you picked?"

Henry stood, pulled a couple of fat peaches off the tree, and tossed one to Ben. "Lunch." He quickly counted his boxes. "I got ten; how 'bout you?"

Ben took a bite, juice running down his chin. "You must've had good trees, I only got nine. I wonder if they'll give me the benefit of the half-a penny."

Henry flopped on the ground. "At this rate, we ain't gonna be able ta make enough ta buy food. We're gonna have ta live on peaches."

A voice floated over from a nearby tree. "You go to dee boxes too much. An' you stay in one place too long."

Henry was too tired to argue. He turned toward the Filipino who'd spoken. "How many boxes have you picked so far?"

A wizened little man came over and knelt beside them. He had his bandana covering most of his face, bandit style, and though he looked to be in his sixties, his movements were that of a much younger man. He said, "Rudy Rivera." It came out sounding like Ribeera. "I pick one hundred and fifty-nine boxes, but I not dee best picker. Dee best picker, he got over two hundred."

Henry stared at the man in shock. "A hundred and fifty-nine boxes?"

Rudy nodded with a gap-toothed grin and waved toward a stack of filled boxes some distance away.

Henry had just started to calculate when Ben said, "Jesus, that's almost twenty bucks. Can you show us how to make that kind of dough?"

Wariness crossed the small man's face. "Danny ees my cousin. He say to take care of you, but he don't pay me for it. I got to pick for myself. You watch me, maybe you catch on."

Four hours later, they called it a day. After watching Rudy, Henry had altered the way he picked. He didn't try for every peach on the tree, concentrating instead on the ones that were clustered together and easy to grab. Moving the ladder took time, so he reached as far as possible to each side before climbing down. The bag cut into his shoulder but he managed to endure the weight until it was full. Now, when he emptied his bag, its contents filled two boxes. His afternoon total was twenty-nine boxes. Added to the ten he'd picked before lunch, he'd earned four dollars and eighty-seven cents for the day. Not good, but better.

Ben came stumbling along and they walked to the bunkhouse together. Henry wiped the sweat off his forehead and winced. "Shit, I'm on fire. I must've got a sunburn."

"Me too, but it ain't sunburn. I had sunburn before an' it doesn't feel like this. This is some kinda rash."

The sing-song voice of their Filipino friend floated from behind them. "It ees dee peach fuzz. Maybe you rub your face? Tomorrow you cover up, don't get so much fuzz."

They stopped and waited for Rudy to catch up. When the three of them arrived at the bunkhouse, the grinning man motioned for them to wait. He moved to the woodpile and carefully started pulling out some old two-by-fours.

As he pulled the wood, a sudden black cloud rose above the pile and the ominous buzz of thousands of bees filled the air.

"Dere ees a beehive in dee woodpile. You be careful when you take dee wood, or dey swarm you."

Rudy shoved a few pieces of kindling into the fire pit beneath the huge kettle and put the larger wood planks on top. With a squirt of lighter fluid, he started a fire.

Pointing to a couple of buckets, he told the boys to bring water from the pump. It took fifty trips to bring the water level high enough for a bath, making their arms almost as sore from pumping as they were from picking.

Thirty minutes later, they doused the fire, and the three of them immersed themselves in the pot to wash away the irritating peach fuzz. They dried off, and while Rudy went to Danny's to get some zinc oxide for their peach rashes, Henry grabbed the roll of toilet paper propped next to the bunkhouse door and headed for the outhouse.

The stench inside was almost too much. At first, he tried holding his nose, then he switched to breathing through his mouth. The sides and roof of the structure were covered with spiderwebs, some intricately patterned with perfect geometric forms, others haphazardly spun. A cloud of flies rose from deep within the pit, thrown into a frenzy over Henry disturbing them. A few bees from the woodpile buzzed around his head but he froze, and they didn't sting him. Finishing his business as quickly as possible, he hauled up his jeans and got out of there.

Ben, who had used the outhouse before their bath, was grinning as Henry barreled out. "I bet you wished you still smoked. It sure cuts down on the stink."

It was still several hours until dark, and Henry was hungry. He waved as Rudy came strolling up with the tube of ointment. "How can we get ta town ta buy somethin' for dinner?"

Rudy squeezed out some zinc and smeared it on Henry's face, neck, and arms. Then he turned to Ben and did Ben's face. He nodded toward the foreman's house. "Danny say in one hour, you come eat wiss him. How 'bout we go fishing till den? When dee sun almost down, dee catfish, dey bite good."

He showed the boys where Danny kept a number of bamboo poles, and they started off for a tributary of the Yuba River that formed the border of Tormino's property.

The river was shaded by huge California oak trees that grew at the water's edge. Rudy pulled a package of soft cheese from his pocket and showed the boys how to roll it into balls and wrap it around their fishhooks. Then he disappeared around a twist in the river. Henry dropped in his line at a clear spot on the bank. His exposed parts still burned, and every muscle in his body ached with a vengeance. He sat down in the soft weeds and gripped his pole with his knees. Using his shoes as a pillow, he let his head sink back, and within minutes, he was asleep.

When the line tugged, he awoke so startled that the thrashing fish almost yanked him into the water. Henry groaned with muscle pain, dug his feet into the bank, and stared as the pole bent into a perfect arc. He yelled for help and hauled on the pole, scrambling backward up the riverbank. The line stayed tight, and suddenly, a foot-long catfish burst from the water and flopped up next to Henry, jerking spasmodically. Henry jumped up and down, screaming, "I got one! Jesus, I got a fish."

Ben ran up and helped pull the hook out of the fish's mouth. Its long whiskers quivered, and its gills pumped feebly as it tried to breathe in the air. Rudy came strolling over holding a string of three fish, each one larger than the one Henry had caught.

It didn't matter. Henry wanted to keep shouting, to scream to the heavens that he'd caught a fish—that from here on out, he, Henry Fox, needed no one, he could feed himself by fishing for his food.

He smiled at Ben and handed the fish to Rudy. Rudy held up the string. "I take dee fish, salt dem, an' put dem on dee roof in dee sun. Pretty soon dey dry out, an' you can eat dem wiss beer like crackers."

Dinner was served at a table in back of the house by Danny's wife, Viola. She was pretty in a plump, comfortable way. Her hair was ginger-colored, and she had the kind of freckled skin that undoubtedly became a misery in the sun.

Rudy was also invited and sat next to Carmen, Danny's eight-year-old daughter. There was fried chicken, mashed potatoes, and green beans. A jug of red wine was brought out, and Danny, seeming to understand that they wouldn't dare do it themselves, poured for the boys.

During the meal, Danny managed a few yeses and noes, but otherwise, said nothing. While Viola cleared away the dishes, he went into the house to get homemade ice cream.

Henry leaned over to Ben and whispered, "I never had no Flip food before."

Ben stiffened. "This is regular American food. And don't say 'Flip.' It's really rude."

Henry flushed, causing his rash to heat up. "You gonna tell me which side of the paper I should wipe my ass with, too?"

Carmen tugged at Rudy's sleeve and pointed an accusing finger at Henry. Her upturned nose quivered with indignation. "He said a bad word, an' I'm gonna tell Daddy."

Later, the boys lay in their cots, kept awake by noises they couldn't identify. Henry stared out the window. "I didn't know 'Flip' was a bad word."

That was as close as Henry could come to an apology. He could feel Ben smiling in the dark and was relieved when Ben said, "It's not that bad. Not like 'nigger' or 'kike' but it's rude. Anyway, we're cool."

An owl hooted and the crickets quieted for a moment. Henry propped his head up with his arms. "This has been the best day of my life. How 'bout you, Benny boy, are you diggin' this as much as me?"

Ben's answer was a muffled snore. The owl flapped away into the night and the crickets kept on chirping.

CHAPTER FORTY-TWO

The next day was much like the first day except both boys now had rolled down sleeves and buttoned at the neck collars.

That evening, after picking, Henry went for firewood from the pile and yanked a two-by-four from the bottom. When the board above it clattered too close to the hive, the bees rose in an angry cloud. A swarm headed for the outhouse and buzzed around it, but after a few minutes, they headed back to the hive. Henry shaved some kindling with his knife and packed it in the fire pit under the big kettle. Then he laid the boards on top and lit a fire.

The pot had to be stirred like a giant bowl of soup or the water on the bottom would be scalding while the top was still cool. Henry shouted over to Ben, who was sitting by the shack door picking at one of the few scabs left over from his bout with chiggers. "I got the wood, you gotta stir."

Ben shuffled over and grabbed the large wooden paddle Rudy had left for them. He stirred until steam started to rise over the surface of the water. Then he got up on the lip of the cauldron, dipped in a toe, and when it didn't scald him, he slid the rest of the way in. "Soup's on."

Henry heaved a bucket of water on the fire, stripped naked, and joined Ben. They were splashing and laughing when Danny's daughter

Carmen came marching up. Her cherubic face broke into an evil grin when she realized that she'd caught them without their clothes on.

Embarrassed, Ben ordered her to leave. When that didn't work, he tried bribery. "I'll give you a dollar if you go home right now."

Her grin widened. Pulling at the clothes the boys had left on the ground, she made a pile of them and sat down. "No."

Finally, Ben threatened to tell her father.

Hands on hips, her eyes narrowed, "I live here an' you don't. I can go where I want. Mr. Tormino told me so."

Henry whispered to Ben that he'd pretend to climb out, figuring that she'd get scared and run home. He put one leg on the lip of the kettle and gripped the edge with his hands. When Carmen called his bluff by not moving, he sank back under the murky water.

They sat for close to an hour as sundown approached. The air temperature dropped, the water cooled, and still Carmen stood, watching them. Ben began to shiver. "What is it you want?"

She rolled her eyes. "I wanna see your weenies."

Henry cupped his hand and tried to splash her, but she was too far away. "You're just a little girl. How would you like it if I told your dad what you just said?"

The smirk was hard to see because it had grown dark, but Henry could hear it in her voice. "I'd tell him you were a liar, and he wouldn't believe you."

In the end, Carman's mother, Viola, saved them. She came storming from around the side of the bunkhouse, screaming her daughter's name. "What did I tell you about stayin' out past dark?"

The boys couldn't tell if she'd heard what Carmen had said, or was just upset that the child hadn't come home on time. They didn't much care. The sight of the brat being dragged off by one arm, getting her bottom swatted along the way, was sweet enough.

The next night, after a day of picking that saw each of them top fifty boxes, Ben suggested they go to the river to clean themselves. Carmen's antics didn't really worry him, but he decided that avoiding her was the wiser course. Henry pretended not to understand why Ben wanted to skip the kettle in favor of a swim, but he, too, had an uneasy feeling when it came to Danny's daughter.

They were walking back from the river when their friend George Red Cloud showed up and offered to drive them into town for hot dogs.

The only place in town that served Frankfurters was a ramshackle place with an open counter that faced the parking lot. A faded sign advertised good food and car service. George grinned and waved them out of the car. "That sign's fulla shit on both counts. Ain't been a carhop here since I was in high school. An' it's no wonder, bad as the food is."

Henry nodded as he bit into his hot dog. The things were tasteless and sort of squishy, with no resistance when you bit into them. For the first time since hitting the road, he had a twinge of homesickness for Chicago. He could almost feel the pop of the skin on the Polish dogs that the Post Restaurant served back home. Ben seemed to agree. He took one bite, made a face, and tossed his in the garbage when George wasn't looking.

Broken Arrow starring Jeff Chandler was playing at the movie theater. They sat in the first row, and when the Apache chief, Cochise, agreed to end the fighting with the white man, George booed.

After the movie, they asked George to stop at the grocery store so they could stock up on potato chips and Twinkies. He shook his head. "Bad idea, rats'll clean ya out two minutes after ya leave for the fields."

*****

On Thursday, Danny sent Rudy over with another dinner invitation. This time, it was rabbit stew, and while they finished off the

249

homemade ice cream, Viola started asking them questions about life in a big city. "I'm just a country girl myself, born an' raised right here in Yuba County. Danny, he's been all over. He was in the Philippines durin' the war, an' he's been to New York City, too. One of these days, we're gonna take a trip there." She turned to Danny and smiled. "Aren't we, honey?"

Danny grunted something unintelligible, but it seemed to satisfy Viola. Carmen kept frowning and staring, first at Ben then at Henry then back to Ben again. Once, Ben caught her eye, and she stuck out her tongue and glared until he looked away.

By the end of the week, Henry was up to sixty-five boxes a day. He secretly counted Ben's boxes and always made sure to fill at least one box more. Ben never seemed to notice.

They were looking forward to getting Sunday off, but it was not to be. A grinning Rudy rousted them out of bed. "Dee peaches, dey doon know 'bout Sunday."

*****

Nine days later, the crop was picked, and there was nothing left to do. Henry had earned sixty-seven-and-a-half dollars, while Ben's take was an even sixty-four bucks. Rudy drove them into town to cash their checks, dropping them off at the bank. He was headed for San Francisco to play the Chinese lottery, and the boys—they were going to stay with George—would have to walk from the bank to the Cheyenne's house.

The bank was tiny, just one teller and a table with deposit slips. Tormino's name on the check seemed to carry some weight because the boys got both checks cashed without any need for identification.

Ben counted his money and added it to the meager amount he had left. "We got a hundred an' fifty between us. Should be enough. Let's hit the bus station to see what bus tickets home are gonna cost us. Then we can figure how much we got left to spend."

They walked down Main, expecting the station to be within walking distance. As usual, the day was baking hot. There were a few trees planted along the street, but they were too stubby to offer much shade. The sidewalk was deserted except for a mother pushing a baby buggy. She smiled and nodded at them as she passed. Traffic consisted of one rattling truck, sputtering its way up the road on fewer than four of its eight cylinders.

After going from one end of town to the other in search of the bus depot, Henry shrugged and gave up. Without checking to see if Ben was following, he was halfway across the street when he realized that Ben had stopped and was looking in the window of a clothing store. Annoyed, he walked back. "How come ya didn't think ta ask where the bus station was when we was at the bank?"

Ben didn't turn around. He kept staring in the window. "How come you didn't?"

There were different sized risers in the window with shirts and ties draped over them and small price tags pinned on the merchandise. Farthest back was a rack with several pairs of black pants and a sign that read, "100% wool." Under that was a price tag. Ben shook his head in disbelief. "Can that be the price? Five bucks for real wool pegged pants?"

Henry had seen the price tag and was already headed inside the store.

The clerk assured them that the price tag was right and they both bought a pair. Henry came strutting out of the fitting room. "I'm wearin' mine."

"It's too hot for wool, isn't it?"

"Just till we get ta George's house. I wanna see his face when he catches sight of us in these cool drapes. I gotta quarter says he'll come buy some before they're all sold out."

When their belts proved to be too thick to fit the narrow loops of the pants, they disguised the lack by letting their shirttails hang out. They transferred their wallets and things into the pockets of their new pants and stuffed their jeans and belts into a bag supplied by the store. Mock-boxing with each other, they strolled back out onto Main.

The first clue that something was wrong came when the woman with the baby buggy they'd seen earlier almost bumped into them. Instead of smiling and nodding as she'd done earlier, she shrank back, spun the buggy away, and almost ran in the opposite direction.

Henry shoved his hands in his pockets and slouched. "What's with that crazy bitch?"

Ben shrugged and they headed for George's place.

Neither boy paid any attention to the police car that passed them going the other way. They didn't see the cop inside do a double-take, but when the car flipped a tire-squealing U-turn, they stopped to see what was going on. The squad car slammed to a stop and the cop came barreling out, waving his gun and hollering "Freeze!"

The order didn't make sense because they weren't moving.

Henry looked up and down the street, trying to figure out who the cop was yelling at, then suddenly realized the cop was coming for them. Both boys were too startled to run. This deputy wore the same uniform as Vince, but there were subtle differences. His holster wasn't tied to his leg, and a baton, flashlight, several cartridge holders, police whistle, and a pair of handcuffs were all attached to his gun belt. His pants were pulled up high, forcing the bulge of his belly to protrude below the belt. While Vince's hat had been set forward on his head, marine-style, this guy wore his hat straight, with the brim pushing down on the tops of his ears.

He cuffed Henry's right hand to Ben's left and forced them into the back seat of the Ford.

"Excuse me, Officer, can I ask what we done that was wrong?" Henry asked, then gave Ben a "See how polite I can be" smirk. Ben sneered.

The cop pulled into the police station without answering.

Ben was surprised at the size of the station. It seemed large for a town as small as Lodeville. Behind the counter were two desks facing one other and a door on the left marked "Chief of Police." To the right, a second door stood open, and Henry could see the bars of the holding cells in back. The deputy removed the cuffs and ordered them to empty their pockets. When Henry realized that the guy wasn't going to pat them down, he cursed himself for adding his switchblade to the pile.

Ben rubbed his wrist and did his best to look older. "Officer, we've got a legal right to know what you're arresting us for."

The deputy pushed them past a swinging half-gate and thumbed toward the dimly lit cell area. "Inside."

The first two cells were locked, each occupied by a snoring man. The reek of beer and vomit was mixed with the foulest breath Henry had smelled since he left his father's house. They shuffled down the corridor to the last cell. Once inside, the deputy slammed the bars shut and turned to go.

Ben tried once more. "My father's an important man. I'm sure he's going to sue you and the town of Lodeville for this outrage."

The cop turned back and faced Ben. "You open that smart pachuco mouth of yours one more time, an' that important daddy of yours won't have enough left of you to worry about. Onlyest thing I hate worse than a badass beaner is a white kid who wants to be just like 'em." With that, he walked out, slamming the door behind him and leaving the boys alone.

"What the fuck's he talkin' about?"

Ben got up and started pacing. "I'm not sure, but he thinks you're Mexican. And for some reason, that says to him that we're criminals." He sat on the metal cot and grinned. "I may move out here. These people are so busy hatin' Mexicans, they don't seem to worry about Jews."

On the back wall between the two cots was a commode without a seat. Henry had just finished taking a leak when the door from the office opened and the cop lumbered in, followed by Vince.

"Got two of 'em. Pachuco assholes walkin' up Main Street, bold as brass. The Mex got a switchblade, but the big white kid wasn't armed. They both was carryin' bags with them thick kind of belts and the buckles was razor sharp."

Vince looked over at the cell. "Aw shit, Calvin."

He stared in at Henry. "What the hell was you doin' in a zoot suit?"

Ben moved up to the bars. "What's a zoot suit?"

"Them pants you're wearin'. The ones with the narrow cuff. Them's zoot suit clothes."

Henry jumped to his feet, but Ben held him back with his hand. "We just bought those pants from a store two blocks from where your friend arrested us. They're in style back in Chicago."

Vince's mouth turned down at the corners, and shook his head. "Let 'em out."

"But Vince, it's against the law to wear that shit in town."

Vince's sigh was deep and prolonged. "The boy ain't even Mexican, Calvin. He's an Indian. An' he's a friend of George Willette. What we *should* do is arrest that moron Charlie Wilton at the clothing store for not tellin' these kids it was against the law to wear them pants. Now let 'em out."

They retrieved their belongings and Vince drove them to George's place. "That knife you're sportin' is illegal in California. You best-better put it in your bag till you get home. There's some funny laws up here, so I suggest you walk a little light till you catch on."

They turned in at George's place and Vince cut the engine. He rolled his finger under Ben's nose. "I'd shave that smudge you got growin' under your nose, an' both of you should trim your hair. Calvin's gonna be gunnin' for you 'cause you made him look like a fool. Thing is, he is a fool, but he don't like bein' reminded of it. Tell George I said 'hi.'"

They got out and watched Vince spray up a cloud of dust as he pulled away.

In the kitchen, George popped the top off three bottles of beer. The boys had changed back into jeans, but Henry wouldn't give up his knife. It went back into his pocket.

George took a deep swig and leaned back. "Pachucos was a bunch of Mexican gang kids who got into trouble durin' the war. They fought with sailors on leave an' wore zoot suits that included pegged pants like the ones you guys bought. I owe Vince for this. Told you he wasn't a bad guy."

Henry rolled the icy bottle across his forehead. "That other guy, Calvin, he's nuts. He pulled a gun on us."

"Yeah, he's nuts, all right. But so's the rest of this town. Pachucos never did come up this far north, but they passed that stupid ordinance anyway. That's not the only dumb law they got. Every time the town sees some kinda problem, one of the council members comes up with a stupid solution. You're lucky you zipped those pants all the way up. If Calvin caught you with a low zipper, he could fine you.

"When the braceros first started workin' up here, they didn't know that just whippin' out their willy and takin' a leak against the side of a building offended people. Instead of passin' a law that says no out-door pissin', these fools decide to fine anyone whose fly is unbuttoned. Five bucks a button and twenty-five for a zipper."

255

Henry laughed and mocked wiping the sweat off his brow. "Benny boy, it's outhouses only from now on. No more pissin' in the street."

Ben smiled and then let a few beats go by before he changed the subject. "Is the dog back under the house? I haven't seen him around anywhere."

George rubbed his forehead and looked down. "No way to sugar-coat this, Ben. The dog's buried out back. Started killin' chickens, an' I couldn't have that. I had to put him down."

Ben felt the catch in his throat that warned of tears. He swallowed and clenched his teeth. "Yeah, can't have that." Pressing a fist to one eye, he stood and turned away.

They polished off another couple of six-packs, and soon, both boys were drunk.

Thinking about the dog, Ben started to weep.

George put his arm on the boy's shoulder. "Some creatures is just wild, Benny, an' there ain't nothin' you can do about it. They can't adjust to livin' domestic."

It had seemed Henry wasn't listening, so Ben and George were surprised when he spoke. "I guess it's like what Grandfather says about our people. Some of 'em, like my dad, just can't adjust ta the white man's ways. Sometimes, I wish someone woulda had the good sense ta put him down."

CHAPTER FORTY-THREE

Henry woke up the next morning with a pounding beer headache and queasy stomach. He followed Ben into the kitchen, where George was already fixing breakfast. "I know I ain't ever gonna end up like my old man. The hangovers would kill me before I got anywheres near as bad as him."

Ben closed his eyes and carefully nodded back.

Grinning, George crushed some shredded wheat biscuits into three bowls. "Next time, you boys should drink a glass of milk first. Coats your stomach." He sat at the kitchen table and covered his cereal with raisins.

"After first pickin', Tormino waits a few days, then sends in a second crew. It's four days of work, and you don't get paid by the box, you get paid hourly. It's slow work, 'cause you gotta use a measuring ring an' make sure no undersized peach gets picked."

George glanced up at Henry and smiled. There was a raisin stuck on his front tooth, making him look sort of clownish, but Henry was in too much pain to care.

"The Filipinos won't work that cheap, so Tormino brings in a bunch of braceros to do it. Danny says if you guys wanna pick, he'll put you on. It pays a buck and six-bits an hour an' all the peaches you can eat."

Henry's face crumpled, the thought of food pushing bile and beer up toward his throat. For a moment, it felt as if he was drunk again. He pushed the cereal away and reached for the cup of coffee George had set on the table. "If I have ta eat one more peach, I'll puke my guts out. After I get back home, I swear I'll never have another one in the house."

Ben rubbed at his temples. "Same here, bro. I'm not even sure I'll be able to keep my food down just touchin' the things. But it's more money per hour than we made pickin', and fifty-six extra bucks would really come in handy. We'd better go for it."

Taking a pen from his shirt pocket, George did some quick calculations on the back of the shredded wheat box. "Four days at eight hours a day is thirty-two hours. Multiply that by one seventy-five... yeah, fifty-six bucks is right." He stared at Ben and nodded approval. Then in a soft voice, he said, "You know, Ben, I'm real sorry 'bout the dog."

*****

This time, they had to share the bunkhouse with six Mexicans, none of whom spoke much English. Some of Ben's freshman Spanish came back, and he tried talking to them. A few words were exchanged, softly at first, then louder, as if shouting would make things clearer. There were a few smiles and a lot of head bobbing, but no real communication went on.

That night, the sounds of owls and crickets were drowned out by heavy wheezing and deep snoring, and each exhale added the smell of peppers and garlic to the pungent mix of sweat and unwashed bodies. Henry slept with his knife in his hand, while Ben hardly slept at all.

In some ways, the work was harder. Fruit with bruise spots and any that passed through their three-inch diameter rings were unacceptable. The peach fuzz and heat were the same.

For the first time, they got to see Tormino. He looked like an egg—short, round and bald—with a sun-wrinkled face that had long since given up on smiling. Ben immediately dubbed him Humpty-Dumpty.

Tormino stalked in and around the trees, sneaking up on the pickers and barking out in fury if he found someone who wasn't working. Rudy and Danny also played at being foremen but neither one bothered the boys. At day's end, they had picked only twenty boxes between them.

Rudy explained that the agreement with the braceros included a nighttime meal. As part of the crew, Ben and Henry were invited. Still wary of Carmen, they again went to the river to clean up. The closest spot was too deep to stand in the water and soap up. Instead, they stripped, splashed each other, and soaped their bodies while still on the bank. Then they dove in to rinse off.

The plunge put out the fire on Ben's skin, and when he surfaced, he started lazily swimming upstream. He fell into an easy rhythmic stroke and lost himself thinking about the future, much as he did when taking a stroll. He thought about finishing high school and going downstate to school. He would live in a dorm or maybe have an apartment like Martin. Economics didn't enter into his plans—somehow, some way, he'd manage.

In the quiet of the river, he heard only his breathing and the slight splash of his arms as he eeled, naked, through the water. His thoughts faded into fantasies of female bodies, and he slid further and further away from where Henry was.

Soon Ben was Tarzan, and an amorphous Jane was swimming lazily beside him. As she solidified, Tarzan rolled over on his back and envisioned his mate swimming next to him nude. Ben had a painful erection, which cut the water like the periscope on a submarine.

Upriver, the stream narrowed, and the sun became blocked by strange deformed trees. On both sides, the eerie trees' heavy roots were exposed and the banks had turned slick with foul smelling moss.

Ben felt something rough and slimy brush against his leg. With a panicked shudder, both his erection and his fantasy of Jane disappeared. Pulling upright near the bank, his feet touched bottom and, to his horror, sank shin-deep in slimy silt. Visions of movies involving death by quicksand gripped him. Terrified, he yanked his feet out and flipped around to swim back the way he'd come.

This time, he sprinted, his arms flailing and his legs churning the muck off the river bottom. Henry watched him haul out of the water. "What's up with you?"

Ben shrugged, embarrassed. "Just in a hurry 'cause I'm hungry." He tried to forget his sudden fear, but the eerie feeling caused by that stretch of the river stayed with him all the way back to their shack.

*****

Dinner was outdoors again, but this time, Danny had set up two tables with benches in the front yard. Viola covered the tables with a flower-patterned oilcloth and served beans with melted cheese on top, Spanish rice, and corn tortillas. Like their other meals with Danny, there was homemade red wine, beer, and water to drink.

Danny, his wife, and Carmen sat with Rudy and the boys, while the Mexican pickers had a table to themselves. Like the last time, Viola chattered away and Danny occasionally grunted. Carmen tattled on everything that the Mexicans had done wrong since their arrival.

At a lull in the conversation, Ben said, "I had a weird experience down at the river. I was swimming along when I felt something touch my leg. Whatever it was, it was big." He shrugged, embarrassed by the silence that had come over the table.

"Probably just seaweed, but it felt really strange."

260

Rudy grinned his monkey grin. "It was dee mermaid."

Henry scooped up some beans with a tortilla, the way he'd seen the Mexicans do. "What mermaid? Whadda ya talkin' about?"

Danny looked like he wanted to say something, but Rudy talked over him. "All water got dee mermaids. Even dee river. Dey grab boys and pull dem under dee water."

Ben sneered. "So, if it was a mermaid, how come she didn't pull me down?"

Rudy snapped the trap he'd set shut. "Dee Mermaids only grab dee good-looking boys."

After the laughter died down, Danny poured himself a glass of wine and looked over at Ben. "Don't listen to that Filipino nonsense. What brushed your leg was a fish, a giant catfish." He paused, took a deep drink of wine, and set the glass down. "But the place you're talking about is an evil place. A man was murdered right there on the riverbank."

Everyone went silent, and the quiet stretched out so long, it seemed as if Danny was trying to decide whether to continue. Henry thought he caught a twinkle in the foreman's eye, but when he looked over a second time, it was gone.

In the hushed voice people used to tell ghost stories, Danny went on. "Back in those days—this was before Viola did the cooking—there was a kitchen shack setup near where you were swimming. The crew ate their meals next to the bank because it was cooler down there."

Danny took a slow sip of wine and stared out toward the river. "The guy Tormino hired wasn't much of a cook, and the men got to razzing him about the food. The more upset the cook got, the more they razzed. It was hot that year, hot and humid. The weather had everyone snarling at everyone else. The cook suffered more than most, what with working in the heat of the kitchen and then having to carry heavy pots of food down to the river.

"This one night, he came out with a huge pan of refried beans and set it on the table. The man closest to the pan leaned over and sniffed at the beans, like a dog smellin' shit. He made an ugly face and shoved the pan to one side. 'Take those beans away and try feedin' them to the hogs, though I doubt they'll eat them.'

"Then he gave the cook the worst insult possible. The cook went bright red. Without a word, he went to his kitchen and got a meat cleaver. When he came back, he hid the cleaver behind his back and asked the man to repeat what he'd said. The fool sneered at the cook and damned if he didn't repeat it. That was it for the cook. With a blood-curdling scream, he brought that cleaver down so hard, it split the man's skull in two. Half the guy's brains splattered into the bean pan and the other half splashed into the water. To this day, no one swims near that spot because they're convinced the man's spirit haunts those waters."

Without gauging the reaction to his story, Danny took another sip of wine and went back to eating.

Henry cocked his head. "What was the terrible thing the guy said?"

Danny looked up, his face completely devoid of expression. He picked up the bean pot and held it. "He said, 'I'd rather eat peaches.'"

CHAPTER FORTY-FOUR

Ben spent the rest of the evening in the bunkhouse, trying to teach the braceros how to count in English. After they went through uno, dos, and so on, Ben worked on convincing them that a dime was worth more than a nickel. Once they got that, the rest of the American coins made sense. Dollars were easier, but Ben didn't know the Spanish words for any number over ten; so he told them not to buy anything priced above nine dollars. He wasn't sure that the merchants on Main Street purposely cheated the Mexicans, but it did seem as if they came back with less goods for their money than they should have.

After the lesson, the crew piled into the back of Danny's truck and Rudy drove them into town. For a few blessed hours, Ben and Henry had the bunkhouse to themselves. The only light in the shack was a single bulb with a pull string that hung down from the ceiling, and Ben had called dibs on the cot closest to it so he could read at night. This evening, he was halfway through a book that Viola had given him.

Henry had been outside, throwing rocks at the beehive. He pushed open the screen door and flopped down on the cot next to Ben. "I guess bees stop movin' around at night. Before dark, they go half nuts when I toss a rock, but once the sun goes down, I can't get 'em ta move at all."

Ben nodded and kept reading.

Henry got up and went over to his own bunk. "What's the book about?"

Ben still didn't look up. "You wouldn't like it."

"Why not, 'cause I'm too dumb ta understand stuff?"

There was a threat in Henry's tone that warned Ben to take him seriously. "Nah, but it's just this new novel about some kid. Viola said it reminded her of us, but she's wacky. This kid gets kicked out of school and decides to run away. There isn't much action, so I figured you wouldn't like it."

"Yeah, 'cause ya think I'm a dummy."

Ben shrugged and closed the book. He got up to turn off the light, but Henry waved him back. "Leave it on for a while. I'm gonna write postcards ta Andy and Mike."

Ben sank back down and tried closing his eyes. The light was too glaring. He decided to read again until Henry was ready for bed. After a few pages, he noticed that Henry was stretched out with his hands behind his head, staring up the ceiling.

"Hey, if you're finished with the cards, hit the light, will you?"

Henry stirred, and in an angry voice said, "You get it. You're closer."

Ben started to get up, then thought better of it. "Nah, you do it. I wanted it out before, but you said to leave it on. So by rights, you should be the one to turn it out."

Henry didn't move. "The thing is, I don't much give a shit if it stays on or not. You're the one wants it out. So you're the one who should get up."

Ben rolled on his side with his back to the light and tried to sleep. It wasn't the light anymore; it was Henry. He was tired of always putting up with Henry's crap and damned if he'd be the one to give in.

Time passed, and Ben could tell by all the rustling noises coming from Henry's cot that he wasn't sleeping, either. "Come on, Henry. Quit bein' so stubborn. Just turn out the fuckin' light."

"Light don't bother me. A couple hours an' the Mexicans'll come back. Let them turn it out."

"Well, it bothers me. You're just doin' this 'cause you're pissed off at me."

Henry was quiet for a few moments, then he said, "OK, Benny boy, I'll compromise with ya. I'm not getting' up, but I'll put out the light. That work for ya?"

Ben started to ask how, when a shoe flew up and smashed the bulb. The bunkhouse went dark and Ben finally fell asleep. An hour later, he was awaked by the Mexicans stumbling around and cursing in Spanish when the light wouldn't go on.

*****

Even though Tormino didn't smile, everyone could tell he was happy. His attitude had brightened, and he actually patted one of the pickers on the back and told him he was doing a good job. Rudy explained that the second picking was filling twice as many boxes as the fat man had expected. "First picking, dee grower geet back dee money he spend. Dee second picking ees all profit."

The praise had them all working harder, but in the end, it backfired. In their zeal to please the boss, the Mexicans put too many small peaches in the crates. Danny flew into a rage and insisted that the boxes had to be sorted, peach by peach, to cull out the undersized ones.

After picking, the boys were hot and, as usual, covered with peach fuzz. Ben was too spooked to go back down to the river, so they decided to wash up in the kettle, keeping their Jockey shorts on in case Carmen showed up. Ben started the filling process while Henry worked on starting the fire. When Henry eased a log from the pile, the bees rose, and with an angry drone, swarmed for the outhouse. This time, they seemed to stay there much longer than they had in the past. They were still buzzing in and around the outhouse when Ben emptied his final bucket into the pot. "That's strange, I thought honeybees went for flowers. How come they keep heading for the crapper?"

Henry kept testing the water, and when he deemed it hot enough, he kicked out the fire. "Maybe they're shit bees. I'll bet the honey they make is brown and stinks."

Ben stripped to his shorts and jumped in before Henry. "Last one in is a shit-eatin' bee.

Henry slid in and sighed at the soothing warmth of the water. "Asshole, ya can't jump in first an' then call it. Ya gotta give the other guy a chance."

Carmen came around the back of the bunkhouse and stood in front of the steaming cauldron. "I heard you both say bad words again, an' I'm gonna tell my daddy. He's the boss, an' he'll make you go away."

Ben cocked his head to one side and barked at the eight-year-old. "How come you're always so mad at us, Carmen? We haven't done anything to you."

She stamped her foot. "My daddy says I have to stay inside and not be around you 'cause you could be bad men."

Both boys just stared. It had never occurred to either of them that Danny might think they would hurt Carmen. They climbed out of the kettle and started drying off. When Carmen saw that they were wearing skivvies, she gave a disgusted snort and flounced over to the outhouse.

Henry watched her walk away. "I'm gonna go tell Danny he's bein' a jerk. We'd never hurt no kid."

Ben snatched the towel from him. "Yeah, you do that. And do it now, while he's still pissed about having to go through the boxes with the small peaches."

Henry scowled, then picked up a fist-sized rock and threw it with everything he had at the beehive. They were both buttoning up their pants when the first scream hit the air. It was an unearthly sound, pitched high enough with pain and fear to set dogs howling. The door of the outhouse flew open, and Carmen staggered out, her panties down around her ankles and a dark swarm of angry bees circling her head.

Henry reacted first. He hadn't put his shirt on, and now he ran to her, waving it frantically, trying to shoo the bees. If anything, it seemed to make them angrier. Some of them turned toward Henry, and his howls were added to Carmen's piteous shrieks. Then Ben moved. The bees had gotten under Carmen's blouse and were stinging her chest and stomach. He ripped off the blouse, then picked her up and threw her into the kettle. Henry put one hand on the rim and flipped in beside her.

As the bees dove for their heads, Henry yelled, "Hold your breath!" and pushed the child under. The bees hovered for an instant, then went for Ben. There was room in the kettle for three, so Ben scrambled in. He took a deep breath and ducked under. Carmen was somehow managing to cry under water. Her mouth was open and she was sucking in the soapy broth. Seeing that she was about to drown, Ben lifted her to the surface. She broke through, coughing and blubbering with fright. Her face was lumpy from forehead to chin, and her body was covered with red welts. Henry moved over and held her, trying to calm her down. "Come on, kid, it's over. The bees all went back ta the hive."

Henry didn't see Danny run up behind him, but he felt the punch. It slammed into the side of his head. Losing his grip on Carmen, he bounced to one side, caromed off the edge, and slid under the water.

Danny shouted, "I'll kill you, I'll kill you both." With superhuman strength, he grabbed the edge of the cauldron and pulled it over. The flood knocked him down and gave Ben the chance to scramble out. Henry stayed on the ground, too dazed to move. His first thought was that Danny knew he'd thrown the rock that caused Carmen to be swarmed. Ben was on his feet and danced back, hands up to defend himself. The sight of Carmen's naked body helped him understand the real problem.

"Danny, it isn't what you're thinkin'. We didn't hurt Carmen."

Danny was past hearing, past reason. He lunged for Ben, but in his haste, slipped and fell to the ground next to Carmen. She was still screaming, and at the sound of his child's cries, Danny reached over and scooped her into his arms.

As Henry stood, the pain sunk in. He'd been stung twenty or thirty times, mostly on the face and head. A rib had cracked when he slammed against the side of cauldron, and his jaw ached from Danny's punch. He scrambled over to his soaked jeans, reached in his pocket, and pulled out his knife.

Danny was on the ground with Carmen in his lap, trying to comfort her. Her cries covered the snick of the knife as its stiletto tongue flicked out.

Ben heard it. Keeping his back to Danny, he moved to block Henry. Shoving him, Ben yelled, "Danny thinks you were trying to rape his daughter."

Carmen's screams faded into whimpers while Danny, his face still infused with rage, scrambled to his feet. Henry motioned Ben aside and held the knife underhand and forward. "I don't give a shit what he thinks. He suckerpunched me."

Ben stammered, searching for calming words that wouldn't come. "Henry, for God's sake, don't! You cut him and we're fucked."

And suddenly, there was Viola. Enraged, she pulled Carmen out of Danny's grip. Holding her daughter at arm's length, she examined the child's face. She spun on Danny. "You can't tell bee stings?" Clutching Carmen to her chest, she rushed to the pump and dug out handfuls of mud from the tiny pool under the spout. She smeared the mud everywhere while Carmen renewed her shrieking.

Ben took Henry by the arm and forced him to close the knife as they went to the pump to wait their turn. Danny walked over, quiet now, and Ben turned to him. "I just want you to know, Henry saved her life. If he hadn't tossed her in the kettle, she would've been stung to death."

The muscles of Danny's jaw bulged out. "And taking off her clothes was part of this rescue?"

Ben shook his head, trying to decide whether an explanation was worth the effort. "She came running out of the outhouse with her pants already down. The bees were everywhere—in her hair, under her blouse, all over her. He had about one second to decide, and what he decided saved her life."

Danny said nothing and his face didn't change.

Ben watched as Henry squatted down to apply the soothing mud to his face and neck. "The thing is, Henry's as crazy as you are. If we stay here, one of you is gonna get hurt. It'll be better for everyone if we leave."

They packed their things, and Viola used Rudy's car to drive them to George's house. As they pulled out onto the road, Ben looked back for one final glimpse of the shack. Standing at the foot of the woodpile was Danny, a can of gasoline in one hand and a flaming stick in the other.

CHAPTER FORTY-FIVE

G eorge asked no questions. When he learned that they hadn't eaten dinner, he pulled out the peanut butter and made sandwiches.

Ben told him the whole story, but George didn't seem surprised at the way Danny reacted. "The one thing he asked me when I first took you guys out there was if I thought you kids would bother Carmen. 'Bout ten years ago, a couple of pickers raped his brother's little girl, and Danny's been scared ever since."

When Henry got up the next morning, he was still in a foul mood. To him, learning that Danny had distrusted them from the beginning was the worst kind of betrayal. In his book, that betrayal tainted everyone in Lodeville—everyone except George.

It didn't bother Ben as much, but when Henry suggested hitting the road, he said it was OK by him. They decided to hitchhike down to San Francisco and catch the bus home from there.

The plan took a small detour when they discussed it with George. "Rudy called before you guys woke up, says Danny's sorry as hell. They got Carmen to a doctor an' the doc said the same thing you guys did. She could've died if you'da let them bees keep stingin' her. Once she stopped cryin', she told Danny that they swarmed her while she was peein' an' that you wasn't the one who took her pants down. Anyways, he said for you an' Ben to hang around for a day or two and he'd get Tormino to cut ya a check for the work ya put in."

They were sitting at the kitchen table after a breakfast of oatmeal and toast. Ben had washed his bowl and gone out back to play with Smoke's mother. George picked the blue enamel coffeepot up off the stove and poured a second cup for him and Henry. "Man's sorry for the way he acted. You gotta get over it."

"It ain't that, George. The truth is, I probably got the damn bees mad in the first place. What pisses me off is that he'd think we'd hurt his kid, like we're some kinda perverts or somethin'. We need the bread, though. So if it's OK by you, we'd like ta hang out here till the check comes."

George's grin and nod was interrupted by the roar of what sounded like a hundred cars without mufflers pulling into his front yard. The noise lessened as engine after engine shut down. Ben came rushing in through the back door. "We got trouble. There's a bunch of motorcycle guys out on your front lawn, an' they don't look happy. If they're lookin' for a fight, we could use a couple of baseball bats or somethin'. You know, to even up the odds a little."

George got to his feet. "Could be friends. How many out there?"

Ben shrugged, then moved to the window in the living room. He pulled at the edge of the curtain and peered out. "Nine in all. Eight of 'em are sittin' on their bikes, an' one of 'em is headed for the front door."

George moved over to his bedroom and came out with a twelve-gauge double-barrel shotgun. He broke the gun open and grinned. "It's a good sign that they haven't fanned out an' only one is comin' ta the door, but it pays to be ready. If they're friendly, they'll understand. If not..."

271

A thundering knock shook the house as George finished ramming in the shotgun shells. He closed the gun and nodded to Henry, who reached over and opened the door.

A wiry scarecrow of a man stood with his hand raised to knock again. He was wearing a sagging pair of filthy jeans, a black leather jacket, and had a red bandana tied on his head. He took a step backward when he saw the shotgun. "No need for that, George." Grinning, he glanced back at his companions. Affecting a somber tone, he raised his right hand and said, "White man come in peace. Besides, you can only kill two of us. The other boys would rip ya to pieces."

George raised the shotgun, aiming it at the biker's face. "Maybe so, Alvin, but you'll be the first to die. I'd enjoy blowin' your head off, just for being an Indian-hatin' wiseass."

One of the men left his bike and walked up behind Alvin. He waved at George and laughed. "Don't do it, George, you'll get mess all over the porch."

The man in back was big, six-three or four, with broad shoulders and huge tattooed arms exposed by a sleeveless shirt. His voice didn't fit the picture. It came out high-pitched and squeaky, like a man trying to imitate a woman.

George looked past Alvin, lowered the gun, and smiled. "I didn't see you back there, Frank. What're ya doin' hangin' with these murder-cycle outlaws?"

Alvin kept smiling, but the way his mouth pruned up made the smile look forced. "You wasn't always so picky, George."

George lowered the gun and stared at Alvin. "I got religion. You oughta try it." They glared at each other for a moment, then George stepped back. "Come on in."

Frank started to shuffle toward the door, but Alvin stopped him with an abrupt hand movement. "We ain't got time. Come for your tow truck. We need it to get Billy Ray's bike out of the gully up by the honey run."

George set the shotgun against the door jamb. "No one drives my truck but me. I'll go with ya to get the bike, an' you'll pay the regular rate. God only knows why you wanna bother. Billy's too dead to need it, an' his bike can't be fixed ta run no more, anyway. Crashin' through the guardrail an' fallin' fifty feet wasn't much good fer it."

Henry wasn't sure what to do. It looked like things were under control, but he didn't trust the one called Alvin. Ben called out, "You want us to come with?"

The biker called Frank smiled at him and stuck out his hand. "Name's Frank. You wanna ride with me? Alvin can give your buddy a ride."

Ben looked over at George, and when George nodded, he shook Frank's hand. "I'm Ben an' he's Henry."

Alvin's smile went even tighter. He watched Ben settle in on the seat behind Frank and frowned at Henry. "You ever been on a bike before?"

Henry shook his head.

Alvin straddled his bike and kick-started it. "Just hang on ta me and sway when I do. Not before and not in the other direction. This here's an Indian Scout, the best bike ever made. It ain't no pussy cycle like that piece-of-shit Harley your buddy's on. We're goin' up on the honey run. It's steep and twisty, so if you're the nervous type, go in the truck with George."

Henry smirked and threw his leg over the bike. "Takes more than a motorcycle ride ta scare me."

Alvin roared louder than his bike. "Ya talk a good game, kid. Now we're gonna see if your balls are as big as your mouth."

Frank and Alvin had their bikes out of the yard and on the road before George and the other bikers could get their engines going.

When they hit the highway, Alvin opened up. The jolt of speed almost dumped Henry, but he resisted the urge to tighten his hold. He took a quick glance back and saw the other bikes and George's truck fade in the distance. Frank was alongside, grinning. With a sudden stomach lurch, Henry realized that he and Ben were in the middle of a race.

They veered left at a turnoff and started to climb. At first, the bikes seemed to labor, but as the road flattened slightly, they gained speed. Henry glanced sideways and saw that there was no guardrail and the drop was suicide-steep. Frank went left and cut in front of Alvin. Alvin reacted by swinging to the right and regaining the lead. The front wheel of the Scout was inches from the edge of the cliff, and Henry made the mistake of looking down. His stomach lurched the way it did in a dropping elevator. There was nothing but empty space, ending far below in a drought-brown valley. Alvin cut back away from the edge at the last instant, and the game of chicken took on even more speed. The exhilaration of being on a bike for the first time momentarily overcame Henry's feeling of danger. He swayed in time with Alvin, shouting "Go, go, faster." The shouting seemed to take some of the fright away, so he kept it up as the paths of the two bikes crisscrossed again and again, missing each other by inches.

Frank's bike appeared to be the faster of the two, but the Indian seemed more maneuverable. Either that, or Alvin was willing to take more chances. The wind was buffeting the bikes as they headed into a series of curves so tight, they were close to U-turns. Alvin cut the angle and pulled ahead as Frank eased up slightly. The bikes were almost parallel to the ground as they rocketed out of one turn and plunged into another. Alvin was in the lead as they came to a straightaway at the end of a series of curves. Without needing to slow for curves the throaty roar of both bikes increased as the drivers opened their bikes up as wide as possible. Henry suddenly realized that if a car had come around the turn at the end of the straightaway, there'd be no chance to avoid it.

Alvin yelled something at the top of his lungs, a savage scream that was drowned out by the thunder of the motorcycle's engine. He crouched down over the handlebars to cut wind resistance, and Henry bent with him. Frank was in the same racing stance. Henry saw a chalk-faced Ben glance over, and he tried to fake a smile, but his face wouldn't cooperate. He clenched his eyes shut, praying that Ben hadn't seen how terrified he was. They stayed neck and neck almost to the end of the straightaway. Then, just as the road curved, Frank roared past Alvin, and moments later, raised his arm in triumph. They were at the top of the mountain, and Frank eased off the gas, bringing his bike to a stop at an area designated as a scenic lookout.

Here, there was a guardrail, but it was bent in the middle and one stanchion was broken off at the bottom. Alvin pulled in alongside Frank. He yanked off his bandana, used it to wipe the sweat off his forehead, and got down from his bike. "The kid swayed wrong an' I had ta ease up. That's the only reason ya beat me."

Before Henry could say anything, Frank shot Alvin the finger. "The kid rode like he'd been ridin' all his life. You're just a pussy loser."

Waving the boys over, he moved to the edge and stared over. They could make out the twisted remains of a motorcycle far below. A few moments later, the others pulled in. George got out of the truck and stood by Henry. "That's what a bike looks like after a maniac hits the railing doing eighty miles an hour."

He backed the truck to the edge, jammed his foot in the hook end of the cable, and let Frank winch him down to the wreck. Within minutes, he had the wire wrapped around the frame of the bike and gave the signal to crank it up. Once the bike was lifted to the guardrail,

Frank and the others picked it up and carried it to the back of the truck. Frank started to lower the hook to help George back up, but Alvin put a hand on the crank. "Let him walk back. By the time he gets home, we'll be long gone. Ain't no sense in payin' if we don't got to."

Frank shook Alvin's hand off. "Get the fuck off me." He again started to turn the crank. Alvin waved at the other bikers, but when they started for Frank, Henry blocked them, and Ben moved alongside. Alvin started to laugh. "Look's like ya got the baby patrol on your side, Frankie. After we scare the shit out of 'em, you'll have ta change their diapers."

Henry fingered his knife. Now there was nothing short of killing him that could make him back down.

Frank kept lowering the hook. His odd, squeaky voice made his words sound boyishly cheerful, but there was steel in his eyes. "Here's the thing, Alvin. You and the others may be able to stop me from bringin' George up. But before we leave here, I'll do a mess of hurtin' on ya."

His glare swept over the other seven bikers. "Afterward, I'll hunt the rest of you down, an' when I find ya, you know what'll happen. Now quit fuckin' around and help me get George up outta that gully."

Alvin's face lost its smile. He shrugged and moved back over to his bike. "Some guys can't take a fuckin' joke." He kicked down the starter and took off, leaving the others to help Frank raise the cable. George came scrambling up. "What the hell took so long?"

On the way down, Ben was quiet. Henry looked out of the truck's windshield and stared at the sheer drop as they edged down the tight curves. "Was ya scared when we was racin'?"

Ben curled his lower lip and laughed. "Me? Hell, no. The only reason I pissed my pants was 'cause I didn't want to wait till we got back to the house."

Henry let out a heavy sigh, "Me too. I was too scared ta scream. When that crazy son-of-a-bitch passed Frank on that curve near the top, I slammed my eyes shut so tight, they hurt."

George downshifted to slow the truck around a curve. "The honey run scares everyone, and every year, it eats a few who were too stupid to admit it. Billy Ray was one of them. The reason they wanted his cycle is 'cause when a rider's killed on his bike, they bury the bike with him. The funeral's tomorrow."

The brakes on the truck squealed and George chewed on his lip. "Frank told me that Alvin wanted to leave me down in the gully. And when he told Alvin to shove it, you two were ready to help him fight them. Courage is one thing, stupidity is another."

Henry took his words as a compliment. "Frank was the one that scared the shit outta 'em. They backed down when they found out he wasn't goin' along with it."

"We go back, Frank an' me. I'm the reason his voice is so funny."

Ben turned to look at George. "I did wonder if he was born that way."

"Nah, he sounded like the rest of us until one summer, we decided to make some money lumberjacking up in Washington. A bunch of Yakima decided this Cheyenne an' his paleface buddy shouldn't come up an' take their jobs away. Both of us wound up in the hospital. I was OK, but Frank got hit with an ax handle across his throat an' it broke something in there, God knows what. Just proves my point—fightin's stupid. Alvin an' his pals could've killed ya."

He was quiet as they negotiated a turn. "Anyway, thanks."

*****

The boys went to the funeral with George and watched as six Levis-clad pallbearers lowered the twisted frame of Billy Ray's bike into his grave and let it fall over onto his coffin. Everyone filed by to toss a handful of dirt into the hole, then Frank squeaked out a few words. When he said, "The good die young," one of the bikers started laughing.

They went to Billy Ray's family home for refreshments. The talk was all about bikes and the incredible feats Billy had performed on his. As the group got drunker, the claims got wilder, and after some heated exchanges, the whole biker group roared off to prove they could do whichever stunts they'd been claiming.

George told Billy's mother how sorry he was. She shook her head and wiped away a tear. "Been a long time comin'."

*****

The boys stayed with George for two more days. Danny brought their checks and nodded at Henry as he handed them over. Henry seemed to recognize that was as close as he was going to get to an apology. He nodded back.

This time, it was Henry who wanted to stay longer, but Ben was anxious to see more of California before they headed home. At the crack of dawn, George dropped them off a few miles south of the city limits. He wanted to get them out of the jurisdiction of Deputy Calvin, just in case the Keystone Kop still wanted to get even. He shook their hands and made Henry promise to give his regards to his grandfather. "You're both a credit to him, an' you can tell him I said so."

With a final wave, he made a U-turn, and trailing a blue haze of exhaust, the truck slowly shrank into the distance.

As Henry watched George's truck fade, it reminded him of Martin. Like Martin, George had been a friend—a friend he'd probably never see again. He turned and looked south. The black two-lane highway was empty as far as the eye could see.

"Seems like we've been here before."

Ben shouldered his bag and they started walking.

CHAPTER FORTY-SIX

They sat on the side of the road, tucked among some oleander bushes, the only shade they'd seen for miles. Henry had stopped sweating a while back and was now so overheated, he felt sick. "One thing I never figured was that California would be so fuckin' hot. I thought it was all beaches an' redwood trees. This place is like Iowa without water. What kind of a place goes more than a whole month without rain?"

Ben licked at his cracked lips and stretched out on the ground, his head resting on his bag. "Maybe we should've grabbed a bus in Sacramento. After getting from Lodeville to Davis with only two rides, hitchin' seemed so easy, I figured why waste the bread on bus tickets."

"I ain't blamin' you. We could probably get a ride if there was any cars on this road. There ain't been one in over an hour. What time ya think it is?"

Ben stared at the sun. "It's way past noon, maybe two or three. I sure as hell don't wanna get caught out here at night. Let's get goin'." He stood, but Henry didn't move.

"A guy could die of thirst out here. I'm so dry I can't spit, an' I ain't been able ta take a whiz since this morning."

Ben grabbed Henry's hand and pulled him to his feet. "Same here. We gotta get some water. Let's stop at the next farmhouse we see an' ask. People can't refuse to give you water."

It was another ten minutes before they came to a house. It wasn't part of a farm. There were no animals or crops that they could make out, just the frame house at the end of a narrow driveway with a truck parked alongside the porch. It seemed pleasant enough, with bougainvillea-covered trellises running up the side of the house and pots overflowing with pink and red geraniums along the porch railing.

Henry decided they should stash their luggage behind a large rock outcropping. "If we carry bags an' stuff, the people might think we're hobos."

Ben didn't argue but he wondered what else they would think when two dust-covered guys showed up begging for water.

They both moved up the porch steps, and before he lost his nerve, Henry softly rapped on the wooden edge of the screen door. The frame was loose and the rattle made more noise than the knock. He stood to one side, next to the one piece of furniture on the porch, a rocking chair. The idea was to be far enough away from Ben to avoid looking threatening but still close enough so it wouldn't seem as if he were hiding. A woman moved into view, partially hidden by the thick mesh of the screen. Her hand was on the main door and she seemed ready to slam it in their faces. "Well?"

"We were headed home an' we run outta the water we brought. Could you spare us a drink?"

The woman released the door and pushed the screen door outward. Henry had to step back or get hit by it. She was big, stern-faced, and wore a shapeless dress with a bleached-out white apron that couldn't hide her rotund figure. Her hair was tied back, but a few wisps had broken free and were plastered to the perspiration on her forehead. A flood of food smells rushed out, hitting Ben so hard, his stomach convulsed. He hadn't eaten since breakfast. The woman's hands were covered with some kind of white powder, which she dusted off against her apron. "Where's home?"

Henry shrugged and nodded back over his shoulder. "Down the road about ten miles, near Davis." He sniffed loudly. "Boy, whatever you're cookin' sure smells good."

The woman's lips tightened. "I'm not cookin', I'm bakin'. It's what I do for a living. I bake pies an' I sell 'em. If you do live nearby, you know that's the way it is around here. Nothin's free. Smooth talk won't get you water, but hard work just might."

Ben started to protest, but Henry nudged him to be quiet and nodded to the woman.

She led them around to the side of the house and pointed to a toolshed. Next to it was a huge pile of wood that was weathered gray. "My friend helped me pull down the split rail fence that used to circle this property. If you want water, there's some saws in the shed. Cut the wood into fireplace-sized pieces an' I'll let you have all the water you can drink."

Henry stared at the pile. "Any bees in there?"

The woman gave him a strange look and walked away without answering.

Reassured, Henry started pulling at the wood. "Might not have to saw it all. We can prop most of it up against that tree stump an' break it in half with a kick."

Ben shook his head. "For a drink of water?"

Henry set one end of the log he'd pulled out on the stump and then kicked down on it. The wood broke in half. "She's bound to give us one of those pies she's bakin'. Did you get a whiff of them?"

They worked out a routine. Henry took over breaking the logs in half, while Ben sawed the halves into quarters. When all the logs were broken, Henry got another saw from the shed, and within half-an hour, they were through.

Ben was about to go tell the woman they'd finished when she came waddling out. She inspected the job, frowned at them, then reluctantly nodded her approval. She pointed to the side of the house. "There's the spigot. Take all the water you want."

Looking sad-faced was easy for Ben. He added a round-shouldered slump and shuffled his feet. "We're sure hungry after all that work. I was hoping you'd spare us one of your pies. They smell delicious."

The woman gave a derisive snort and turned away. "I sell pies. I don't give 'em away."

Henry watched her until she disappeared around the back door of the house. He shook his head at Ben. "I'm sorry, I should have known she was trouble the minute she started mouthin' off about how I was tryin' to sweet-talk her. Fat old bitch looks like she eats all the pies herself."

They turned on the water and drank until they could drink no more. Then they poured water all over each other. The relief from thirst was beyond any sensation either boy had ever felt. Cool for the first time in hours, they sat against the side of the house, unwilling to leave the spigot.

Henry wrung the water out of his T-shirt and put it back on. "Now that I ain't thirsty no more, I'm starvin'."

Ben ran his comb through his hair. "Whadda you say we offer to buy one of those pies?"

Before Henry could answer, they heard the sound of a truck coming up the drive. Curious, they moved to the front, but stayed hidden by a stand of bushes. A panel truck was alongside the woman's truck, and the woman was standing next to it talking to the driver. They could see that she was grinning. "I know you were counting on getting paid for cutting the fence wood, but I got a couple of dumb kids to do the whole job for a drink of water."

The driver reached out and patted the woman on the shoulder. "Good for you. It's too damn hot for me to be cuttin' wood, anyway."

Henry poked Ben in the ribs and whispered. "Dumb kids? She played us for suckers." His voice took on an accusatory tone. "Wouldn't a happened if John was here." Henry's jaw bulged as he clenched his teeth. Suddenly, he stood and snapped his fingers. "You keep 'em busy as long as ya can, then ditch 'em and head for the road. I'm goin' inside the house."

Ben whispered back. "Don't get crazy on me. Whadda you gonna do?" Henry was already headed for the back door. He looked back at Ben and grinned. "I'm gonna be crazy like a fox. Just keep the baker lady and her pal out of the house."

Shaking his head, Ben moved around to the front of the panel truck. He forced a smile. "That water sure was good on a hot day. You got any other chores to do? My friend and I would sure like to get somethin' to eat."

The woman and the driver stared at him. She cocked her head and frowned. "I'd have thought you'd be on your way by now."

Ben took his time answering, trying to give Henry as much time as possible. "No, ma'am. While we were drinking that water, I noticed we'd put a few logs in the pile that were too long. Because you were so nice to us—giving us water an' all—I thought maybe we should stick around and finish up the job."

The woman kept staring at Ben, her eyes flitting between him and the front door. "Luke, something's fishy here. There's two of 'em, and I don't know where the other one went. Hold this little liar here while I go check in the house."

Ben kept smiling as the driver got out of his truck and moved toward him. He was almost as big around as he was tall, and the front of his bib overalls strained to hold in his watermelon stomach.

The screen door slammed behind the woman, and the sudden noise gave Ben the slight distraction he needed. He dodged past Humpty Dumpty and ran full-out for the back of the house with the man huffing in pursuit. Circling the house, Ben looked back to make sure the truck owner was following him. Fatso was only thirty feet behind. He bounced after Ben looking like a giant balloon dressed up in a man's clothing. Shocked at how close his pursuer was, Ben put on a final burst of speed and headed for the panel truck. Just then, Henry came barreling around the other side with the woman behind him, shaking her fist and screeching, "Stop, thief!"

Ben reached in the driver's side window and grabbed for the truck keys. The fat man wheezed up and snatched at him, but Ben—truck keys in hand— dodged and headed for the road, laughing so hard he could barely run.. Henry, arms filled with boxes, was loping along a few hundred yards father up.

Ben pulled up next to Henry, and as they reached the end of the driveway, they sprinted back toward where they'd stashed their luggage. "I got the fool's car keys, an' the lady's truck is blocked. That tub of lard'll have to push his truck out of the way before they can come after us. The thing is, if they decide to come on foot, we got no place to hide. They're bound to catch us. Let's stop an' gobble down at least one of the pies while we can."

Henry nodded and they ducked into an outcropping of oleander bushes. They could hear the woman screeching, but it was clear she wasn't sure which way the boys had gone. Henry had six boxes, each one holding a freshly baked pie. They hunkered down and had just started to open the top box when a convertible came into view, heading back in the direction of Sacramento. Both boys jumped up and frantically threw out their thumbs. The car stopped.

CHAPTER FORTY-SEVEN

I n the driver's seat of the brand-new Olds convertible was a slender, toothy young man with a dark, wavy pompadoure, long sideburns, and sunglasses. His grin was infectious. "Hop in, boys, this baby hates to idle."

Henry handed the pies to Ben and vaulted into the back seat. Ben opened the door and slid in the shotgun seat. "Uh, it would be really cool if you'd get moving. We're sorta bein' followed." As if to emphasize his point, a truck pulled out of the woman's driveway and headed in the opposite direction.

The driver of the Olds glanced in his rearview mirror and said, "Freakish, man," just as the woman's truck screeched to a halt and started a three-point U-turn. He dropped the Olds into gear and took off, smoke and the odor of burning rubber following them for a few hundred feet.

The driver let out a yell and started pounding on the steering wheel. "Rocket 88, don't hesitate, just be cool, and lose that fool."

The Olds quickly pulled ahead on a straightaway, but when they hit a series of blind curves, the fat man began to catch up. He seemed to know the twists in the road and made better time by not riding the brakes. As they powered through a couple of sharp turns, Ben looked back. The truck was close enough for him to see the furious red face of the fat man behind the wheel.

Ben handed Henry the set of keys he'd taken from the truck. "Waggle them at Porky Pig, then toss 'em out." Henry laughed and dangled the set of keys on the end of his finger, making sure the truck driver could see them. He taunted the man like you would a dog with a bone, waving them and making *"come and get 'em"* motions with his other hand. Suddenly, the truck was on their bumper and it looked as if the driver was going to ram them.

"Quit screwin' around, Fox throw the fuckin' keys."

Henry flipped the truck driver the bird and tossed the keys into the ditch that ran alongside the road. The truck slammed to a stop, and the Olds pulled away for good.

"That was a gas, man, way too much. How come the citizen was chasin' you?"

Ben opened one of the pies and broke off a piece. "Fatso wanted our pies." Stuffing a wedge in his mouth, his face took on a look of pure ecstasy. "I think it's apple, but…" Handing a piece to the driver, he said, "You'd better taste it to make sure."

*****

The driver's name was Marco. At first, he professed to be a talent scout for a Hollywood studio. But later he hedged, admitting it was just a line he used to get women. "All the chicks wanna be in flicks." He next claimed he was an assistant to a California state senator. "I got heavy juice with the people that produce." Then he made vague references to a film project he was working on. "Lookin' for a star that's big and bad, like Alan Ladd." At that one, Ben gave Henry a wink and got a knowing smirk in return.

They stopped at a roadside café and parked in the rear lot. Marco pulled out a sack of what looked like green tobacco and started to roll a cigarette. "You boys like the wacky weed?"

Neither one of them had ever had any marijuana, but Ben didn't want Marco to think they were sissies. He gave Henry a nudge to be quiet and nodded. Marco fired up and sucked a lungful before handing the reefer to Ben. Ben tried to copy Marco, got smoke in his throat, and started a hacking cough. He passed the cigarette to Henry, who didn't fare much better.

Marco smiled like a benevolent uncle. "Suck air with the smoke an' go for broke."

They passed the stick back and forth until it was too tiny to hold. Marco took out a pair of tweezers and got one last hit. He put the ember out by pinching it with his fingers, then popped the stub in his mouth, grinned,and swallowed it.

They strolled into the diner and sat at the counter. Ben was disappointed. It was his first experience with grass, and he felt nothing. At first, he stared at the menu, trying to decide what to eat. Then a chocolate cake on a pedestal caught his attention. There were flies trapped under the plastic top, and they seemed more intent on escaping than eating the cake. Ben couldn't take his eyes off the flies. There was something profound about the way they bounced against the plastic, trying to find their way out of the trap. He started to ask Henry about it, but before he could come up with the words, he forgot the question.

The waitress stood there, pad in hand, and time seemed to stand still. When she was gone, the wooziness began to fade a bit, and Ben realized he was starving. "I'll have a burger with fries and a chocolate milk shake."

He heard Henry say something that sounded like, "Another one?" and then they were outside in the car, giggling.

Ben woke up just as they pulled into Sacramento. He reached over to the front passenger seat and shook Henry awake.

Marco had pulled over to the curb. "Hey compadres, rise and shine, end of the line. Been a gas but all must pass. I got me a date with a freakish filly. I'd share but there ain't enough there."

Dry-mouthed and groggy with sleep, they crawled out of the car. Ben leaned in the passenger side window and asked, "Can we ante up for gas?" The offer earned him an elbow from Henry, but Marco waved it away. With a silly grin on his face, he said, "No bro, don't want your dough. Just leave the pies, you'll be my guys." With that, the Olds peeled rubber and was gone.

They watched the Olds pull away, then Ben started walking. "Wonder why he was spinnin' all that bullshit? I can't figure any percentage in stringing us along."

Henry fell in alongside. "Guy reminded me of Johnny. It'd be an insult for him ta tell a straight story. Where we headed?"

"Lookin' for a phone booth. I'm callin' your buddy George an' beggin' him to come get us. We left our clothes behind that rock at the pie lady's house. We don't have the bread to buy all new stuff. And if we buy a bus ticket to Frisco, it won't leave us enough to get home."

"I hate callin' George. We already bummed too much offa him. Maybe we should just head home from here."

"All this way, an' the only part of California we get to see is Lodeville and a peach ranch. I'm sayin' we make the call. I know he was your grandfather's friend, but now he's sorta our friend, too."

Ben spotted a pay phone next to a gas station, and they pooled their change so Henry could make the call.

The worst part was that George didn't laugh. "Sorry you guys are havin' so much trouble. Time was ya could just stick out a thumb an' the next car would stop. Nowadays, people are either too selfish or too scared ta stop. Hang out by that phone an' I'll call ya right back. I may be able to solve your problem without draggin' ya all the way back here."

The minute they hung up, a woman insisted on using the phone and threatened to call the attendant when Ben protested. "OK, lady, you win, but could you make it short? We've got someone callin' back."

Her voice was shrill, a teacher lecturing kids on right from wrong. "It's a public phone for outgoing calls, not your private line." She closed the door to the booth and spun the dial slowly, smirking at them righteously with each digit.

Ben stood with his face pressed against the glass door, glaring at the woman as her call went through. "If the old bag wants privacy, she'll have to go somewhere else."

The woman finished her call and slammed open the accordion door. She started to say something, then seemed to catch the menace in Henry's eyes and backed away.

Henry tried George again. This time, the line was busy. They sank down next to the booth, exhausted, and waited silently until finally, the phone rang.

"Got some good news and some bad news. The good news is I got ya two a ride all the way to San Francisco. The bad news is, it's not till tomorrow. You'll have to find a place to crash for the night. The ride's with your buddy Rudy, Danny's cousin from the peach ranch. He's goin' to the Chinese lottery an' he says he'll be glad for the company. Gimme the cross streets where ya are, an' he'll pick ya up around ten in the mornin'."

Henry was beaming. "Hey, George, you're a real pal. We'll grab some sleep at the Greyhound bus station. It's kinda on the way, so maybe Rudy can pick us up there."

In the morning, Rudy Rivera pulled up in a four-door De Soto sedan. He leaned out the window and grinned at the look of wonder on the boys' faces. "I win money for dee car in dee lottery. Now I go back

290

to get more money from Chinese so I don't got to work in dee fields no more."

The boys had already cleaned up in the bus station bathroom, so they were ready to go. Henry went around the car, opened the front door, and slid in. "You're gonna give it all back is what you're gonna do."

Ben got in the back and Rudy took off. "No, I know what numbers goin' to come up. Last time, I look at all dee sheets from dee whole day, an' I pick dee numbers dat come up most. I win two thousand dollar dat way. Dis time, I bet even more."

They told Rudy about the pie place and he insisted on going to San Francisco on that same highway. "When we get dere, you hide, an' I grab you tings."

When they got back to the pie lady's house, Rudy drove a few hundred yards past the driveway and pulled the De Soto to the side of the road. The boys described where they had stashed their bags and Rudy walked briskly to the rock outcropping. Ben raised up just far enough to peek out the back window. He watched as Rudy retrieved the two bags and headed back to the car.

The woman seemed to fly out from nowhere. She was shrieking something Ben couldn't understand and waving a finger in Rudy's face. The little man stood quietly and listened, then he began to speak. The woman seemed to get even angrier. She stamped her foot and waved one arm in the direction of Sacramento. Rudy shrugged, but before he could say anything else, the woman stalked off.

Rudy threw the bags in the trunk and got behind the wheel. He pulled slowly away, giving the retreating figure a wide grin and a finger wave. When they were far enough away, both boys sat up. Ben reached over and tapped Rudy on the shoulder. "What did you say to her?"

Rudy smiled. "I tell her she ees ugly pig an' dat I would not make fuckin' with her. I say lots of tings but I say eberyting in Tagalog. She tink I don' speak English."

Henry put his arm on the back of the seat and grinned at Ben. "She sure was givin' ya hell about somethin'."

Rudy nodded. "She say look out for teeves on dee highway. She say don't pick up hitchhikers, two teeves stole all her pies an' dey ees very dangerous."

Ben felt a surge of pride. He leaned forward and gripped Henry's shoulder. "That's us," he said, "Crazed pie bandits, unarmed, and very dangerous, especially when hungry."

CHAPTER FORTY-EIGHT

Rudy drove down to the East Bay. As they passed the town of Berkeley, Ben begged him to stop so he could see the California campus. To Henry's relief, Rudy shook his head and laughed. "Dat place for smart peoples, not dumb fruit pickers like you."

They came to the toll booth of the Oakland Bay Bridge and Rudy handed the toll collector a quarter.

As they crossed the bridge, Ben hung his head out the back window and the wind carried away most of what he was saying. "...and when the bridge was finally built, it was the longest suspended deck bridge in the world. It's actually two bridges, 'cause they built it over an island. The island..."

Henry was leaning out the front window. "Benny, you're makin' my brain hurt. Shut the fuck up so I can enjoy the view."

At Third Street, Rudy turned north and crossed Market, explaining to the boys that he was headed for Chinatown. He zipped up one narrow street and down another, finally coming to a stop next to a grungy, three-story brick building. Rudy led them down to the basement. At the door, a young Chinese man held up a hand to stop them. With a questioning look, he nodded at Ben and Henry. Rudy stood between the two boys and reached up to put his arms around their shoulders. "Dees my friends. Dey come from Chicago to see how dee lottery ees run."

The man smiled politely and waved them in.

Henry's eyes flitted back and forth, taking in everything. "I guess the door guy didn't figure us for cops."

Rudy led them into a room filled with rows of chairs facing a long counter. "Policemans don't come to Chinatown. Chinese people take care demselves."

Behind the counter, Henry counted six wizened Asians hunched over like tellers in a bank, each with a cigarette dangling from his mouth. The air was so thick with smoke, it was difficult to make out their faces. Rudy moved immediately to a table with blank lottery tickets and the winning sheets from the day's previous drawings. He didn't bother to explain the system to the boys. Instead, he marked his choices on a sheet and took it to one of the tellers. At a speed too fast to follow, the old man copied the numbers with a Chinese ink brush onto a regulation sheet. Rudy carefully checked to make sure the numbers had been copied correctly, then he stepped back.

After a few minutes, the customers stopped milling around and the place went quiet. The man who had taken Rudy's bet went to a chuck-a-luck machine filled with ping-pong balls. He flipped it a few times, and then, with his head averted, he started drawing numbers. Once they had all been drawn, another one of the old men made a bunch of template sheets by punching out the winning numbers. Rudy grabbed a copy and placed it over his sheet. Only a few of his numbers showed through. He crumpled the losing sheet and turned away in disgust. "I play too fast. Forget to check numbers dat win earlier."

He left the boys standing in the middle of the room and went back to the table that held the blanks. He studied the winning numbers of the past games for a long time. Finally, he marked several sheets and presented them to one of the cashiers. The old man squinted out of one eye behind the rising trail of his cigarette smoke. He took out a brush, dipped it in ink, and slashed the new numbers that Rudy had picked. Rudy made sure they were the right numbers, then paid and pocketed the sheets.

"We don' got to wait. I come back later, collect my money den. Now we find you place to stay."

Rudy drove them a few blocks to Jackson, then down a side street where a brightly painted sign embellished with a frigate announced "Hotel John Paul Jones." The sign was the only thing that had been painted in years. The lobby floor was made up of the tiny white hexagon tile that the boys were used to seeing in public restrooms. At the reception counter, which was caged in with chicken wire, sat a cigar-chewing white man. He frowned at them as they approached. "No kinky crap. Ya wanna play with kids, ya gotta go somewheres else."

Henry looked confused, but Rudy understood. "I don' stay. Dees boys from Chicago. Dey need dee room."

The rate was two dollars a night. "You're on the third floor. The other floors are off limits, so don't let me catch ya wanderin' around."

As they started up the stairs, a chubby Chinese man and two heavily painted Asian women with blonde hair were coming down. One of the hookers smiled at Henry and winked. Henry smiled back, and they continued going up. The next floor was noisy with the clink of coins and the voices of men arguing in a language Henry figured was Chinese. Henry gave Ben a questioning look. "Whadda ya figure?"

Ben smirked. "First floor whores, second floor gamblin', third floor rooms. Who knows what's on four? This place is like a department store of wrong shit."

At the third floor, odd smoke with a sickly-sweet odor came drifting down from the floor above, answering Ben's question.

Their two dollars got them a small room with one double bed, a window, and a bathroom down the hall. There was a sink next to the bed, and from the stench, it was clear that it had been used for a lot more than washing. Pinching his nose, Ben went over and ran the water until most of the stink was gone.

Rudy started to leave, but Henry stopped him. "How 'bout getting us somethin' ta drink before ya go? We'll pay ya."

His eyes wary, Rudy shrugged. "What kind ting you want?"

"Anything, whiskey, brandy, gin, anything ya can get in half-pint bottles so's we can carry it."

Rudy nodded, accepted a five-dollar bill, and left.

Ben flopped down on the bed. "You think he's gonna win at the lottery?"

Henry crashed beside him. "Gambling's strictly for suckers. I know a bunch of bookies back home, an' none of 'em are broke."

The wisdom of the statement impressed Ben. There were times when Henry acted like he had more inside than just muscle. "Now that Rudy's got our bread, think we'll ever see him again?"

"I got a feelin' Rudy's a straight shooter. I don't figure him ta rip us off."

An hour later, Rudy was back. He handed over four half-pints of Jim Beam and grinned a good-bye "Danny say he sorry 'bout de ting wit Carmen. He say you come back next season, he let you pick."

Ben walked him down the stairs to the front. "How'd you do with the lottery?"

Rudy grinned a sheepish grin and with a shrug, was gone.

CHAPTER FORTY-NINE

Having spent most of their nights since leaving Chicago sleeping on cots, couches, or floors, the hotel bed was a luxury. They slept till noon.

Henry woke up eager to get out and see San Francisco. Ben would have just as soon caught a few more hours of sleep, but Henry was determined to sight-see and Ben didn't want to stay in the room alone. They dressed in T-shirts and jeans and went downstairs.

A different man was behind the chicken wire. This guy was younger. He was slender and frail and didn't seem as threatening as the cigar chewer who'd checked them in. Henry stopped at the cage and asked the guy where they could get breakfast. The string bean stared at Henry and wet his lips. "Depends on how strong your stomach is. There's a dump one block over that ain't too bad."

Henry motioned to the left with his thumb and cocked his head to one side. The clerk kept staring and nodded. "Just follow your... uh...nose."

"We ain't from around here..."

The guy grinned, and purred, "No shit."

Because the guy was smiling, Henry decided not to take offense. "An' I figured you could give us some ideas of what sights to see."

"Well, you're too young to see the real sights, but I can give you the lowdown on some touristy things." He wrote out a short list with some directions, and as he handed it to Henry, his smile faded. "Keep your hands in your pockets and don't make eye contact with anyone. With those sweet faces, the freaks in this neighborhood will be all over you."

Henry took the piece of paper and thanked the clerk. As he and Ben stepped outside, the wet wind hit. The temperature, plunging from triple digits inland to the fifties in the city, sent them scurrying back upstairs for warmer clothes. Money was too scarce to go buy new coats, so they made do by putting on every shirt they owned under the light jackets they'd brought with them. Even so, when they hit the road, they were huddled over, shivering in the cold.

Henry turned and started walked backward. "Chicago in the winter ain't as cold as this."

Ben zipped his jacket up to his chin. "It's the damp, the damp and the wind. When the wind blows, it makes the moisture evaporate an'…"

Henry stopped and Ben had to pull up to keep from running into him. "You're drivin' me crazy. Will ya please quit bein' a smartass? No one gives a crap."

The hamburgers they splurged on helped the boys forget the peaches and peanut butter sandwiches they'd been living on for the past few weeks. Henry wanted to order a second one, but Ben talked him out of it. "We aren't home yet. Let's watch our money, just in case."

Afterward, they walked to Coit Tower, climbed to the top, and stood staring out at Alcatraz.
The view of the prison seemed to affect Henry like universities did Ben. He whispered, almost in awe, "I'll bet there're some bad-asses in there."

Ben drew in his chin and looked over at him. "I guess."

North Beach was another one of the desk clerk's recommendations, but they couldn't find it. They found the streets he'd mentioned, but there was no beach anywhere near.

Ben had wanted to ride on a cable car, but even though they found the tracks, they didn't see a single car. Hoping one might come along, they followed the tracks downhill until they reached Fisherman's Wharf. Unlike the concrete piers they were used to, this pier was made of heavy wood planks and stank of fish. It was lined with outdoor vendors selling souvenirs, dishes of shrimp, and cups of clam chowder. They strolled to the end and looked out at the bay.

The water was almost black, and a foul odor came up every time a wave lapped at the pilings. Henry didn't bother to hide his disappointment. "Let's get outta here. The stink of this place is too much."

A little after four in the afternoon, they went back to the hotel and crashed on the double bed. "We musta walked ten miles. My feet are killin' me."

Ben kicked off his shoes. "Same here. This town's a bust. Whadda you say we hitch down to Los Angeles? We could go to Hollywood. I think it's somewhere near there, an' it's a lot warmer than this. The distance to Chicago is about the same from L.A. as from Frisco, so bus fare can't be too much different."

Henry sat up, grinning. "Sometimes you bein' smart ain't so bad. That happens ta be one of your great ideas. How much money we got left?"

Ben pulled out his wallet and counted the bills. "Over a hundred and twenty bucks. Should be plenty."

Henry headed for the door. "It's about six in Chicago. I'm gonna call Grandfather an' let him know we plan on coming back from L.A. instead of Frisco. Maybe I can talk him inta telegramming a few more bucks so's we can have some bread ta spend in Hollywood."

299

Ten minutes later, Henry was back. His head drooped and his shoulders sagged. There was no question that the news was bad. "I gotta head home. Grandfather says my old man won't listen to anyone. He checked himself out of the hospital an' is drinkin' again. Grandfather says it's gonna kill him an' he says I gotta be home before he croaks. As if I give a shit."

The news got worse. "And I can't take the bus back with ya. Grandfather's buyin' me a plane ticket 'cause the bus takes too long. I begged him ta front ya the bread, but he said he was short from payin' my dad's hospital bills." Henry flopped down on the bed. "He's gonna ask your mother. Ya think she'll spring for a ticket? That way we could fly home together."

Ben shook his head. "No way, she'll probably pay me to stay here."

They sat in silence for a moment before Henry said, "I never asked before, 'cause I figured it was your business, but this is different. Do you got a dad? Maybe he could help."

Ben shook his head. "No luck there, either. Got no idea where he is. During the war, when I was about nine or so, a soldier showed up at my school and took me out of class. His name was Lenny, an' he claimed to be my father. We walked around the block a few times, and the only thing he said to me was that I had my pants belt too tight and that I'd get a stomachache if I didn't loosen it. I never saw him again. When I told my mother that this guy Lenny came to school and told me he was my father, she laughed and said, 'How would he know?' You wanna know a funny thing, Henry? Ever since that time, if I tighten my belt, I do get a stomachache."

Ben got up, unzipped his pants, and started to pee in the sink. "How much is the plane ticket, anyway?"

Henry thought a moment. "I think Grandfather said ninety bucks. It's a non-scheduled airline called North Star." He brightened,

300

sitting up excitedly. "Ya know what? We got over a hundred bucks between us. I'll loan ya forty bucks outta my share an' ya could come with."

Ben grabbed one of the half pints of Beam and unscrewed the top. He waved the bottle toward Henry and toasted. "Here's to a real friend, Henry Fox. Soon as I get a job, I'll pay you back." They each slipped two of the half-pints in their jacket pockets and went out for a last night on the town.

Their first stop was a Chinese restaurant. The Chinese restaurants they were used to in Chicago had chop suey, chow mein, and egg foo yong. This menu had all kinds of other dishes, things they'd never heard of. They played it safe and ordered chicken chow mein.

Ben kept reading the menu. "I wish I knew what some of this other stuff is. Like this mu shu pork. It might be good."

Grinning, Henry sprawled back in the booth. "Ya seen any cats around here? Better stick with chicken chow mein."

By the time they hit Market Street, they'd finished a half-pint each. Henry was flushed and a little unsteady, and Ben was flat-out drunk. Staggering and yelling, "Chicago, Chicago, Chicago, that toddlin' town," he threw his arm around Henry's neck. "You're the best pal a guy could have. We're goin' home tomorrow, an' we're goin' together, 'cause you're the best pal a guy could have."

A shop without a door promised a girly show, and Ben guided Henry inside. The clerk, a tall skinny creep with a face like Frankenstein, was reading a magazine and didn't look up. He thumbed them out. "Come back when ya got hair on your balls."

Henry started to argue, but Ben had seen a couple of what looked like girls walk by, and he yanked on Henry's arm. The girls turned out to be women in their thirties, but by then Ben was so drunk it didn't faze him. He downed most of his second bottle and tried to whistle at the women. They ignored him.

Still hanging on Henry's arm, he began to follow them.

"Hey schweety, how's about we get together?"

One of them turned around. She was a mean-looking bleached blonde who might have been pretty once. "Go home, sonny. I don't know who got you drunk, but if a cop sees you, you'll wind up in jail."

Ben grinned the grin of all drunks and took her words to mean she was interested. Henry had finished his whiskey and gone quiet.

He was as drunk as Ben, but with Henry, drunk wasn't happy, it was serious.

"Let's get outta here 'fore the cops come."

Two sailors in uniform approached the women. "These punks bothering you?"

The blonde who had spoken to Ben smiled and put her hand on the nearest sailor's arm. "We were hoping someone would come along to save us." They paired up, laughing.

Ben had started to turn away when he heard Henry snarl, "Who the fuck you callin' a punk?"

After that, Ben lost all focus. The sailors were coming, and Henry hit someone, and someone hit Ben. He tried to fight back, but the sailors wouldn't hold still. Then he and Henry were running and the whole world turned into a kaleidoscope of faces, neon colors, and strobing lights. He wanted to stop, but Henry wouldn't let him. In a fog, he heard Henry yell, "There's only the big one still chasin' us. We gotta split up."

And then Ben was alone in the girly shop, and the Frankenstein guy was slapping him. After that, he felt his feet leave the ground, and then he was face down in an alley. Later, he was puking, and that was all he remembered.

When Ben woke up, the first thing that came clear was the tile on the floor. It was the same as the tile in their hotel's lobby. His head was pounding so hard, he thought his ears were going to bleed. When he tried to move, nausea roiled his stomach and forced up a mouthful of bile. He was in a toilet stall with his arms around the commode. He dry-heaved and spit until the wave passed, then he tried to stand. The room whirled and he had to sit on the toilet and wait for the dizziness to pass. Finally, when he felt steady enough to move, he staggered out of the stall and went to the washbasin. After soaking his head in cold water for as long as he could stand it, he dried off with a paper towel and finger-combed his hair.

When he walked out of the restroom, he realized he was in the Greyhound bus station. Reeking of vomit, he was too embarrassed to ask passersby for directions. Instead, he wandered up and down streets, trying to find one that seemed familiar. Even though San Francisco wasn't a large city, it was hours before he stumbled across Jackson Street and managed to find the John Paul Jones Hotel.

The skinny clerk barely gave him a glance as he moved past. "Hey, young blood, you guys movin' out today?"

Pain shot through Ben as the booming voice crashed into his ears. He nodded and kept moving.

"Check-out time is noon. Later than that, I gotta get another two bucks."

Something was blocking the door to their room. Ben pushed hard, but the door refused to open. Finally, in exasperation, he slammed his body against it with all his might. There was a moan and the door pushed ajar enough to let Ben slide in. The obstruction had been Henry's head. It was obvious that he had staggered into the room and passed out, falling backward with his head against the door. Ben moved to the bed and slumped onto his side.

Henry sat up. "Jesus, it feels like someone beat me over the head with a baseball bat."

Ben stared at the ceiling. "Probably just the hangover."

Henry ran his hand through his hair. "Do ya get lumps from a hangover? Damn, if my old man feels like this after a bender, no wonder he wants ta beat the shit out of everyone."

Ben propped his head up on one elbow. "Maybe he slapped your mother around and that's why she split."

The sun in the window was behind Ben and it hurt Henry's eyes to look up at him. "Dad says she was a tramp. A few months after I was born, she cleaned out his wallet an' split."

Ben rubbed at his eyes. "I'll bet you remind him of her an' that's why he's so rotten to you."

Henry seemed to give it thought, then shook his head. "Nah, she was white. What time is it?"

The sun began to heat up Ben's back. He got up and pulled down the shade. "It's after eleven, an' we gotta be outta here by noon. What time does our bus come?"

Henry moved to his duffel bag and started shoving his clothes in. "Not till three, so we can get somethin' ta eat before we go."

Ben started to nod, then thought better of it. Keeping his head still seemed to help. He reached into his pocket for his wallet and froze. The wallet was gone.

Face the color of chalk, Ben sat back down on the bed. "I guess you're on your own as far as the bus is concerned. I've been rolled. I think it was the tall freak at the girly shop. I sorta remember him slappin' me around and tossin' me out in the alley." He dug in his other pocket and pulled out three crumpled dollar bills and some change. "I don't suppose you've got a hundred or so stashed away somewhere."

Henry sat on the bed and sank his head into his hands. "I got

304

about a buck. Maybe ya should let the fruitcake at the desk blow ya. I figure he'd be good for bus fare."

"The guy wasn't after me. He was dead in love with you." Ben paced over to the window and stared out. "If we were home, we could let the guy make a pass and roll him. Most times, the fairies are too scared to go to the cops. The thing is, I don't think we oughta take a chance in this town. We've seen a lot of fairies, and they don't bother to hide it as much as they do back home."

Henry went to the door. "I'm gonna call Grandfather an' tell him ya ain't even got enough for bus fare. He's gotta come up with somethin'."

He left the room while Ben packed his bag. One thing was for sure, he wasn't going to waste his last two bucks on a room when there was a perfectly good bus station to sleep in.

Henry came back grinning. "A miracle. Grandfather's gonna get ya a ticket. I couldn't understand what he was sayin', somethin' about gettin' a better price there in Chicago. The thing I can't figure out is where he got the bread. I guess your old lady fronted the money after all. Anyway, ya got a ticket. We're both booked on North Star Airlines and headed for Chi-town. We'll straighten out the rest of it once we get home."

They checked out and went to Market Street. As they walked Ben kept pounding his fist into his hand. "I wanna see the girly shop guy again. I'll be able ta tell if he was the one who grabbed my wallet."

The sign said the shop was closed and wasn't scheduled to open again until 5:00 p.m. Ben stood and brooded, trying to think of some way to get even. His headache was still pounding, and the persistent nausea had him moving at a snail's pace. No way could he smash a window and get away; two steps at a run and he'd collapse. He searched in his pocket for change and found only dimes and quarters. "Gimme a nickel."

Henry handed over the coin. "Whadda ya gonna do?"

"Probably no good, but I'll feel better if I try."

They found a diner and ordered oatmeal. Then Ben went to the phone and called the police department. When the desk sergeant answered, Ben dropped his voice and used an Irish accent. "This is Father O'Brian at Saint Thomas. That girly shop on Market, the one near Sixth Street, is sellin' marijuana an' letting minors in. And them within a few blocks of Civic Center. It's a disgrace to this city, an' the good people of San Francisco won't put up with it."

Before the cop could answer, Ben slammed down the phone. "The cops are probably on the take, but at least I can pretend to myself that I got the bastard in deep shit."

When the bus to the airport rolled up at exactly five, Henry threw his arm around Ben's shoulder. "I never thought I'd be sayin' this, but I'm glad we're goin' home."

CHAPTER FIFTY

T he bus driver had all the passengers call out which airline they were flying on, and the boys discovered they were the only ones using North Star Airlines.

The guy in the seat across the aisle, a crew-cut, square-faced man with serious acne, sneered. "I wouldn't fly one of those non-scheds if they offered the seats free. They fly those C-47s that was in the big war. Those damn planes are flyin' coffins."

"Don't scare the boys, honey." His seatmate was a plump, cozy-looking blonde. She munched on potato chips and offered the bag to Henry. He took a handful, thanked the woman, and passed the bag to Ben. Still feeling hungover, the smell of the greasy chips almost got Ben dry-heaving again. He shook his head and passed the bag back.

The blonde took the bag, dug out a chip, and popped it in her mouth. Talking and chewing at the same time, she leaned toward Henry. "We're goin' home to Boston on TWA."

Henry gave her a slight smile, then put his head back and closed his eyes. The bus rolled south, and within minutes, the motion put both boys to sleep.

When the driver shook them awake, they were the only ones left on the bus. "We're at the freight area, boys. This is where you get on the non-scheduled airlines. North Star is through the door on your right."

Even though North Star was just one room with a boarding gate, it was plush compared to a bus station. The woman behind the ticket counter found their names on a manifest and waved them toward a row of seats. "I'll call you when we're ready to board."

They sat for over an hour with half-a-dozen other passengers. Finally an attendant in brown pants and a wrinkled blue uniform jacket showed up and led the group to the waiting plane. There was a rolling stairway pushed up against the fuselage, and Ben and Henry struggled up, bags in hand.

The plane had a center aisle with nine rows of bucket seats, two per row, on either side. Ben grabbed the window seat and Henry piled in next to him. A smiling stewardess came slowly up the aisle, stopping occasionally to help passengers stow their luggage and to check everyone's seat belt. She was dressed in a blue uniform with a short skirt and wore a hat tilted to one side with wings pinned on it. Henry kept staring at her legs.

"Uh, once we get up in the air, can I move so's I can get a window seat?"

Seeming amused by the effect her body was having on Henry, the stewardess smirked at him. "Not if you want to sit beside your friend. Our first stop is going to be Los Angeles. After that, we'll be full."

Ben groaned. "We're flyin' to Los Angeles first? That's four hundred miles south of here and out of our way." The stewardess shrugged and kept moving up the aisle.

Henry got up and grabbed a window seat one row up. "I'll come back just before we land."

The one engine Ben could see from his porthole window began to sputter and spew smoke. Finally, after some high-pitched whining, it caught with a thunderous roar and the propeller began to spin. He hoped the one on the other side was working as well. The noise became even more deafening as they bounced across the runway. Just when it seemed as if the whole plane would shake itself to pieces, it lurched into the air. After hanging for a moment, it dipped down, lurched up again, and was finally airborne.

Ben tapped the back of Henry's seat. "That scared the shit out of me. I thought we were goners."

Henry had kept his eyes on the stewardess. She sat in the front of the plane in a fold down jump set, facing them. Throughout the take-off, she had calmly filed her fingernails. "I watched Miss Legs the whole time. I figured as long as she wasn't panicked, things was OK."

The lights of the city winked at them as they headed downstate. Ben tried to crane his head toward the back to catch sight of the bridges, but they were already too far south. He pounded on Henry's seat. "This is so cool. I can see everything from up here. Man, I am never gonna drive anywhere again. From now on, it's all flyin'."

Within minutes, the lights faded, and only an occasional yellow glow from some desolate farmhouse showed from below. Then the plane pushed above the low clouds. The engine noise smoothed to a low roar and there was nothing but dark gray mashed potatoes clouds to see. They fell asleep.

*****

It was after ten when the sensation of falling woke Henry. He moved back next to Ben. "Either we're gonna crash, or we're comin' inta L.A."

They bounced their way onto the ground and the stewardess told the boys they could deplane. "Stay in the terminal. We're behind schedule, so we'll be leaving as soon as we pick up our L.A. passengers."

Once inside the terminal, they lay on the floor, resting their heads on their bags. The benches had arms every thirty inches, so stretching out on them was impossible. It was almost midnight when the loudspeaker announced, "North Star Airlines now boarding at gate three."

They ambled over and got in a line of soldiers being rotated home from Korea. Most of the khaki-clad men reeked of alcohol and had trouble standing without swaying from side-to-side. Their window seats were gone, taken by a pair of grim-faced sailors who sneered when Ben asked them to move. The stewardess came by, looking harassed and angry. Her hat was off and the jacket of her uniform was unbuttoned. Before the boys could complain, she directed a standing soldier to an aisle seat, and when he argued, she snarled at him. "We have thirty-six passengers aboard and another twenty waiting for the first available flight. You want me to call the captain and have you tossed off? Sit down, or we'll never get this damned plane off the ground."

Ben and Henry took the hint and grabbed the last two empty aisle seats.

This takeoff seemed better, probably because they knew what to expect. The moment they were airborne, half the servicemen raced for the one toilet in the rear of the plane. There was the sound of retching and the smell of vomit as the plane bumped its way east. Ben had dozed off, but awoke to a terrible stench and a blinding headache. Henry was staring toward the back of the plane. "The toilet's overflowin' with puke an' shit. Lucky we had ta leave those seats back there, it's flowin' right next to 'em."

At five in the morning, they landed in Albuquerque, New Mexico.

Ben's head was pounding so hard, he could barely walk. The stewardess was too frazzled to care. "Sorry, sonny boy, it's off the plane for you. We've got to clean up this mess and get some new toilet tanks, or we're not going anywhere. I'll see about an aspirin when we get back in the air."

In too much pain to even nod, Ben put his hand on Henry's shoulder and staggered off the plane. The effect of the warm, dry air was immediate. It started working on the headache, and by the time they got in the terminal, the worst of the pain was over. They stood by a huge plate glass window and watched the crew work to get their plane ready to fly. "I'm gonna move out here when I'm outta college. This air is just what I need for my headaches."

Henry gently bumped Ben with his hip. "I thought ya was gonna move ta Tahoe."

"Right. Tahoe in the summer an' Albuquerque in the winter, an' I'm gonna fly back and forth."

The sun was breaking over the desert when the announcement came to get back on the plane. A dozen passengers had either reached their destination or the smell had forced them to find other transportation, so there were now several window seats available. Henry gazed down at the fluffy clouds and decided they looked like huge globs of whipped cream instead of mashed potatoes. Both visions fueled his hunger pangs.

When the stewardess brought Ben two aspirin and a glass of water, Henry reached over and touched her arm. "We ain't had nothin' ta eat since yesterday. Any chance of getting us somethin'?"

She didn't even look at him. "St. Louis in five hours. You can buy food there."

They reached St. Louis just past noon Central time. They hit the bathroom in the terminal, then headed for the airport cafeteria. Except for a few potato chips from the blonde lady, Henry hadn't eaten since the oatmeal the day before. He figured Ben must be in worse shape, since he hadn't even had the chips. "How much bread we got?"

Ben fished in his pocket. "Two-seventy. That oughta be enough to fill us up."

Henry was walking fast and Ben had to hustle to keep up. Henry called back over his shoulder, "Might as well blow it all, we'll be in Chicago in a couple of hours, an' my grandmother'll probably feed us when we get home."

They sat at the counter of the airport diner, and Henry stared at the menu. "I can't believe it. The prices are three times what we been payin'. Look at this—chili con carne's a buck, Coke is thirty-five cents."

Ben shrugged. "I'm too hungry to argue. We got exactly enough for two chilis an' a couple of Cokes."

They ordered and wolfed down their food. Henry asked for extra crackers and the waitress grudgingly put one additional packet on the counter. When Ben ordered water, she turned her back and walked away. The check came to two dollars and seventy-five cents instead of the two seventy Ben had figured. He'd missed the tax.

"We ain't got enough. Whadda we gonna do?"

Ben grabbed the check and went up to the cash register. "What can they do, toss us in jail for a nickel?"

Their waitress came over to ring up their meal. She grabbed the money and rang up the sale before she realized they were short. "Another nickel."

Ben pulled his pockets inside out and tried a sheepish grin. "Didn't know there was tax on the meal. I'm flat broke."

The waitress slammed her hand down next to the register. "Why the hell didn't you tell me when you put the money down? Now I gotta make up the nickel from my own pocket." Looking around to include the entire restaurant in her complaint, she shouted. "Goddamn kids, no tip, an' it's gonna cost me on top of it."

She waved her hand dismissively, and still in a loud voice said, "Next time, read the menu, you deadbeats. Get the hell outta here."

Burning with anger and embarrassment, Henry grabbed Ben's

arm and they went down to the gate. "I wouldn't never hit no broad, but I sure wanted ta shut that bitch up. Why'd she have ta pitch a fuckin' fit over a nickel?"

Ben picked at his teeth with a toothpick. "Because she can, that's why. She probably takes guff from people all day long. Guys hittin' on her, pinching her ass when she walks by, and treating her like a piece of meat. Her boyfriend probably smacks her around, and she's probably gotta suck off the boss to keep her job. So she figures, here's my chance to give some shit back. I'll take it out on these kids."

Henry started walking faster. He looked over at Ben and shook his head. "Ya know what? You think too much."

Ben shrugged. "And you don't think enough. Your brain is smart but the rest of you is dumb."

Henry nodded. "Yeah? Well, I may act dumb, but inside, I'm smart enough ta know that I'm sick of bein' the one who gets shit on. When we get back, things are gonna be different."

Three hours later, they stepped off the plane at Midway Airport.

Henry's grandfather and Ben's mother were standing in front of the line, waiting for them. Henry's dad, a wizened, older version of Henry, stood behind them with his head down. Grandfather placed a hand on each of Henry's shoulders. "It is good to have you home. I hope you learned much on your journey."

Henry slightly bowed his head and tried not to smile at the old man's formality. "I learned what it means to have friends who respect you. George Red Cloud sends you his greetings."

Ben's mother cocked her head to one side and examined Ben. "Jesus, we've been waiting for over three hours." She reached up and grabbed his chin, turning his head in each direction. "You look like hell."

CHAPTER FIFTY-ONE

They all piled into Grandfather's Buick Roadmaster, with the boys in back. Henry's father twisted around to face Henry. His voice was hoarse, and barely above a whisper. "Your Grandfather missed work because of your stupid trip."

Henry stared out the window. "You sure as hell didn't."

He locked eyes with his father as the man straightened and formed a badly shaking hand into a fist. "You watch how you talk to me, you little punk. I can still give you the beatin' of your life."

Henry did his best to make his look of disdain more insulting than his words. "No—ya can't. I'm not a kid anymore. If you get drunk enough ta take a swing at me, I'll break ya in half."

"I'm sick, not drunk. Once I get back on my feet, I'll teach you not to talk back to your father."

Henry gave a derisive snort. "Sick! Yeah, you're sick, all right. The only reason you're sober is 'cause you're shakin' so bad, ya can't hold onta a glass of booze long enough ta get it up ta your lips."

Grandfather's stern voice stopped his grandson from taking things further. "Henry! Do not speak to your father like that."

Henry said, "Yes, sir," and fell silent.

Grandfather drove at a steady speed down Garfield Boulevard and caught a green on every light until they reached Cottage Grove.

Ben talked to the back of his mother's head. "Thanks for frontin' the money for the plane ticket. I'll pay you back soon as I get a job."

Her head swiveled around so fast it looked as if it would detach. "Are you crazy? Even if I had the money, which I don't, I wouldn't waste it on getting you home. As far as I'm concerned, you got yourself out there, so it was your job to get yourself back."

Ben sat back. "Then who...?"

Grandfather downshifted and turned right on Harper Avenue. "The person who paid your way was a boy named John. He came to my house and gave me the money for your ticket."

Ben started to ask more questions, but Henry put his hand on Ben's arm and whispered, "Later. Don't put your business in the street."

*****

Life on the stoop hadn't changed. When Henry and Ben came out the next day, Andy, Mike, and John were already there. John grinned and got up to lag. "So, how was California?"

Henry pretended to think about the question. "They eat potatoes for breakfast."

John turned to face him. "No shit?"

Henry nodded. "I shit you not. Hash browns or home fries, they'd probably serve 'em mashed if ya asked. Benny was so impressed, he vowed he was gonna move out there first chance he got."

John spun a quarter and it hit exactly on the line. "Well, I'm glad you guys are back." He pointed toward Mike. "This loser ran outta money a week ago, an' Andy's been broke for as long as I can remember. I ain't been able to make any dough laggin' since you guys left." He threw another quarter and waited for Ben to join him.

"Joke's on you," Ben said. "We're so flat broke we had to stiff a waitress in St. Louis for a nickel. Which reminds me, I got a few

315

questions for you. Where'd you get a hundred bucks to loan me? An' how'd you know I needed it?"

No one else seemed to want to lag, so John picked up his money. He sat between Ben and Henry. "Andy told me."

Ben started to say something, but John held up his hand. "Gimme a chance, an' I'll tell you the whole thing." He glanced up and down the street as if what he was going to say was confidencial. "It went down like this. The first thing Henry's father did when he got out of the hospital was to go out drinkin' with Andy's old man. He told Andy's dad that Grandfather was gonna buy Henry a plane ticket. An' 'cause you don't got the dough, you're gonna come back by bus. Andy's old man told Andy, an'…"

Andy jumped up to face Ben. "An' I went an' tol' Johnny."

John smiled tolerantly. "An' I hotfooted it over ta Grandfather's place with the airfare. I had the dough just sittin' around 'cause I made beaucoup bucks over the summer."

Ben tried to stay tough, but he couldn't pull it off. His voice broke. "I'll make it up to you, Johnny, I swear I will. I'm gonna pay you back every cent, with interest."

The emotion seemed to embarrass John. He looked away and shrugged. "You'd do the same for me. Anyway, as soon as I gave the dough to Henry's grandfather, I figured out a way to make up for the loss."

"How'd you do that?"

"When I got back from giving the bread to Henry's grandfather, I tol' Andy to call Maxine Sommers an' tell her I was locked up an' needed a hundred bucks for bail. She put up the cash, thinkin' she'll get it back when I show up in court. I don't need her money, but when she finds out I scammed her, it'll be payback for the nickel tip she gave me when I delivered ice cream for Edelstein."

"I didn't even know you two were friends."

"We met in Benton Harbor, at the resort I was workin' for. There was an old lady who had me push her wheelchair out on the porch every afternoon. She'd scratch my palm—you know, dirty-like, then cackle like a hen, an' slip me a dime. Turns out she was Maxine's great-aunt. I ran inta Maxine an' told her what the old lady did. She pretended not to get it, so I scratched her palm to show her. She looked down at her hand an' said, 'Don't scratch for it like a dog, John, ask for it like a man.' So, I asked for it like a man, an' after that, we made out every chance we got. She's nuts about me."

Henry smiled at Ben, and Ben smiled back. It was good to be home.

*****

Ben spent his after-school hours searching for a job. He got some delivery work around Christmas, but it was only for the holiday. Through January and February, he tried every business in the Hyde Park, Kenwood, and Woodlawn districts, and was turned down by all of them. One time, he thought he had a nibble, but the job disappeared when he told the employer his name.

He figured maybe it was because the guy didn't like Jews but then again, maybe not. Things were tight, and jobs were scarce. Being broke was affecting everything he did. His grades suffered, and it seemed as if he was always fighting with his mother. Because she had no current boyfriend, she was increasing the pressure on him to help out with the household expenses.

To add to his misery, John hadn't said a word about paying him back for the plane ticket. Somehow, that made his lack of money worse. He could still hear the airport waitress shouting, "Deadbeat!"

*****

317

It was dry out, but bitterly cold. The wind off the lake found the tiniest open spot on Ben's clothing and burrowed in. Huddled over to conserve warmth, he waited at the bus stop for Henry and Andy. The CTA bus that ran the route to and from Chicago Vocational pulled up, and his two friends piled off.

Ben's daily job search had kept him off the stoop, so he and Henry hadn't seen much of each other. As he stood alongside Henry, he suddenly realized Henry had grown. He was within inches of Ben's height. "You're getting taller."

"It's 'cause I quit smokin'. I'm tryin' ta get the squirt here ta quit so's he can be a six-footer."

Andy shook his head. "It ain't smokin', it's bein' on my feet all the time. Crushes me down. If I could just stretch out for a nice twelve-hour nap once in a while, I'd grow."

They walked back to the Castle and stood in the doorway. It was too cold to sprawl out on the stoop. Mike's mother leaned out of the window and yelled down to them, "Why don't you bums get a job instead of clutterin' up the front of the building?"

Ben didn't bother to look up. "The thing is, the old bat is right for once. I gotta get a job to pay you for the money I lost the night we got drunk, an' Johnny for the plane ticket. I don't give a shit what I have to do, as long as I can make some money."

Henry took out a toothpick and rolled it into the corner of his mouth. "I know this guy, name's Nicky Costas. He's Outfit. One time, before you came around, we was laggin' nickels an' this big Lincoln drives by. There's one guy sittin' in back, an' one guy in front drivin'."

"Like a chauffeur?"

Henry frowned, a huff of fog coming out of his mouth as he spoke. "I'm freezing out here. Ya wanna hear this, or ya wanna interrupt so's we can both freeze ta death? No, not like a chauffeur, like a guy drivin' a Lincoln for a mob guy."

Ben shrugged.

"Anyway, just as the car gets next ta us, the back door flies open, an' this pudgy hood, all duded up in a fancy suit, jumps out an' scoops up the nickels. He's laughin' like it's the funniest joke he's ever pulled, an' I get pissed. The car pulls away, an' I chase after it. When his driver stops for the light at Lake Park, I catch up an' pound on the back window. I say, 'Gimme back my bread,' an' the guy says, 'You know who I am?' An' I say, 'Yeah, I know who ya are, you're the thief what stole my money.' The guy starts laughin', an' he says 'You got a lot of moxie, kid. When you grow hair on your pair, come see me.'"

Andy stood to go inside. "I remember when that happened. Tommy was still alive. Him an' Mike was sure Costas was gonna kill ya."

Henry reached over to ruffle Andy's hair, but Andy pulled away. They exchanged mock punches, and Andy pushed through the Castle door and went up the stairs.

Ben moved to face Henry. "Andy isn't a 'booger nose' anymore. Maybe you didn't notice, but under his earmuffs, his hair was combed."

They were quiet for a moment, and a queasy feeling came over Henry. Things were changing, and he hated change. He shook off the feeling and remembered where he'd left off in his story. "Anyway, before we went ta California, I done some errands for him. Small stuff, like when they ran the big Greek poker games down at the Post, I'd go out an' get food for 'em. Stuff like that. Now I'm almost seventeen, I figure maybe I'm old enough ta start doin' some serious work. Costas does some loan sharking, runs a string of hookers, and sells most of the drugs in the neighborhood. But the big slice of his pie comes from his bookmaking operation. If ya really don't care what ya have ta do for money, I'll ask him for some work an'put in a good word for ya."

*****

Nicky Costas put Henry and Ben to work immediately. As a courtesy to his heavy betters, the mob boss had his people deliver any winnings directly to them. He started the boys out with payments that amounted to less than a thousand dollars. Henry figured it was a kind of test to see if they were dumb enough to try to steal some of the dough. The job paid ten bucks per delivery. And because the payments were going to winners, tips were a definite factor.

After a half-dozen trips with no problems, Costas turned all the payment work over to them. It was clear that the mobster had taken a liking to the boys. Even so, he would only use them for payments—never pickups.

Ben seemed to be thinking out loud. "The big money is in pickin' up from the losers. Costas pays as much as a hundred for that kind of action. I wonder why he won't give us a crack at that?"

They had just delivered a package and were heading for the park to see if any of the guys were around. Ben fired up a cigarette and answered his own question. "Maybe Costas figures we aren't tough enough. Sometimes a pick-up guy has to use muscle on the guy he's collectin' from."

Ben knew it was the wrong thing to say the instant the words were out of his mouth. Henry stopped and jabbed a finger in Ben's chest. "If that's what he thinks, he's got another think comin'. I'm tougher than half the goddamn pussies he's got collectin' now. I ain't gonna ask him, Benny, I'm gonna tell him. We're ready ta take on the big money jobs. If he don't like it, he can get another couple of guys ta do his delivery work."

Ben grabbed Henry's hand to stop the jabbing. "Look, do me a favor, Fox. Don't screw this up. You piss Nicky off, and we'll lose what we got. I already paid John off, and I almost got enough to pay you back."

Henry's eyes narrowed, and he stared down at Ben's hand holding him. Ben let go. "Ya don't owe me nothin'. If I hadn't got drunk with ya, ya wouldn't a gotten rolled."

They started walking again, but Ben could tell something had changed. He'd crossed some kind of line with Henry. Despite what Henry said about repayment, the obligation remained, and Ben had a feeling Henry enjoyed having him at a disadvantage.

"Come on, Henry. Just hold off for now. I promise, soon as the time's right, I'll go to Nicky with you." He glanced over to see if he was getting through. Henry had on his poker face, the face that revealed nothing. A hint of panic crept into Ben's voice. "You know, we'll have a better chance with Costas if we go together and back each other up."

Finally, Henry grunted. It wasn't complete agreement, but at least it was a breather.

CHAPTER FIFTY-TWO

Mike sat on the back of a park bench with his feet on the seat. Ben idly practiced lagging quarters while Henry, fresh out of money, sat on the bench next to Andy and ignored the challenge. The benches were across the street from the Post Restaurant. Behind them was a thick row of head-high bushes, and past that, a large grassy field. It was a good place to hang out because they could see the street in both directions and make a quick escape into the park if there was trouble.

Andy first bummed a cigarette, then a match from Ben. Ben stopped lagging long enough to hand one over and light it for him. "You want me to smoke it for you, too?"

A grin flashed on Andy's face, then faded as quickly as it had come. "I'm droppin' outta school. Shit, I ain't learnin' nothin', an' I ain't gonna go ta college. I'm better off workin'."

Ben picked up his coins and sat down. "You've only got a couple of years left, and it might be tough findin' a job without a high school diploma."

"I already got a job. I'm workin' at the new A&P supermarket as a delivery boy."

Mike looked over as if he'd just realized Andy was there. "What's it pay?"

"I get paid by the customer. Two bits a delivery."

Mike shook his head in disgust. "You jerk, you're gettin' robbed. The regular guys get half-a-buck an hour for delivery."

Andy was sorry he'd mentioned his job. He looked away and, under his breath, told Ben, "I get tips, too, an' the manager said if I do good, he'll put me on as a stock boy."

Ben felt guilty at the thought that stock boy was all Andy could ever hope for. "You're gonna have to go to continuation school."

"Nah," Andy said, "I just stopped goin'."

Henry was incredulous. "Ya can't do that. They'll come after ya."

"They called a few times at the house. But after Sissy moved out, I started answering the phone. Once, the school called, an' this snooty broad says, 'Is Mr. Beauvue there?' an' I says, 'Nah, the whole family moved downstate.' An' she says, 'Does that mean that Andrew Beauvue will no longer be attending school?' An' I says, 'How am I supposed to know?' The same lady called again the next day, an' I tol' her to stop botherin' me, 'cause I work night shift an' I gotta get my sleep. Then my old man stopped payin' for the phone an' they took it out. It's been since before Easter, an' ain't nobody come around to check, so I think they gave up."

"Smooth," Ben said, and the four of them lapsed into silence.

The day had been a warm one for April, and even with a cold wind blowing in off the lake, the temperature was still in the mid-fifties. Henry hadn't been able to talk his grandfather into letting him take the Buick. And John, the only one of the group who had his own car, hadn't shown up. They were without wheels, and no car meant nothing to do.

Five minutes later, John's three-year-old '49 Ford made a right turn onto Stony Island and screeched to a halt in front of the bench. He had removed the hood ornament, repainted the car candy-apple red, and added white wall tires with wire wheel sport rims. He'd told Ben that he wanted to drop a Cadillac engine in it. "That'll make it a Fordillac. I could pretend it was just a Ford and cream half the rides on the street. They'd never know what hit them." Ben knew it wouldn't happen. Long before John got a project like that under way, he'd lose interest and buy a new car.

If the guys were glad to see him, they didn't let on. Once he was out of the car, Ben gave him a lazy wave. "What's shakin'?"

John was smiling. "Ain't nothin' shakin' but the leaves in the trees, an' they wouldn't be shakin' if it weren't for the breeze." His smile got broader and he went around to the trunk of his car. "I lied. I got some big haps right here in the trunk of this fine automobile. Get off your asses an' come on over here."

He waved them to the back of his car, lifted the trunk lid, and stepped back.

Andy, too curious to maintain his cool, was the first one to see it. There, in the trunk, was a sixteen-gallon keg of beer. It was frosted at the top and covered with rivulets of condensed moisture.

"What's that?" Mike asked, as he walked over and stood beside Andy.

The corners of John's mouth turned down in disgust. "It's a keg of beer, stupid."

"Is it empty?" Mike asked.

"No, it's not fuckin' empty." John wearily shook his head. "Why would I cop an empty beer keg?"

Ben and Henry sauntered over. Even though Ben suffered from the cold more than the others, the thought of an icy beer appealed to him. "Put it over by the bench and pump it up. Let's see what we got."

Henry and Ben wrestled the keg out of John's trunk and rolled it on its edge over to the bench.

"Pump it, pump it up," Andy chirped, almost dancing with excitement. John hooked up the pump and started pushing the plunger in and out. While he was pumping, Henry went across the street to the Post and borrowed half-a dozen water glasses. By the time he got back, the keg was pumped up, and they were all waiting. Ben tossed out the first spurts of foam and let the golden liquid flow into his glass. Drinking deeply, he solemnly pronounced it "beer," and belched.

They moved the keg back into the bushes where it couldn't be seen from the street, and after filling their glasses, went back to the bench. Henry, always amazed by John's scams, asked the obvious question. "How'd ya get it?"

John smiled broadly and looked over at Ben. "Benny ain't the only Jew in the group, what with Edelstein making me an honorary member of the tribe."

He took a deep swig of beer and settled back, nursing the story for all it was worth. "I heard from Edelstein's kid Barry about this fancy Jew party at the South Shore Country Club, an' I decided to crash it. I was thinkin' maybe I'd run inta a rich girl or something."

Ben grinned. "Like Maxine Sommers?"

John gave a grimace of disgust. "She ain't no real Jew. She's was born an' baptized in the church of full-blooded bitches. Now shut up an' let me tell it. Anyway, I get there, an' all the ladies are really old. Mostly college age. So, I figure the night's wasted, an' I'm startin' to leave when I see three beer kegs lined up next ta the bar waitin' to be opened. I take out my notepad..." At this point, John pulled a spiral note pad from his pocket and proudly waved it in front of Henry's face. "An' makin' sure no one's watchin', I copy down the number on the last keg.

I'm too dressed up, so I take off my tie and jacket. Then I roll up my shirt sleeves to look like a workin' guy, stuff a pencil behind my ear, and I pull my car inta the entrance. I says to the guard, 'South Shore Liquor, we got a call to pick up a busted beer keg.' The guy don't even look at me, just waves me in. I get the car as close as I can, an' I head straight for the bar. Pullin' out my pad, I walk up like I'm readin' from it. I says to the bartender, 'I gotta pick up keg number 1709. It wasn't supposed to be sent. According to my boss, it's got a air leak in the top an' the beer's probably flat.'

"The guy's not a regular bartender. Just some guy they got to volunteer for the night. No hesitation at all, he comes out from behind the bar an' starts lookin' for the right keg. While he's lookin', I see a couple, three guys standin' next ta the bar talkin', so I go up to 'em an' I say, 'Could you guys gimme a hand here?' They come over just as the bartender spots the keg. I grab the pump an' they carry the keg to my car, an' here I am."

John leaned back and chuckled, letting the worship of the others wash over him as he sipped his beer.

Henry couldn't control himself. "Johnny, ya got balls the size of cantaloupes." He raised his glass and said, "A toast ta John, the best thief in the neighborhood."

The others laughed and everyone clinked glasses.

For a time, the group sat quietly drinking. Pete, the young counterman from the Post who had loaned them the glasses, came over on his break to see what was going on. They gave him a glass of beer, and when he left, he promised to come back after the Post closed.

A car cruised by with some kids from Vocational, and Henry jumped up to talk to them. After that, the word spread. Within an hour, there were a dozen or so neighborhood kids all swilling beer. When Pete came out, he brought a couple of bottles of Ouzo as a party offering.

"This is Greek liquor, and it's really good." Pete's family was from Athens, but unlike most of the Greeks in the neighborhood, he didn't mind associating with non-Greeks. He was in his early twenties, and he immediately started trying to score with Mary Ryan, one of the girls who had shown up.

A portable radio came out and someone tuned it to Al Benson, the rythum and blues disc jockey. The Clovers, Ruth Brown, Earl Bostic—the music poured out nonstop and they danced to it and drank, and danced some more, and drank some more.

Pete disappeared into the back of the now-closed restaurant with Mary. Henry, a little drunk and very pissed off at her, snuck into the back seat of John's car with a girl named Cindy. The original keg was emptied, the Ouzo finished off, and half-pint bottles of Seagram's Seven were being passed around when the police finally showed up.

CHAPTER FIFTY-THREE

There was only one car. It screeched to a stop and the two uniforms barreled out yelling orders and waving their flashlights. "All a ya, hold it right there. Hands up, hands up."

No one listened. Instead, the party scattered in all directions. Mike was too drunk to run and would have been caught, but Andy and Ben grabbed him under the arms and dragged him toward the bushes.

As they plowed through, Mike started puking, and Andy knew if they kept running with Mike, the cops would catch them. He motioned to Ben, and together, they pulled Mike under a large bush, hidden from view. On the other side of the row of foliage, they could hear the jangling of the cops' equipment and their shouted curses as they tried to chase the fleeing teenagers.

Ben leaned down to Mike and whispered, "If ya keep quiet, they won't know you're here."

Mike groaned. The smell of vomit was overpowering, but Mike seemed too far gone to care. Before the boys were ten feet away, they heard the sound of heavy snoring.

Andy headed across Stony Island with Ben right behind him. They climbed over the bars of the revolving exit turnstile at the 57th Street Illinois Central Station and ran up the stairs onto the train platform. Two middle-aged women with jackets over their nurse's uniforms were seated on a bench waiting for a train. Reeking of beer, Andy sat down next to them and smiled politely. Ben stood off to one side. He kept looking back toward the stairs and nervously shifting from foot to foot. The women rose and walked to the far end of the platform.

From the elevated platform, Andy could see the police car and the two cops as they searched the park. John's car was still parked in front of the bench, and Andy was guessing Henry was still in the back seat with his latest girl, Cindy. The cops didn't seem to notice that the windows were steamed over. All the other kids had gotten away, and Andy laughed, letting the thrill of the chase wash over him.

When the cop car left, they walked back down the stairs and headed for home. Suddenly, Andy stopped, "Shit, we left Mike in the bushes."

Ben stared at him as if he thought Andy had lost his mind. "The last thing I'm gonna worry about is what happened to Mike. Besides, he's probably home by now."

Andy shook his head. His jaw knotted and he pursed his lips. "He was too drunk. We gotta go back for him."

"You're either drunk or crazy if you think I'm goin' back. Sometimes, the cops just pretend to split. If they come back, they'll nail us for sure." Ben opened the door of the Castle and went inside without a backward glance.

Andy stood outside, huddling against the cold. He felt woozy, but he was sure he was sober enough to fool a cop. He turned and retraced his steps to the park.

Back at the bushes, he circled around until the smell of vomit led him to the right spot. Mike was just where they'd left him. Face down in the dirt and snoring loudly, he resisted Andy's attempts at getting him up with angry grunts and unintelligible muttering.

Andy stood to full height and was trying to figure out what to do when a flashlight clicked on and caught him in its beam. Instantly, he dove for the park side of the bushes. He crashed through and ran out onto the grassy area, unknowingly saving Mike by attracting the cop's attention. There was only one cop, and he bulled his way through the bushes, shouting for Andy to stop. Instead, Andy reversed direction. Momentarily out of the cop's sight, he moved to a bench, dropped down, and rolled under it. He froze like a fox gone to ground and stayed under the bench for half an hour, motionless except for an occasional shiver from the cold.

By now, Andy was really feeling the alcohol. The world was spinning out of control, but worry over Mike finally forced him to move. He rolled out from under the bench and stood brushing off his pants and tucking his shirt in. Then, with a conscious effort at control, he made his way back to where he'd left Mike. He decided that if the cop was still there, he would just walk by as if he were out for an evening stroll.

The cop watched him coming and broke out laughing. Andy felt himself weave but couldn't make his legs behave. He shoved his hands in his pockets and tried to strut nonchalantly, but the movement was too tricky. He staggered and would have fallen if the cop hadn't grabbed his arm. The cop, still laughing, cuffed the boy and pushed him into the patrol car.

*****

They hauled Andy to the Hyde Park Police Station, a filthy, two-story building with walls that attracted dirt like a magnet. Just inside the double front doors was a high counter, behind which sat the duty sergeant. Andy was brought in and hustled up to the desk. The arresting officer said in a bored tone, "Drunk and disorderly, underage."

The sergeant thumbed them toward the back, and Andy was shoved into a small room at the end of the corridor. They snapped off his cuffs, searched him, and took down his name and address. When they finger-printed him, they kept slapping his head repeatedly because his fingers wouldn't hold still long enough to let them get a decent print. They took away his belt and shoelaces, escorted him to a cell with three other prisoners, and left him standing trancelike, holding onto the bars.

"Hey, you got a cigarette?" A middle-aged Negro dressed in a rumpled suit shuffled over to Andy.

Without answering, Andy fumbled for his pack and handed it over.

"You better learn not to do that, boy. You better learn to just hand over a cigarette. Other guys gonna take the whole pack, you do that."

"Yeah," Andy said, "Thanks."

The Negro went back to where he had been sitting, and a large white guy who outweighed Andy by forty pounds ambled over. Even in his drunken state, Andy could tell the guy was bone-mean.

"Hey, how ya doin', kid? How 'bout sharin' one of them smokes with me?"

The colored man called out something, but Andy didn't hear what he said. He reached into his pocket for the cigarettes and was digging one out to give to the guy when a punch from the other white member of the cell group slammed his head against the bars. Andy sagged to his knees, and the warm wetness of blood started running down his neck.

The two men were searching his pockets when, through the dizzy haze, Andy heard someone shout, "Guard, guard, help! Help!" The Negro was shaking his head as if he couldn't believe what the two had done. "He's just a kid, I think you kilt him."

In a low, ominous voice, the large man said, "Shut the fuck up, nigger, or you're next."

Andy never carried a wallet, and the few dollars he had were tucked deep in the pocket of his jeans. With a curse, his assailant aimed a kick at him, but Andy's head had cleared up enough for him to roll to one side.

Jingling keys, the guard wearily strolled over to see what all the noise was about. Andy got to his feet. By the time the guard reached the cell door, Andy was standing holding onto the bars, the way he'd been when the guard put him in. The guard saw the blood. With a snort of disgust, he opened the cell and pulled Andy out by the arm. "What the fuck happened to you?"

"He fell," the white guy said, and his grinning partner nodded.

"He did, like hell," the Negro said. "They punched him, just a kid, an' they beat him up for his money."

The guard took Andy to an empty cell two doors down and roughly pushed him in. "You mess up this cell, an' I'll kick the shit outta you. I gotta clean it." He turned and walked toward the door that led out into the corridor.

"Hey," the colored man called. "That kid needs a doctor."

The guard looked at his watch. A call for a doctor would mean a report, and a report would mean staying past his shift.

"He'll live."

"Well, what about me?"

"Whadda 'bout you?"

"You ain't gonna leave me in here with these two. They'll start ta beat on me."

"That's tough shit. Next time, mind your own fuckin' business."

Andy's new cell was smaller, with only one metal cot hanging from chains attached to the wall. In the back was a commode without a seat and with no toilet paper. The commode was stopped up, and the floor around it was covered with a combination of urine, vomit, and water. At first, the smell was so bad, Andy was afraid he was going to throw up. As he became aware of the sounds of fighting coming from the other cell, he stopped thinking about the smell. He sat on one of the cots with his legs curled up and listened to the colored guy's shouts for help. They seemed to last forever, but finally, the cries turned to moans and then went quiet.

*****

In the morning, the guard brought Andy a cup of black coffee and a piece of stale white bread with a thin slice of baloney on it. He tried to eat, but his hangover and the stench coming from the commode were too much. An hour later, the guard came back and told him to turn around with his back to the cell door. When Andy he did, the guard opened the door and handcuffed him. He pulled him out to a waiting paddy wagon and they drove to the courthouse.

Andy sat in a holding room, waiting for his case to come up. He'd taken his jacket off earlier to keep it from getting messed up, but now he put it back on to hide his bloody T-shirt.

A kid close to his age sat down next to him. "Whadda ya in for?"

"I got drunk."

"Ya do any damage?"

"Nah."

"Hurt anyone?"

"Uh-uh."

A knowing look crossed the kids face. "Twenty-five bucks."

"Twenty-five bucks?"

"Yeah, twenty-five bucks an' out ya go." The kid seemed to know what he was talking about. For the first time since the cop had slapped the cuffs on, Andy felt as if things were going to be OK.

"What's with all the blood?"

"Some guys beat me up in jail."

The boy shook his head. "Aw, that's rough, man. Maybe you can catch up with 'em on the outside."

"Yeah."

The boy's look of compassion faded away replaced by a wistful frown. "Hey man, could ya do me a favor? My shirt's really dirty an' the judges don't like to see ya dirty. Maybe you could loan me your jacket for when I see the judge. I'll give it back to ya as soon as I'm through. Then you can use it ta hide the blood on your shirt."

Andy's jacket was dark blue cotton, cut Eisenhower-style. It had been one of the first things he'd bought with his own money. He hated parting with it, but the other kid told him that impressing the judge with a clean jacket could make the difference between jail and probation.

"I wouldn't care so much, but my mother's got cancer, an' she really needs me ta help her."

Andy peeled off the jacket.

The boy still hadn't come back by the time Andy's case was called, and as he walked out, he asked the bailiff where the other kid had gone.

"He went home."

"But he's got my jacket," Andy complained as he was led past the bailiff out into open court.

The judge glared at him and pounded his gavel. "Silence in the court."

The bailiff read the charge, "Drunk and disorderly."

The judge leaned forward and looked down. "How do you plead?"

Andy shrugged. "I was drunk but not disorderly."

A few spectators laughed, and the judge pounded his gavel again. "Making jokes isn't going to do you much good in this court, young

334

man. Just look at you. Your clothes are in disarray and there's blood all over you. It's obvious to everyone in this court that you've been fighting, and I can't think of a more disorderly thing than fighting. Now how do you plead, guilty or not guilty?"

Andy heaved a deep sigh. "Guilty."

*****

The jacket thief had been right. Andy was sentenced to a twenty-five-dollar bail, which would act as a fine if he didn't show up in court. The problem was, Andy didn't have twenty-five dollars. That meant he would be spending the next thirty days in county jail.

He was sent back to the Hyde Park Police Station to await transfer. They took the cuffs off and put him in the cell he'd been in earlier. His head started bleeding again. When he asked to see a doctor, the guard told him to shut up.

At three, he was again told to turn around and face away from the cell door. Again he was cuffed and led out into the main room of the station. There, standing at the sergeant's station, were John and Ben. John had posted Andy's bail.

Ben took Andy by the chin and turned his head to see the cut. "What the fuck did they do to you?"

"Some guys in the drunk tank sucker-punched me."

"You're sure it wasn't the cops?"

"Nah, it was just some guys. They wanted ta roll me."

Ben probed the edge of the cut to see how deep it was. He grinned and put his arm around Andy. "You need stitches, but you'll live."

Andy nodded and his eyes turned to slits. "Yeah, that's what the guard said."

*****

A few days later, Andy walked into the Post Restaurant. The whole left side of his head was bald and a circular bandage covered his

335

stitches. He smiled shyly when he saw the guys and pulled a chair up to the booth. "Hi."

Henry grinned at him. Nudging Ben, he pointed to Andy's head. "From this side, he looks like a marine. He could probably get some pussy if he told the chicks he just got back from Korea."

John and Ben laughed, but Mike turned away and got to his feet. "Dig you later."

"You just got here," Ben said, surprised.

"Yeah, but that was before he showed up." Mike was pointing at Andy.

"Whadda you got against me?" Andy asked.

Mike walked to the door and turned back. He looked at all of them, one by one, and ended with Andy. "My mom told me, I can't be seen with jailbirds."

CHAPTER FIFTY-FOUR

In the spring of 1952, Ben's mother suddenly decided her role in life was to take care of Ben. She set a ten o'clock curfew and refused to allow any of "those bums with whom you associate" in her house.

Since he had become too sick to work, Henry's father was always home. The elder Fox might have been too sick to work, but he wasn't too sick to get drunk. His angry presence kept the group from hanging out at Henry's place.

Mike's parents kept his apartment off-limits, and Andy was too ashamed of his place to let them in. John didn't even live in the Castle.

In their younger days, Gus had tolerated them hanging around in the hallways of the Castle, but now that they were older and smoking, he routinely booted them out. So with no apartment to go to and the Castle off limits, the Post Restaurant become the group's official hang-out.

*****

Henry and Ben sprawled in the back booth with John and Mike across from them. Outside, winter was trying to make a late-April comeback. The sky, black with storm clouds, was alternately dumping icy rain and sleet. The wind kept trying to get in, howling in frustration while buffeting the huge windows lining the east wall of the restaurant. Pete had the heat on full blast, making the air foul with the stench of wet wool from overcoats. There was no relief in the forecast.

Henry gobbled down his last fry and pushed his plate to one side. "Any of you guys ever been ta the Neighborhood Club in the basement of that church over on Dorchester?"

The question came on the heels of Mike's, ubiquitous, "So, whadda you guys wanna do?"

Ben was busy finishing up his dinner. He looked sideways at Henry and let his shoulders sag in boredom.

"I heard about it." Mike said, "But the guys from 47th Street kind of run it, don't they?"

"Nah, "Henry said. "There's lots of 'em that hang out there, but the priest makes sure there's no trouble. He ain't really a priest, I mean, he ain't Catholic."

John cocked his head and squinted. "If he ain't Catholic, I don't think he can be a priest."

Henry hated to be contradicted. It was bad enough that ever since their return from California, Ben seemed to think he could correct Henry anytime he felt like it. Now John was doing the same thing.

"Shows what the fuck all you know. The guy's a piskin'palin. They're just like regular priests except they can have wives."

"Episcopalian," Ben said. "They're Protestants, and they're all rich."

Henry smiled with his lips only. "Shit, too! I thought all the Jews were rich till I met you, Benny." He shoved Ben, not too gently, with his shoulder.

"Benny knows all about those *piskin'palins.*" Henry smirked. "He was singin' in their choir. Our Jewboy Benny was a choirboy for the Protestants."

Ben flushed deep red. "It was a long time ago, and it was a job. I got paid to sing."

He turned his head away, hoping Henry would drop it.

But Mike picked it up and wouldn't let it go. "I remember that. I seen him in his red robes with a white collar, just singin' away at the top of his lungs. My mother said he looked like a little angel. We had to go to the Episcopal Church once 'cause Ben's old lady asked her to come an' hear her little Benny boy sing."

John looked over at Ben. "Whadda you mean, it was a job? Did ya really get paid?"

"Yeah, fifteen bucks a month."

John whistled. "Just for singin', that's really cool. How come you quit?"

Ben relaxed. Thanks to John, the teasing was over. "My voice changed. No more high-pitched songbird, more like a low-croakin' frog."

Everyone laughed but Henry. "So whadda ya say? You guys wanna go over an' see what's goin' on at the club? They're supposed ta have good sounds. It could be freakish, an' it's something ta do."

No one answered, but Henry stood up and started walking toward the doorway. Ben moved with him, and the other two fell in behind. They huddled under the Post awning, out of the sleet but chilled in the damp air.

Ben stared out at the cold. "It's too ugly out. I'm for goin' back inside."

Smirking, Henry strolled to his grandfather's Buick and unlocked the door. "I didn't know pussy freezes."

Henry climbed inside and pulled up the buttons. Mike elbowed Ben out of the way and raced over to grab the front seat.

Ben shook his head in disgust. "He still acts like a goddamn kid."

As Ben and John slid in the back, Henry turned sideways in his seat to face them. "I need some gas money."

Mike was trying to find a station on the radio. "It's four fuckin' blocks. How much gas does that take?"

Henry was still in a bad mood over what he saw as a threat to his leadership from John and Ben. He sure as hell wasn't going to take any crap from Mike. He raised his top lip above his teeth in a parody of a smile. "First I'm gonna take up tap ta get us some booze, an' then I'm gonna drive ta the club. You don't wanna put in some bread, then get the fuck out."

Mike dug into his jeans and pulled out a dollar.

"Hit me harder," Henry snarled. "I wanna grab a couple a half-pints."

With a flourish, John produced a five, and Ben dropped in three ones. Mike came up with another crumpled bill, and Henry started to drive to Harper Liquors.

On the way, he stopped at Mary Ryan's building and ran inside. In less than a minute, he came back out with Billy one of Mary's older brothers close behind. The sleet had turned to rain, and the rain had diminished to a cold, steady drizzle.

Billy Ryan stood at the car window, wet and shivering. "Ya didn't tell me ya was buyin' for all of Kiddyland. These punks'll get fucked up and then squeal ta their mommies that I got 'em a taste." He turned to walk back, but Henry grabbed his arm. He leaned in close and mumbled something. Ryan shook his head "no" a few times, but Henry kept talking, and finally they both headed for the car.

The passenger side door was yanked open and when Mike didn't move, Billy barked, "Shove over, asshole." Mike slid to the middle, and they drove the rest of the way to the liquor store in silence.

Minutes later, Billy came out with four half-pints of Seagram's Seven. He kept two and handed the other two in through the window to Mike.

Mike looked as if he couldn't believe what was going on. He stared at the bottles. "Just for walkin' in an' gettin' the booze, you get half?"

Billy leaned in and put his face almost nose to nose with Mike. His voice was almost too soft to hear. "Whadda tryin' ta say, Fuck Face? I ain't worth two half pints?"

Mike didn't squirm away. Instead, he seemed to be trying to stand his ground. His voice shook slightly. "I'm not sayin' you ain't worth it. I'm sayin' it's too much for such a small job."

Billy stared at him, trying to gauge the situation. He turned to Henry. "The deal was two half-pints. Ya goin' back on your word?"

Henry said, "Shut up, Mike. Ya only put in two bucks. Ben an' John ain't complaining', an' between 'em, they ponied up eight."

Satisfied, Billy Ryan hunched away from the window and Henry pulled out into the street.

Once Billy was far enough away, Mike shook his head. "I still think it was too much to pay. One time, Andy's brother got some gin for me for nothin'."

Henry slammed on the brakes, bringing the car to a skidding stop in the middle of the street. "Either shut the fuck up about it or get out."

Mike turned his head away, saved from answering by the blare of a horn from the car behind them.

As they pulled into the church parking lot, the big wooden doors flew open and a large group of kids came pouring out. The first few were complaining loudly, waving their arms and clearly upset about something. Henry recognized one of the girls and waved her over. "What's goin' on, Annie?"

Ben stared as an olive-skinned girl turned and ran over to the car. She had a long coat slung over her shoulders, cape-style, and wore a low-cut, embroidered white peasant blouse tucked into a skirt with crinoline slips. The girl held a soggy magazine over her head as she peered into the car. Then, recognizing Henry, she grinned and opened the back door. She shoved in next to Ben and tossed the wet magazine out the window. Ben moved over, but not quickly enough to avoid the touch of her thigh as she sat down. Her classic Italian face was outlined in the light coming from the street lamps. Ben stared, deciding she was, hands down, the most beautiful girl he'd ever seen.

Annie shook her head ruefully. "Some of the Basement Boys started a beef with a couple of the Dorchester guys, and we all got kicked out."

Henry and John had been sipping from one of the two half-pints while Ben and Mike were working on the other.

Henry took the bottle from John and finished it. "Damn," he said. "This night has been a total bust. I finally talk my guys inta comin' over here, an' they shut the place down."

Annie said, "I'm freezin'. Isn't someone gonna offer me a drink?" With a toss of her head, she flipped her long, auburn hair away from her face and smiled directly at Ben.

He looked into her almost-black eyes for a long moment, then took the bottle out of Mike's hands and handed it to her without a word. It was almost full, but Annie tipped it up and drained it without stopping. Mesmerized, Ben watched the loveliest throat he had ever seen bob up and down, swallowing whiskey, and at that precise moment, he fell insanely in love.

"Damn!" Mike shouted. "You downed the whole fuckin' thing." He reached over and grabbed Annie's arm. "That whiskey cost me two bucks. You're either gonna pay for it, or I'll take it out in trade."

Ben reached past Annie and backhanded Mike in the mouth. It was more of a slap than a punch, but it snapped Mike's head back. "You, watch your filthy language. You're talkin' to a lady."

Henry started to laugh, then choked it back when he realized Ben was serious.

Mike rubbed at his lip and licked a bit of blood off his fingers. "You sucker punched me. I oughta kick the crap outta you for that."

Ben's anger eased. "As if you could. Just watch your foul mouth and there won't be any more trouble." He reached in his pocket and pulled out two dollars. "Here's your two bucks. Take it and shove it up your hole."

Now Henry did laugh. "That's the best offer you're gonna get, McMann. Push any harder, an' you'll probably wind up without the cash and a busted face ta boot."

Mike turned to Henry. "You're always tryin' ta start some trouble, maybe someone oughta kick the crap outta you."

Henry raised his upper lip again. This time, it wasn't anywhere near a smile. "I don't see no anchor up your ass. I guess the only thing holdin' ya back is fear."

Mike opened the car door and got out. "Fuck all of you, and fuck her, too," he said, pointing at Annie.

He took off running, but Ben didn't follow him. He turned to Annie and said, "You gotta excuse him. He's just real ignorant."

Annie Taloni had two older brothers. Both of them acted as if their role in life was to slap their sister into line. Her father was usually too busy beating on her mother to interfere, but occasionally, he joined in the fun. No one had ever come to her defense before.

She said nothing, but her face softened and she gazed with wide-eyed admiration at her hero. She held out her hand. "Annie Taloni."

Ben just stared.

CHAPTER FIFTY-FIVE

At eighteen, Andy was a year older than the rest of the gang. His once square face had lengthened, his shoulders had broadened, and with the upright posture, John had taught him, he looked taller than his actual five-nine. No one would ever call Andy handsome, but the sadness in his eyes and his shyness appealed to the more maternal type of woman.

Working instead of going to school had the effect of alienating Andy from the Castle group. He labored as a stock boy at the new A&P until six in the evening and was usually too tired to hang out. Armed with a phony driver's license and draft card, he frequented the local bars with some of the older guys who had also dropped out of school.

*****

Andy and a guy he worked with at the A&P, Wally Campbell, sat in one of the back booths of the Tip Top Tap, nursing their beers. Smoke from a dozen cigarettes filled the air, and the only light came from the neon signs reflecting off the back bar mirrors.

Wally was a butcher's apprentice. He was also a fence. He held the package under the table and slid the gun halfway out.   "I'll sell it to ya cheap."

The *it* in question was a .45 caliber Army Colt automatic. Perfect in its shiny blue-blackness, it rested in Wally's hand and seemed to Andy to be throbbing with coiled power.

Andy couldn't take his eyes off it. "Where'd ya get it?"

"It's better if you don't know." As a buyer and seller of stolen goods, Wally never asked where the merchandise came from. He had purchased this particular item from a stranger. Guessing that the gun was hot, he'd offered the thief twenty dollars and finally paid thirty. Now he was hoping to turn a profit.

"How 'bout it? Seventy-five bucks an' it's yours."

Andy hesitated. He had no idea what he'd do with the gun. The only thing he knew was that he wanted it. "Yeah, OK, I got fifty on me. You'll get the other twenty-five when I get paid."

Wally knew Andy was reliable. He'd held the job at the A&P for six months and had a reputation as a hard worker and stand-up guy. They exchanged palm slaps on the deal, and after Andy swore never to tell where he got the gun, the paper bag with the weapon inside changed hands.

*****

Andy loved his gun. Some evenings, he'd stand in front of his bureau mirror and quick-draw it out of his waistband, waving it menacingly at his reflected image. Draw, posture, wave, over and over. On ocasion, he'd tuck it behind his hip and prowl the neighborhood, hoping someone would try to rob him. He envisioned the mugger's face as he pushed the gun under the guy's quivering chin. Back home after his walk, he'd clean the gun, making sure the unmarred surface was clear of every speck of dust. Finally, he'd reluctantly wrap it in a felt cloth impregnated with Hoppe's gun oil and stow it away under his mattress.

Constantly playing with the gun made discovery inevitable. Sooner or later, someone, either Andy's brother or one of the guys, would find out about it. The someone turned out to be Andy's sister.

Sissy, unable to tolerate how her brothers lived, would occasionally come over to the apartment to clean up. On one of her visits, she surprised Andy and saw him quickly stuff a bag under his mattress. Curious, she changed the graying sheets on Andy's bed and discovered the gun.

"Are you crazy?" she hissed, trying to sound stern, but she couldn't disguise her fear. Sissy sank down on the edge of the bed, then jumped when she realized she was close to the weapon. With a look of revulsion, she slid to one side. "My God, why would you bring a thing like that in the house?"

Andy worshipped his sister. She was the only person who had ever cared for him, and the last thing he wanted was to upset her. He couldn't explain why he loved the gun so much, so he tried to think of an answer she'd accept. Shrugging and staring down at his shoes, he said, "I'm just holdin' it for a friend."

"Look at me, Andy." She reached up and made him turn his head toward her. "I know you're lying, I can see it in your eyes. Our dad's a drunk. He could come over and find that thing and go nuts with it. You've got to get rid of it." Sissy began to cry. "It scares me, Andy. It scares me bad."

No one in the entire world except Sissy could have persuaded Andy to part with his treasure. Even she would have failed if it weren't for her tears. Andy crumbled. "Yeah, OK, I'll get rid of it, Sissy. I promise."

*****

Andy tried to sell the gun back to Wally, but Wally wouldn't pay more than thirty-five bucks. Finally, Frankie Dee, an older hood from 47th Street, offered him the seventy-five it had cost Andy in the first place. Making a decision that would change his life, he reluctantly sold the gun to Frankie.

*****

It was an unusually warm night in early May. Drunk and hopped up on bennies, Frankie Dee and his pal Tonto drove past the Hyde Park Police Station. Tonto, just slightly less drunk than Frankie, was at the wheel. Through a whiskey-induced fog, Frankie recognized the station. With a wild shout, he pulled out the gun he'd been carrying tucked behind his back since he bought it from Andy. He leaned out of the window and began waving it at two cops who happened to be walking out the front door. He shouted, "Bang, bang!" and went into hysterical laughter when the cops froze and then hit the ground.

Twenty minutes later, after a weaving car chase that was doomed from the start, Frankie and Tonto were spread-eagled on the sidewalk with their hands cuffed behind them. Frankie was still laughing.

He stopped laughing back at the station.

*****

"Where'd ya get the gun, Frankie?" The question was preceded by a sharp slap. Frankie wiped the blood from his nose with the back of his hand. He sat in a straight-backed chair in the center of the interrogation room and stared at the drying blood. The walls were a dirty, flat green, and the only illumination came from an overhead lightbulb that had a shade over it but no globe to soften the glare.

Frankie leaned back and looked up at the ceiling trying to clear his head, but the light bothered him and he quickly turned away. "I'm bleedin'."

There were two plainclothes cops working on him, but only one did the talking. The other cop just stood facing him and stared. He was the one who had slapped Frankie. He hit him again, this time with his fist. "It's gonna get worse, Frankie. You tried to kill a cop."

347

Frankie started crying, tears mixing with the blood and snot running along his upper lip. "I was stoned, just fuckin' around. I swear I wasn't gonna shoot."

"How do we know that, Frankie? The gun was loaded. Tell us where ya got it."

Frankie had spent the night in a cell, throwing up. Dirty, unshaven, and stinking of vomit. Now the extent of his stupidity was finally seeping through the drug and alcohol induced fog of his brutal hangover. He sniffed in and wiped at his face with the back of his hand. "I bought it offa guy."

The cop who was doing the talking stopped his partner from hitting Frankie again and then walked over to the door that led back into the squad room. As if the thought had just occurred to him, he said as he went out, "OK, Frankie, have it your way. The piece was stolen from a gas station during a holdup that wound up with the gas station guy being shot. Robbery an' attempted murder, an' we're gonna make you for the job."

It took a moment for the information to penetrate. Then discomfort turned to full-blown panic. "Hold it. I didn't do none a that shit. I'll give ya the guy I bought it from. It ain't like squealin' 'cause the fucker should've told me the gun was dirty in the first place."

*****

When the police came, Andy's dad was in the apartment nursing a hangover. He opened the door, and two plainclothes cops shoved him aside, pushing past him. One of the two was Delaney. Delaney knew Andy from the neighborhood, and without stopping, he called out, "Andy, get your ass out here."

Andy came out of the kitchen, confused. He was shoeless, dressed only in jeans and a sweatshirt. Before he could say anything, the other detective spun him around and tried to put handcuffs on him. Andy

348

squirmed and brought his hands forward. The cop grabbed his hair and pulled his head back. "Hold still, you little fuck, or I'll cuff you between your legs."

Delaney put a hand on his partner's shoulder. "Let the kid get his shoes before you cuff him."

He nodded at Andy's father to go get the shoes. Once Andy had them on, Delaney pulled his arms behind his back and the cuffs snapped shut.

"What's goin' on?" Andy's father asked. No one answered him. He shrugged and didn't ask again.

They led Andy out the side entrance of the Castle and pushed him into the back of their car. Several neighbors stopped to watch, but the occurrence was common enough, and the observers lost interest as soon as the cruiser pulled away.

"Whadda I do?" Andy asked.

Neither policeman answered.

"Whatever it is, ya got the wrong guy," he said, trying to keep the whine out of his voice. Near tears, he kept wracking his brain trying to figure out what was happening. He clung to the thought that this was a mistake.

Once at the station, they pushed him past the desk sergeant and into the back room. He was searched, photographed, and fingerprinted. This time, it went smoothly because Andy was sober. After sitting on a scarred wooden bench for almost an hour, he was led into the interrogation room.

"Where'd you get the gun?"

"What gun?"

Delaney played angry. "Don't fuck around, Andy. Frankie Dee gave you up. We know you sold him the gun."

Andy dropped his eyes. "Oh, that gun. I bought it offa guy."

"What guy?"

"I don't remember."

Delaney was patient. "Andy, the gun was stolen, an' the guy that stole it shot someone. You better give us a name."

Andy shook his head. "The guy I got it from wouldn't rob it. He fences stuff, he don't steal stuff."

Delaney smirked. He came around to stand directly in front of Andy. "Listen to me, you stupid shit. If you don't tell us who you got it from, we'll have to pin it on you."

Andy couldn't look at Delaney. Shoulders slumped forward, he kept his eyes fixed down. He folded his hands in his lap the way he had been taught in school and shrugged. In a voice so soft the cops had to lean in to hear him, he said, "I can't rat the guy out."

They put the cuffs back on and forced him to shuffle, falling out of his laceless shoes, to night court. The weary judge set a trial date for two weeks later and agreed to let him see a public defender. The charges were grand larceny and illegal possession of a firearm.

Delaney had lied about the shooting to scare Frankie Dee and Andy, but not about the robbery. The gun had been stolen from a gas station while the owner was out pumping gas. Delaney was pretty sure the theft was an inside job, and that should've let Andy off the hook. But the assistant DA wasn't as impressed by Andy's unwillingness to squeal as Delaney was. He went for the maximum and complained when bail was set at only $1,000.

The Castle gang dug deep, and between Ben, Henry and John, they came up with fifty dollars, half the money the bail bond service wanted. The other fifty came from Sissy.

*****

Henry was beside himself. "Ya fuckin' jerk! You're eighteen, so you're gonna go ta Joliet if ya don't give up that punk Wally."

350

"Maybe not. It's the first time I ever been in trouble."

They were parked in Grandfather's Buick in the Museum of Science and Industry's parking lot. Henry and Ben sat in front, and Andy was in back. They were drinking from a gallon jug of Gil's beer, a beer that claimed it "never goes flat." Henry joked that the beer was flat when you got it. Still, it was only a buck a gallon, it got you drunk, and Gil's would sell to minors.

"That first offense shit don't mean nothin' when a gun's in it, an' don't forget ya got a drunk an' disorderly on your record." Henry looked back to Ben for confirmation.

"He's right, Andy. What the fuck, Frankie Dee gave you up. No one would blame you for giving Wally up."

"I promised."

And that was that. Henry knew that arguing with Andy was a waste of time once his mind was made up.

Ben reached forward, and before Andy could stop him, he mussed his hair. "I'll come and visit you in the shithouse. Bring you some cigarettes."

He said it with such finality that Andy finally realized there was no hope of his beating the rap.

Henry confirmed it. "You're gonna do a stick for sure, so we'll have a whole year ta come see ya."

Andy was about to answer when the interior of the car was lit up by a spotlight.

Henry looked in the rearview mirror and whispered. "Shit, it's the cops, an' we got beer."

"Ditch it," Ben whispered back.

"Where the fuck am I gonna ditch it?" Suddenly, Henry realized what this could mean for Andy.

He reached up and slipped the bulb out of the overhead light so that it wouldn't go on when the door opened. "Andy, when they come ta my side of the car, you slip out an' crawl over into the bushes."

Andy said nothing. He slouched down in the seat and quietly cracked the back door open.

The cop wasn't in uniform. His face was backlit, made indistinguishable by the glare of his flashlight. He walked slowly over to the driver's window as Andy slipped out the passenger side back door. Once on the ground, Andy started crawling on all fours toward the row of bushes that lined the parking lot.

He'd covered about six feet when a shoe was slammed down on his back. A tired voice that was all-too-recognizable said, "Andy, you are one stupid asshole."

The smell of oily asphalt sickened him as his face pressed into the hard surface of the parking lot. Almost choking with the effort, he fought against his tightening throat, knowing that if he cried now, he'd lose what little pride he had left.

Delaney stood over Andy, pinning him to the ground with his foot. He pushed his shoe into Andy's spine, and the pain forced Andy back into the moment. The urge to weep evaporated. In its place came a feeling of hopelessness, and with an exhale of breath, he simply gave up.

The other cop had Ben and Henry out of the car, sitting on the curb. The almost empty gallon jug was beside them.

Delaney stepped back and pulled Andy to his feet. With a tone that sounded resigned to continual disappointment, Delaney turned toward Henry. "The only chance this moron had of gettin' probation was his almost-clean record. Now that's fucked 'cause here he is with you hoodlums, gettin' drunk."

Fuming with what seemed like honest indignation, he turned back to Andy, "You're so stupid, I won't even waste my time kickin' the shit outta you."

Andy tried to look at Delaney, but he couldn't meet his eyes. He said nothing. Delaney sighed and walked over to where his partner stood. The other detective had picked up his car radio transmitter to ask for a wagon.

"Skip it," Delaney said.

"Whadda you mean?"

"Just skip it. It ain't our job, anyway, an' I ain't got the energy to write it up. The kid I pulled off the ground is due in court on a gun beef. He's gonna do some time, but if we bust him for drinkin', the judge'll toss the key away. Old man's a drunk, mother skipped out early. I know the sister. She says he's a good kid in with a bunch of bums. Just kick him in the ass an' let him slide."

Delaney's partner was stunned. In the two years they had been together, Delaney had never given anyone a break. He shrugged. "It's your call."

The two cops got back in the unmarked car and Delaney leaned out the window. "Andy!" He said loud enough for the others to hear him. "This is your last warning. Keep hangin' around with these fucks, and you're gonna end up a loser like them. They're nothin' but trouble. Next time I catch you with them, I'll act like the prick you always figured me for."

CHAPTER FIFTY-SIX

After a sleepless night filled with terrifying visions of prison, Andy got up, dressed, and stuffed his bag with everything he owned. He was waiting outside Edelstein's drugstore when Barry came to open up. "You need something?"

Andy shook his head. "Just wanna make a phone call." As soon as Barry unlocked the door, he rushed to the phone booth in back and called Sissy.

"Delaney caught me drinkin' in the park last night, an' instead of runnin' me in, he let me go."

Sissy's voice was thick with sleep. "Andy, why would he do that? I know Delaney, he brings his cleaning to the shop I work at. He always comes across as a really mean cop."

"I dunno. Last night, he cut me a break. He told me to keep away from the guys. Said if I stay here, I'm bound to get in trouble."

Sissy gave a huff of exasperation. "Well, he's right about that. That Henry Fox, and the other one, what's his name?"

"You mean Ben?"

"Yes, Ben. I heard from Dad that they're both working for mobsters."

Andy wanted to defend Henry, but thought better of it. "I think Delaney was tryin' to tell me to get outta here."

"What do you mean, get out of here? You've got to go to court."

Taking a deep breath, Andy looked around to make sure Barry wasn't listening. "Sissy, the time I got drunk and spent the night in jail, it almost drove me nuts. I can't take a chance on some judge decidin' to send me to Joliet. I'm gonna jump bail and split."

"Oh, baby, if they catch you, it'll be a lot worse."

"Henry says I'm gonna do a year. I can't do it, Sissy, I just can't. As soon as I get somewhere, I'll call you, an' I'll send you and the guy's money to pay for the bail dough."

Sissy's tone softened and there was a catch in her voice. "Andy, you're my baby brother, and I'll always love you. Forget about the money, your friends will understand. Don't call me or any of them, don't even write. The police'll be watching, and the bail bondsman will be lookin' for you, too." She paused. "You're the best of a really bad lot, and you deserved better than you ever got from our family. Take care, baby."

The phone went dead, but Andy stayed in the booth, holding the receiver until he finally stopped crying.

*****

The first ride he hitched took him to downtown Chicago, and the next one went west to the city of Lombard. From there, he walked for a long time, resting periodically and inhaling the fragrance of the lilacs that grew in abundance throughout the town. As he walked the unfamiliar streets, he was struck by the impact of his decision. Completely alone, he was leaving his friends, his neighborhood, and his sister, the only person who had ever cared for him. Self-pity threatened to start him crying again, and he had to fight off the urge to turn back.

It was dark by the time he caught his next ride. It was a truck headed for Rockford. He threw his bag on the floor of the cab and climbed in next to the driver.

"Where you headed?"

Andy stared out at the night. "As far as you'll take me."

"I'm goin' inta Rockford. That OK with you?"

"Yeah."

"You know anyone in Rockford?"

"Nah."

The driver gestured to Andy's bag. "Where you from?"

Andy studied his fingernails. "Chicago."

"You plannin' on gettin' another ride when we get to Rockford?"

When there was no answer, the driver glanced over. "Well, which is it? Are you plannin' on movin' on or stayin' in Rockford?"

"Don't know for sure."

"You sure don't like to talk much, do you?"

"I ain't got much to say."

The driver gave up, and they rode the rest of the way in silence.

*****

On the outskirts of Rockford, Andy got down from the truck and thanked the driver. He got a grunt in return and the truck pulled away. Three of the four corners at the intersection were gas stations, and the fourth was a late-night diner.

Andy hadn't had any food since leaving home, so he headed toward the brightly blinking sign that ordered him to "EAT."

He took a seat at the counter, pulled a menu out of the rack, and, knowing that he had to make his money stretch as far as possible, tried to figure out what to have.

A plump, middle-aged woman with a gentle air about her wiped her hands on a starched white apron and came over to take his order.

When Andy tried to confirm that the stew came with crackers, she got a soft look in her eyes.

"You go sit in a booth, sonny. I'll bring your food over."

Andy was puzzled, but he was used to following orders, especially from women. When he was seated, the woman served him a huge bowl of vegetable soup and a basket of bread and crackers. He knew he hadn't ordered it, but too shy to speak up, he ate it anyway.

Before he was finished, a salad appeared and Andy got nervous. He couldn't afford to waste money on a salad. "Hey, I didn't order this."

"It comes with the stew, honey," the woman said.

Andy finished the salad. While he ate, the woman leaned against the coatrack that was attached to the side of the booth.

"Where you headed, honey?"

"I'm not sure," Andy said. "Is this a nice town?"

"Oh, it's like most small towns; some good, some bad. You thinkin' of stayin' here?"

"Maybe, if I can find a job."

"What kind of work you lookin' for?"

"I don't know. The last job I had was in a supermarket."

The woman smiled indulgently. "Well, there aren't a whole lot of supermarkets in Rockford." As an afterthought, she added, "But the town's growin' fast."

A teenage girl came out of the kitchen carrying a huge plate of pot roast and mashed potatoes. She set it in front of Andy and turned away without a word.

Andy panicked. "I can't pay for this." He pushed the plate away and started to get up.

The woman reached out and took him by the arm.

"Honey, it's on the house. One look in those puppy eyes of yours, an' I can tell you're down on your luck. Believe you me, I've been there. Now you eat and don't worry about the check." With that, she straightened up and went back behind the counter.

Andy was six when his mother left, and his memory of her was vague. He'd put together a combination of warmth, tenderness, and love, and had come up with a mental picture of what a "mother" should be like. The woman behind the counter fit the image perfectly.

He ate slowly, enjoying the first full meal he'd had since getting out on bail. When he was through, he walked over to the counter and asked the woman what he could do to pay for his meal.

She seemed distracted at the question, as if she'd been thinking of something else. She said, "How'd you like to work here?"

"You mean like a real job?"

She smiled. "Yes, like a real job. You'd wash dishes, wait tables, and generally help me run the place while my husband's on the road. He's a truck driver. I run this place while he works. It wouldn't pay much to start, but you'd get your meals and enough to get a room somewhere. Whadda you say?"

Andy's face scrunched up and he choked back tears. Then he swiped at his eyes and grinned. Nodding rapidly, he said, "Yeah! I mean yes, ma'am!"

CHAPTER FIFTY-SEVEN

J ust past the garbage bins outside the rear door of Stavros's grocery, the alley behind the Castle took a right turn and continued on another fifty feet until it was blocked by an eight-foot-high brick wall. Pushed up against the wall was a derelict '39 Chevy that Henry's dad had once owned.

After taking out a lamppost during one of his drunks, Fox Senior had lost his driver's license, and with an arrest for drunk driving, he became afraid to drive. The solution Henry's father came up with was to have his son repair the car and drive him wherever he wanted to go.

Henry had laughed in his face. "The day I decide ta be a fuckin' chauffeur, it won't be for a drunken bum like you."

Instead, Henry called Ben, and the two of them pushed the car off the street and dumped it in the alley behind the Castle. They put the car up on blocks and sold the tires, keeping the battery so they could play the radio.

Next to the car, tucked under the porch stairs and close enough to hear the radio, Ben set up a half-dozen wooden milk crates for the group to sit on. He convinced the others that despite the garbage smell, it was a great place to smoke, drink beer, listen to jazz, and talk.

*****

"I think my old lady's goin' nuts." Ben smiled at Henry to show he wasn't serious.

Mike and John leaned back against the wall, balancing on the edge of their milk crates. When they didn't interrupt, Ben took it for interest.

"You know how she's always tryin' to get rid of roaches, puttin' roach powder all over an' sprayin' everything? An' how the roaches, hip to her action, just move downstairs for a while an' then, when the coast is clear, they crawl back, thicker than ever?"

Mike gave Ben a languid head nod. "Yeah, so? Everyone's got the same problem."

"So yesterday, she decides it's time to clean the kitchen. When she gets in a cleaning mood, she acts really goofy. She tears everything apart and scrubs like a maniac. This time, she decides to replace the paper on the shelves an' in the drawers. I'm sitting at the kitchen table watchin' her work on the drawer next to the icebox when, suddenly, she gets this wild look on her face an' slowly pulls the drawer all the way out. She sets it next to me on the kitchen table. I'm just about to say somethin' when she puts her finger to her lips and hisses for me to shut up. She tiptoes over to another drawer and pulls out a rolling pin. Then she carefully lifts everything out of the drawer that's sitting on the table. When she's got it completely empty, she slams the rollin' pin down into the drawer and starts rolling it back and forth really hard. She's shrieking and laughing and rolling, and I'm about to put in a call to the loony bin when I see a roach crawl out from under the paper and run for its life. Turns out, she found a whole nest of the fuckers under the paper."

John smiled. "Don't expect me to eat anything that's made with a rollin' pin at your house."

They all laughed, and Mike said, "I hate roaches. I wish I'd been there." He spit in the dirt as if to rid himself of the thought.

They were quiet for a while, each seeming to drift into their own thoughts.

Henry broke the silence. "Did ya hear that Jack's dead?"

"Jack Moran?" Ben asked.

"Yeah, the gooks got him in Korea."

"Damn, that's fucked," John said.

Mike pushed forward from the wall, bringing the crate upright. "Bullshit, it was his own fault. He shouldn't of enlisted."

"He didn't enlist," Henry said. "He volunteered for the draft."

Mike's brow furrowed. "What's the difference?"

Henry wasn't very clear on the difference himself, but he wasn't going to let on to Mike. "If ya volunteer for the draft, ya go early, but ya still gotta do four years."

"So I still don't see the difference. Both ways are the same."

"Nah," Ben said. "It's like this. If you enlist, you go in right away. They've got you for four years, but you get your pick of which service you wanna join. If you volunteer for the draft, you…"

"Me, I'd join the navy," John said.

Henry turned toward John. "Let him finish."

"Yeah, shut up an' let me finish." Ben grinned. "Anyway, if you volunteer for the draft, you can't choose your service, an' you gotta go in for four years. But it's a good deal if a guy wants to get it over with."

"Yeah," John said. "Like Jack. He got it over with, all right."

Henry reached over and took Mike's cigarette out of his hand. He took a deep drag and handed it back. "He didn't have a choice. He got nailed with a nickel bag in his pocket and the judge told him, either join up or do time. That's the way they broke up the Dorchester gang, take your pick, jail or the army."

Ben slammed his crate forward. "They can't do that. It's not legal."

Henry did his raised upper lip sneer. "Yeah, you tell 'em, Benny. Just like it's illegal for Delaney to give ya a slap for bein' a wise guy. Me, I'll stand by an' keep my mouth shut."

Mike stared over at Henry and took a drag on his cigarette. "Delaney ain't such a bad guy."

They fell silent again. Henry got up and went over to his father's car. He reached in the window, turned on the ignition switch, and the radio came on. Ruth Brown was in the middle of "R.B.'s Blues."

Ben listened to the pulsing beat for a moment. "Can I borrow the car tomorrow night?"

Henry nodded. "Make sure ya leave it clean."

"Cleaner than I found it, I promise." He turned to John. "It's a date, so that means you an' Mike gotta make yourselves scarce."

John shrugged, but Mike objected. "Shit, Henry, you can't give him the car. Where're the rest of us supposed to hang out? It's the Memorial Day weekend. We can't hang at the park, it'll be full of people, an' the cops'll be all over the place."

Henry looked at Mike as if he couldn't believe his ears. "Jeez, that's funny, I thought the car was mine. Anyway, the car is for when ya got a date. If you ever get a date, which I doubt, I'll let ya use it."

John turned to Ben. "How late you gonna be?"

"All night, so do me a solid an' keep Nosey McMann away."

The three of them knew that Ben would be with Annie Taloni. An all-night date made Henry wonder how far Ben had gotten with her.

Mike wondered, too, and he was rude enough to ask. "You an' Taloni doin' it?"

Ben flushed. "That's none of your business. It's ignorant to even ask."

John said, "That means no," and they all laughed.

*****

Ben spent most of the next day getting the Chevy ready. After emptying the ashtrays, he pulled out the seats and went over the interior with a whisk broom and a wet rag.

While he was working, Andy's older brother Karl showed up with the three quarts of Schlitz Ben had asked him to buy. A date with Annie meant good beer, not the cheap Gil's crap they usually drank. Ben handed over a five-dollar bill, three bucks for the beer and a deuce for Karl.

"You heard from Andy?" Ben asked.

"Fuck no, an' I hope I never do. Him an' my freakin' sister can both keep outta my life forever. The cops been practically livin' at the house since the little freak jumped bail. The old man says Sissy was the one what put the idea to split in his head. He sure as shit wasn't smart enough ta figure it out for himself."

Karl leaned back against the car. "How 'bout you guys, you got an idea where he went?"

Ben slowly shook his head. He hadn't heard from Andy, either, but if he had, he wouldn't have told Karl. The word on the street was that the bail bondsman had offered a cash reward to anyone who'd let him know where Andy had gone. Ben figured Karl would turn in his whole family if there was money involved.

"Well, if ya hear from him, let me know. Forget what I said before, I'm really worried about the little guy."

Folding the five and stuffing it into his pocket, Karl pushed away from the car and walked toward the entrance of the alley. "Don't get too drunk on all that beer."

*****

Later that evening, Ben covered the back seat of the car with a blanket he'd pulled from his bed. He splashed Mennen's aftershave all over the interior of the car to cut the stale smell and opened two packs of Lucky's. He pushed the open packs in the armrest ashtrays.

*****

The guys called her Ample Annie, but never in front of Ben. Annie was barely five feet tall, and that made her chest seem larger than it was. Her body was full and softly curved, causing heads to swivel when she walked by. She was pretty in an overblown way. Her hair was long and teased, even when short and perky was in style. She used too much makeup, and the colors were a shade or two darker than what was popular.

The Talonis lived on 56th and Blackstone, a couple of blocks from the Castle. Taloni Senior hated the fact that she was dating a guy who wasn't Catholic, and her two older brothers referred to Ben as "Annie's fuckin'hebe."

The response from her father when they said that was, "Don't say fuckin' in front of your mother."

*****

Hoping that neither of Annie's brothers would answer, Ben tapped softly on the Talonis's door. Muffled angry sounds came from the apartment. Ben backed away a step and stood clenching and unclenching his fists while he waited for the door to open.

When it did, it was only wide enough for Ben to see Annie standing there. Her face was framed by auburn curls, and her dark eyes sparkled in the hallway light. She smiled, Ben smiled back, and they stood for a moment just looking at each other.

Suddenly, the door was pulled open the rest of the way, and Annie's brother Vincent stepped into the doorway next to Annie. Whadda ya starin' at, ya sheeny freak?"

Before Ben could answer, Annie shoved her brother back into the apartment and yanked the door closed. Laughing, she grabbed Ben's hand and headed down the stairs. They raced side-by-side, pushing and bumping hips, each trying to reach the bottom first. Vincent leaned over the banister and screamed curses down at them, but their laughter and pounding footsteps drowned him out.

Their first stop was Nicky's for pizza—double sausage, extra cheese. From there, they walked to the lake and sat on the rocks, watching the waves. They talked quietly, discussing plans for graduation.

Ben draped his arm across her shoulder. "Are you mad at me 'cause I don't have enough money to take you to the prom?"

"No, you gotta save for college. But when we have kids, we'll pay for them to go, won't we?"

"Yeah; by then, I'll have a good job an' we'll be able to afford anything we want."

"Not going's OK, really it is. Most of the kids who go are a bunch of snobs, anyway."

They started to kiss, but another couple came over and sat within a few feet of them. They stopped and watched the waves for a few minutes more. Then, without speaking, they got up and left the park, walking hand in hand.

In the back seat of the car, they finished a quart of the beer and relaxed. The noises in the alley had become so familiar, they no longer paid them any attention. The scurrying sounds of rats searching for garbage, an occasional screech of an outraged cat, and the muffled fragments of conversations from the lower floors of the Castle—none of it bothered them. With the windows closed, the door buttons down, and snuggled in each other's arms, they were safe.

The radio played softly and Ben straightened up, trying to strike a pose that Annie would think of as manly. When she leaned toward him, he put his hand behind her head and kissed her. He pushed his tongue against hers and was shocked to feel her aggressively push back. This was new. When they had made out in the past, Annie had always been passive, even reluctant. Now she seemed to be encouraging him. He slipped his hand up the back of her blouse and undid her brassiere. She kissed him harder and took his hand. He thought she was going to shove him away, but instead, she pulled his hand under her blouse and up to her breast.

The temperature inside the car rose with body heat and the windows fogged over. For a brief time, the rest of the world disappeared.

Annie's skirt had inched above her knees. When Ben saw her bare thighs, he took his hand from her breast and slid her skirt all the way up. She didn't seem to notice, so he began to stroke the inside of her thigh, lightly touching the moist outside of her panties. He reached inside and began to rub his fingers in her downy fuzz. Annie moaned and Ben started stroking harder, covering his fingers with her wetness. He tried to push his finger inside, but her panties were in the way. Using his other hand, he tried to reach up and pull them off, but her legs moved together and stopped him.

Her breathing was labored, and when she spoke, her voice sounded as if she were exhausted. "Tell me how much you love me."

Ben gripped the top edge of her panties and started to peel them down. "I love you."

"How much?"

He stopped and looked in her eyes. "I love you so much, I'd die for you."

That seemed to do it. She stroked his cheek, reached under her skirt, pulled her panties all the way off and tossed them into the front seat. Then she undid the buttons on her blouse, revealing her breasts. Ben's heart was hammering so hard it felt as if it might explode. Unable to speak, he leaned forward and started to kiss her, managing to move his finger into her at the same time. He started quickly shoving it in and out the way the guys told him to, but Annie stiffened in, what was clearly pain, and he slowed down. For a short time, he was content to kiss her breasts and have his finger in the warmest place.

His love lay back on the seat and Ben pulled away, drinking in the sight of her body. He wondered if she'd know that he'd never done it before.

"Can you do something so I won't get..." Embarrassment stopped her. "You know, have a baby."

"I heard you can't get pregnant if it's your first time, but I brought somethin' anyway." He reached in his back pocket and removed the condom he'd been carrying for over a year, just in case. He unrolled the rubber onto his penis, grateful for the instinct that had made him practice putting one on. He'd even masturbated wearing one just to see how it felt.

Finally, with the rubber in place, he leaned over to Annie. He was sitting in the middle of the seat and she didn't seem to understand that she would have to slide toward him.

Ben knew their position was wrong. He fumbled with his pants, first pushing them down to his ankles and then deciding to remove them completely. Naked from the waist down, rubber-shrouded erection sticking straight out, he roughly pulled her sideways on the seat, not noticing in his haste that she did most of the work. She was impossibly small down there and when he tried to shove inside, she let out a squeal of pain.

Scared, he pulled back. "Jesus, it's so small. Maybe we'd better not."

"Yes," she said, "Do it." And she turned her head away.

He tried again, and with a sharp thrust, he burst into her. This time, her cry was much louder. She hollered, outraged by the unexpected pain, but by now, Ben was beyond stopping. With a frenzied motion, he pumped frantically for less than a minute. Then he shivered and moaned and his pulsating liquid rush ended their first lovemaking.

Except for the night noises, the alley was quiet. Ben took off the filled condom, opened the door a crack, and threw the thing under the car. While he pulled on his pants, Annie turned away and wriggled back into her clothes.

At first, they just sat there, not touching. Then Ben reached over and took her gently into his arms. She lifted her head to look in his eyes and her voice quivered slightly. "Are you going to tell everyone?"

"Whadda you take me for? Of course I'm not gonna tell. An' we'll get married as soon as I graduate."

"What about college?"

"I can go at night. It's gonna be OK."

He smoothed her hair and kissed her lightly on the cheek. She smiled contentedly and snuggled closer. "You're going to Illinois, like you always wanted. We'll move downstate, and I'll get a job waitressing. With tips, it's really good money. You can get a part-time job and between us, we can make enough to live on while you get your degree." She gripped his hand and kissed his palm. "I love you, Ben Kahn."

"And I love you, Annie Taloni."

*****

Later, as he lay in his bed, Ben wondered how he could go about getting more rubbers. He knew he couldn't buy them outright because he was still under twenty-one. He toyed with the idea of asking John to get his replacement at Edelstein's to steal some. He considered it for a while, then decided against it; as soon as he asked John for rubbers, it would be like telling the world that he and Annie were doing it. He wondered if it would be safe to just pull out before he came and have Annie douche afterward. Having no one to ask kept him worrying until he was too tired to think. As the sun was coming up, he finally fell asleep.

*****

The next night, Ben went down to the alley. John was alone and he passed Ben a half-filled gallon jug of Gil's beer without speaking.

"Where's Henry?" Ben asked, more to open conversation than to really find out.

John shrugged, avoiding Ben's eyes. "He's been hangin' out on 55th a lot. Could be doin' some sellin'."

"Weed?" Ben asked.

"Nah, there's no money in weed. I think he's dealin' smack. His old man is gonna die any day now, an' he needs bread to live on."

Ben shook his head. "No fuckin' way. I know Henry, he wouldn't sell that shit no matter how much bread he needed."

They fell quiet. Ben tilted back his crate and leaned against the wall. He wanted to share the way he was feeling with John, to tell him that he'd become a man. He held his tongue for a couple of reasons. It was bound to get back to Annie, plus he'd have to admit that all the other times he'd bragged about sex had been lies.

He took a long pull at the beer jug and wiped his mouth with the back of his sleeve. "The first chance I get, I'm gettin' out of this armpit. I'm goin' downstate to school. Fox and you can let this neighborhood rot your brains, but I'm gonna get my degree an' make somethin' of myself."

John took the jug and held it in his lap. "I like it here. Lots of ways to make a dishonest dollar." He tilted the bottle up and finished it off. Mindful of the fifteen-cent deposit on the empty jug, he carefully set it down next to his crate. "If you ever do get to Illinois, I hope they teach you how to shove used rubbers all the way under a car, 'cause down there, you won't have buddies like me to do it for you."

CHAPTER FIFTY-EIGHT

When Henry got off the bus from school, Ben was sitting on the Miller Building stoop. They hadn't seen each other for a few days because Henry had been staying later at school to take his finals. He'd been suspended for three days for fighting during the regular exam period and needed special permission to take the exams he'd missed.

Intending to go up to his flat to change clothes, he gave Ben a halfhearted wave and headed across the street.

Ben got to his feet and shouted, "Where you headed, Fox, to sell some drugs?"

Henry turned, a stunned expression on his face. "Jesus! Are you nuts? Hold it down." He ran back and stood a few feet from Ben. "Anyway, what if I am, what's it to you?"

"Sellin' drugs is fucked. That's what it is to me. I never thought you'd mess with that shit."

Henry's voice took on a pleading quality Ben wasn't used to. "Ya don't understand. College may be your ticket outta here, but I ain't goin' ta no college, an' I ain't gonna spend my life workin' in no god-damn factory. If my way outta this slum is workin' for Costas an' sellin' drugs, then I'll work for Costas an' I'll sell drugs. I ain't using an' I ain't gonna start, so what's the harm?"

"The harm is, it's wrong," Ben said quietly. "And you're gonna get caught."

Henry put out his hand, palm up. "Look, Benny, if I didn't sell the shit, someone else would. The guys I sell to are already hooked, an' it's worse for them if they don't get their fix. I'm not gonna get busted, I'm just a little guy. The cops go for the biggies."

Ben kept shaking his head. "We both know better. Sooner or later, one of those junkies will rat you out to keep out of jail. Besides, I still say it's wrong."

Henry sighed. He stuffed both hands deep in his pockets and looked straight into Ben's eyes. "Ya know somethin', Benny? You think ya got all the answers. You're always so goddamn sure you're right. One of these days, you're gonna find out that things ain't always cut an' dried like ya want 'em ta be. Anybody can get pushed inta doing stuff that's wrong, Benny, even you."

There was more Henry wanted to say, but Ben's face flushed with frustration. He looked ready to either explode or cry. "I don't know what you're talking about."

Henry turned as if to go, then hesitated and faced Ben again. "Maybe ya don't know what I'm talkin' about 'cause I'm sayin' shit you don't wanna hear." Without waiting for response, Henry turned away.

This time, Ben let him go.

*****

It was two weeks before graduation, and Henry wouldn't be among those graduating. He'd taken and passed his make-up exams for all of his classes but one. His civics teacher, angered by the fighting, had refused to let him take a late final. He would let Henry take the test in summer school, but wouldn't let him graduate with his class. Another argument with Ben had started when Henry told him that he was going to just skip it. "No one ever checks ta see if ya

371

really graduated. An' anyway, I'm gonna work for Costas. He don't give a shit about high school diplomas."

Ben had exploded, going off again about how wrong it was to be selling smack. Henry couldn't figure Ben out. It was OK for the two of them to beat people half to death for Nicky Costas, but it was wrong to sell someone a jolt of pure joy.

*****

Using the fake draft card he'd gotten from John, Henry bought a quart of beer and walked down to the bench across from the Post Restaurant to think and drink in peace. It was a balmy evening. The sun was fading behind the buildings, and one by one, the streetlights started blinking on. He crossed his legs at the ankles and stretched out, one hand on the back of the bench and the other holding the beer.

A car pulled up and came to a stop. It was a brand-new, pearl-white Studebaker convertible with the top down. The driver smiled at Henry, but said nothing. Henry ignored him.

The driver shut off the engine and shifted to face Henry. He still said nothing, but his smile was phony, and it seemed to Henry as if the guy was having trouble maintaining it.

Finally, Henry looked over at him. "I know you?"

The driver shook his head no, but the smile became a leer, and Henry caught on. The driver leaned toward him and in a soft voice said, "No, but I'd like to get to know you."

Henry's first thought was to tell the fag to beat it. His second was to beat the shit out of him for thinking he was the kind of a guy who'd go with a fairy, and his third was that the guy probably had money.

He walked to the passenger side of the car and opened the door. When the driver nodded, he got in. The car had tuck-and-roll white leather seats, and a small Kewpie Doll hung from the rearview mirror.

Tight-lipped and frowning, Henry leaned back in the plush seat. "So whadda ya want?"

The leer broadened. "You're very beautiful in a cruel sort of way. I want to kiss you," he said, with a nod of his head toward Henry's crotch, "down there."

"Ya got any money?"

After a moment's hesitation, the man reached into his pocket and pulled out a twenty-dollar bill.

Henry grabbed it. "Ya can't blow me an' drive at the same time. Better let me drive."

He slid over as the man got out and walked around the back of the car to the other side. Grinning, Henry dropped the car in gear just as his admirer reached the passenger door.

"So long, sucker," he shouted over the screech of tires as he peeled away. In the rearview mirror, he watched the guy frantically wave and yell for Henry to come back. He rounded the corner just as the waving hand curled into an angry fist.

Henry laughed, and for the first time that night, felt good.

He drove to 55th Street. He cruised past the bars between Harper and Lake Park, past the church at Kimbark Avenue, past the University Tap where a bunch of freaks called the Compass Players were packing in the crowds, and on up to Cottage Grove. He made a U-turn and rolled back down toward the lake. Just his luck, the one time he had a decent ride, there was no one around to admire it. Taking a left, he drove down Lake Park as far as 47th and was about to give up and ditch the car when he spotted Billy Ryan standing on the corner next to Lola's Tavern. He pulled over and nodded with pride when Billy did a double-take on the car.

Grinning, Henry said, "Hop in, I'll give ya a ride."

Billy flipped himself over the car door without opening it and settled in the seat. The smell of weed hit Henry immediately and he asked Billy for a hit. Billy giggled and raised his hands, palms up. "All gone."

Henry said, "Shoulda caught ya sooner."

As they drove, Henry told Billy about the fairy and how he got the car. Billy didn't seem to care. He pulled out a half-pint of Jim Beam and offered Henry a swig. After grabbing a swig himself, he recapped the bottle and pushed it back into his pocket. They drove down to the lake and pulled into the 53rd Street parking lot.

Henry pushed the seat back as far as it would go. "Ya ever finish high school?"

Billy laughed. "I didn't even finish up at Ray Elementary. I got sent ta juvie, an' by time I got out, it was too late."

Henry shook his head in sympathy. "You can still tell people ya graduated. They never check."

Billy nodded. "Yeah, but I can't write so good, so I gotta keep away from writin' jobs."

"Ya can always work in the steel mill," Henry said, and they both laughed.

"Yeah, but first, I gotta learn ta talk Polish."

They sat there for what seemed to Henry like a long time. Billy began to fidget. "So whadda ya wanna do?"

Henry shrugged. "We gotta either ditch the car or get outta the neighborhood. By now, the little faggot's gone ta the cops."

"Maybe not," Billy said. "Sometimes queers are too scared ta squeal 'cause the cops don't like 'em."

"You're nuts," Henry said, staring out into the blackness of the empty lot. "Fag or no fag, no one's gonna give up a ride like this."

Billy took another swallow of whiskey and passed the bottle to Henry. Henry finished it and opened the car door.

"Where ya goin?" Billy's voice was slurred and his eyes seemed to wander.

"Might as well just leave the car here, we're close ta home."

Billy tried to snap his fingers, but no sound came out. "We could go up ta the North Side. I know these really cool broads livin' there. They might put out for guys with a car like this."

They drove up the Outer Drive and exited on Montrose Avenue. Once off the Drive, they headed west. At almost every intersection, Billy made Henry turn either left or right, saying, "This is it for sure." Finally, he giggled and admitted he couldn't remember where the girls lived. They kept driving up and down dark side streets, going as far west as Pulaski.

Every house looked pretty much the same, and with each frustration, Henry got more annoyed. "Shit, we'll never find 'em. Let's head home."

Billy shook his head. "I know it's around here somewhere." They started driving back toward the lake. When they passed Avers Avenue, Billy wiggled his finger at the street sign.

"That's it, that's the street."

"You been sayin' that for the last hour," Henry grumbled, but he slammed on the brakes, backed up, and made a left turn. It was a one-way street, and a cop car was passing through the intersection just as Henry pulled across. The cop's light flashed, and without thinking, Henry punched it.

If he'd been completely sober, he would have stopped and tried to talk his way out of things, but Henry wasn't sober. The smoke and stink of burning rubber filled the air, and with a scream, the Studebaker fishtailed forward. The cop flipped on his siren and was right behind them. They turned at the corner and went into a skid that threw them sideways. At first, Henry fought the skid, then turned into it and regained control. He drove straight up the street, ignoring the stop signs at the end of each block. He barreled down alleys, skidded onto main streets, and even drove through a corner gas station, but the cop stayed with him. The cop was the better driver, and after a dozen more blocks of squealing tires and near misses, Henry knew he wasn't going to get away.

"We gotta ditch the car. I'm gonna pull over." He shouted over the roar of the engine. "The minute I hit the curb, we'll flip out an' run. There's only one cop in the car, and if we split up, he can't chase both of us."

Billy was laughing and he seemed too relaxed. "Cool," Billy said. "Real cool."

Henry was out and running before the car stopped, and the Studebaker's momentum pulled it over the curb and into a tree. He heard the crunch of the bumper smashing, and when he looked back, he saw Billy calmly walking away. Henry cursed and kept running. He spun across a manicured lawn, turned onto a path alongside the house, and flipped a gate that led to the backyard. Lying flat, he was able to watch the action through the opening at the bottom of the gate.

He saw Billy cross the street and slide under a parked car. The police vehicle had come to a stop behind the Studebaker, and Henry could see the boots of the cop as he stepped out.

The tactic of hiding and freezing had worked in the past, but Billy had been too slow. The cop had seen him roll under the car. He stood for a moment taking in the scene, then walked over to where Billy was hiding and told him to roll on out.

This North Side cop wasn't like the ones in Hyde Park. He didn't smack Billy or rough him up in any way. He just put the cuffs on and walked him back to his squad car. He even held Billy's head to keep him from getting bumped when he pushed him into the back seat.

Leaning in the driver's side window, he picked up the radio and mumbled something into the mike. What came back sounded like pure static to Henry, but the cop seemed to understand. He turned to Billy, and in a voice loud enough for Henry to hear, he said, "The guy you stole the car from reported it. You're up for grand theft auto."

Billy was pushed back into the seat. Henry couldn't hear what he mumbled but he figured Billy must be giving him up.

Again the cop's voice was loud enough for Henry to hear. "What's this other guy's name?" The cop's tone sounded bored, as if he didn't care if Billy answered or not.

Billy said something and the cop laughed.

"Yeah, I figured you wouldn't know his name."

Henry got up, crossed the yard, and crept along the other side of the house. If Billy had given him up, things would have been different. As it was, he knew he had to do the right thing.

Under his breath, Henry groaned, "Shit," and walked out onto the street. The cop was working the radio and didn't see Henry coming.

"He's tellin' the truth. He didn't know the Studie was hot. I picked him up hitchin'."

The policeman was startled. He jumped back and pulled his gun. "Lie face down on the ground." He waved the gun and pointed, but Henry didn't see it because he had already dropped down.

"Hands locked behind your head."

Henry obediently laced his fingers and put them behind his head.

"Don't move," the cop said to Henry. A few moments passed in silence and Henry understood the cop's dilemma. Two suspects, one set of handcuffs, and no back-up. The cop yanked Billy out of the car and took off the cuffs. With a shrug, he motioned for Billy to take off. "This is your lucky night. Beat it."

Billy looked down at Henry, then turned and quickly walked away. When he was out of sight, the cop put the cuffs on Henry. "Pretty decent of you, but you're still up for grand theft auto."

Henry let out a huge sigh. "Guy didn't give me no choice. I copped a lift from him, and he turned out ta be a fairy. When he started grabbin' at my privates, I asked if I could drive, an' when he got out ta go around, I took off."

The cop helped Henry into the car. "Damn queers make me sick. I wish I'd known before I called it in. Now I gotta book you. Tell the judge your story, an' he might go easy on you."

*****

The station was brightly painted and very clean. Henry was put in a cell by himself and given coffee with cream and a baloney sandwich on toast. Through a bureaucratic mix-up, he stayed at the Montrose station for three days. Finally, a guard came and explained that they had been waiting for someone from Hyde Park to come and pick him up, but no one had bothered to show. The next day, a very pissed off Montrose cop drove Henry to the South Side. "We make the bust, they take the credit, and I gotta drive halfway across town to deliver their prisoner."

Henry put his head down and fought to keep the smile off his face. "Ya could just let me go."

The moment he got out of the car, he was grabbed and shoved toward the entrance by a cop he didn't know. "Move it, asswipe."

He was pulled past the desk sergeant and subjected to the full routine. They took his fingerprints, photographed him, stripped off his belt and shoelaces, and shoved him into a cell.

An hour later, he was hauled out for a lineup. He shuffled onto a stage, trying to keep his laceless shoes from falling off. There were three other men standing on the stage, all Negros. The owner of the Studebaker quickly identified Henry.

378

In the morning, Henry was taken by bus to court for arraignment. The day was bright with sunlight and he looked out between the bars on the windows of the Black Mariah. People were rushing everywhere on their way to work, school, maybe just shopping. He figured a bunch were just out because it was a beautiful day. Traffic was moving, horns were honking, lights were blinking, and the city was filled with life.

There were times when Henry had seen the paddy wagon go by, but he'd never given a thought to the people locked inside. He turned to the slender white man chained next to him. The guy's face was bruised and his plaid shirt had spots of blood on it. "You ever been in one a these before?"

The man said nothing.

"First time for me," Henry said, but there was still no response.

"What, is it against the rules ta talk?"

The man turned to face Henry. "No, asshole, it ain't against the rules, but when you ain't got shit to say, it's best to shut your hole." His breath was stale with cigarette odor and unbrushed teeth. Henry shrugged and went back to staring out the window.

When the bus arrived at the court building, a guard approached Henry and pulled him out of line. They stood on the sidewalk while the rest of the prisoners went inside the building. A fat, gray-haired man in a dark blue suit with a huge leather briefcase came over and tucked a twenty in the guard's pocket. He smiled. "Two minutes, Ed."

The guard nodded and stepped to one side.

Setting the briefcase down, the fat man pulled a handkerchief out of his pocket and wiped the sweat from his forehead. "I'm your lawyer, kid, compliments of Nicky Costas. You say nothing. You let me do all the talking. If the judge asks how you plead, you say not guilty. Nothin' else, just not guilty. Got it?"

Henry nodded and the lawyer motioned the guard back over.

*****

"This is the young man's first offense, Your Honor. According to the arresting officer, he gave himself up. He was hitchhiking and had the misfortune to be picked up by a deviant who tried to molest the boy. In fear, he managed to trick the deviant and get away in the car. The owner of the car is a predator who would just as soon forget about the whole thing. He is not pressing charges, nor is he seeking restitution for the damage."

The judge wasn't listening. He looked over the report in front of him and frowned at Henry. He hunched over and rapidly wiped his finger back and forth under his nose. "You think because a person's homosexual, you can steal his car?"

Henry knew better than to answer. He put his head down and tried to look sorry.

"Your Honor, this boy has never been in trouble before. He—"

"You mean he's never been caught before." The creases in the judge's face deepened and his graying eyebrows met in a V above his nose. He nodded and looked at the lawyer. "Isn't that what you mean? He's never been caught before."

He stared down at Henry and said, "Well, you're caught now. How do you plead to the charge?"

Before Henry could answer, the fat lawyer put his hand on Henry's shoulder. "There is one other thing, Your Honor. I hesitated to mention this because the boy has been lost in the system for three days and his family was unable to give him the tragic news." The lawyer turned away from the judge and faced Henry. "Son, I'm sorry to have to tell you like this, but your father passed away two days ago."

If Henry had been a professional actor, he couldn't have played the scene better. He let his head droop down and wiped at a nonexistent tear. "Well, I guess it's for the best. Poor Dad, he's finally out of pain."

The judge shook his head. "Died while his son was sitting in jail for stealing a car." He slammed the gavel down. "All right, in light of this bereavement, I'm going to give you a break. This case is continued for thirty days, and you are free on your own recognizance. If, during the thirty days, you were to seek enlistment in the service of your country, I would be forced to suspend your sentence. I want to be perfectly clear—the decision is yours. In thirty days, your lawyer can either come back to this court and explain to me that you are not available because you are a member of the armed forces, or he can bring you back here and you'll go on trial for auto theft. Understood?"

Again, the judge pushed his finger back and forth under his nose, and this time, he finished off by sharply pinching both nostrils. He looked at Henry's lawyer. "Understood?"

Both Henry and the lawyer nodded in unison. The judge banged his gavel again, and Henry was released.

The lawyer was visibly upset. "Crap, just my luck to draw the only pansy judge in Chicago. Mr. Costas is gonna be really angry about this. It's a break for you, but it means you won't be around for four years."

CHAPTER FIFTY-NINE

Henry's attendance at his father's funeral was a must. Grandfather took him to a second-hand clothing store and helped him pick out a dark suit. The jacket had to be tightened at the waist and the pants shortened, but the shop owner was a master tailor and the result was a perfect fit. The single-breasted suit had wide lapels and had three buttons instead of the tuxedo-cut, one-button roll kind Henry wanted. It was the first suit Henry had ever owned, and despite his grumbling, he secretly thought he looked cool.

At the burial, Henry struggled to feel some kind of regret at his father's passing—struggled and failed. A part of him wished his father was still alive so he could beat the bastard to death. As they lowered the coffin, Henry dropped his head to his chest, thought about maggots feeding on his father, and to please his grandfather, pretended to pray.

*****

The news that Henry had to join the army to avoid going to jail sent a chill through Ben. It wasn't the first time a judge had delivered that kind of ultimatum, but Ben had assumed Nicky Costas's connections would be enough to get Henry off with only probation.

Each member of the Castle group had their own idea of what Henry should do, and they weren't shy about advising him. John was for risking a trial. "The pansy already said he wasn't gonna testify. With Costas's lawyer, you could beat the rap easy."

Mike had a different take on it. "You gotta go in the army sooner or later. At least this way, you can join the navy an' stay outta Korea. Even if the fightin's over, that place is still a hellhole."

Ben, who was wary of seasickness, recommended the air force.

*****

A week after his father's funeral, Henry still hadn't made up his mind which service to join. He was sitting on the park bench across from the Post Restaurant with Annie and Ben. It was graduation night, and the hip party to go to was the one given by Maxine Sommers. John had wangled invitations for the group, and everyone except Henry was going.

Ben was worried about his friend. Since his court date, Henry had alternated between mildly down in the dumps and out-and-out morose. Going to the party without him seemed like desertion.

"Hey, I'm serious. We don't have to go. We'd rather just hang out here with you." Ben looked sideways at Annie for confirmation. She sat between him and Henry, perched on the edge of the bench as if she were ready to flit away at any minute. Her pixie smile faded just enough for Ben to know that she was really looking forward to going. "Or you could change your mind and come with us."

The park lawns had been mowed earlier in the day, and the smell of freshly cut grass still filled the air. Henry put his arm around Annie's shoulder and gave both of them a forced grin. "I'd feel funny goin' ta a graduation party an' me not graduatin'. You guys go ahead. Maybe I'll catch ya later."

Ben and Annie were dressed for the party. Ben was wearing the dress slacks and the sports jacket he'd worn under his graduation gown. "No one cares if you graduated or not. This might be the last chance for a lot of the kids to see you before you join up."

"I'm cool," Henry said. "But you an' Annie are all prettied up, an' I ain't dressed right. I'll go home an' change an' meet ya there."

Smiling, Annie bounded to her feet and did a quick spin, letting her skirt flare out. She gave Henry a kiss on the cheek and then turned to grab Ben's arm. As they walked away, Ben caught Henry's eye and knew that Henry had only agreed to go to get rid of them. He started to turn back to argue, but Annie tugged on his sleeve.

With a slow wave, Ben walked away with his arm around Annie's waist. Henry watched them until they turned the corner. He retrieved the paper bag he'd stashed under the bench just before Ben and Annie had shown up. Hiding the beer was a cheap trick, but a quart wasn't enough for three, particularly when one of the three was Annie Taloni. The bag was rolled down enough to expose the neck of the bottle of Schlitz.

The night was warm, almost hot, and Henry thought about going down to the beach to catch the lake breeze. He leaned back on the bench, took a pull at the beer, and had a fleeting desire for a cigarette.

A few moments later, a brand-new '53 Olds pulled up, and Mary Ryan got out of the passenger seat. She waved at the guy driving and the Olds sped away. Standing in front of Henry, she shuffled from foot to foot as if she was unsure of her welcome.

"Hi."

Henry smiled. "Hi, yourself."

Mary looked good, really good. She wore tight jeans and a pale yellow sleeveless blouse that accented her cone-shaped breasts. Strawberry-blonde and freckle-faced, her bright red lips broke into a broad, toothy grin. "Thanks for what you did for Billy."

Henry gave her an, *it was nothing*, shrug and motioned for her to sit down.

Mary perched on the edge of the bench seat. "How come you never come around no more?"

Henry shrugged again and ignored the question. "How come ya ain't at one of the graduation parties? Ya graduated, didn't ya?"

She gave him a wry smile and pointed to the Schlitz. "The neighborhood punch don't get invited to parties."

Henry handed over the quart. "Ya shouldn't talk like that. Ya ain't no tramp. In my book, you're as good as anyone around."

Mary took a small sip and handed the bottle back. "I heard about the army thing. If you want me to, I could write you letters…I mean, if you want me to."

The wind came up and rustled the leaves in the trees above the bench. Henry inhaled and thought it odd that the city smelled worse after dark. The earlier smell of newly mowed grass had faded completely, replaced by the damp stink of leafy mildew. He debated making a pass at Mary, then decided against it. She was talking so seriously, it made trying something seem wrong.

"Yeah, a letter would be good. I ain't much for writin', so if ya don't hear back, don't get upset."

She stared down at her shoes. "I could wait for you."

"Whadda ya mean?"

"I mean, I could wait for you to get out. Not fool around anymore. And when you get out, we could be together."

Henry shifted his body away from her. "Nah, it's gonna be four years, an' I don't even know if I'm comin' back here."

She turned away, and Henry could tell she was crying. "Yeah, you're probably right. Four years, I'll probably be married and have a couple of kids. It was just a joke, so forget I said it, OK?"

With a quick wave, she stood and started across the street toward the restaurant. "See ya around, Henry Fox. You have a good life."

He saw her through the window of the Post as she went to the counter and sat down. Pete the counterman hustled over and with a goofy smile, grabbed her hand with both of his.

CHAPTER SIXTY

Four of them were drinking at Lola Blues Tap. They were huddled around the curve at the end of the bar, with John and Henry at a right angle to Ben and Mike.

It was late afternoon, and the dust mote filled rays of the sun streamed in the front window. The wall-to-wall carpeting was so spattered with wine and beer spills that the resulting pattern looked intentional. To most people the place would have seemed shabbier in sunlight than it did under the subdued lighting of the evening, but to Ben the worn and weary look of afternoon gave the bar a more comfortable feeling.

Blue, Lola's longtime man, stood at the sink, wiping a glass and staring out of the window.

John took a swig of beer. "You know that Jap kid who won all the math stuff?"

"Yeah, Mas Matsuta, we're tight. What about him?"

"He got a scholarship to MIT. Four full years, and he turned it down."

"You gotta be shittin' me. What would he do that for?"

"His old man's sick. He has to help out the family."

Ben slowly shook his head. "College is the ticket out of this shit-box neighborhood. Turn down a scholarship? The guy must be insane."

Henry had chugged the VO he'd ordered and was sipping at his water back. "I know that guy, Mas. His people own the garage on 47th an' Lake Park. He's a fuckin' math genius."

"Yeah," John said. "All them Japs are smart. One of my teachers told me that they had a quota on Japs so no class could get too many of 'em."

Henry motioned to Blue and pointed to his empty shot glass. "That's stupid, why would they do that?"

"It's true," Ben said. "Japs push up the class average. If the teachers go by the curve, all the regular guys flunk."

Mike nodded knowingly. "I heard it, too. I also heard that some teachers fight to get 'em in their classes 'cause they're so smart, they make the teachers look good."

Blue set down his towel and sauntered over. He poured Henry his shot, then questioned the others with his eyes. John nodded, and after Blue had poured and turned away, he took a swig and sighed. "I had this physics teacher who was a marine. He hated Japs, so he gave the other teachers his quota."

"Now, that's really stupid," Ben said. "Mas an' the other Japs who live here are Americans. There's even some who fought in the war."

John looked at Ben, and in a sing-song voice, said, "Oh, Mr. Ben, can't you see? I'm jes' tellin' you what the motherfucker told me."

It was a paraphrased line from a dirty poem called "The Signifying Monkey." They all smiled, even Ben.

Mike stared down at his drink. "I got a job at Buick Aircraft, out in Willow Springs."

If Mike's news took the others by surprise, they didn't show it.

"What's it pay?" Ben asked.

"Two twenty-five an hour."

"That's pretty good bread."

387

"Yeah. I'm startin' in spare parts, but the personnel lady told me I could move up to the line if I did good."

Henry sneered. "They always say shit like that ta get ya ta work harder."

Mike shrugged. "Hey, whadda you care? You're gonna enlist. Anyway, now that I'm outta school, my folks are chargin' me rent."

The door swung open and Rick Dolan, a friend of Henry's from Golden Gloves, staggered in. He crowded in next to Henry and started pounding on the bar. "Bartender, bartender, I need a drink."

Blue was big and black and he never smiled. He gave Rick the dead-eye stare, and drunk as Rick was, he seemed to get the message.

They sat in silence for a few minutes. Finally, John said, "Lemme get the next one. I'm holdin'."

Rick smiled and tried a whisper that came out too loud. "Yeah, you're holdin'. You're holdin' all the bread I had to pay you to get this phony ID." The other three nodded in agreement.

John preened with pride. "Ain't that stuff the best? Draft card, driver's license, the works—all for twenty-five bucks."

Mike shook his head. "I still can't figure how you do it. That shit looks real. Ben's got his picture on a chauffeur's license, and he can't even drive."

They were all still laughing when Lola strode in. A former *Ebony Magazine* model, she was tall, elegant, and whipcord tight. Lola ran Blue and the bar with an iron hand.

She clocked them for ID, frowning at the perfect licenses they produced. After checking them all, she stared at Rick. "You drunk; gonna get me in trouble. Whyn't y'all hang out somewhere else?"

Rick smiled. "Because I love you." It came out, "Becush I wuv you."

Lola didn't smile back. She shook her head and walked through the curtain to her living quarters. The four of them followed her generous rear with their eyes. Blue came over and wiped the bar in front of Rick. "Don't be smart-mouthin' Lola."

Blue was looking straight at Rick, but the message was for all of them. They nodded in unison.

"Whadda you got that has a kick?" Rick asked.

Blue looked at him with sad eyes.

"Lola say you too drunk."

"Then give me somethin' strong an' I'll pass out. That way, you don't gotta worry 'bout me."

Blue shrugged. "Your funeral. Got anythin' you want, up ta pure alcohol."

Ben said, "There's no drink that's pure alcohol."

The blue neon light of the Pabst sign glinted off the hairless dome of Blue's head. His face was devoid of emotion. "White lightnin' gets close, 190 proof."

"Gimme some," Rick said, grinning at the others. "I wanna try it."

Blue pulled down a dusty bottle of clear liquid from one of the top shelves. He slowly wiped the bottle clean, then placed a glass on the counter. Without looking, he filled the glass almost to the brim. "One'll make you crazy, two'll make you brave, three'll rot your insides, put you in de grave." Pulling out a cigarette lighter, he touched the flame to the edge of the glass and the drink caught fire.

"That proves it's the real shit, when it burns like that," Henry said. "Drink it."

Rick reached down and lifted the glass. His hand shook slightly as he raised it to his lips.

He seemed to be about to take a sip when Ben called out.

"Blow the flame out first, for Christ's sake. You'll burn yourself."

Rick tried, but he blew too hard and some of the burning liquid spilled onto his hand. At the same time, he was raising the glass to his lips and his hand began to shake even more. The fire sloshed out, lit the fingers holding the glass and chased the liquid running down his arm. Screaming, Rick dropped the drink and it crashed onto the bar, spewing flame along its surface. Everyone at the bar recoiled, knocking their barstools over backward. Mike grabbed a towel and began to swat at the fire. The towel immediately became soaked, and with each back-swing, the liquid flew in all directions. Now the flames were on the wall and the ceiling.

Mike lost his cool and started shouting, "Fire! Fire!"

Lola came out of the back and stood surveying the scene. It seemed as if fire was everywhere, on the bar, up and down the walls, and on the towel Mike was still ineffectually waving. With a look of pure disgust, she pulled the towel from his hand and shoved it into the soapy dishwater in the sink. She smothered the flames on the counter, then using the wet towel as protection for her hand, she picked up the shot glass and threw it in the sink. By now, most of the liquid had burned off, and the rest of the fire went out without causing any damage.

The boys stood around, looking sheepish, but Lola was enraged. "Get out, all y'all! Get out, an' don't come back."

Blue slunk into the back, and his retreat seemed to calm Lola. She stood with her hands on her hips, steely-eyed, and watched until the boys had filed out of the front door.

Out on the sidewalk in front of Lola's, Ben blinked in the glare of the sun's final gasp and shuffled from foot to foot. Rick waved his singed hand and started weaving his way up the street.

"You fuckin' moron," John laughed, looking at Mike. "Why'd you start shouting an' pick up the stupid towel?"

Mike snarled something under his breath, and with an angry shrug, he too started walking away.

John went after him and put his arm around his shoulder. "Mike, you're a total fuckup, but you're our total fuckup." Bursting into laughter, the two of them kept going without saying good-bye to Ben or Henry.

Henry watched them disappear around the corner. "Lola got so pissed, she forgot ta nail us for the tab."

They started walking back to the Castle. Henry went on, "It's a good thing, 'cause I'm really hurtin' for bread. I gotta get some dough before I sign up."

Ben nodded. "Maybe I can come up with something.

*****

The next day, Ben banged on Henry's door. "Got some good news. I talked to Costas like you said an' asked him for some higher-payin' jobs. He said we deserve a shot, and he gave us a thing that pays five hundred bucks."

Pushing past Henry, Ben moved into the apartment. For a stunned moment, he stood swiveling his head in all directions and gaping at the scene as if he couldn't believe his eyes. The place was neat and clean, and for the first time in Ben's memory, it didn't stink of puke and alcohol. "You are a wonder, Fox, a real wonder."

"There was no sense in tryin' ta keep things clean before. The old man would just come home, toss his cookies, and tear the place up." Henry led Ben into the kitchen and broke out two cans of beer. "Watch this, ya ain't gonna believe it." With that, he yanked at a ring on the top of the can and it pulled out a wedge of metal, opening the can. "No church key necessary."

Ben took the can and inspected the opening. "Man, that is really cool."

Henry nodded. It wasn't often he impressed Ben. "So, what's Costas want us ta do that's worth five big ones?"

"The money's to send a warning to a deadbeat they call Weasel. We bounce the guy around a little and collect the bread."

"I know this ain't your thing, Benny. Are ya just goin' along ta keep me from dealing smack?"

Ben turned away to cover the flush that was starting to crawl up his neck. "What difference does it make? It's two hundred and fifty bucks for you to go be a soldier on. Besides, some of it's personal. That prick Weasel tried to nail my mother, an' when she shut him down, he said some bad shit about her." Ben grinned and nudged Henry. "The shit was true, but there's a principle involved. So whadda you say?"

"I say Weasel should have kept his mouth shut.

CHAPTER SIXTY-ONE

The strong-arm job should have been a cinch, but it didn't turn out that way.

Costas told them that Weasel was staying at a dump called the Pearl Beach Hotel. The next evening around dinnertime, they staked out the flophouse from behind a parked car. Within twenty minutes, Weasel came slinking out the front door with a cigarette dangling from his lips. Jacketless in the warm June air, he looked both ways before turning down Cornell Avenue.

Henry took off running at top speed in the opposite direction, circling the block so he could wind up facing their victim. Ben let the deadbeat get twenty feet ahead, then fell in behind him. As Henry ran up, Ben closed the distance. And before Weasel could react, Ben had him pinned from behind. Henry slammed in a gut punch and followed it with a hard right hook to Weasel's head. Ben let go, and Weasel went down, curling forward and gasping for air.

Henry said, "Nicky Costas sends his regards."

Between gasps, Weasel began to wail. He went into a prayer position, pleading for another chance. "I'll pay. Tell Nicky I got a job, an' I'll pay double fer bein' late."

Henry grabbed Weasel's hair and pulled his head back. "I'll tell him. But if you're shittin' me, the next time, it's gonna be way worse. Nothin' personal, but I gotta do some damage so we'll get paid. Hold still, an' I'll make it quick."

That's when the job went to hell. The final punch landed just as Detective Delaney's unmarked car happened to roll by. Delaney slammed into the curb, and both boys took off running. The detective didn't have to chase them; he knew who they were. Screaming at his partner to call it in, he chased them anyway. When they split off in different directions, Delaney went for Ben, knowing he could never catch Henry. Ben ran full, out, passing under the Illinois Central viaduct. He was hoping to lose himself in the shadows of Jackson Park. As he crashed past the bushes and started across the Inner Drive, Delaney was right behind him. A squad car responding to the call from Delaney's partner blocked him off, and when Ben spun around, he ran his nose right into Delaney's fist.

The back of the squad car smelled of sweat, leather, and fear. Because they had cuffed Ben's hands behind his back, he couldn't stop his nose from bleeding. He tried putting his head back, but the blood ran down his throat and started to choke him. He finally gave up and let it drip on the car seat. Ben watched as Delaney, penlight tucked under his chin, wrote something on a pad. The police radio crackled with disjointed phrases and static.

Still writing, Delaney spoke without looking up. "That was Fox doin' the hittin', wasn't it? Don't bother denyin' it. I recognized the punk."

Ben turned his head away and stared out of the window.

"Go better for you if you be straight with us. Word on the street is you're a pretty savvy kid. Fill us in on who paid you two to dance on Weasel, and we'll try to get the judge to go easy on you."

The bleeding let up a little, and Ben tried putting his head back again. His nose began to throb and a crushing headache was forming behind his eyes. He said nothing.

Delaney sighed. "OK, kid, if that's the way you want it."

They picked up Henry at his apartment the next day. There was no Costas lawyer this time. Supplying a lawyer would have let the police know who had ordered the assault. Because the boys were over seventeen, they were both tried as adults. At their arraignment, they claimed they could not afford a lawyer, so a public defender was assigned to their case. The lawyer asked that the cases be separated but his request was denied, and he was stuck defending both of them.

The boys sat behind a thick glass partition and listened to the man who was supposed to be their lawyer. "You've got to waive a jury trial. If you don't and you lose, the judge will throw the book at you. I spoke to the ADA who's prosecuting your case, and he says if you throw yourselves on the mercy of the court, the judge will be lenient."

Whether the PD lied to get the case over with quickly or was just plain stupid, they never found out.

*****

The courtroom was almost empty. Delaney sat in the first row, ready to testify if necessary. Henry saw Grandfather sitting in the back row. His face was expressionless, but Henry knew the old man well enough to understand the deep shame he must be feeling for what his grandson had done. None of the neighborhood kids showed up because no one had bothered to tell them when the trial was to take place. Ben found out from his mother that Weasel wouldn't be there. He'd refused to press charges, but it made no difference because Delaney had caught them in the act. Neither boy would give up Costas.

The narrow-nosed judge sentenced Ben first. He peered down like a hawk about to devour his prey and intoned his decision as if it were the word of God. "I've taken into consideration your excellent academic record and factored in your stated desire to attend college. I'm going to give you a six-month trial continuance in Cook County to give you a taste of jail. If you stay there and don't try to bail your way out, after six months, I'll put you on probation and dismiss the charges against you."

Henry was a different story. The judge knew that Henry was already facing an earlier charge of grand theft auto and had been out on his own recognizance when he committed the assault. He accepted Henry's plea of guilty to both offenses and pronounced his sentence: one to five years in Joliet State Prison.

Henry's public defender acted shocked. "But, Your Honor, the lad just turned eighteen. A full year in Joliet will turn him into a hardened criminal."

The judge sneered. "The sentence is one to five years, counselor, because he's already a hardened criminal."

The bailiff separated the boys and started to lead them away. Ben tried to catch his mother's eye, but she was already on her way out of the courtroom. Henry flashed him a quick smile. "At least I didn't have ta join the fuckin' army."

Ben nodded and grinned, trying to hide his terror.

Grandfather came forward and stood in front of his grandson. "You struck out on the first pitch, Henry."

Henry wanted to tell the old man how sorry he was, but the shame was so overwhelming, it turned him defiant. "That's all you know. A guy can't strike out on the first pitch. He can ground out or fly out, but in baseball, it takes three strikes ta make an out."

There was no change in Grandfather's expression as the bailiff led Henry past him. "Life isn't baseball, Henry."

CHAPTER SIXTY-TWO

B en was cuffed with his hands in front and led to a bus with barred windows for the trip to Cook County Jail. Although the vehicle was full, there was an eerie lack of conversation that lasted the entire trip. The man in the seat in front of Ben had his face pressed against the window as if he were hoping there would be someone out there waiting to say good-bye. He was a small, balding guy with wire rim glasses, and his face was streaked with tears. In the seat next to the crying man was a muscle-bound giant. The guy looked to be six-foot-four or five, and Ben figured he'd tip the scales at three hundred plus. Ben expected the big guy to have some kind of reaction to the cry baby, but the giant just ignored him.

The jail was on California Boulevard, so when a neighborhood guy got locked up there, he was said to be in California. Ben smiled ruefully at the irony. His vow to return to California someday had turned into a pathetic joke.

Once inside, the group was told to strip for physicals. Holding his rolled up jeans and T-shirt in one arm, Ben turned his head and coughed while a doctor pushed on his testicles. Blood was drawn, and he was shoved along with the rest of the busload into a gang shower. A pair of baton-wielding guards paced behind them to make sure they got clean. After the shower, the doctor ordered Ben to bend over and shoved a finger up Ben's asshole, looking for drugs. Butt greasy with lubricant, he was allowed to get back into his clothes. Ben went through the process overwhelmed by the shame of his helplessness. Like all the other prisoners, he kept his eyes on the floor and didn't say a word—not to the guards, not to the doctor, not to anyone.

His first night was spent in a six-by-eight-foot quarantine cell with bunk beds. It was a gray metal box with a solid steel door that operated electronically. A kid was already stretched out on the top bunk when Ben was let in. He glanced at the kid and then tucked into the bottom bunk, using his loafers for a pillow.

A pimply face peered over the edge. "How old are ya?"

Ben looked up. The word in the neighborhood was you had to come on tough or you'd wind up someone's trick. "Whadda you supposed to be, the fuckin' FBI?"

Pimples didn't seem to take offense. "If you're under eighteen, ya get to go on a kids' tier. If you're older, ya gotta go with the men."

Ben thought about it and softened his tone. "Which is better?"

"The kids' tier. On the old guys' tier, they try to fuck you up the ass."

Ben's sphincter tightened, and he could still feel the lubricant from the exam. "I'm seventeen now, but I'll be eighteen by the time I get out."

"Cool. I'm eighteen, but I got a habit, so they won't put me with the men. I'm gonna go to Lexington an' get straight."

Ben didn't comment, and within a few minutes, the sounds of snoring came from the upper bunk.

In the middle of the night, the kid began to make a fuss. He shouted and pounded on the door until a guard came and took him away. Ben never saw him again. In the morning, Ben was moved to the holding cell of tier H2.

The main dayroom of the tier had four large tables with benches and a separate enclosed room called the kitchen. There was also a gang bathroom with showers, but it wasn't visible from the cell in which Ben and three other white kids had been placed. They stood staring through the bars, waiting for the duty guard to open the door and let them onto the tier. The forty prisoners inhabiting the dayroom crowded around the front of the holding cell, hurling insults and threats. About a third of them were colored, and the rest were either Mexican or white. The Negroes were the more vocal of the group.

"I like the little pussy-lookin' one back there, he's gonna be my special bitch."

"No, motherfucker, he mine. Ain't you, bitch?"

An open hand with wiggling fingers came through the bars. "Gimme a cigarette, motherfucker."

The four of them backed away.

A black man pushed up and grabbed the bars. "Look at them shoes, them's my shoes, ain't they, bitch?" This last was directed at Ben. He'd worn his new loafers because he'd been told that shoelaces weren't allowed. Now he cursed himself for not scuffing them to make them look old. He turned away and tried to ignore the hecklers.

After an hour, a guard came and pushed a button that opened the cell door electronically. As soon as it slid back, the crowd moved away, and the newcomers walked into their new home.

A light-skinned Negro about Ben's size approached the newcomers and, one by one, gave them each a little speech. When he got to Ben, his tone left no doubt that he was accustomed to obedience.

"Name's Newby, I'm the kitchenman." He pointed over to the small, enclosed cell. "The food comes up in a dumbwaiter three times a day. The guard opens the kitchen cell, and I go in there and lock myself in. Everyone gets in line, and I pass out the food. After you eat, you return the plate and the spoon to the kitchen cell. Don't try to keep a spoon, because they're all counted. If one comes up missing, the tier goes on lockdown until they find it. At ten, the door to the sleeping cells opens. You go down the corridor to your cell. Go inside and sit on your bunk until the door closes. Lights go out at eleven. Six in the morning is wake-up." His voice tightened. "Get this straight, I run this tier. Start some shit, and you'll answer to me."

Ben said, "Name's Ben."

Newby looked at him for a moment, frowned, then waved him away.

Ben moved to the other end of the dayroom and sat on one of the benches. He leaned forward, elbows on his knees, and avoided making eye contact with anyone.

A stocky black man moved in front of him, the guy who'd wanted his shoes. "You got a smoke?"

Ben looked up. "I got a few, but I need 'em for myself."

"That ain't the way it works, fish. You gots to share." The man held out his hand.

"What's your name?" Ben asked.

The man looked confused. "Walker. Why you ast?"

Ben ignored the question. "Mine's Ben. You know what, Walker? I'm not givin' you my cigarettes."

Walker stepped back as if he'd been slapped. He turned to include the rest of the tier and laughed at Ben. "You fuckin' white punk-ass motherfucker. You ain't shit."

Ben swallowed and tried to hide his fear. *Tough act tough or they'll run all over you.* "Yeah, you're right, Walker, I'm not shit."

Newby walked over and pulled Walker's arm. "No fightin', Walker. We just got off lockdown 'cause a y'all, an' I ain't lettin' you put us back on. You dig?"

Walker pointed at Ben. "Somebody better tell this ofay mother-fucker ta keep his mouth shut or I'm gonna fuck him up." Fists clenched, he stood and stared at Ben. When Ben stared back, Walker snarled a curse and turned away.

The kitchenman waited until Walker was out of earshot. "You've made a bad enemy. Walker doesn't like white people."

Ben shrugged. "Been white all my life. There's not a whole hell of a lot I can do about it now."

Newby nodded. "You play cards?" He fanned a deck open into a full circle with one hand, then fanned it back closed.

"Some," Ben said, grinning at the way Newby handled the cards.

"We play whist, bid whist. I'll teach you the game. If you're any good, we can partner up."

"Sounds OK, but only if you play for money."

Now Newby laughed. "I like you, Ben. You just might be cooler than you look."

*****

At ten o'clock, the lights blinked, signaling the return to the cells. The doors opened, and everyone rushed down the corridor to get to their bunks before the night guard, Mr. Brown, walked the sweep. Word was that if Brown caught anyone out of their cell, he'd whip them into it with the thick leather strap that carried his keys.

The doors to the cells were solid metal but the side opposite was made up of bars. A walkway encircled the tier, and the night guard would stroll past the cells at given intervals. When Mr. Brown was on duty, he would occasionally flick his flashlight on and off in the eyes of a sleeping inmate until the sleeper woke up. Then he'd grin and walk on.

There were forty-four individual cells on H2. Cells one through twenty-two were called the low side, twenty-three through forty-four were the high side. Ben was on the high side, in cell number thirty-three.

It was Ben's second night on the tier. A few minutes earlier, Mr. Brown had walked the corridor, and now the doors began to close electronically. Bang, bang, bang, first the low side, then the high side. Ben waited as thirty-two other doors slammed shut. Then his door closed and the bad feeling started. Ben tried to block it out by listening to the other convicts yell at each other.

"Hey, dat motherfucker next ta me jackin' off."

"Better not let Mr. Brown catch yore ass. He don't like no dick-yankin' on his tier."

"It ain't me, it's da cell next ta me. He be goin' at it so hard he gonna break it off."

"Shut up, motherfucker."

"Who you tellin' ta shut up?"

"You, I be tellin' you."

"Motherfucker, now I'm gonna tell you somethin'. You better meet me before you meet your oats in da mornin'. I'm gonna hurt you bad."

"Yeah? We gonna see who gets fucked up."

Ben lay on his bunk and stared up at the ceiling. His first night, he'd taken the threats and catcalls seriously. The next morning, he'd learned it was mostly joking.

He took a drag from his cigarette and fingered the lone dollar bill he had in his pocket. If he wanted to keep smoking, he would have to use his only buck to pay the candy cart man five times what a pack of Lucky's cost on the outside. Cursing, he got up and moved over to the small sink attached to the wall of his cell. He urinated, turning the water on at the same time to cover the sound.

"Some motherfucker's pissin' in da sink. I kin hear him."

"Call Mr. Brown. He don' like no sink pissin' on his tier."

Laughter came from a few cells. Then the tier fell silent.

Newby said, "This here be Newby talkin'. Any you fools know da words ta 'Crying In The Chapel?'"

Lying back down on his bunk, Ben said, "You saw me cryin' in the chapel, the tears I shed were tears of joy."

"Yeah, I gots dat part, what come after?"

Ben grinned. Newby only spoke like a colored man when the other coloreds on the tier could hear him. "I know the meaning of contentment now, and I'm happy with the Lord."

Newby said, "Das' it. Das' da part I's missing. Dat you, Ben?"

"Yeah."

"How 'bout 'Purple Shades?' You know da words ta 'Purple Shades?'"

The lights went out and Mr. Brown's voice boomed out. "Next one ta talk gets da belt."

Ben shut his eyes against the closed-in feeling. He tossed and turned for hours until he was so exhausted that his night terrors could no longer keep him from sleep.

When the flicking of the flashlight failed to wake Ben up, Mr. Brown banged it loudly against the bars. Ben sat up, rubbing his eyes, and Mr. Brown laughed. "Jest makin' sure y'all wasn't dead."

CHAPTER SIXTY-THREE

For Ben, life on the tier was like slogging through heavy mud. There was nothing to fill the dreary hours—no work details, no weight-lifting rooms, and no yard activities. Each day plodded by in slow motion, a repeat of the day before. Up at six, breakfast of oatmeal or farina, optional gang showers and face scrapings with a razor that had already bloodied at least forty chins, then sitting around till lunch. Lunch was followed by five hours of nothing to do until dinner. Then the meal provided a brief respite from the boredom, followed by four more empty hours until bedtime.

Nights were especially bad. Each time the door slammed shut, Ben's claustrophobia increased. He did jumping-jacks until his legs burned, then dropped to the floor and did push-ups to exhaustion. He lived in fear of the day some idiot would screw up and the tier would go on lockdown. The thought of staying in his cell around the clock for days on end was too terrible to imagine.

One way to pass time in the dayroom was to play cards. Newby taught him bid whist and they partnered up. They seemed almost able to read each other's minds, and as a result, they rarely lost. The stakes were usually cigarettes, and their winnings helped Ben keep smoking.

On Ben's third day in jail, one of the white guys challenged Newby. The routine for fighting was to shove the tables against the bars and set the benches on top. That left a floor twice the size of a traditional boxing ring for the combatants. This fight didn't last long enough to even start moving the tables. The white kid took a swing at Newby, and the kitchenman slid under it, throwing the guy off balance. Before he could pull back, Newby slammed him with three hard shots to the body, the last one in the solar plexus. The kid dropped to the floor, clutching his stomach and gasping for air.

Later, Newby told Ben that before getting busted, he'd gone 11 and 0 as a middle-weight. Ben had watched Newby's eyes during the fight, and he could tell that Newby's boxing skill wasn't the only reason he was feared. Henry Fox used to say there were three kinds of guys: those who didn't want to hurt people, those who enjoyed hurting people, and guys like Henry, who just didn't give a shit. Newby was like Henry. He didn't give a shit, and that made him really dangerous.

Walker, on the other hand, was the kind who enjoyed hurting people—and he hated Ben.

"Just keep away from him," Newby said. "He's bad news."

Ben shrugged. "Can't dodge forever, no place to hide."

Newby shook his head ruefully. "Walker's just plain evil. Mean to the bone and evil." He leaned close so they couldn't be overheard. "Before you came to the tier, I had another partner. Nice kid named Ricky Washington. Whenever Ricky trumped in a whist game, he'd stand and lean over to slap his card down hard. This one day, Walker came up behind him and before Ricky sat back down, Walker put a rolled up newspaper on Ricky's seat. None of us paid any attention and we went on playing. A few minutes later, Walker sidled over and lit a match to the newspaper. Ricky had his shirttail hanging loose, and when the paper flared up, the shirttail caught on fire. By the time we got the fire slapped out, his back was damn near burned up. I could see big circles of pink under where the skin was gone. I looked over at Walker and he was grinning like a maniac. He was too excited to laugh, but I could tell he wanted to. When they carted Ricky off to the hospital, he told me that watching Ricky scream gave him a hard-on."

Ben nodded. "I've met guys like him before. The one thing I know is you can't let 'em get ahead of you. You've always gotta be out front."

Newby rubbed at his eyes. "Just keep away. If something goes down between you two, I can't take sides."

Keeping away wasn't easy, but Ben tried. When Walker approached, Ben moved aside. And when he wasn't able to put distance between them, he made sure to keep his mouth shut.

Life was so boring on the tier that Ben began going to church services on Sunday. It was something to do. Anyone who wanted to attend was marched single file—"Eyes down, hug the wall"—down to a room dubbed "the chapel." The preacher was colored and was backed up by a choir of older prisoners. After his sermon, the choir would sing a few hymns. The program always ended with one of the men singing the Lord's Prayer. The soloist had a broad range, moving from tenor to bass effortlessly and blending the words of the non-rhyming prayer so smoothly that it sounded as if it were written to be sung. Ben decided it was the most beautiful thing he'd ever heard.

Walker also went to church, probably for the same reason, boredom. He razzed Ben both during the service and after. "Hey, Rev, y'all know you got a Jewboy here? Maybe the Jewboy done found Jesus."

The reverend ignored him and so did Ben.

One day, Ben was staring out the window of the dayroom. There was a guy making odd hand motions at him from the tier across the way. He asked Newby what the guy was doing.

"He's sending a kite. A few of the guys can do the alphabet with their hands. They rap out a message and tell whoever reads it where they want it sent. We can rap to F tier and G, and they can rap to C tier and D, and so on. Kites can get to any tier in the place."

Newby taught Ben the sign language alphabet, and Ben started hanging around the window, either sending or receiving kites.

Three weeks into his six-month sentence, Ben was receiving a message for one of the older guys. The guy's rap partner across the way on F2 was worried that his pal was going to roll over on him. "Tell Willy he better—." Before the message was finished the sender was yanked away from the window, and another con signaled, "Urgent!"

Ben called out. "Newby, we've got an 'urgent.'" Newby came over to the window and they both watched as the message formed.

"SQUEALER ON H2...NAME WILSON." The message was repeated, but Newby had already turned away.

"What's it mean?" Ben asked.

"When The Man wants to know what's goin' down on a tier, he puts in a squealer. They'll cut some time off the guy's sentence in exchange for information. Wilson came here a week before you. Couple of days after he showed up, we were put on lockdown, and when The Man searched the cells, he found all kinds of shit."

Ben motioned with his head toward Wilson. "Whadda we gonna do about it?"

Newby looked over at Wilson, who was playing cards at a nearby table. "Shower day tomorrow. We'll fix it then."

*****

After breakfast the next day, some of the tier went in for their scheduled showers. Newby held Ben back until Wilson had gone in. Then, along with two others, Newby and Ben stripped and went in. One of the others had taken four mop buckets out of the storage area, and they all held one as they walked into the shower room.

Wilson had his back turned. He was a tall, skinny Negro with a badly pocked face. His ribs showed when he bent over, and his buttocks were crisscrossed with keloid scars.

When the first bucket of water hit, he hardly seemed to notice. But when the second one slammed into him, he turned around, annoyed.

"That's it?" Ben asked, "We're just gonna stand here and throw water at him?"

Newby didn't smile. His face was grim and hard. He answered without turning. "Just watch." Another bucketful hit Wilson.

They formed a bucket brigade and kept emptying the buckets on Wilson as fast as they could fill them. When Wilson tried to leave, they pushed him back inside. Eventually, he sunk down and sat with his bony back to the wall. When the water filled his mouth and nose, he could barely breathe. He curled into a ball and tried to keep his face covered. They moved around him and kept throwing the water from all sides. Wilson started to cry, and still the water came. He tried to plead with them to stop, but when he opened his mouth, they aimed their buckets at his face.

Newby took a pail from one of the guys and emptied it at Wilson's crotch, hard. He snarled, "Squealer."

Wilson was crying uncontrollably. He covered his private parts, but that left his face open. He swore he never squealed, but the water just kept coming.

Two hours after the torture started, the guards noticed that some of the inmates were still in the shower room. Armed with belts, four of them went in. Wilson was crying and blubbering incoherently and he could barely stand. The guards tried to calm him down, but he was too far gone. Two of them finally propped their shoulders up under his arms and half-walked, half-carried him, naked, off the tier.

"I can't figure out how that worked," Ben said.

Newby looked thoughtful. "I'm not sure. Some of it's not bein' able to breathe; makes the guy think he's gonna drown. But I think the serious damage has to do with the hate. When the water keeps coming, each bucketful says to the guy, 'You're a piece of shit and we hate you.' Eventually, it works on his mind."

"If it was me, hate wouldn't be enough. I could take hate," Ben said

Newby stared into Ben's eyes and nodded. "I believe you could."

CHAPTER SIXTY-FOUR

The days behind bars grew longer and lost their meaning. Ben almost missed a church service because he didn't know it was Sunday. John came to visit. They sat him in a booth with a two-way phone, but the phone didn't work, so they couldn't talk. Ben knew better than to complain. After trying shouting, lipreading and hand gestures, John shrugged and put his hand against the glass. Ben matched him and they just stared at one another for the rest of the visit.

To Ben, the loss of control over his life was the worst part of being in jail. Sleeping, eating, showering, shitting, everything was at the whim of some unseen force.

One morning, a kid was told to pack up to go home. The boy was ecstatic. He had been on the tier for three weeks waiting for trial on a burglary charge, but the guard assured him that the papers he'd been given said the kid was to be released.

"Maybe your lawyer pulled a fast one."

After passing out his money and cigarettes to his friends, the kid was marched away, only to return an hour later, in shock. Someone had made a clerical error.

The incident preyed on Ben's mind. What if someone made a mistake the other way around? What if, when Ben was to be released, some clerk decided he had to stay another year or ten years or forever? A cold terror settled in. Recognizing that others could control his fate caused a worse fear in Ben than any other he'd ever felt. And he knew that this fear would be with him for the rest of his life.

Newby's assistant in the kitchen, a two-time loser named Harvel, left the tier to go to trial. He knew he wasn't going to beat his rap and was pretty certain his next stop would be Joliet. Ben gave him a message for Henry. "Tell him I'll make it out there to visit after I'm released. An' tell him…uh, tell him I'm OK."

Newby suggested Ben take Harvel's place in the kitchen. "It's only 'cause you're gonna be here longer than most of the others. I'm sick of breaking in a new guy every two weeks. I've got five months left, so you could be the last guy I need to deal with. All you have to do is hand out the plates at mealtime and make sure each plate comes back with its spoon. Whadda ya say?"

Assistant kitchenman was the second most important person on the tier, and Ben knew that Newby's choice of a white man could lead to serious trouble. Ben stared over at Walker, then turned back to Newby and nodded. "Cool."

At mealtimes, the door of the kitchen opened electronically. Newby and his assistant would slip inside, and the gate would slam shut again. At a signal from Newby, the meals would start coming up by dumbwaiter from wherever they were prepared. Newby's job was to pull the plates off the dumbwaiter and count them as he handed them to his assistant. The assistant would stand at the opening in the bars and pass the meals out to the inmates. It was the assistant's job to ensure that no prisoner got more than his share. Cups of coffee were handed out the same way.

On Ben's first day, Walker stood at the head of the line. He ignored Ben and called over to Newby.

411

"How come that white motherfucker get ta be assistant?"

Ben handed him a plate.

"Newby, I ast you a question," Walker said, scowling through the opening.

Newby didn't turn away from the dumbwaiter. "Move on, Walker, or I'll tell The Man you fucking up the flow."

Stiffening his shoulders, Walker reluctantly stepped aside and sat down to eat his oatmeal. When breakfast was over and all plates and spoons had been sent back down to the main floor, the door clanked open and Ben and Newby stepped out.

Walker pushed up to within inches of Ben. "I still wanna know why the gray boy gets special shit with you." Ben tried to walk past, but Walker cut him off. His lips were curled back in anger, and he pushed his face almost nose-to-nose with Ben.

Ben found himself staring, mesmerized, at Walker's teeth. The teeth were perfect—snow white, straight, and set in the pinkest gums he'd ever seen. Then Walker started to talk, and the spell was broken.

"Maybe you suckin' Newby's dick. That it?"

Ben looked up into Walker's eyes and swallowed his fear. Fighting to keep his voice steady, he said, "Yeah, but you get to suck off the rest of the tier, so you shouldn't feel too left out."

Newby laughed, and Walker clenched his fists. He bumped against Ben's chest. "You an' me, motherfucker. You an' me, right now!"

Ben looked over at Newby, and Newby glanced at the outward curve in the bars that formed the observation area. A guard would occasionally sit there and watch the action in the dayroom. This morning, the chair was empty. With a nod to the other prisoners, Newby signaled his approval, and the tier came alive with activity. The tables slammed against the bars on each side of the room, and there was a scramble to get the benches up onto the tables. Once the benches were in place, the audience grabbed seats based on the tier pecking order.

Ben and Walker stood in the center of the room and Newby stood between them like the referee in a boxing match. "It works like this: everything goes below the neck. No punching where it shows. You keep goin' until one of you quits. Then it's over. If a guard shows up, the fight stops an' you can pick it up later after he leaves."

Most of the prisoners wore jeans, but Walker was different. He wore a wrinkled pair of green slacks and a tight T-shirt. Every muscle bulged as he raised his arms and reached back to pull the shirt over his head. He outweighed Ben by at least thirty pounds. Remembering Henry's words about big men—"Big don't mean shit; heart is what matters"—Ben unbuttoned his denim shirt and stripped it off. Walker's smile twitched slightly as a look of doubt briefly crossed his face. Ben was thin but wiry, with clearly defined muscles that had been hidden by his long-sleeved shirt.

Suddenly, the other prisoners, who had been stamping their feet and shouting incoherent instructions, went quiet. All eyes turned to the observation area. It had been empty, but now Mr. Brown sat calmly in the chair.

The guard smiled. "Gonna have you a fight?" He tilted the chair back and put his feet up on the bars for balance. He smiled again, this time directly at Walker. "Jes' don' kill the poor white boy, you hear?" Then he righted his chair and got up. Laughing, he turned his back and walked away.

Walker curled his hands into fists and started toward Ben. The way he came on told Ben that Walker wasn't trained as a boxer. The man had his hands too far apart, and he held then down around his waist. Instead of circling, he came straight on. Walker swung a round-house swing that would have broken something if it had landed.

It didn't land.

Ben moved to his right and ducked under. Walker swung again, and Ben fell back. Walker chased him, trying to force him up against the benches, but Ben kept moving in a circle, bobbing and weaving. Frustrated, Walker rushed forward, this time swinging both arms wildly in an effort to land a punch. Ben closed and came up under the flailing arms. He landed a short, glancing right on Walker's jaw. The punch was too close to do any damage, but Walker fell back, stunned.

Someone yelled, "He hit above the neck." Newby jumped down off his bench. He moved between Ben and Walker and held out his arms.

"You can't hit in the face. If a guy's marked, The Man's gonna put us on lockdown."

Ben kept his hands high and danced from foot to foot. "Yeah, I'm really gonna worry about that when I'm fightin' this big son-of-a-bitch. I'll tell you what, Newby. It doesn't matter if I hit him in the face or not.I'm gonna hurt this bastard so fuckin' bad, he'll wish to God he'd never been born. The way he'll be bleedin', The Man's gonna know for damn sure he was in a fight."

It was pure bravado, and Ben prayed that Walker didn't catch the quiver in his voice.

Newby dropped his arms and got back up on the bench. He turned to the others and shrugged. No one was going to interfere.

Now instead of pushing forward the way he had been doing, Walker waited nervously for Ben to come to him. Ben just stood there, swaying slightly and forcing himself to grin. Finally, Walker charged, but this time, Ben refused to dodge away. This time, he resolutely stood his ground. Walker's first punch caught him high on the cheek, but he managed to slip most of it and countered with a hard left hook to Walker's ear. The punch was thrown off balance and couldn't have hurt, but Walker acted as if he had never been hit before. Sensing some kind of change in his opponent, Ben attacked. His next two punches were body blows to the heart. This time, Walker dropped his arms and quit. He staggered back just as Ben landed an uppercut into the big man's gut that should have ended the fight.

Ben watched Walker double over, but he couldn't stop. Something snapped inside and a blind rage took over. He alternated hooks to Walker's head. Walker's cheekbone cracked and Ben's hand came away just as Walker's mouth flew open, spewing spit and blood. Now Ben seemed insane. As Walker sank down, Ben used uppercuts to get a few more shots in before Walker was flat on the floor.

Ben had drawn back his leg to kick Walker when Newby stepped in and pulled him away. Newby wrapped his arms around Ben, pinning his arms to his sides. Insane with rage and fear that Walker might still get up, Ben struggled, but Newby started talking low in his ear. He couldn't tell what Newby was saying, but the crooning sound of his words calmed him.

*****

The tier went on lockdown. That meant no time in the dayroom, no showers, no mail, no store cart, and no chapel for a week. They were only allowed out of their cells for bathroom breaks and meals.

Ben spent the first few hours trying to control the shaking that had started the minute the cell door slammed shut. When the shaking subsided, he began pacing back and forth, banging against the walls and mumbling to himself. A part of him knew he was acting crazy, but he couldn't stop.

Newby's voice came floating in, calm and soothing. He spoke loud enough for the entire tier, but Ben knew by his use of proper English that the message was meant just for him.

"Get in your bunks and take deep breaths. These people can imprison your body, but they can't imprison your mind." He paused for a moment, as if to let his words sink in. "Don't think about getting out. Think about being out. Let your head take you away from here to somewhere nice. Do that, and you'll be all right."

The lights went off, and Ben drifted into a kind of trance. He thought about the 57th Street Beach, and in his mind, transferred the sandy beach to the tree-lined shores of Lake Tahoe. He put Annie there in the one-piece red bathing suit she'd bought just before he was arrested. They stretched out on a blanket and slowly undressed, kissing and caressing, day after day.

When the weeklong lockdown ended, Ben couldn't remember eating, sleeping, or using the bathroom. Newby said that had happened to him once. "Kinda like bein' hypnotized."

Walker didn't come back to the tier, and the word was that they put him on another tier at his request.

*****

The dayroom routine picked up again as if nothing had happened. The other prisoners seemed so relieved to be rid of Walker that Ben was forgiven for having caused the lockdown. Besides, the fight had been a great one. Ben was now top man next to Newby.

Newby flipped the trump ace and took the last trick. "Was that some kind of act when you was fightin' or did you really lose it?"

Ben counted his tricks. They had made their bid with one extra book to spare. "I really lost it. I was so scared he'd get back up, I figured I'd better kill him."

Newby shook his head. "But you acted like you knew you could beat him."

Ben tried to smile, but the fight was still too fresh. "All my talk about really fuckin' him up was woofin'; just an act. Don't know what I would've done if it hadn't worked."

Their opponents in the whist game paid up two cigarettes and decided to quit playing.

Newby leaned back and put his hands behind his head. "When I get outta here, I'm gonna go to work for my uncle. He runs most of the numbers on the South Side. How 'bout you? Whadda you gonna do when you get out?"

Ben took out a cigarette. Because matches were even harder to get than cigarettes, he tore one from the book and used his fingernail to split it lengthwise. Placing one of the halves back under the striker, he lit his cigarette with the other half and shuffled the cards. "I'm goin' to school, college. It's all set. I'll start in January, soon as I get outta here."

Newby sneered, "Get serious. Where's a slum rat like you gonna get the bread to go to college?"

Ben trusted Newby, but he'd heard too much about jailhouse snitches to open up completely. "My lady's gonna wait tables."

Newby grinned. "Sure you aren't thinkin' of turnin' her out? Waitin' tables doesn't pay all that much."

It wasn't that he didn't feel comfortable with Newby. There were just some things you didn't talk about. Telling him that Nicky Costas had offered to pay his first year's tuition as a reward for keeping his mouth shut wasn't in the cards. "Let's just say I've got a rich uncle."

Newby laughed. "Soon as you get out, you gotta introduce me."

*****

Annie was the only one who had been visiting regularly. Each time she came, he managed to be first on the single razor blade allotted to the tier. Even so, his nervousness at seeing her usually left his face dotted with tiny bits of toilet paper. The indication that this visit was different came when the guard announced that he had two visitors. Ben expected to see one of the gang, John or even Mike. He was unable to hide his shock at seeing his mother.

She picked up the phone and pushed close to the Plexiglas barrier. "What, I'm such a bad mother, I won't go to see my jailbird son?"

Her voice was loud and shrill, forcing Ben to pull the phone away from his ear. "Yeah, hi."

With a look of disgust, Ben's mother gave the phone to Annie. Tears started down Annie's face, and she pressed her hand against the glass between them.

Ben pressed his own hand on the glass. He thought his heart would explode. "Please, baby, don't cry. It's gonna be OK. I promise."

Annie sobbed harder, then pulled her hand away and ran it through her pixie-cut hair. She wouldn't look at him, staring instead at his mother. "My family kicked me out. I had no place to go, so your mom let me stay with her."

Ben glanced at his mother's frowning face; it was clear she hated the intrusion. Annie's head came back up. The tears stopped and she stood straighter. In a defiant tone, she said, "I'm not going to be able to wait tables while you go to school. I'm pregnant."

CHAPTER SIXTY-FIVE

I n January, exactly six months from the day that Ben had been sentenced, a guard unlocked his cell, handcuffed him, and led him off the tier. After a maze of hallways, they wound up in an office where a clerk checked him out. The clerk turned to the guard while he handed Ben an envelope with his watch and personal items inside. "Deal was, if the guy didn't bail out, the judge would cut him loose. Givin' him his things now'll save us hauling him back here."

The guard didn't like it. "Yeah, well, what if the judge changes his mind an' he gets sent back here?"

The clerk shrugged. His face was devoid of expression, but there was a sneer in his voice that told Ben the guard had asked a stupid question. "Then we'll check the guy back in."

The guard flushed, and without a further word, pushed Ben toward a door that opened onto an outside platform and the cold Chicago winter. Ben had only the thin summer jacket he'd worn when he was sent to jail. Now he shivered in the below-freezing air and grinned. It was the first time he'd been outdoors in six months. The Black Maria driver recuffed Ben with his hands in front and shoved him aboard the bus for the ride to court.

*****

When Ben came out of the holding room, Annie started to sob. The bailiff frowned at her and put a finger to his lips in a silencing gesture.

The judge put Ben on two years' probation. "Keep your nose clean, and at the end of the probation period, your record will be expunged. Is that understood?"

Ben looked down and gave a brief nod. The judge banged his gavel. "I can't hear a nod."

If the judge had been able to read the hatred in Ben's eyes, he would have sent Ben back to jail. "Yes, Your Honor."

The clerk had been right. Ben was released on the spot. He walked up the aisle to Annie, and the two of them left the courtroom. "Stop crying. I don't wanna give those bastards the satisfaction of seeing you cry."

"I think it's the baby. You know I never cry. Your mom said that pregnancy can cause mood swings. I tried to stop sobbing when that mean son-of-a-bitch shushed me, but I just couldn't."

They stopped at the women's restroom and when Annie came out, Ben pulled her around to face him. "You look terrific. How come you're not all fat?"

Annie started crying again. "I'm wearing a heavy girdle and a full skirt. Underneath, I'm a tub of lard."

*****

The next day, Ben went to Lola's. Blue frowned when Ben showed up, and the frown deepened to a scowl when, a few minutes after he'd poured Ben a VO, John and Mike sauntered in. Business was slow, so he served them. Because it was afternoon, none of the neon signs were lit; the only light was the muted winter gloom that seeped through the front window.

The boys exchanged shy hand slaps and settled in at the bar. No one spoke for the first few moments. Instead, John ordered a drink, and Mike settled for a draft. All three lit cigarettes. Blue had vacuumed just before Ben walked in, and the exhaled smoke gave substance to the floating dust motes.

John came halfway off his stool and leaned toward Ben. "So Benny, what's the good word?"

Ben's face was devoid of expression. He spoke to the mirror. "White wine goes with pussy."

Mike forced a laugh. "I don't eat no pussy."

John elbowed him. "Shit, you don't get any pussy, period. If you ever do, try kissing it first. Makes for an easier slide." He turned to Ben. "Tell me, oh, wise one, what's your take on the subject?"

"You know what they say. 'A pretty lady'll make a slit-licker out of you.' An' my Annie is one pretty lady."

John gripped Ben's shoulder and squeezed. "Most guys would lie, but not our Benny. Man, you ain't changed a bit."

Ben shrugged John's hand away, his stare hard. "Yeah, I have."

They locked eyes for a moment, then John looked down at his drink. His voice dropped an octave. "It's good to have you back. I'm sorry I didn't get up to see you more."

Ben shrugged. "At least you came. You and Annie were the only ones."

Mike took a sip of his beer. "I know you mean me. I'm sorry, but my mother said she'd kick me out of the house if I visited you. If she knew I was here, there'd be hell to pay."

Ben shrugged again. "So go home, mommy's boy. Who needs you?"

They sat until the silence was too much for John. "Hey, did you hear about Polack getting busted?"

"Who's Polack?" Mike asked.

"You know, Stan Raymond."

"I didn't know he was a Polack."

"It's a nickname."

Mike signaled Blue for another beer. "You mean like Hiro Naguchi, the guy they called Chink?"

John shook his head. Leave it to Mike to get lost in the details. "Nah, that was 'cause everyone hated the Japs during the war. Chink pretended to be Chinese an' it stuck. Stan's called Polack 'cause his mother's Polish."

Before Mike could interrupt again, John said, "He was caught with smack."

"Was he sellin' or usin'?" Ben asked.

"Using."

Ben squirmed and again spoke to the mirror over the bar. "He was one of Henry's customers before we got busted." There was silence as Mike and John digested the information. Blue came over, dropped a fresh coaster on the bar and set Mike's beer on it. Then he took away the empty glass and started getting the bar ready for the evening business. "Y'all better drink up fast an' get outta here 'fore Lola comes on. Y'all know she don' allow y'all in here."

John dropped a ten on the bar and finished his drink. He made a circle motion with his finger to let Blue know he was buying. "So what if Henry did sell him the shit. He's already in Joliet."

"Bein' in prison doesn't mean they can't charge you with a crime you committed before you went in. Maybe Stan'll rat him out."

"No fuckin' way," John said. "Stan's the toughest fucker on 55th Street. He'd never fink on no one."

"Don't be so sure about that. Faced with hard time, he might try to cut a deal. And Joliet is hard time."

Blue tossed John's change on the bar and John scooped it up. "When those bad boys run inta Stan, they'll find out they ain't so bad after all. He knocked out both of the Darcy brothers with one punch."

Ben finished his drink and they all started for the door. "Thanks for the drink, Johnny."

It was still afternoon, but the winter gray made it feel later. All three boys shoved their hands in their pockets and started walking back toward the Castle. Ben curled forward against the bitterly cold wind. "That story about the Darcy brothers isn't true. I know what really happened 'cause I was there.

"Timmy Darcy knew that Stan was fucking his sister Ruthie, and both Timmy and Earl put out the word that they were lookin' for Stan. At the same time, Stan put out the word that he was lookin' for the Darcys for spreading shit about him and Ruth. Right around then, he was startin' to date Soda, an' he didn't want her to hear about Ruthie and break up with him."

"Who's Soda?" Mike asked.

"Noreen Olsen" Ben answered. "Her brother gave her the nickname when she was little. He really called her Baking Soda 'cause her arms were huge like the lady on the baking soda box. But only the Soda part stuck."

"Didn't she an' Stan get married?" John asked.

"Yeah, his being married is one of the things that makes this bust so bad."

"OK," John said. "Finish the story."

"Yeah. So this one day, Stan an' me are standin' on the Big Nickel, near Kimbark, and along comes both of the Darcys. I figure Polack is gonna ask for my help, but instead, he just walks right out in front of the two of them. And before they can say a word, he says, 'Make way for a real man.' He draws back his arm and gives Timmy a backhand slap that sounds like a gunshot. Timmy sees the slap comin' and jerks sideways tryin' to duck, but instead, he cracks his head against

Earl's head. They come together so hard that Earl goes down, an' he's so dazed he don't know what hit him.

"Meanwhile, Timmy is staggerin' from the slap and the head-bumping, so Polack finishes Timmy with a straight right to the gut. The Darcy brothers are on the ground; Timmy's grabbin' at his stomach and Earl is flat on his back, dazed. Polack stands over them an' says, 'I musta made a mistake, I thought you was tough guys.'

"Then he walks over to me like it's no big deal, an' says, 'Catch ya later,' an' he splits. Polack definitely knocked out Timmy, but Timmy's fat head was what knocked out Earl."

John liked the story because he admired Stan Raymond. He gave a knowing smirk. "I know someone a lot tougher than Polack."

Ben bit. "Bullshit. Who?"

"His wife, Noreen."

"You mean Soda?" Mike asked.

"Yeah, Soda. I seen her in action at their wedding reception. I wasn't invited, but you guys know I like parties, an' I figured Stan's too much of a good guy to throw me out. An' I was right. It was one hell of a party. Great homemade Polish food, a good band, and lots of booze.

"When I first saw Stan an' Soda together, they looked kinda funny. You know, her being four inches taller than him an' all. But I could tell that they really liked each other.

"After the reception had been goin' on for about six hours, Noreen starts sayin' to Stan, 'Let's go home.' He's really smashed. His tie's undone, he's all smeared with lipstick an' grinnin' from ear to ear. He's havin' the time of his life, an' he don't wanna leave.

"He's sayin', 'Just one more dance, honey,' an' 'One more drink, honey,' an Noreen's gettin' really steamed. She grabs his arm an' announces that they're leavin', an' they head for the door. Just as they're about to go out, Edna Reilly spots Stan leavin', an' she runs up, grabs him around the neck, an' pulls him back out on the dance floor. He's still grinnin' an' he ain't resistin', so they start doin' the dirty boogie.

"Noreen stands there, both hands curled inta fists, an' at first, I think she's gonna knock Edna out. Instead, she heads for the food table where there's a kettle of water that was filled with Polish sausage when the party started. Noreen picks it up, an' when Stan bops by with Edna, she hoists it up as high as she can an' empties it over Stan's head. Everything stops, even the band. Polack's got cold, dirty water all over his tux. An' that yellow sausage grease you get from Polish dogs is in his hair an' runnin' down his face. He stands there drippin', tryin' ta figure out what happened. We all figure it's all over for Soda. She's gonna get killed on her wedding night. Instead, Stan seems to wake up. He grins at the crowd and says, 'I guess I gotta go now.' The whole place breaks up laughin', an' the two of them head out the door, hand-in-hand."

John smiled sadly, remembering. "Now he's headed out the door for the shithouse."

Ben nodded. Then, loud enough for Mike to hear, he said, "I wanted you guys to know Annie's knocked up, so we're gettin' married."

CHAPTER SIXTY-SIX

Ben and Annie were married by a Justice of the Peace in Crown Point, Indiana. An extra twenty dollars changed hands, and they were given a Certificate of Marriage dated eight months prior. Ben's mother came dressed in a gray wool suit, the nicest thing she owned, and Ben was grateful. She stood to one side, smoking and forcing a smile. The Talonis weren't there.

After the proceedings, the three of them took the train back to Chicago and had dinner at Valois Cafeteria. There was no reception, no celebration, and no gifts except for a set of towels from John.

*****

On the Ides of March, after twenty-eight hours of labor, Annie gave birth to a healthy six-pound girl they named Kitty. After a few weeks under the same roof with Ben's mother, it was a relief to move into a thirty-five-dollar-a-month apartment of their own on the second floor of the Castle.

John went to work for Maxine Sommers's father at his Ford-Lincoln dealership. Though John was good at selling cars, in his spare time, he kept doing what he did best—scamming. He fenced stolen goods, sold cigarettes with counterfeit tax stamps at discount prices, and ran high-stakes poker games in the back room of the Post Restaurant.

Mike got a job driving a truck for Buick Aircraft. He liked the freedom of the road and started saving for his own rig. When an opening came in the spare parts division at the Buick plant, he talked his supervisor into hiring Ben.

After Henry was paroled in June, his parole officer got him a job in a paper mill near Chicago's downtown loop. With Grandfather's help, he rented an apartment on the Near North Side. On his first Sunday off work, loneliness drove him back to the Castle.

*****

More than a year had passed since Henry had been arrested. John, Mike, and Ben were sitting on the stoop outside the Castle when Henry sauntered up. He smiled at their stunned expressions. He was dressed in pegged tan chinos and a short-sleeved white shirt with the tails out. The front wave of his dark hair was stylishly slicked upward, but because of his Indian blood, he had to forego sideburns. "So, what's the good word?"

Ben jumped to his feet. "Never do push-ups on the sidewalk with a hard-on." They gripped wrists then slapped palms, grinning like a couple of idiots. He looked appraisingly at Henry. "You finally grew, an' you're a lot heavier."

Henry yanked up his shirt and flexed. His abdomen tightened into clearly defined cords and his pecs and lats bulged with the strain. Relaxing, he spread his arms to allow the shirt to fall back into place. "Five-foot-ten and a hundred-eighty pounds of rust colored iron."

Mike slid over, and Henry went to his place at the top of the stoop as if he'd never left. "So, Benny, how was it in County?"

So much had happened in the six months since Ben had been released that it took a moment for him to focus. "Let's just say that the judge's plan worked. My taste of jail was enough to make me quit Costas and go straight. I'm workin' a lunch-box job at Buick Aircraft."

Henry's face went hard. "Yeah, prison worked for me, too. I ain't never goin' back, 'cause I ain't never gettin' caught again. I got four years on parole, and after that, Costas is gonna make me rich."

He stared at Ben as if daring his friend to argue. When Ben said nothing, Henry shrugged. "So what about your big college plan?"

Ben sighed and looked away. It was clear that college wasn't a subject he liked talking about. "The baby takes every nickel I make. In another few months Annie's gonna go waitress part-time, but even then, we'll barely get by. Maybe I'll go when the kid is old enough for kindergarten."

John asked, "When'd you get out, Henry?"

"Couple of weeks ago. Got a job, an apartment on the North Side, and in a few weeks, Grandfather's gonna come up with enough scratch ta get me a car."

John nodded. "I can help with that. I'm sellin' cars for Maxine's father. So, if you ain't got wheels, how'd you get here?"

"I took the bus ta the Randolph Street Station and grabbed the IC."

It was hot and humid, typical for late June. The sun had just cleared the Miller Building and was glaring down on the stoop. Mike squirmed and looked up at Henry. "It's gettin' too hot. Whadda you say we go to Lola's an' shoot the shit?"

Henry shook his head. "I better not. If I'm seen with you guys—particularly Benny—I go back inside and do four more years."

Mike rubbed at the sweat on his face with the sleeve of his shirt. "Then how 'bout we get outta the neighborhood? We could go swimmin' at the quarry. We ain't done that in a long time."

Henry stood up. "Things have really changed around here. Mike's gotten a whole lot smarter. He just came up with a good idea."

Mike stood and nudged him with his shoulder. "I'm glad you're here. Now things can get back to normal."

428

Ben said, "I can't go. I'm supposed to take care of the baby. I promised Annie I'd give her a break so she could spend some time with her folks."

"Where's the quarry?" John asked. He'd never been there but was willing to go anywhere just to get moving.

"The Lemont Quarry," Mike said. "It's really clean water and deep. You can do lots of dives 'cause the walls are about fifty feet high."

Ben clasped his hands behind his head and leaned back. "More like thirty feet, but it feels like fifty when you're divin'. Damn, I really wish I could go."

John snapped his fingers as if he'd just had a great idea. "Why not bring the kid along? We gotta go home to get bathing suits, an' I can pick up my Thermos jug. It's big enough for a bottle." He turned to Henry. "I think my brother's about your waist size; I'll grab his suit for you. We can take my car, an' I'll even pop for gas."

An hour later, they piled into John's '53 Merc and headed for Lemont.

John opened the wind wings all the way, and the breeze helped make the drive a little more pleasant. Ben sat in the back feeding the baby, and Mike sat next to him. The baby cooed, burped and spit up while they sang, *Ninety nine bottles of beer on the wall*. Henry was really enjoying the drive. Except for when Grandfather drove him home from Joliet, it was the first time he'd been in a car since the night he was arrested. He decided that when he got his own car, it would be a Mercury.

John had one hand on the wheel and the other out the window. "So, what was it like?"

Henry shrugged. "Would've been a lot worse if Costas hadn't put out the word ta treat me right. Even so, it was bad enough. I got in a couple of beefs, one on the first day. This one guy, a lifer named Ray, gets in my face askin' for cigarettes, an' when I tell him ta fuck off, he takes a swing. I'm dumb enough ta think it's gonna be a one-on-one fight. That's when his three buddies jumped me. Just when I figure I'm a dead man, a couple of guys come over an' break up the party. This one guy, a big ugly moose, says, 'I'm your bodyguard, compliments of Nicky Costas.' After that, the other cons pretty much left me alone. A few weeks later, I had ta fight Ray again, but I clocked him a couple of times an' he decided it was better ta be friends. That was pretty much it. The rest of the time, we just sat around liftin' weights and waitin' ta get out."

John kept his eyes on the road. "I'm sorry I didn't get out there more often. I got no real excuse."

Henry made a fist and tapped him lightly on the thigh. "You and Grandfather were my only visitors. I can't tell ya how much easier life was with the money you sent me. In the joint, ya can get just about anything ya want if ya got money."

Ben didn't say anything, but he felt a wave of warmth for John. In addition to visiting, John had sent him money too.

The hum of the tires finally lulled the baby to sleep, and Ben tucked her in on the seat between him and Mike. "Henry, you remember when we used to go to Olson's butcher shop an' buy necks and backs to eat?"

Henry smiled at the memory, but he didn't turn around and he didn't answer.

"I think he knew we weren't buyin' the stuff for my mom."

Now Henry turned to look back. "How do ya figure?"

"Annie an' I went shoppin' the other night. We go to the A&P, even though my old lady says we should boycott 'em."

"What's a boycott?" Mike asked.

"It's like when you don't do business with someone because you're pissed off at them," Ben explained.

"How come your old lady is pissed at the A&P?"

Henry threw a disgusted look at Mike. "Will ya shut up an' let him tell it?"

Mike looked away and fell silent.

"She's not, it's just that she doesn't like how all the little shops are goin' outta business. First, the Greek went under, then Olson had to close up the butcher shop. My old lady says there oughta be a place for the little guy."

Mike laughed. "Your mommy's a commie. Anyway, it ain't true about the Greek. He closed up 'cause he had ta get outta town. He got caught bangin' some guy's wife, an' the guy was gonna kill him."

Henry gave Mike a murderous look. "I guess things haven't changed as much as I thought. You're still an asshole. Go ahead, Benny. Mike ain't gonna interrupt again. Right, Mikey?"

"Yeah, right."

"Well, we sorta snuck in, hopin' we wouldn't see anyone who might tell my mother. When we got to the meat counter, Annie spotted a guy cutting meat behind the glass. 'Isn't that Mr. Olson?' she says. An' sure enough, that's who it was. Mr. Olson was workin' as a butcher at the A&P. He acted just the same. Didn't look at anyone, didn't smile, just chop, chop, chop."

"I don't get it," Mike said. "What's the big deal about Olson workin' at the A&P?"

"Shut up, just shut the fuck up." This time, Henry emphasized his words with a swing at Mike. He missed, but the shout woke the baby, and she started to cry.

"Now see what ya done," Henry said. "She'd still be sleepin' if you'd just shut up."

Ben lifted Kitty up to his shoulder and jiggled her until she calmed down. Then he set her on his lap.

"Annie started to pick out a few things, ground beef and stuff, and was lookin' over at the chicken. The A&P has packages of parts so you can buy what you like without having to buy the whole bird. She was checking prices when Mr. Olson came out and started fillin' up the bins. I smiled an' nodded hello, an' he nodded back. Course he didn't smile. I don't think anyone has ever seen Mr. Olson smile. I started to turn away when he motioned with his head to a package he'd just put down. On top of a pile of chicken breasts was a package of necks and backs, and the price on the package was five cents a pound. He knew it was us buyin' all that stuff back then, not our mothers. I took the package and went to thank him, but he was already back inside, cuttin' up more meat.

Henry sat quietly thinking about Mr. Olson. "Ya could be right. I'll bet he knew all along we were on our own an' just hungry."

"Lemont comin' up," John said. "Which way do I turn?"

*****

They went to the highest part of the quarry rim and jumped in. Each one would take a turn sitting with Kitty, letting her watch the others play in the water. Instead of trying to dive, John jumped feet first on his initial turn. Afterward, he got up his nerve and did a few straight dives, including a fair jackknife. Henry topped him with a perfect swan.

Ben and Mike continued jumping, each secretly glad the other wouldn't dive.

When Mike jumped, he allowed his body to plunge all the way down to the quarry bottom. Then, bending his knees, he would push off and shoot up to the top. Ben would spread his legs as he hit the water to stop his downward motion.

Each one of them became a serious adult when it was his turn to hold the baby. Between times, they laughed and played in the water like the kids they still were.

*****

Mike didn't feel the razor sharp slice as he rocketed off the bottom and swam to the surface. He pulled up onto the rock ledge and started to climb back up for another dive. Looking down to make sure of his footing, he saw the gush of blood, and then the pain hit him.

John said it must have been a broken bottle because the cut at the base of his big toe was so clean. When Mike started moaning, Henry shook his head in disgust.

"OK, I know it's deep, but ya don't have ta act like you're dyin'."

In a fog of fear, Mike heard Ben say, "He's scared, Henry. He'll be fine once we get him to a doctor."

They made him sit down, and John tried to stanch the blood with a towel. It kept seeping through the cloth, and with each new stain, Mike's face went a shade paler. Afraid of Henry's reaction, he choked back the hysteria that threatened to start him screaming. He gripped John's arm and pulled him close. "You can tell me the truth. Is my toe still on?"

Henry heard him and snorted with derision. John knelt down and peeled back the towel. "It's a deep cut, but it's clean. A couple of stiches'll fix it up perfect."

Mike stood, hopped over to the car, and crawled into the front seat. Tremors shook his body, and no amount of reassurance on John's part could calm him down. John was lying, he was sure of it. His toe would be gone, and if the bleeding didn't stop soon, he'd bleed to death.

Still in wet bathing suits, Ben and Henry pushed the driver's seat forward and got in the back. John fired up the Merc and they headed for the nearby town of Lemont. The baby had fallen asleep, but the engine noise woke her and she got fidgety. Ben tried giving her a bottle, but she sucked for a while and then started fussing again. "She crapped. I gotta change her." As Ben pulled off the soggy diaper, the pungent odor filled the car. John pushed his head out the window while Henry held his nose and turned away. "If I ever get married, my old lady is gonna do all the shit work. No way am I ever gonna do what you're doin'."

While Kitty cooed, Ben undid the safety pins. Taking her tiny ankles in one hand, he raised her bottom and removed the soiled diaper. Using the clean part, he wiped her as best he could, then wrapped the messed diaper in waxed paper and changed her into a fresh one. "Stop at the Texaco station. I'll wash the crap out of the diaper in the men's room toilet. Henry can check the phone book for a doctor at the same time."

Still holding his nose, Henry snarled, "I ain't got no bread, an' I know this cripple's flat broke. Who's gonna pony up for a doc?"

John shrugged. "Guess I'm elected."

With her diaper changed, Kitty quieted. She seemed fascinated by Mike's groans and kept turning to look at him. She seemed most interested when he was at his loudest.

They stopped at the gas station, and Ben hustled off, trailing a vapor of baby-shit that had the pump jockey staring at him. Henry went to the phone, copied three numbers out of the book, and started making calls. The first number he tried was disconnected, and the same was true of the second one. The nickel wasn't returned after the second call, so Henry had to go back to the car to get another one from John.

Mike's moaning got louder, and he tugged at John's sleeve. "If we have to wait till we get home, will I get gangrene?"

Henry'd had enough. "Shut your whining trap, or so help me, ya won't have ta worry 'bout no gangrene 'cause I'll kill ya."

Mike sank back into the car seat and quieted down. A flood of relief hit him when John handed over a second nickel.

Henry tried the third number, and a woman answered. "I'll get the doctor," she said. "He's out in the backyard." Her words were clipped and she sounded annoyed.

The doctor came on the line and listened to Henry's explanation of what had happened. "Are you sure you can't just drive back to Chicago? I'm on my first day off in three weeks."

"The cut won't stop bleedin', an' the guy who's cut is freakin' out." .

The doctor gave them directions to his office.

As Henry helped Mike hobble toward the front door, he faked a worried frown. "Geez, I made it sound a lot worse than it is, Mikey, an' the doc had ta drive all the way from home. I hope he ain't so pissed off he takes it out on you."

Mike clamped his jaw shut and turned his head away. He seemed about to faint.

Ben glared at Henry and got an innocent smile in return. Kitty started crying again, and Ben took her back to the car while John came around and put his shoulder under Mike's other arm.

John laughed, "The baby must be disappointed 'cause Henry made Mike quit making those noises."

Giving up on Mike's pathetic attempt to hop, the boys used a fireman's carry to get him the rest of the way into the doctor's office. They stumbled through the empty waiting room and into the surgery where a young man in a golf shirt was scrubbing his hands. They sat Mike down on the examining table, and as the doctor bent to inspect the cut, Mike whimpered and drew his foot away, staring at Henry. The doctor glanced up and seemed surprised to see Henry and John against the wall, watching. With a dismissive wave, he sent them back to the waiting room.

Once they were gone, the doctor put a gentle hand on Mike's shoulder. "I'm going to have to take a look."

435

Tears streamed down Mike's face. "Are you gonna have to cut my toe off? Please don't cut my toe off."

The doctor pulled up a stool and gently probed the injury. He smiled and looked up at Mike. "No amputations today. That's a deep cut, but it can be closed with sutures."

Mike didn't seem to hear. He kept crying and muttering to himself.

Out in the waiting room, Henry and John started matching quarters. When the door swung open and Ben walked in, they quit.

"I'm glad ya showed up," Henry said. "Another ten minutes an' Johnny woulda had me workin' for him for life."

Ben sat down and laid the baby in his lap. "She's about to doze off, but I wanna keep her awake so she'll sleep on the drive home." He started to coo baby talk, then looked up, red-faced, when he realized the others were watching him.

Henry smiled. There was something about the way Ben handled the baby that made him think having kids wouldn't be so bad. Just then, a squeal of pain came from the behind the closed surgery door. "Ya think Mike's gonna get outta here without having a heart attack?"

John shrugged and Ben shook his head. Henry got up and started pacing. "What makes him like that?"

Neither John nor Ben answered.

Inside the surgery, the doctor set up an instrument tray for the repair job on Mike's toe. "There's two kinds of fear. The kind that's real and the kind that isn't. This is real. In a minute, I'm going to sew up that cut, and to do it, I'm going to numb the area. I'm not gonna lie to you; the shot is going to hurt. Some of my colleagues will tell you it's going to pinch; others'll say it's going to sting. I've even heard some say it will be uncomfortable. That's baloney. It's going to hurt, and what I need you to do is grit your teeth and hold still."

Mike nodded and a needle went into the wound. He held his breath and stifled the yell that was building in his throat. When he tried to pull his foot away, the doctor held his ankle. "Steady now, it's almost over." Then the toe went numb and the doctor started cleansing the wound.

With the total lack of sensation, Mike's fear eased up. He watched as the doctor sawed a toothbrush back and forth, scrubbing the open wound. "How come I'm such a chicken?"

The doctor didn't look up. "Everyone's chicken. Some just hide it better than others."

"My buddy Henry isn't chicken. He's not afraid of anything."

The doctor snipped the end of the thread. "If your friend's never been afraid, something's wrong with him. Fear's a warning. Only fools ignore it."

Mike nodded, remembering when Delaney had said there'd have been two funerals if Mike had gone in after Tommy that day at the rocks.

"The trick is to heed the warning and stay in control."

The doctor wrapped Mike's toe and part of his foot in gauze and slapped him on the back. "Stitches out in a week to ten days. No swimming; keep the foot dry. It would be a good idea to have your own doctor check you out when you get back to the city." He turned away and started cleaning up. "About your friend—it sounds like he might be afraid of being afraid."

The doctor helped Mike into the waiting room, where John paid him.

Henry looked uncomfortable. "Sorry about the way Mike acted, Doc, an' thanks for takin' us. We tried both other names in the phone book, but neither one answered."

The doctor frowned at Henry. "You don't have to apologize for the actions of someone else. Once Mike calmed down, he was a perfect patient."

Waving them out the door, the doctor locked up, then joined them on the sidewalk. "The reason why the other two doctors didn't answer is because both of them are gone." He smiled. "They used to be partners, but they had a big falling out. One of them, Doc Tucker, was kind of hot-tempered. He told his partner, Doc Walters, that if he knew how to build a bomb, he'd blow up the office and Walters with it. So, to call his bluff, Walters bought Tucker a book on how to build bombs. According to Doc Tucker's wife, Tucker was afraid Walters would think he was a coward, so he decided to go ahead and build a bomb. He worked on it in the office, but before he could finish, the thing went off and killed them both. So, because a guy was too proud to admit he was scared, I'm the only doctor for thirty miles around."

"No shit...uh, I mean, shuck?" Henry said as he climbed into the car.

"No shuck." But the doctor had a huge grin on his face as he closed John's car door and waved good-bye.

"Was that the truth?" Ben asked.

"I think the story's too crazy to be a lie," John said.

Henry laughed. "I think that country hick just suckered four big-city guys."

Back at the Castle, they separated—Henry for the Illinois Central Station, John to a poker game, and Ben to home, with the baby in one arm and Mike leaning on his other. Henry cooed a good-bye at Kitty. "This was a really great day. Just like old times."

Mike turned to look at him. His eyes tightened shut, his nostrils flared, and he thought about the way Henry had bullied him most of the day. "Yeah, it was, Henry. Just like old times."

CHAPTER SIXTY-SEVEN

M ike was alone. He sat on the park bench across the street from the Post, sneaking an occasional pull from a quart bottle of Schlitz. The stitches had come out of his toe a couple of weeks earlier, and the injury to his foot was all but forgotten. It would take a lot longer to forget the way he'd embarrassed himself in front of the guys.

It was early evening and still light. The summer heat had been oppressive all day, but now, with the lake breeze picking up, the temperature had finally dropped below ninety. Mike was just beginning to wonder if any of the guys would show up when John pulled to the curb in his new '54 Olds 88. The car was a two-tone hardtop with a jet-black body, candy-apple red top, and balloon white wall tires.

John had sold his Merc to Henry after being thrashed in a quarter-mile drag race by an Olds just like the one he now drove. The flashy car bothered Mike. Even though he worked forty hours a week and put in overtime whenever he could, he was the only one in the group who didn't have wheels. By the time he helped out with family expenses, there wasn't any money left over for luxuries.

John slid onto the bench next to Mike and smiled. "What's happenin?"

Without answering, Mike handed him the beer. John tipped it back and took a long swig. He handed the bottle back, and they sat quietly for a few minutes.

Finally, John asked, "Any of the guys been around?"

Mike shrugged and shook his head. "I ain't seen Henry since we went to the quarry, an' Benny told me he had to take Annie to the drive-in. She was really pissed about his goin' to the quarry with the baby. Said a three-month-old had no business bein' on a trip like that. I guess the rest of the neighborhood guys are either out with broads or at Lola's, drinkin'."

John looked up and down the street as if to verify that Mike was telling the truth. "I guess you're it then." He paused and smiled a smile that was more of a smirk. Then he put his hands behind his head and did an elaborate stretch. "Yeah, I guess you're the one who just got lucky."

Mike knew he was about to be conned. He wished he could just ignore John, but curiosity got the better of him. With a rueful shake of his head, he gave in. "OK, spill it. Lucky how?"

John took the bottle from Mike. "I got a date tonight, an' she's got a friend."

Mike grimaced. "That's what you call lucky? No, thanks. I'm tired of gettin' set up with a bunch of dogs."

"This ain't no dog, bro. My lady says this is one foxy broad."

"Yeah, well, if she's so foxy, how come she's gotta get her girlfriend to fix her up?"

John turned away from Mike and took a long pull on the beer. "Well, uh, she's sorta got a boyfriend. But he's not around right now."

"Hey, if the guy's in Korea, I ain't gonna cut in on his stuff."

"Nah, he ain't in the army, he's just away. This lady's supposed to be real cool. She just gets bored and wants to have a little fun once in awhile. You never know, you might even get your cherry busted."

Mike flushed bright red. He turned toward John with clenched fists, but before he could explode, John raised his hand. "I was just kidding. The thing is, you ain't doin' nothing but sittin' around. Why not give it a try? I mean, whadda you got to lose?"

They picked up the girls half an hour later.

*****

John's date was a tiny redhead nicknamed Perky. She had huge eyes, large breasts, and lived up to her name, by being a nonstop talker who was in constant motion. Everything she saw was either "cool" or "freakish." John seemed to tolerate her with an attitude that bordered on parental. When she squirmed too much, he'd reach over, pat her arm, and tell her to calm down. That would work for a minute or two, and then she'd be off again.

Lisa, Mike's date, was the opposite. She was on the tall side, a silvery-haired blonde with soft blue eyes. She smiled shyly at Mike and sat quietly, speaking only when asked a direct question. John's lady had been right; Lisa was a stone fox.

John drove out to the Indiana Dunes State Park, taking Route 12/20 and turning off at Tremont. From there, the park was only a few miles. There was no ranger on duty at the gate, so John pulled straight into the main parking lot. He found a space facing the lake, parked, and cracked open a couple of quarts of beer.

For a while, they just sat and passed the bottles back and forth. The pavilion was lit up and soft music filtered out into the still, warm night. The shadows of couples dancing played on the concrete sidewalk in front.

"How 'bout you an' Lisa go for a long walk?" John said. "Me an' Perky are gonna lay down a blanket on the dune, and we could use some time alone."

441

Perky blushed, but for once, she didn't say anything.

Mike led Lisa out and they walked toward the beach. He awkwardly reached for her hand, but she had pushed slightly ahead and didn't notice. Reluctantly, he let his hand drop back to his side. As they neared the pavilion, Lisa seemed to come to life.

"Let's walk over by where the music's playing. I'd like to watch them dancing."

The open-air pavilion looked like a set for a movie with its arches and pillars supporting the dome-shaped roof. The main attraction was the brightly lit dance floor, and it was packed with couples. As the slow, romantic music poured out of the hi-fi, most of the dancers just held onto each other and swayed back and forth, hardly moving.

In the light streaming out from the pavilion, Mike decided that Lisa was the most beautiful girl he'd ever seen. She was like a younger, blonder version of Lauren Bacall. He stared at her, too enthralled to speak.

Suddenly, Lisa spun around to face him. "Do you know how to slow dance?"

When Mike shrugged, she pulled him by his arm toward the pavilion. She wanted to go inside, but Mike resisted. "It's too crowded on the dance floor. The music's just as loud out here."

Lisa smiled, agreeing to stay outside on the sidewalk. She held out her arms and they fumbled for a moment, getting their position just right. Mike had trouble picking up the tempo at first, but after a slight hesitation, they were dancing. The phonograph was playing "Vaya con Dios," and Lisa began to hum the tune. At first, Mike just swayed back and forth like the others, then decided to try a few steps. His first forward move caught Lisa by surprise. She stumbled slightly, causing him to miss a step, and he dropped his arms to his sides, red-faced.

Instead of quitting, Lisa took his right arm and wrapped it around her waist. Then, holding his other hand down alongside her hip, she kept on dancing. "Hold me tighter. That way, it's easier for me to follow your moves."

Mike began to experience a kind of warmth that had nothing to do with the summer heat. The softness of her breasts pressed against him, and the touch of her bare arms around his waist caused a feeling so intense, he was sure she could hear the pounding of his heart

Lisa began to sing, "Wherever you may go, I'll be beside you. Whether you are near or far away."

Mike wondered if she was thinking of her boyfriend, the one who was off on vacation somewhere. When the music stopped, Mike closed his eyes and kept on dancing.

Lisa stepped back. "The song's over," she said, smiling up at him. "Let's walk down by the water."

Mike grunted, "Uh huh." He could still feel the impression of her breasts against his chest.

He started out onto the sand, but Lisa held back. "I'm gonna go get the key to the car. I want to get some beer and a blanket for us."

"I'll go," Mike said, but Lisa held up her hand.

With a mischievous smirk, she said, "You'd better let me do it. I don't want to embarrass Perky."

She came back, giggling. "It's a good thing I went when I did. A few more minutes, and I'd have needed some ice water to throw on them."

Mike was stunned to hear a girl say something that sexy. He tried to laugh, but it came out strangled, and he gave up. Carrying two quarts of beer and an old army blanket, they started walking east along the shore.

The waves rolled high up onto the beach. At first, they skipped out of the way, but eventually, they took off their shoes and let the water cool their feet.

There were a few stars out, and Lisa stopped and pointed upward. "Look, it's the Big Dipper."

Mike looked up but he only saw a clump of stars. "Where?"

Instead of trying to show him in the sky, Lisa drew the seven star configuration in the wet sand. "It looks like that. Over there, back toward Chicago."

Mike picked out the cluster and broke out in an excited grin. "Wow! I never saw it before. Show me some more stuff."

She smiled and kept walking. "That's the only one I know."

As they walked farther up the beach, the lights of the pavilion faded and the night sky seemed to grow closer.

"I got this friend, Ben, he knows a lot about the stars. He reads a lot too. The guys all rag on him about being smart, but I think they're just jealous. Sometimes, I wish I could be like that. Knowing stuff, I mean."

Lisa nodded. "So do I. Girls are supposed to be giggly and not care about learning. When I told my mother I wanted to advance my education, she said it wasn't necessary, that I could find a good man in the neighborhood. She thought the only reason a girl would go to college would be to find a husband."

Mike looked over at her. "I really like the way you talk. Not exactly snooty, but high class."

Lisa flushed with pleasure. "You're the first person to mention it. I've been trying to speak properly. I think that's the mark of an educated person."

Mike nodded and silently made a vow to clean up his own speech.

The wind off the lake picked up slightly, and so did the size of the surf. The moon was almost full, and its silver glow flickered off the white-capped waves.

Lisa bent down and swished her hand in the water. "It's not cold. Wanna go swimming?"

Mike shook his head. "No bathing suit."

"I don't have one either," Lisa said. "We can go in our underwear. I won't look if you won't."

The heart-thumping heat came back, and Mike started to stammer, but Lisa was already pulling off her blouse. She wore a pink bra, and when she stepped out of her jeans, Mike saw that her panties matched.

"You weren't supposed to look," she said, laughing. "Come on in." With that, she turned and ran into the water, hitting an incoming wave and disappearing into the surf.

Mike peeled off his pants and shirt and stood uncertainly in his boxer shorts. He tried to spot Lisa, but it was too dark. He called to her, but she didn't answer. Suddenly, the memory of Tommy hit him. This time, he wasn't going to be afraid. Ignoring the first shock of the water, he crashed in screaming, "Lisa! Lisa!"

When the water was almost chest-high, a rogue wave caught him standing sideways as he tried to spot Lisa. The sand beneath his feet seemed to disappear as he thrashed frantically, lost his balance, and fell backward. His back scraped the bottom as the wave sucked him down and rolled him over and over. Just before full panic set in, a hand gripped his arm, and he was able to struggle upright. Coughing and sputtering, he came up alongside Lisa.

If she was aware of his near drowning, she didn't show it. Grinning broadly, she stared at him. "Looks like you decided to go without the underwear." Mike glanced down and realized that the wave had pulled down his shorts. Frantically, he pushed into deeper water, watching Lisa as she almost choked with laughter. The shorts were still wrapped around one leg and he was able to yank them up before wading back toward the beach. Lisa began to giggle again. "Those shorts don't hide much."

He stared back at Lisa. The outline of her nipples showed clearly through her wet bra and the crotch of her panties clung so tightly he could see the outline of wiry pubic hair. "You should talk," he said. This time, they both laughed.

He took her hand and led her back up onto the sand.

They picked up their clothing and moved to the base of the nearest dune, where they spread out the blanket. Mike thought about getting dressed, but Lisa immediately dropped down and started drying her hair with her blouse. Taking that as an invitation, he put his clothes to one side and stretched out beside her.

Lisa finished with her hair while Mike rolled over on his stomach to hide his erection.

When she spoke it was in a subdued voice, almost a whisper, and he had to sit up in order to hear her.

"I'm having a really nice time," she said.

"Me too."

His head was tilted toward her and she looked directly into his eyes. "Have you ever been in love with anyone?"

He pulled back a few inches. "When I was really young, I thought I was, but now I think it was just puppy love."

She sighed and reached up to stroke his face. "Sometimes, I think I just need to have someone love me. And if he really did that, then I'd love him back."

Mike was quiet, searching for words to describe what he was feeling. Before he could speak, Lisa reached over and pulled his head down to hers. She kissed him, and when he lightly probed her lips with his tongue, hers came forward to meet his. The touch was like an electric shock, and the taste of spearmint flooded in with the kiss.

Mike had French-kissed a girl before. He had even gone as far as stroking a girl's breasts, but this was different. This time, he knew they were going to go all the way.

Lisa slipped her bra straps down. Twisting it so that the hooks were in front, she undid the clasp. Her breasts were small and shaped like orange halves. The nipples were hard and erect. Mike used his body to push her down and began to roughly suck at her right breast.

Lisa slowly moved her hand, blocking his mouth. "Gently, like licking an ice cream cone."

Mike nodded and followed her instructions. Lisa moaned and took his hand, pushing it under the waistband of her panties. She guided him as he stroked her gently, then he pulled down her panties and rolled between her legs. He pushed inside and felt the wetness and incredible warmth. Within seconds, a burst of sensation forced him to groan in violent relief. He started to push off, but Lisa held him tightly and he stayed atop her, panting, until she finally sighed and released him.

Spent, they turned away from each other and quickly dressed. Then they settled back to lie side by side, staring up at the sky.

"This was your first time, wasn't it?"

Mike's first instinct was to lie, but Lisa's voice was so non-threatening, he told the truth. "Yeah."

"I'm glad it was with me." She leaned in and kissed him lightly. "Are you mad because it wasn't my first time?"

Mike didn't say anything. He pushed up on his elbows and looked out at the lake.

Lisa turned away. "I only did it with one other guy. I started seeing him when I was fifteen and I thought I really loved him. Now I...I just don't know. Things have gotten really crazy."

Mike put his arm around her. "I wish I'd been the first. All the guys say a girl always loves the first one."

They sat quietly, holding each other. After a while, Lisa curled onto her side and fell asleep. Mike propped his head with one arm and spooned next to her. He didn't even bother closing his eyes. For him, sleep was out of the question.

Throughout the small hours of the night, waves rhythmically lapped at the beach. Too soon for Mike, the dawn broke out over the lake in soft pinks and muted golds. He watched as seabirds pecked along the shoreline and scolded each other in raucous tones.

Lisa awakened, and they watched the sky change colors. She started to hum and then sing softly. "Now the dawn is breaking on a new tomorrow. But the memories we shared are there to borrow."

They were sitting next to each other, gripping their knees, when Perky and John walked up.

*****

They dropped Perky off first, and John waited in the car as Mike walked Lisa up to her door.

After a deep kiss, Lisa told him she couldn't see him again.

Mike fought to keep from crying. "I don't get it. Last night was—"

Lisa put her hand on his mouth and stopped him mid-sentence.

"I was someone else last night. It was the nicest night I've ever had, but I shouldn't have even gone out."

Mike had felt love and then right afterward, loss. "But I…I'm crazy about you."

Lisa was crying. She stepped inside her apartment and started to close the door.

Mike put his hand out to stop her, but she shook her head "no," and he moved back. Tears running down her face, she said, "I love you, too. Vaya con Dios, my darling." And the door clicked shut.

Mike stood for a moment, trying to decide what to do. Then the impatient bleat of John's horn made his decision for him. He turned and slowly walked down the stairs.

They drove back in silence. As they stopped in front of the Castle, John reached over and gripped his arm. "You really fell for her, didn't you?"

Mike nodded. "She gave me the brush-off. Says she was a different person last night an' she can't see me no more."

John nodded and seemed to come to a decision. "There's somethin' I gotta tell you."

Mike turned toward him and waited.

John seemed almost unable to form the words. He looked both embarrassed and frightened. "The guy she's goin' with…the guy who's away…he's been in juvie. He's almost done his time, and pretty soon, they're gonna let him out."

"Yeah?"

"Yeah, and the guy…it's Roger Shaw. Remember what he did to Andy just because he brushed him back in a softball game? And that was when he was a lot younger and not so evil. Lisa knows if he found out about last night, he'd kill the both of you."

Mike was too stunned to say anything. He slid out of the car and softly closed the door.

John put the car in first and started to pull away. He glanced back at Mike and saw that he hadn't moved. So he braked, leaned over, and rolled down the passenger window.

"I'm really sorry, Mikey."

Mike nodded, then turned and walked slowly to the Castle's front door. Pushing inside, he began to climb the stairs. Under his breath, he said, "Yeah, I'm sorry, too."

CHAPTER SIXTY-EIGHT

N ow that everyone in the Castle gang was through with school and had started working, the seasons lost their importance. There were no more two weeks off at Christmas, no spring breaks, and summer just meant it was hotter in the car driving to and from work. On weekends, if the weather wasn't too bad, Henry would risk going to the South Side and the group would gather for a poker game.

"Ante a quarter." Henry shuffled and offered the deck to Ben.

Ben reached over, took five or six cards off the top, and set them next to the pile. "Cut 'em thin, you're sure to win."

Henry dropped the larger pile on top and laughed. "So far that shit ain't been workin' for ya, Benny boy." He picked up the deck and started to deal. "Seven-card stud."

Mike groaned, "I never win at stud."

They were playing at Ben's house while Ben watched Kitty. It was Annie's night out. The baby had been too excited to go to sleep, so she sat in Ben's lap and watched.

Everyone focused on the game as the first two cards were dealt face down. Ben, John, and Mike lifted the edges of their hole cards and looked. Henry didn't.

Henry dealt the next card up. He snapped the cards as he flipped them around the table, calling out their number and suit. "Nine o'clubs, seven o' diamonds, big ace of clubs for Ben. An' the dealer pulls a pitiful three of hearts."

John looked again at his hole cards. "Didja hear about Mary Ryan?"

The table grew quiet, and Ben glanced at Henry. Henry seemed not to have heard. He took a swig of beer and said, "You're high, Benny."

"What about Mary Ryan?" Mike asked.

Ben threw in a dime.

"She's gettin' married," John said, tossing in his dime.

Henry looked over at John. "Ya took a second look at your cards an' you're bettin' outta turn. Means you're trying ta make us think ya got a good hand."

"Who'd marry that punching bag?" Mike said, folding his cards.

Henry's face flushed as he threw in his own dime, but Mike didn't seem to notice, and he went on talking. "I mean, she's balled half the guys in the neighborhood."

John's second card was another nine, and he bet a quarter. "She's marryin' Pete."

"You mean the Greek?" Mike asked.

"Yeah, you know, Pete, the counterman at the Post."

Henry's second card was a king of hearts. He decided it was time to check his hole cards. After a quick look, he slid his quarter in. "Mary's a good kid," he said softly. "I wish 'em both the best."

Ben and John both nodded.

Mike was quiet for a time. Then, with an odd quiver in his voice, he asked. "Would you go for a broad that wasn't cherry? I mean, could you be really serious about her?" He addressed the question to the table in general, but he was asking Henry.

Henry dealt the third up card, and Ben dropped. "Didn't have shit except the crummy ace."

John nodded. "Good hand to bluff with."

Henry looked at Mike. "I dunno. I'm not sure I could get the picture of other guys fuckin' my wife outta my mind."

"Yeah," Mike said. "An' they say a broad always loves the first guy who nailed her."

John groaned. "What moron made that one up?"

Mike looked as if John had somehow betrayed him. "You fuckin' damn well know what I mean. Guys say it, people say it. Shit, everyone says it."

John tilted back in his chair, balancing it on two legs. "Well, I don't say it. Perky was with other guys, an' now she's with me. She don't care about some fool just because he nailed her before she found out what Mr. Good Dick was like."

They all laughed. Mike crushed an empty potato chip bag into a ball and bounced it off John's head.

John grabbed it and threw it back at Mike. "Seriously, you figure if a broad gets raped, she falls in love with the guy who raped her? It's stupid."

"Bein' cherry isn't such hot shit," Ben said. "A broad can be a virgin an' still be a raging bitch."

John grinned. "You talkin' from experience, Benny?"

When Ben didn't smile, John turned away, peeking at his hole cards again.

"Ya think the cards are gonna change?" Henry snarled, dealing the last up card.

Henry had a pair of threes, a king of hearts, and a ten of hearts showing. He had a three in the hole. John was showing two nines, a seven of hearts, and a jack of clubs. John bet a quarter.

"I read a book by John Steinbeck," Ben said, "*Cannery Row*. The guy in it marries a hooker."

"No shit?" Mike said.

"No shit, an' he says that workin' girls are best, 'cause they know how to really please a man. And they ain't gonna screw around 'cause they've already tried lots of guys, so they're not curious."

"Man's got a point," Henry said. Then he wistfully added, "I wish I'd read a book like that, some things mighta been different."

He dealt the last card down.

Mike started to say something, but John touched his arm. "For once just shut up, OK? I wanna finish this hand."

John bet a quarter and Henry raised. "I think you're bluffin'."

John saw the raise and raised another quarter. Henry called.

"Whadda ya got?" John asked.

"I paid ta see you." Henry's face was grim, but Ben knew it had nothing to do with the cards.

John showed a full house, nines over jacks. Henry turned his cards down, and as John raked in the pot, Henry looked down at the floor.

The baby started getting fidgety, and when Ben got up to put her in bed, Henry shoved back from the table, signaling the end of the game. He put on his coat and gloves, pulled on a pair of earmuffs, and walked to the door.

"It's a long haul back to the Northside. I'll catch ya later."

Ben came back into the room just as the front door closed. "She's out like a light. Where's Henry?"

"He split. I think he was pissed about somethin'." John said, then picked up the cards and shoved them back into their cardboard container.

Ben sat down and shook his head. "I thought you knew. Mary Ryan got his cherry way back in grade school. I think he had a thing for her, but he couldn't get past her being with other guys."

"No shit? If I'd known that I woulda kept my mouth shut about her gettin' married." John frowned. "I really fucked up."

"Nah, he would've found out sooner or later. The way he acted, though, I think he's really sorry he let her go."

Mike looked down at his hands. "An' I said that stupid shit about Mary bein' a punchin' bag." He got up to go, looking over at Ben as he opened the door. "You really think being with other guys is no big deal?"

Suddenly, John caught on. "Wait a fuckin' minute, you ain't thinkin' about seeing Lisa, are you?"

Mike shrugged.

"You date her, an' you're gonna have a lot more to worry about than whether or not she was cherry. Shaw's due ta get out any day now. If he gets wind of you messin' with his girl, you'll end up dead."

Deep in thought, Mike seemed not to have heard. He nodded emphatically as if just coming to a decision and walked out the door.

CHAPTER SIXTY-NINE

Ben was well on his way to getting drunk. He waved both arms, almost knocking over John's drink. "You know, it's spring out there. Birds are singin', trees are sproutin' new leaves, the world's comin' awake after a long winter. So"—it came out "shoo"—"how come we're spendin' the afternoon indoors?"

John finished off his drink and signaled Blue for a refill. "I love a bar. When I get enough bread, I'm gonna own one." Blue came over and poured a double shot of bourbon into John's glass. "You can come work for me, Blue. I'll need a good bartender."

As he moved away, Blue's unsmiling face didn't change. "Lola catch yore ass in here, we both be needin' lots more den a job."

John sipped his whiskey. "So, aside from gettin' it regular, how's it really goin', Benny?"

"Regular, my ass. I get it whenever Annie wants it. If she isn't fussin' with the baby, then she's too tired, and if we do try to get it on, the baby wakes up and ruins the scene. I think the kid can hear us if we're just thinkin' about sex."

"How old is Kitty now?" John asked.

Ben frowned at him as if insulted by the question. "You can't even remember her first year? She was a year old last month."

"What about the Talonis? They still hate your guts?"

"Things aren't so bad now that her fucking brothers are out of the house and have decided to have nothing to do with us. Her mom and dad came to the baby's birthday party, but the only one in the family we see regular is her Uncle Gino. He's cool. Annie started workin' as a waitress at night, an' when Gino found out, he gave her a little .25 caliber pistol to carry in her purse."

John smiled knowingly. "Better not get caught with that piece. If it comes from a Taloni, it's either hot or been used to kill someone. They're in tight with the Outfit."

Ben laughed. "They just like you to think that. Gino's pretty straight. He does a little bookin' on the side, but it's so small, the big boys won't have anything to do with him."

John fingered his drink. "Maybe you should loan the gun to Mike. He's still seein' that broad of Shaw's, an' Roger's due out of the shithouse any day now. When he finds out, he's gonna put some serious damage on Mike."

Ben looked cautiously around the bar until he was satisfied that no one was paying them any attention. Reaching into his pocket, he slipped out the tiny automatic. It had once been silver, but long use had worn off most of the finish. The black plastic handle grip was cracked, and there was a piece broken off one side.

John lightly pushed the gun downward. "Put it away."

Ben ignored him. He pulled at the slide to show John that the action was jammed. "I'd be glad to loan it to Mike. Maybe he'd off Roger an' do the world a favor. Trouble is the damn thing's jammed. Annie gave it to me to get it fixed. You know anyone around here who does that kinda work?"

John took the gun and quickly slipped it into his jacket pocket. "I'll get it fixed an' give it to Mike. If Rog is gonna go after him, he'll do it as soon as he gets out. We should know if Mike's got a problem within a month or so."

Ben smiled. "OK, I'll square it with Annie, but if she gets raped in the meantime, she'll come lookin' for you."

John laughed. "I pity the poor son-of-a-bitch who tangles with Annie. She'd kick his ass from here to Cottage Grove."

Ben shook his head. "That's my lovely wife you're talkin' about. But you're right. Growing up with those two moron brothers of hers made her tougher than a horse-meat steak."

*****

John brought the gun to a pawnshop that dealt in illegal weapons. The pawnbroker looked at the weapon and gave a slight sneer. A .25 caliber automatic wasn't a gun that men respected. It was of no use except at really close range. Because it was small, it was considered a lady's gun, and because ladies carried them in their purses, they were always jamming up from dirt and lint.

John was embarrassed. "It ain't mine. I'm gettin' it fixed for a broad I know."

The pawnbroker shrugged and pushed the gun back under the cage wire to John. "This piece of crap ain't worth fixin'. You give a shit about this broad of yours, you'll get her a gun that'll do some damage."

John shoved the gun back. "She ain't my broad. Just fix the thing so it shoots."

The pawnbroker had sharp, owlish features and bifocals that slid down his nose. He peered at John over the rims. "Five bucks, an' no guarantees."

John nodded. As he left the shop, he heard the pawnbroker mumble, "Fuckin' thing ain't worth five bucks."

The repaired weapon was ready a few days later. John dropped a five-dollar bill on the counter. To show the old fool that he knew what he was doing, he slammed the clip into the handle of the gun, jacked a round into the chamber, slipped on the safety, and dropped the piece into his jacket pocket.

The wind off the lake picked up in the late afternoon, and by evening, the temperature had dropped to almost freezing. John huddled in his jacket with his shoulders hunched and his chin down to hold in the warmth. If his head hadn't been lowered, he probably would have seen Frankie Dee and Tonto. As it was, he almost walked into them.

Frankie said nothing, but Tonto smiled through rotten teeth. When John tried to go around, Tonto blocked his path. "Johnny boy, how ya holdin'?" His tone was wheedling and threatening at the same time. He glanced back at Frankie for encouragement, but Frankie looked away.

"Get outta my way, asshole." John moved sideways, but again, Tonto cut him off.

Tonto was small and skinny. His two front teeth had decay on both sides and stuck out, forcing his upper lip to protrude. When he was little, the kids called him Ratty, but when he started hanging around with Frankie Dee, who was a tough guy, he became Tonto. Even though his nickname meant he was just a sidekick, he liked it. Being called by an Indian name made him feel dangerous, and feeling dangerous made him dangerous.

John heard the snick of the knife, but its tip was cutting into his throat before he could react. Tonto was holding it point first, but the edge of the blade was angled to slice at a flick of his wrist. He leaned close to John's face and exhaled. His breath stunk of something dead.

"Did you call me asshole?" The wheedle was replaced by a slow drawl that carried as much menace as Tonto could create. "I'm gonna have ta cut this fucker's throat, Frankie. Whadda ya think?"

There was a time when John had considered Frankie a friend. They had done business together, and John couldn't believe Frankie was letting Tonto rob him.

Frankie shook his head nervously. "We're stone broke, Johnny. Just give him your money an' we'll split."

Tonto turned the knife sideways and pressed hard against John's neck with the dull side. "Nah, he called me an asshole. I gotta cut him."

John was pinned against the wall of a building. A small trickle of blood was working its way down his neck from the tiny cut made by the point of the knife. He couldn't move his head, but he put his hands up as if he were surrendering.

The knife edged back slightly and John took a breath. "Let me get to my wallet. I got a few bucks I can let you have."

Tonto pushed the knife forward and the blade cut deeper. "A few bucks? A few bucks? You're gonna give us everything you got. Including your watch, that nice jacket, and anything else I want. And then, I'm gonna give you somethin' ta remember me by."

John's heart was thumping so hard, it felt as if his blood was going to start spewing from his nose and ears. He was truly terrified, more frightened than he'd been in his entire life. Slowly, he lowered his hands and as he reached back for his wallet, he remembered the gun. He carefully pulled the wallet out, trying not to move, and offered it to Tonto. Tonto grabbed it with his left hand and tried to flip the wallet open. But the action required two hands and forced him to put the knife aside for an instant.

John drew back and yanked out the gun. He slammed it directly between Tonto's eyes. Relief flooded over him, followed immediately by a blinding rage. He cried and screamed at the same time. "You motherfucker! You dirty motherfucker! You cut my throat, you dirty motherfucker!" Pushing the gun on the bridge of Tonto's nose, John forced the bug-eyed thug down onto his knees. Frankie started toward him, but John pushed harder against Tonto's head. He was still screaming. "You move, Frankie, and I'll kill you right after I finish off this piece of shit."

All John could think about was how scared he'd been. His hand shook, and he pulled the trigger, wincing in anticipation of the blast. Nothing happened. John yanked at the trigger again, and still, the gun wouldn't fire. His frustration exploded and he began smashing the gun, butt first, into Tonto's face. Tonto went down, blood seeming to spurt from everywhere. John was focused on killing Tonto, and Frankie Dee used the opportunity to take off running.

Tonto was on the ground, head covered with his hands, when John stopped kicking him. He stepped back and tried once more to shoot the gun, but it still wouldn't fire. With a final drop-kick to Tonto's ribs, he turned and walked away.

As he headed for Lola's and a badly needed drink, he shoved his hands in his pocket to hide their shaking. He'd tried to kill a man. Not once, but several times. He'd pulled the trigger, done his best to send a bullet crashing into Tonto's brain. The only thing that had kept him from being a murderer was a broken gun—a broken gun that had just been repaired.

Blue was at the bar shining a glass when John staggered in. Otherwise, Lola's was empty.

"Y'all OK?" Blue set the glass down and leaned forward. He'd been a bartender too long not to recognize trouble.

John kept his hands in his pockets, still not trusting his ability to keep them from shaking. "Yeah."

"You looks like shit. I gon' get you a bandage for dat neck."

Blue reached under the bar and pulled out a first aid kit. He handed it to John and motioned toward the back.

A minute later, John was in the men's room looking in the cracked mirror over the sink. The nick wasn't as deep as he'd thought. He cleaned the cut, covered it with gauze and adhesive tape, and went back to the bar.

Blue asked no questions. He poured John a double shot of VO and popped open a can of 7-Up. John downed the VO and waved off the chaser, motioning for another VO. Blue poured.

"You believe in God, Blue?"

Blue's face didn't change. It was as if he were asked the question every day of his life. "Some."

"I just started tonight." John downed the whiskey, and Blue poured him another one. "Tonight, God stopped me from fuckin' up my whole life."

Blue nodded. "That happens sometimes."

"I tried to kill a guy tonight, an' God stopped me."

The glass was half empty, and Blue filled it. "Best keep dat stuff ta yourself." He moved back up the bar and started straightening the bottles that lined the back wall.

A few minutes later, Ben walked in and sat down next to John. "What's happenin', my man?" Ben caught Blue's eye, made a drinking motion, and pointed to John's glass.

"Nothin' shakin'. I got your gun, but there's no sense in givin' it to Mike. It still don't work."

"What happened to your neck?"

"Cut myself shaving."

Ben looked unconvinced, but he didn't pursue it. After Blue set down Ben's drink, John waved him over to a booth so Blue wouldn't see the gun. He pulled it from his pocket. "I paid five bucks ta get the slide fixed, but I tried to shoot the damn thing, and it won't fire."

461

Ben took the gun and tried to pull back the slide. It wouldn't budge.

"See?" John shrugged.

Ben turned the gun over and flipped off the safety. He again pulled the slide, and this time, it slid back and ejected a live round.

"You left the safety on."

John knocked back his VO and tried not to cry.

CHAPTER SEVENTY

Ben looked up from his coffee as Roger Shaw walked into the Bottomless Cup Diner. "Don't look now, but guess who just walked in."

John twisted around, and his mouth tightened in disgust. "Jesus, I was hoping that fucker would pull some other shit and go back in. How long's he been out?"

"Jeez, I told you not to turn around." Ben took a quick glance and saw Roger doing a one-eighty of the room. "He's been out for a while. I heard his parole officer wouldn't let him come around the neighborhood."

Ben lowered his head and stared down at the cigarette burns on the Formica tabletop, hoping Roger wouldn't see him. It did no good. Striding past the counter where Ben's wife, Annie, was taking a customer's order, Roger charged straight for their booth.

Roger Shaw had grown in the three years since he'd been sentenced to the detention facility at Saint Charles. Now at six-two, two-hundred-and-twenty pounds, with huge, iron-pumped chest and arms, Bad Roger looked badder than ever.

Ben kept his head down and whispered, "He's bigger, but he doesn't look all that mean. Maybe he's changed."

John snorted. "He was a vicious bastard when he left. Being locked up with a bunch of other vicious bastards wouldn't change him."

A man stood up in Roger's path, putting on his coat. Roger moved straight ahead, forcing the guy to jump aside to avoid being barreled into.

When Roger got to Ben and John's table, John nodded. "Rog, howzit goin'?"

Without being invited, Roger sank down onto the green plastic seat next to Ben. Ben shied away an inch or two. Then, figuring that the move might be misunderstood, he gave a nod and a slight smile to show he meant no insult.

Acting as if John weren't there, Roger turned sideways to face Ben. He spoke in a hoarse voice. "Uh, look, man, I know we ain't never been friends, but I need a favor."

It wasn't a flat-out demand, and Ben wondered if maybe John was wrong and the guy had changed after all.

"Sure, Rog. What can I do for you?"

Before answering, Roger locked his eyes on John. "Why don't you take a hike?"

John started to rise, but Ben reached across the table and held his arm. "John's my friend. You ask your favor in front of him or not at all."

If Roger was surprised, he didn't show it. "I heard ya did some time while I was gone. Looks like ya picked up some attitude." His voice gave no indication that he'd given in, but his words told a different story. "OK, he stays. But if he tells one fuckin' soul, I'll kick his nuts off."

Turning to Ben, his face went hard and he half-whispered what he wanted. "I…need ya to…to make a phone call."

Puzzled, Ben just nodded.

Roger got up, motioned for Ben to follow, and started toward the pay phone near the back wall. Ben gave John an open-armed shrug and fell in behind Roger. Annie caught his eye and he shrugged at her, too.

Roger took the receiver off the hook and handed it to Ben. "Go ahead."

"I need a nickel an' the number," Ben said, trying to keep his voice neutral. There was no sense in pissing Roger off with sarcasm.

"Oh, yeah." A crumpled piece of notepaper came out of Roger's pocket. Carefully smoothing it against the wall, he handed it to Ben. "I ain't got no nickel. Lemme tap ya for one."

It wasn't really a request. Ben dug down into his pants pocket and pulled out a few coins. Extracting a nickel, he lifted the receiver, dropped the coin in the slot, and started dialing the number.

Roger pulled forward and watched Ben's every move. At first, Ben thought the guy was concerned that he would dial wrong. He stood back from the phone to give Roger a better view. Extra careful to get the number right, he finished dialing.

Roger stared at the phone with a puzzled expression, as if he were wondering what to do next. In a flash of insight, Ben understood what was going on. He also understood that he was chosen because Roger knew he wouldn't blab it all over the neighborhood.

In a subdued tone, he said, "It's ringing, Rog."

Roger grabbed the phone and waved Ben away with a dismissive gesture. As Ben walked back to his table, he heard Roger say, "Lisa?"

"What the fuck was that all about?" John asked as Ben sat down.

"He's calling Lisa."

"Yeah, it figures, but how come you had to dial the number?"

Ben didn't answer. He shook his head and looked out the window at the traffic. A slight drizzle wet the streets, and the passing cars were reflected in the dark asphalt. It wasn't quite cold enough to turn into snow, but it was still early evening.

Annie came over with a pot of coffee and filled their cups. The warm aroma wafted up, and Ben smiled at her. Then the moment passed as a counter customer called out, "Hey, girly, can I get some service here?" Annie ruffled Ben's hair and turned away.

John poured too much cream in his coffee and it overflowed onto the saucer. He leaned down and took a sip without picking up the cup. "Come on, Benny. Don't make me beg. Why'd he make you do the phonin'?"

Before Ben could answer, they heard the loud crash of Roger slamming down the phone. Without a glance in their direction, he ran to the front, stiff-armed the door, and stormed out onto the street.

Ben shook his head. "That poor fucker. Around the time Shaw got sent away, the phone service changed. Remember back a few years, when you picked up the receiver and the operator would say, 'number please,' and do all the work for you? Well, while he was gone, they modernized the system. I'm pretty sure he didn't know how to use a dial phone and was too embarrassed to ask me to show him. Instead, he let me dial and watched me. You can't help feelin' sorry for the guy."

"The guy I feel sorry for is Mike. From the way Rog blew outta here, it looks like Lisa gave him the air."

Ben peered through the fogged up window and saw Roger Shaw standing alone on the corner. He was hunched forward, hands in his pockets and shoulders rounded against the wind. "She might have told him they were over, but I'll guarantee she didn't mention Mike."

"Doesn't matter, someone's bound to let it slip. Henry told Mike to come up to the North Side and stay with him until this blows over, but he won't leave Hyde Park because he's afraid Shaw will go after Lisa. As if Mikey could do anything about it."

Ben nodded and signaled Annie for their check. "He gave the gun back to Annie. Claimed carryin' it made him more nervous than it was worth."

John stood and gave a slight shudder. "Can't say as I blame him. Still, you gotta admit the guy grew a backbone since he got together with Lisa. Gun or no gun, he knows he ain't got a chance against Shaw, but he ain't runnin'."

*****

The telephone dialing system wasn't the only new thing that threw Roger Shaw. The first time he took a bus, the driver had snarled at Roger's stupidity when he tried to hand him the fare. The CTA had started using coin meters a year earlier. Hanging onto the upright bar, Roger had fought to keep from smashing his fist into the driver's sneering face. Now he avoided buses altogether and either hitched or walked where he wanted to go.

Of all the things Roger had to put up with, the worst ones were the changes in the people he had known. While he had marked time behind the walls of Saint Charles, most of his friends had either gone into the service or gotten jobs. The ones who were left were either paired up or married, like the Jewboy.

Lisa had paired up, too. She wouldn't tell him the name of the guy who was cutting his time, but it didn't matter. She was his first target. He'd get even with her, and when her boyfriend tried to interfere, he'd hurt the guy, hospital-bad.

The streets were filled with cars, and they all seemed to be moving at breakneck speed. Roger had been too young to get a driver's license before the judge sent him to juvie, so he didn't know how to drive. It was a fundamental skill in the neighborhood, and he was ashamed to admit it was one he didn't have. That meant lessons from friends were out of the question. If he'd had the money, he would have gone to a driving school, but without a job, he couldn't afford it. When he first got out, his PO had found him a job in a warehouse, but he'd only lasted a week. Punching out the warehouse manager hadn't been entirely his fault. The guy had pushed him around, acting as if giving him the job was some kind of big favor.

Out on the Nickel, 55th Street, Roger huddled under an awning and went over his options for the evening. He could go over to Lisa's house, grab her by the neck, and drag her out with him. Maybe if he showed her a good time, she'd change her mind. They could go to a fancy restaurant or a nightclub to dance. Thinking about it, he shook his head in frustration. Restaurants cost money.

Darkness came over the city as Roger, seething with anger, wandered aimlessly up Kimbark Avenue toward the University of Chicago. Between 58th and 59th, he passed a chubby female headed in the opposite direction. As he turned to watch, her canvas shoulder purse swung along with her, stride for stride. The motion of the purse was hypnotic. Like a golden pendulum, it rocked forward and backward, promising a big, fat wallet.

The girl was dressed like a co-ed, with a pleated skirt, plaid coat, and shawl over her shoulders. She moved in a choppy fashion, brisk and unfeminine. U of C students made easy targets; they usually had money and were so unaccustomed to violence that they rarely fought back.

Unseen, Roger turned and followed her. She went right on 57th Street and climbed the steps up to Woolworth's, the university bookstore. Roger waited, pretending to read the notices pinned on the tree outside. Within minutes, the girl came back out, holding a large book under her arm. Slowing for a moment, she stuffed her wallet and the receipt into her purse. Then, pulling her purse back over her shoulder, she set off back the way she'd come.

The dim yellow streetlamps didn't throw their light beyond a few feet. Huge, leafless trees with spider-leg limbs blocked what little glow they gave off and created pockets of near darkness. Roger stalked quietly, a predator hunting with mounting excitement as he closed in on his kill. This co-ed, he told himself, had a rich daddy paying for her school, and she had a lot more money than she needed.

As she stepped out of a lighted area, Roger struck. At an all-out run, he hurtled by and grabbed her purse. He had pictured her standing, stunned, as he disappeared into the night.

Instead, the girl caught the thick cloth strap of her purse as it slid off her shoulder. She clutched at it and the strap twisted around her wrist. Roger kept on going. The iron hold he had on the purse yanked the girl to the concrete sidewalk, knees first. When she hit the concrete, there was a sickening thud, and her book went flying.

Now there was an anchoring weight on the end of the purse. Suddenly, Roger was like a dog that had rushed to the end of his leash. Abruptly, the purse was jerked back and he lost hold of it, staggering and barely managing to stay upright.

Regaining his balance, he grabbed the purse off the ground and tried to pull it free by breaking the strap. The violent tug almost wrenched the girl's arm out of its socket, pulling the strap around her wrist even tighter. She screamed in pain, trying to let go of the purse. Roger kept yanking, dragging her face down on the ground. Still screaming, the girl swung her legs around in an effort to regain some kind of balance. Roger kept pulling and her skirt rode up obscenely, revealing chalk-white thighs.

Roger was enraged. The rich bitch wasn't going to get away with cheating him out of his prize. "Gimme the fuckin' purse!"

The girl fell over on her side and instinctively curled up in a ball. She was too stunned to undo the tangled strap that kept her tethered.

Completely out of control, Roger continued trying to yank the purse free. His side-to-side motion dragged her across the cement walk, scraping a hole in her coat and tearing at her already injured shoulder.

Getting nowhere, Roger stopped pulling for an instant and tried to calm down.

The girl quieted, staring up at Roger and shaking in terror. Roger stood above her, backlit and menacing in the dim streetlight. He figured he must look like Satan himself, and the fear he knew he was inflicting brought him a hot flush of victory. He bent toward her, convinced that her fright was so paralyzing, she'd let him simply unwind the purse. Instead, she started screaming again.

"Help! Rape! Rape!" The girl's voice had grown hoarse and her screams were barely audible. But to Roger, they were deafening.

He couldn't think. He knew it was only a matter of time before someone heard her. He needed to shut her up, to stop the deafening sounds coming from her throat.

"Shut the fuck up, ya stupid bitch."

Roger wanted to explain that he had no intention of raping her. He wanted to tell her why he had to have her purse, why the whole thing was her fault for holding onto it.

Her exposed thighs were smeared with blood from her scraped knees, and that only made him madder, because in Roger's mind, the girl's injuries were self-inflicted. All the chaos of his life seemed to be centered in this one insane moment—the hysteria, the blood, the need to cover up his actions. He took her head in his hands, one hand on her chin and the other hand gripping her by the hair. One twist, and the noise would stop. One twist, and she wouldn't be able to tell anyone lies about rape and how he'd hurt her.

He was about to do the snapping motion that would break her neck when the headlights hit him. Roger let go of the girl and stared

470

with confusion into the blinding light. Then instinct took over, and he whirled away as the police car screeched to a stop.

Roger could still hear the screaming girl, but now there was a new note in her tone. The fear was gone and she sounded elated. "He's right there, he tried to rape me." As he spun toward an alley, he saw her rise to her feet and start coming after him. She was shouting and pointing toward the alley. "There, that's him! Get him, kill him."

The cop at the wheel of the squad car had already caught sight of Roger. The patrolman slammed to a stop, blocking the entrance of the alley, and the doors of the cop car flew open. The two patrolmen charged out, one on each side.

Roger was trapped. Unfamiliar with the block, he'd picked an alley that had no outlet. When he reached a high brick wall at the end, he knew it was over. He stopped and put his hands up in the air, his fingers spread open to show the police that he didn't have a weapon.

The first cop to reach Roger began swinging his baton while still running.

*****

Roger Shaw's public defender wasn't given his client's file until they were walking into the courtroom. It was one of nine cases to which he'd been assigned that day. He told Roger to keep the bandage on his head so the judge could see what the cops had done to him and suggested a court trial instead of a jury trial. He was convinced that for a single count of purse-snatching, he could get Roger off with one to five, no more. Without time to read the complaint, the PD was relying on Roger's version for his facts.

As things turned out, Roger's version was nothing like the victim's. She wasn't really a girl: she was a thirty-year-old woman. She wasn't even a student; she was a professor's wife. And the charge against Roger wasn't simple purse-snatching, it was felonious assault and attempted rape.

The papers went crazy. Editorials deplored the deterioration of the neighborhood and compared the situation in the 5th Ward to the lawless days of prohibition. They derided law enforcement and called upon the mayor to begin a full-scale investigation of the police department.

For its part, the University of Chicago was concerned that the increasing pattern of violence in Hyde Park would scare away students. Determined to send a message to the lower elements, they applied pressure all the way to the govener's office, and Roger Shaw was sentenced by a politically-motivated judge to a term of fourteen years to life.

Lisa was in the courtroom when the verdict was handed down. As he was being led away, Roger looked over at her and couldn't understand why she wasn't crying.

*****

It was one of Lola's rare nights off. The boys snuck in when she wasn't around, and as long as she didn't catch them, it seemed to be OK with Blue.

Ben made wet circles with his soda back. "It doesn't pay to screw around near the university. I heard they spent a fortune making sure Roger would get the toughest sentence possible."

John nodded. "Yeah, he shoulda known better. Fourteen years, he'll be an old man by the time he gets out."

He finished his drink and motioned to Blue for a refill. Blue sauntered over and filled the shot glass. He wiggled the bottle at Ben and Mike, but they both shook their heads.

"That's if he gets out. The judge said fourteen to life. If he acts the fool in Joliet, he'll be in a lot longer."

Mike nodded, but said nothing. He stared down at his empty glass and smiled.

472

CHAPTER SEVENTY-ONE

Henry folded the *Chicago Times* article in with his letter to Andy and slipped them both into an envelope. The article was a rehash of Roger Shaw's trial and the subsequent formation of the South East Chicago Commission. The paper went on to laud the commission and the city for finally taking action against the criminal elements who ruled Hyde Park. Millions would be spent tearing down entire blocks of crowded slum tenements and replacing them with middle-class housing.

In his letter, Henry let Andy know that the Castle was on the list of condemned properties. He figured Andy wouldn't much give a shit, but he thought that the kid would want to know. It wasn't as if the building they'd grown up in was worth saving, but they'd had some good times there. "I think the biggest reason the university wants the neighborhood torn down is to keep out the colored and the poor," he wrote. "They closed the Beehive, and the word around was that there were too many dark faces making the scene. I don't know where all the guys are headed. When I find out, I'll let you know."

*****

Once the massive Hyde Park urban renewal project was approved and funded, Ben was given ninety days to vacate his apartment in the

Castle. He began knocking on neighbor's doors to organize a protest against the way the city was tearing everything down. A few people agreed to sign his petition, but when the 5th Ward alderman explained that their moving expenses would be paid for by the city, any thought of protest ended and negotiations to find out which moving company would give the largest kickbacks began.

Ben's mother rented an apartment in South Shore, and Ben and Annie moved in with her temporarily.

When Ben read in the *Hyde Park Herald* that it was the Castle's turn for the wrecking ball, something drove him to go and watch. He joined the crowd standing in the vacant lot that had once been the site of the Miller Building.

Most of the Castle was gone by the time Ben spotted Henry. They hadn't seen each other for months, and for a moment, he shrank back, feeling a strange need to be alone with his memories. Then Henry caught sight of him and Ben casually waved. Henry nodded and sauntered over. "What's happenin', man?"

Ben's reply came back automatically. "Nothin' shakin' but the leaves in the trees."

"An' they wouldn't be shakin' if it weren't for the breeze," Henry finished.

They both smiled. Henry didn't look at Ben when he spoke. Instead, he stared across the street at the Castle. "Did ya hear Parker died?"

"Who?"

"Parker, Charlie Parker. The Bird."

"No shit?"

"No shit, 'bout a year ago. They say he was sick, but the guy who told me claims he OD'd."

"Man, that's too bad. Parker was great."

The huge iron wrecking ball swung toward the Castle in a wide arc. The ball's slow motion ended as it slammed into the northernmost red brick wall, the last wall standing. The impact caused a visible shudder that subsided almost immediately. A slight fog of dust hung in the air, but otherwise, the wall appeared undamaged. The crane drew the ball back for another blow, and the operation was repeated.

Now the blows seemed to be coming faster, and with each hit, Ben gave a sort of low moan. He muttered "Jesus" and winced again, as if he were the one being hit.

It was late afternoon, and the glare of the summer sun was blocked by the mound of debris that had once been the building. The street became even more crowded as people returning from work stopped to watch the spectacle. Most stood across the street, but a few pushed up against the fence—a fence made up of the building's doors.

The doors had been stripped from inside the Castle and nailed together by the demolition crew to create a safety barrier. There were front doors, bedroom doors, bathroom doors, closet doors—a pastel rainbow collection of doors that had once opened and closed on people's lives.

Henry thought he spotted his old bedroom door and crossed the street to check. Returning, he shook his head. "Nah, no dart holes, couldn't be mine."

Ben saw his front door. It was the only varnished door in the line, and it still held the taped-on card that read "Kahn."

The discovery seemed to satisfy whatever need they'd had, and they looked no further. Now the brick wall was visibly shaking with each blow. All movement among the spectators stopped as they waited silently for it to come down.

The boys shifted a little further back to get a better view just as the bricks gave way and began to crumble. Before the wall could complete its fall, the iron ball struck again. There was a roaring sound, a huge cloud of dust, and it was down. The roof had collapsed earlier, and with the destruction of this final wall, the Castle was reduced to a pile of smoky rubble.

"I gotta go," Henry said, as he turned and headed toward the 1953 Mercury John had sold him. "I ain't supposed ta be here."

"Hey, wait up." Ben ran to get in front of Henry and blocked him. Ben didn't know exactly what he wanted to say. He looked back at the building and shuffled his feet uncomfortably. "Parker's dead, man, that's really fucked."

Henry's eyes seemed unfocused, as if he were staring at something far away. "Remember when he came outta the Beehive that night?"

"Yeah." Ben paused a moment. "When are you gonna be off parole and start workin' for Costas?"

The air was still heavy with dust, and Henry coughed to clear his throat. "I just saw Costas an' I told him I was thinkin' of doin' somethin' else. I, uh, met this guy at work." Henry seemed to be having trouble getting at what he was trying to say, and Ben didn't know how to help him. "This guy, Jesse, he's a colored guy, acts kinda like a father to me. He talked ta me an' straightened me out. Asked me if I was OK with beatin' on innocent people, especially women. An' I figured I wasn't. So I told Costas "Thanks, but no thanks. This Jesse, he's a great guy. You'd really like him."

Ben felt a shock of jealousy. He'd tried to get Henry to go straight, but Henry hadn't wanted to listen to him. "I thought you didn't like colored people."

Henry's eyes went squinty. "Where'd ya get that idea? I ain't like that. Shit, if there's any kind of people us Indians should be against, it's white guys."

It was so ridiculous, Ben started to laugh. "What about me? I'm white."

"You ain't white. You're a Jew."

Ben laughed again and let it go. "How about the drug thing? You still gonna deal?"

"Nah, I seen too many strung-out junkies in the joint ta get back inta that shit. Anyway, I got a big promotion at the mill. I'm the dock foreman now an' makin' good bread."

Most of the dust had settled, and Henry moved to his car. He leaned over to brush the driver's side of the windshield clean.

Ben went around to the passenger side and wiped at the window with his sleeve. "Annie an' me, we're pullin' out. Gonna head out West while Kitty's still too young to go to school. I was gonna call you to say good-bye."

They came together in front of the car. Ben put out his hand palm up, and Henry slapped it lightly, then held on. "I know we ain't seen too much of each other lately, but I'm really gonna miss ya. Mike's leavin' too. Him an' Lisa are headin' downstate. The jerk wants ta be a farmer. Can ya beat it? Mike a farmer."

Ben nodded. "He told me. Johnny's movin' to South Shore. Frankie Dee's been shootin' his mouth off about getting even for his pulling a gun on Tonto. Johnny figures it's best to get scarce an' let things cool down. You heard from Andy?"

Henry seemed lost in thought. "Andy? Oh, yeah, Andy. I meant ta tell ya. He's still in Rockford, hidin' out. He told me he ain't never comin' back, an' he's gettin' married."

"Married?" Ben gave a wry grin. "Who'd marry Andy?"

"Believe it or not, his boss's daughter. He claims she's a real looker."

They went quiet again. Henry opened the door of the Merc. He had that odd, faraway look in his eyes again. "It's funny, I didn't know how good it was till it went bad. I got this feelin' we'll never see each other again." He turned to Ben. "You walk light, man."

Ben nodded, too upset to talk. As he slowly turned to go, his eyes dropped to the ground and he stopped in mid-motion.

"Jesus, look at that," he whispered. "The ground's crawlin' with 'em." He pointed down.

At first, Henry had no idea what Ben was talking about. Then he slowly became aware of movement on the street. With a shiver of disgust, he realized that the asphalt was covered with fleeing cockroaches. As common as they were, his skin prickled at their sheer numbers. He stepped on a bunch and watched as the others swept around his shoe, pushing toward some obscure goal. He dropped into the driver's seat of his car as they streamed by and in a wistful voice, said, "I wonder where the hell they're gonna go?"

CHAPTER SEVENTY-TWO

Chicago 1981

H enry went down his list and made all the calls but the last
one. He asked Julia to call John's mother and Perky because
he knew they would cry, and Henry had problems with hearing women
cry. Afterward, Julia came up behind him and started massaging his
shoulders. "You haven't called Ben."

Henry nodded. "I know, I know."

Julia found a knot in the middle of Henry's trapezoid and dug in
hard. "Ben was John's closest friend. You've got to call him."

It felt wrong to be enjoying the massage so much. Henry reached
back and pulled Julia's hands down around his neck. "I'm working up
to it, tryin' to figure out how I can talk to him without getting pissed
off."

Julia leaned in close to his ear. She kissed him and whispered,
"Don't swear, Henry."

*****

The insistent jangle of the phone shattered the twilight state
that was as close as Ben had come to sleep lately. His body reacted
before his brain, and he started to grab for the receiver, hoping to
silence the ringing before it woke Annie. Then, as he reached

toward the nightstand from the middle of the king-sized bed, he remembered that Annie was gone, that they'd been separated for a long time. The pain of her loss hit him and started the tightening in his throat that threatened tears.

He stared at the phone and had to take time to swallow before he could talk. Then, resting back against the pillow, he pressed the phone to his ear and grunted, "Yeah?"

The voice on the other end was gruff and instantly recognizable. "Hey, Benny, It's Henry." A hesitation, and then, "Long time."

Ben glanced over at the clock radio and watched as the last green digit changed from an eight to a nine, 6:29a.m. Even fuzzy with fatigue, he knew this couldn't be good. "Yeah."

"Got bad news. There was a car accident last night, Johnny's dead. I got a call from a friend of mine…"

Ben, still groggy, tried to make sense of what was being said. "A friend called? What friend?"

"What difference does it make what friend? Wake up, Benny. I'm tryin' to tell you, John's dead."

Ben kicked back the covers and swung his legs over the edge of the bed. He rubbed his face, trying to get his brain working. When had he finally dropped off? Three, four? Deep sleep had been rare lately, and his twilight sleep dreams usually seemed so real that, for a moment, he thought this might be one of them.

"John's dead?"

Henry sounded as if he were ready to explode. "Yeah, Benny, John's dead. Now wake up an' quit makin' me repeat myself."

Suddenly the radio alarm went off. Ben pushed the snooze button to stop the buzzing and came fully awake. The phone was still in his hand and this was no dream. "A car accident, you said a car accident?"

"The cops at the scene said it looked like John fell asleep at the wheel. He went off the road and crashed in a ditch. The car caught fire, but the cops said the crash killed him."

"Shit! I can't believe it. John's dead."

"Julia talked to his mother. She's going to have the body sent to Cacher's mortuary. Soon as I hang up, I'm gonna go over and help her and Perky with the funeral details. I know you're gonna be payin' big bucks for airline tickets, but it can't be helped. I called Mike and Andy first. They're both still here in Illinois. Mike's downstate and Andy's in Rockford. You're the only one who's gotta fly." A note of contempt crept into his voice, "Kinda serves you right for moving to L.A."

Ben rubbed his face again, letting the enormity of the thing sink in. "How'd you find Mike and Andy?"

"The same way I found you. I'm in the detecting business."

Ben felt an urge to weep, but it wasn't for John, it was for himself. There were too many things crashing in on him all at once. Having to face the nightmare memories of the old neighborhood seemed almost too much to bear.

His voice rasped with the effort to keep out the tremor. "I don't really wanna go."

Henry seemed to be keeping a lid on his anger. "You what? Whadda you mean?" There was a long pause, and Ben wondered if maybe his friend had changed, had learned with age to control his temper. Then the moment passed, and Henry snarled. "Fuck that bullshit! Solberg was our friend, more your friend than mine. The guy saved your pitiful life. You forgotten that? You're comin' to his funeral if I gotta go out there and drag your ass back."

Ben took a deep breath—a cleansing breath, his karate instructor would say—and managed to regain control of his voice. "We're not kids anymore, Fox. Don't threaten me, and don't tell me what I should or shouldn't do." He waited, letting the message sink in. "I didn't say I wasn't going, I said I didn't want to. I'll fly into O'Hare tomorrow."

Henry's voice lowered. "Sorry, Benny-boy. I knew you'd come through. You just caught me by surprise. Don't bother renting a car. Call me with your flight number, an' I'll come get you."

After Henry hung up, Ben sat on the edge of the bed and waited for the grief that wouldn't come. He vaguely remembered that Annie exchanged Christmas cards with John, and that she'd sent a wedding gift when John dumped Perky to marry the bimbo who waited tables at the bar he owned. Henry was right. John Solberg had once been a close friend, but, through no fault of John's, there hadn't been any personal contact for the past couple of decades.

The hassles of arranging a last-minute trip started churning in his mind. Normally, his secretary made his travel arrangements, but she was on maternity leave. Her replacement was a pool secretary whose skills had yet to be tested. He couldn't take a chance on her screwing it up, so he'd have to take care of the details himself. He ran through his mental in-basket. Union contract talks were set to begin next month, and he'd already scheduled a meeting with the corporate labor lawyers for today. That would have to be postponed, as would the finalization of the plans for the new shipping facility. The rest of his duties could be handled by his assistant. The main task would be keeping the other half-dozen vice-presidents at Unitron Corporation from cutting his throat while he was gone. It was bad enough that Ben Kahn was going to take some personal time off; if his worst nightmare came true and they tumbled to his background, the sharks would smell blood in the water and begin circling.

He went into the bathroom, turned on the shower, and tried to remember what John looked like. The face was there, but he knew it wasn't a real memory. The image of his friend was two-dimensional, straight from Annie's photo albums. Without waiting for the water to warm up, Ben stepped under the stream. With the cold water came the unwanted memory of the winter they'd gone down to the lake and he'd fallen through the ice. John had saved his life that day.

The icy water did little to soften Ben's hangover. He stood, letting the sting of the spray hit him, and tried to force back the blackness that was now part of everyday life. "John, you stupid fucker. Why didn't you let me drown?"

CHAPTER SEVENTY-THREE

"**D**addy says you can't go." The childish whine that Andy had thought was so cute when she was seventeen was ludicrous in a middle-aged woman.

Sally leaned against the doorjamb of their bedroom with one leg propped up and her hands tucked behind her back. The pink silk robe was tightly cinched at the waist but loose enough up top to partially expose her breasts. Andy recognized it as her coquette pose, a technique that had been ineffective for years. Still, she clung to it as if nothing had changed.

When they first married, Andy'd had trouble understanding how a beauty like Sally could settle for a toad like him. Sally was still beautiful and he was still a toad, but it no longer mattered. Andy ignored her and kept packing.

"Daddy says he needs you to run the new restaurant, and he says his decision is final."

Carefully folding a dress shirt into his suitcase, Andy turned to his wife. The asinine edict from his father-in-law wasn't her fault. He spoke calmly, adult to child. "Sal, honey, your father is my business partner, not my boss. Point of fact, he's a junior partner. You and me, we own seven of the nine restaurants outright. I know you never met

Johnny Solberg, but he was my friend, and I'm going to his funeral."
He turned back to his suitcase and closed it. "I'll only be gone three or
four days. Till then, Bert'll just have to struggle along without me."

Reaching for a tissue she had tucked into the sleeve of her robe,
Sally dabbed at her eyes, and Andy watched, unmoved, as she let the
tears flow. "What about me? I'm all alone."

He took his wife by the arm, sat on the bed, and pulled her down
beside him. "Come with me. Once the funeral is over, we can make a
vacation of it, stay as long as we like. I'll book us into one of the fancy
downtown hotels, room service every meal, shopping on Michigan
Avenue, the nightlife. We'll have us a time, baby."

He became carried away with the idea of it, of how it would look
to the others when he showed up with a woman this beautiful on his
arm. "You've never been to Chicago. It's the greatest city in the
world."

Sally pulled the lapels of the robe to cover her chest and stood.
Her bleak expression didn't discourage him. Sally never smiled anymore. Andy had asked her about it a while back, and she patiently
explained that when she smiled, her face wrinkled, and wrinkles made
her look old.

"You said you couldn't go back there, that they'd throw you in jail
if they caught you."

Andy gave an exasperated huff and got to his feet. "Jesus, that was
twenty-eight years ago. There's such a thing as a statute of limita-
tions."

*****

It was almost noon when he left. He tossed his suitcase in the
trunk of the Beammer and slammed it shut. Sally stayed upstairs in her
room and didn't wave good-bye.

Driving through the city, Andy made note of every new construction site along the way. Rockford hadn't just grown in the last twenty years, it had boomed. There was still room for a few more "Home Cookin' Kitchens," but he knew the time was coming when he'd have to branch out to nearby towns. Keep growing or die was the rule in the fast-food business.

When he hit the tollway, he headed east. Sparse traffic, cruise control, and a couple hours of driving ahead—he had nothing to do but listen to the radio and think. A light rain started up, just enough to keep the wipers on the slowest speed. The rhythmic pause, swish, and pause faded into the background as a strange mix of guilt and excitement took over. He wondered why it had taken someone's death to get him back to the old neighborhood, and he wished that it had been anyone but John. Who would be there? Henry, of course, and Ben. Ben had been closer to John than any of them, so he'd fly in—but what about Mike, would Mike come? It would be like a reunion, the kind of reunion he'd dreamed about. Going back to the city in his silver BMW, rich and successful, showing all of them that Andy the fool, the little snot-nose, had made it.

As the rain lightened, he switched off the wipers and changed the radio station from one playing a whining Willy Nelson to one that played soft jazz. Ignoring the mellow mood set by the insipid sax of Kenny G. Andy glanced in the rearview mirror to make sure there were no cops around, pulled into the left lane, and floored it.

CHAPTER SEVENTY-FOUR

The sun was just past the horizon as Mike McMann jumped down off the tractor and headed for the house. The work had warmed him, and he was perspiring even though the cold air turned his breath into billowy white clouds. He'd gotten all of his four hundred acres plowed, and it felt good to be ready for planting. No more organic nonsense, no more marigolds instead of insecticide. This year, the bugs weren't going to get half his corn crop.

He shook his head ruefully. That wasn't fair to the natural food folks. The truth was that last year, he hadn't been around to give the crop the care it needed. Trying to make ends meet on a family farm had turned out to be almost impossible, so he'd been forced to keep driving his truck for a living. Thank the good Lord he hadn't listened to the banker who suggested selling his rig to pay down the mortgage.

Buying a farm had been his and Lisa's dream since moving down from Chicago. Three years earlier, the Butler spread had come on the market. The instant they'd laid eyes on the place, the two-story frame farmhouse—painted white with a north-facing veranda that would catch the early afternoon breeze—became their home. It had taken all their savings, but even now, after three tough seasons, he wasn't sorry.

Peeling off his work gloves, Mike strode up the gravel path, noticing that the huge oak next to the house was beginning to bud. A few
robins had shown up earlier in the week, and the flowers Lisa had
planted in front of the house were starting to show some green. Adding
to his good mood was the sight of his wife wrapped in a heavy wool
sweater on the porch rocker, waiting for him.

"Coffee?"

He shook his head. "Beer would be good."

Lisa smiled and went inside while he settled in the chair next to
hers. Moments later, she came back out with two cans of Schlitz. They
popped the cans together and sat sipping their beer, comfortable with
the silence.

"So, you think I should go?" Mike didn't wait for her answer
before he started in on all the negatives. "The field's ready for
planting, but there's still so damn much to do around here. I ain't even
got the storm windows off the house yet. The tractor needs a tune-up,
and Charlie Simmons wants to trade some carpentry work for five tons
of alfalfa."

He sipped his beer and waited, but Lisa said nothing.

Mildly annoyed, he used his thumb to point toward the barn.
"You see the way that loft is saggin'? If I don't get workin' on the
repairs, the damn thing'll cave in an' kill the cows."

Lisa was still silent, and Mike did his best to shut up. He only
lasted a few minutes. Scratching at the stubble on his chin, he leaned
back and tilted his chair so it rested against the side of the house. "Luke
Hanson from Interstate called last week and wanted to know if I was
still hauling. Claims it's been so long since I took a run, he thought I'd
given up truckin' altogether."

Lisa rocked quietly. Mike knew she was aware of his every mood,
knew all the devils from the past that haunted him. Everything he told

her was true, but not true at the same time. Going to the funeral would mean his being away for only a few days, and they both knew that none of his excuses were urgent.

Fidgeting with his beer can, his voice dropped to almost a whisper. "Besides, I'd be stuck havin' to see the guys."

He again rubbed at the stubble and squinted at her. "Henry, who the whole neighborhood thought was gonna spend his life in prison, has this big-deal detective agency. Benny's a hotshot vice-president of an outfit in California, an' even Andy got rich. He owns a whole chain of coffee shops. The three of them are gonna know I'm a flop, just a dumb hick farmer. We bust our asses on this piss-poor farm, barely breakin' even, and I'm gone half the time, drivin' a semi to bring in a little cash."

Mike lifted his John Deere cap with one hand, ran a hand across his scalp, then tugged the hat back in place. Lisa grabbed it by the bill, pulled it off and ruffled his graying hair. "Face it, lover, you are a hick farmer, salt of the earth and all that."

She stood, her hands on the railing, and looked out at the plowed field. "Half the people in the country would give anything to have what we have." He moved alongside her and she turned to kiss him. "Go— go to Chicago and say good-bye to your friend."

A part of Mike did want to go, but guilt over spending the money was eating at him. "It'll cost a few bucks, what with having to get a motel room and all. You sure we can afford it?"

Lisa reddened slightly and seemed to be avoiding Mike's eyes. "Now, don't go getting all mad at me. When your pal Henry called this morning, I knew this was going to come up. I talked to Luke, and he needs a driver to pick up a load in Chicago and run it over to St. Louis. You'll have to dead-head up there, but at least you'll have a load coming back. Your buddy Henry gave me the number of the hotel where that Andy guy, the one who lives in Rockford, is staying. He drove down to Chicago this morning. When I called, he got all excited and offered to have you stay with him. That way, you won't have to bunk in the rig. With the money from the load, and not having to pay for a motel room, we can make it."

Mike wanted to argue, to explain how cheap mooching a room—especially off Andy—would make him feel. Instead, he dropped back down into his chair with a thump and frowned. "So you're telling me I should take what's left of my balls and just go?"

Lisa knelt in front of him. "Don't say things like that, honey. I was only trying to help. The truth is, you've got no choice. Saying good-bye to John is mandatory."

Mike pulled her into his lap and kissed her, loving the way she enjoyed using big words. "You wanna come?"

She wriggled into a comfortable position and put her arms around his neck. Her head shake no was too immediate, and Mike misunderstood. "Hey, it's been over twenty years. There's no need for you to be afraid of your old boyfriend. I'll bet Roger Shaw's forgotten all about you."

Lisa rubbed against him, kitten-like. "If you and I parted ways back then, would you have forgotten me?" She laughed, letting him know she was joking. "No, it'll be easier without the ball and chain hanging around. You go see all your old friends, get drunk, and make an ass of yourself, and I won't be around to nag you. Besides, your hot-pants daughter Stacy needs parental guidance. Leaving her alone would be begging for early grandparenthood."

Mike winced. "She's only fifteen, for Christ's sake. You think she's fooling around? I'll ground her for life, I'll—"

Lisa kissed him on the lips, effectively shutting him up. "Big talk. One blink of her baby blues and you roll over like a puppy. No, she's not fooling around, and I'm going to ride herd on her to make sure she doesn't." She went country on him, mimicking the Southern Illinois accent. "Y'all go on up to Chicago and show them thar city folk how much better it is to be a downstate redneck."

Mike sat for a moment, nuzzling her neck, unwilling to give up her soft warmth. Then the screen door swung open and their daughter Stacy bounced out, the spitting image of Lisa when Mike first met her. She cocked her head and frowned at them. "Ewww, that's disgusting," she said, and the spell was broken.

He left the next morning. Lisa stood in the yard and waved as he climbed into the cab of the semi. He called to her, knowing she wouldn't change her mind. "You're sure?" Then he saw she was crying. He climbed back down and gathered her in his arms. "What is it, baby?"

She sniffed and gently pushed him away. "I was just thinking about John. Without him, I wouldn't have met you."

CHAPTER SEVENTY-FIVE

Ben was the first of the Castle group to arrive at the church. He spotted Edelstein sitting in a back pew. Always somewhat egg-shaped, the druggist's age-rounded shoulders and bald head now accentuated the image. Ben knew that Edelstein had opened a drug-store in South Shore after the urban renewal project wiped out the one he had on 57th Street, but he hadn't heard anything about him since.

He nodded and Edelstein slowly got to his feet. The quizzical look on the druggist's face convinced Ben that Edelstein didn't know who he was.

"How's it going, Mr. Edelstein?"

Still seeming befuddled, Edelstein gave a tentative bob of his head. "Oh, now I remember you. You're the friend, the one who bossed the others around."

"No, that was Henry. I'm Ben, Ben Kahn."

Edelstein rubbed at a watery eye and shrugged. "By the time you get to be my age, you've seen lots of faces. Who could remember them all?"

Ben gave him what he hoped was an understanding smile. "How's the new store, the one you opened after they tore down Hyde Park?"

Edelstein shook his head. "The new store is twenty-five years old, and it was never like the old one. The old store was a way of life; the new one…" Edelstein gave another shrug. "It was a business. I gave it to my son Barry five years ago. I'm retired now."

Edelstein stared up the center aisle at the closed casket beneath the altar. "You know, he always pretended to be Jewish."

Coming from out of nowhere, the statement puzzled Ben. "John?"

"Of course, John. Who else is being buried today? He pretended he was Jewish because he thought I cared. I could have told him I knew, that he didn't have to pretend, but…why embarrass? What he was didn't matter. John Solberg, he had a Jewish heart. I would have loved him if he was an Arab."

As they talked, John's widow, Vivian, dressed all in black, staggered past them. Her double-handed grip on the arm of John's older brother Roy seemed to be the only thing keeping her upright. Behind her, a frail old lady walked unaided. It wasn't until the three of them were seated in the front row that Ben realized the old lady was John's mother. He looked around for John's mistress, Perky, and found her quietly praying in one of the middle rows. He patted Mr. Edelstein on the shoulder and moved down to Perky's row. As Ben slid into the pew, Perky looked up at him. The grief that poured off of her was so intense, Ben could almost smell it. Her already swollen eyes began to fill again, and suddenly, Ben's throat clutched as a wave of anguish for her loss swept over him. He took her hand in his and let her bury her face in his shoulder.

Henry strode in, leading his wife, Julia, and Ben's—soon to be— ex-wife, Annie. Ben nodded at him and the three of them came to sit in the same row. Annie pushed in next to Ben and reached across to stroke Perky's hair. At that moment, Vivian looked around and caught sight of them. Her eyes narrowed and the grieving widow look was replaced by a glare of pure hatred.

Kenny, the bartender at John's bar, sat a few rows behind. The patrons of the bar who had attended seemed to gravitate toward him, probably because of his familiar face. Soon, an entire section was filled with mourners who had obviously fortified themselves with alcohol before coming.

Julia nudged Henry, who looked back in disgust and said, "Shit, don't anyone light a match. If all those drunks exhale at once, the place'll explode."

She gave a slight grin and whispered, "Don't swear, Henry."

Andy entered the church, followed by Mike. They spotted Henry's wave and stood in the aisle while Henry motioned for the others to slide toward the wall to make room. Again, there were solemn exchanges of grief with Perky.

Mike leaned toward Ben. "If the minister asks, are you gonna say something?"

Mike was the only one not wearing a suit. Instead, he wore a corduroy sports jacket and tan chinos. His tie was askew and clashed with his plaid shirt. Ben shook his head. "I don't think that's on today's agenda. We'll do our own eulogies afterward."

A black-suited man with a cleric's collar stepped up to the altar, and a hush fell over the church. "Let us pray."

Everyone's head went down and there were a few moments of silence. Then the minister's head came up, and he launched into a long, rambling speech. It was clear that the man hadn't known John, because the person he eulogized was approaching sainthood. The minister's soliloquy was followed by a series of sappy platitudes from John's brother Roy, after which a soprano sang *"Nearer My God to Thee,"* accompanied by the theatrical wailing of John's widow.

Ben, Henry, Andy, and Mike were four of the six pallbearers. The other two were John's brother and one of his cousins. Once the church was emptied, they carried the coffin to the waiting hearse. Then they got in their cars and followed the hearse to the cemetery. When the pallbearers arrived, they were instructed by an aide from Catcher's Mortuary. Sliding the coffin from the back of the hearse, they gripped the sides and began the slow walk to the grave site. Because the burned condition of the body had made embalming impossible, there was a strong odor emanating from the coffin. An attempt to mask the smell with some kind of deodorant had made it even more pungent, and the stench became almost overpowering.

"Remember how freaky Johnny was about smellin' bad?" Ben said.

John's cousin shot him a disapproving look, but Ben went on. "He used to damn near take a bath in the men's room after he took a leak."

The casket was heavy, and sweat began to appear on the cousin's face. He glared at Ben, trying to put as much menace into the look as possible.

Ben stared back at him. "If Johnny knew how bad he smelled now, he'd wave the six of us off an' walk himself to the grave."

Henry looked down, stifling his laugh, but Andy started openly giggling. By the time they reached the grave site, the four of them were choking with the effort to hold back their laughter.

As they centered their burden on the platform, they had almost regained control. That's when John's brother tried to shush them. He stepped back, placed a forefinger across his lips, and hissed loudly. Roy had fleshy lips and false teeth, and as the shushing escalated, his teeth threatened to slip out. He slammed his mouth shut to hold them in, and his attempt to shush sounded more like the passing of gas. It was the wrong thing to do, at precisely the wrong time. Ben exploded in laughter, and the other three lost it.

Kenny caught Ben's eye and couldn't help chuckling, and even though the drunks from John's bar didn't know what was going on, they joined in. Within seconds, half the people in attendance were either smiling from ear to ear or laughing outright. The widow's face convulsed with rage, and John's mother put her hand over her heart, swaying as if about to faint. Edelstein gave Ben a mildly disapproving shake of his head. Still fighting back laughter, Ben signaled the other three to step away.

*****

They sat in a booth at Lola's—Annie, Julia, and Perky on one side and Andy, Mike, and Henry across from them. Ben sat in a chair at the end. Perky sipped at her white wine. Her voice shook and she angrily wiped at her eye. "I had to arrange everything. John's mother was too feeble, his brother too busy, and Vivian too emotionally exhausted. Funny thing, she wasn't too emotional to tell me afterward that she didn't want me at the reception."

Julia put her arm around Perky's shoulder. "It might have been awkward. I mean, if Henry was in love with someone other than me, I wouldn't want her around to remind me."

Perky smiled a tight-lipped, bitter smile. "That isn't why she hates me. She never gave a damn what John did, as long as he paid the bills. She's angry because my lawyer just informed her that I'm sole owner of the bar. John put it in my name when he bought it. Some kind of tax thing. I never did understand it."

Ben cocked his head to one side and nodded. "That was just like John, always a scam."

Andy raised his glass. "A toast to Johnny. He taught me how to walk like a man and bailed me out of jail not once, but twice. God only knows what my life would have been without him." Tears rolled down Andy's face. "And he wouldn't have cared that we laughed. In fact, if you'd listened close, you coulda heard him laughing with us."

Lola came over and stood with her hand on Ben's shoulder. In her mid-fifties, she was as spectacular as she had been when they were young. "Blue wants to buy y'all a drink in honor of your friend."

Mike shrugged. "Lisa cried when I left to come up here. She reminded me that without John, we never would have met."

There were nods, and everyone turned to Ben. He fingered his beer glass, staring down at the table. "John Solberg was a hypocrite. A miserable, lying hypocrite of the first order. He pretended to be a con man, but he made sure his cons never really hurt anyone. He pretended to be a thief, but when you became his friend, he couldn't steal from you. And he pretended not to care, but when any one of us got in trouble, he was the first one there to help. He loved us all, and he let us love him back. Like the rest of us, he was a product of this filthy neighborhood. But unlike us, he liked it here and never wanted to get away. If I had one wish, it would be to see him one more time, just to say thanks."

The silence was almost painful. Ben raised his glass. "I give you our friend, John Solberg." And they all drank.

*****

Ben left for Los Angeles that afternoon. He sank back into his seat in first class and let the euphoria wash over him. He'd gotten away without making a bunch of stupid promises he wasn't going to keep. The no-smoking sign went off and he fired up a cigarette. Outside, the thick layer of cotton clouds beneath the plane obscured the land below.

He had nothing in common with the old gang. Andy might have made some money, but he still sucked up to Henry and acted like a jerk. And Mike, for Christ's sake, was a truck driver and a farmer. Henry was the worst one of all. Even though he ran what he claimed was a legitimate private security agency, he'd never grown out of the neighborhood. For God's sake, the man acted as if his finest hour had

497

been when he was the leader of a gang of street punks. He even said that he wished there was some way his son and daughter could have his experiences so they'd learn street smarts. What did that mean, street smarts? How to steal, lie, cheat, strong-arm, hot-wire a car, roll queers for their money, deal drugs, and survive in the sewer they were raised in? That was what Henry wanted for his kids? Hell, the only positive thing Ben could think of that he had learned in the neighborhood was how to spit.

He smiled, remembering how Henry had taught him to curl his tongue and hit a target eight feet away with a wad of mucus. The smile died. He'd been second best at spitting, never quite able to match the ten-foot range Henry had. He sighed and sipped his double scotch. The past was dead, and silently, Ben Kahn vowed to keep it that way.

Click...beep. "Hey, Benny, it's me. You'll never believe what happened after you left town. Andy bailed on his old lady an' hit the road. He stopped downstate to see Mike an' told him he sold out to his father-in-law 'cause he wanted to see the country. Mike says to him, 'What're you gonna do for money?' An' old Booger-Nose says, 'Maybe you didn't know it, but I've got plenty, and if I run out, I'm a great short-order cook.' There's a lot more to it, so call me." *Beep... click.*

Click...Beep. "Hey, buddy, how come you haven't called? I talked ta Mike. He says Lisa got him ta sell the semi. Says they're gonna make it as full-time farmers or die trying. Gimme a call an' I'll fill you in." *Beep...Click.*

Click...beep. "All bad news, Benny. Grandfather passed last week. He almost made it to ninety, so it wasn't so bad, but Delaney's not even sixty, and he's got cancer. Did I tell you that Delaney an' me got to be partners? Anyway, he's got the lung kind, an' it don't look good. I always told you smokin' was bad. I ran into a guy who did time with Roger Shaw. He told me that a week after Shaw got out of Joliet, he was killed. Some guy shoved a bottle in his throat, an' he bled out. There was one bad luck guy, had it all an' blew it. Hey, what's up with you? It's been a couple of months. How come you haven't called me back? I know you're a busy big shot, but you could break away for five minutes to give me a 'How ya doin?'" *Beep...click*

Click...beep. "Hey, asshole. I guess you didn't know that your ex an' Julia really hit it off. They talk a lot, an' Annie finally told Julia why you haven't answered any of my calls. She claims you got a whole new make-believe life, an' that talkin' to me reminds you too much of the past an' the things we did when we was kids. Says you think you're too good for people like us. Well, in words of one syllable, Benny boy, fuck you! We did what we did, an' we paid for it. Growin' up in the Castle was hard, but it made us strong. Alone, we weren't shit, but together, we were a family, brothers who looked out for each other. You never would've scammed your way into that big-deal job if you hadn't known me an' John an' learned how to hustle. I can see why Annie dumped your phony ass. I won't call again. You ever wanna talk to me, you know my number.

Beep...
...click

499

To the following readers, helpers and cheerleaders,
my heartfelt thanks.

Suzy Batta, Darian Bleacher, Sharla Cella, Ken Cline,
Mike Dornhecker, Jo Ann Hahn, Jennifer Hocutt,
Jim and Loretta Rivera, Sheila Ross, Susan Scott, Paula Sorce,
Jack Taylor, Dan Weinstein and Don Weller.

CPSIA information can be obtained
at www.ICGtesting.com
Printed in the USA
FSOW01n2331110717
36047FS